Beneath the Honeysuckle Vine

Center Point
Large Print

Also by Marcia Lynn McClure and available from
Center Point Large Print:

Dusty Britches
Weathered Too Young
The Windswept Flame
The Heavenly Surrender
The Light of the Lovers' Moon

This Large Print Book carries the
Seal of Approval of N.A.V.H.

Beneath
THE
Honeysuckle Vine

Marcia Lynn McClure

CENTER POINT LARGE PRINT
THORNDIKE, MAINE

This Center Point Large Print edition
is published in the year 2017 by arrangement with
Distractions Ink.

The text of this Large Print edition is unabridged.
In other aspects, this book may vary
from the original edition.
Printed in the United States of America
on permanent paper.
Set in 16-point Times New Roman type.

ISBN: 978-1-68324-619-0

Library of Congress Cataloging-in-Publication Data

Names: McClure, Marcia Lynn, author.
Title: Beneath the honeysuckle vine / Marcia Lynn McClure.
Description: Center Point large print edition. | Thorndike, Maine :
    Center Point Large Print, 2017.
Identifiers: LCCN 2017041668 | ISBN 9781683246190
    (hardcover : alk. paper)
Subjects: LCSH: Large type books. | GSAFD: Love stories.
Classification: LCC PS3613.C36 B46 2017 | DDC 813/.6—dc23
LC record available at https://lccn.loc.gov/2017041668

To Debra,
For true and everlasting friendship.
You are the rarest sort of treasure found on earth!

—and—

To my husband . . .
Kevin from Heaven!

PROLOGUE

Vivianna stood next to Mrs. Turner—tried to ignore the bitter sting of hot tears brimming in her eyes. She must be brave—or at least appear braver than she had been months before when Samuel and Augustus left to enlist. She had been too weak then, wildly sobbing with heartache at watching her dear brothers ride off to war. She knew now her weakness and sobbing had made leaving all the more difficult for Sam and Augie— more difficult for her mother to remain poised and courageous in the face of sending her sons to battle—more difficult for her father to stay behind and watch them go. So she would compose herself now in this moment of further heartache—of near heartbreak. She would keep her tears from streaming over her cheeks for as long as she was able. Even when they did escape—and she knew they would—she would not sob. Rather, she would weep genteel, the way Savannah Turner now wept as her two elder sons embraced her.

Yet as a balmy breeze brushed her face—as the scent of autumn in Alabama caressed her tender senses—Vivianna Bartholomew thought of all that was, sorely missing all that had been. Where were the hot, airless days of sun, when lingering under a tree to share its shade brought hours of stillness

7

and tranquility of mind? Where were the warm nights fragrant with honeysuckle and gardenia, sweet with the calming melody of bug noises to gently sway a body to sleep on dreamy waves of contentment? Were they lost forever to the worries and heartache, the pain and suffering of war?

What happy, carefree days Vivianna had known as a child! In the company of her elder brothers and their friends the Turner boys, Vivianna had played, laughed, and lived a life of sweet joy and innocent satisfaction. She closed her violet-blue eyes a moment and remembered the pollywogs in the pond not so many summers past—the summer before her brothers had gone. She remembered sitting on the pond's bank, slipping bare feet into the cool mud, giggling as the pollywogs playing in the shallow water darted back and forth, tickling her ankles as they frolicked and her brothers and the Turner boys fished, lazily basking in the sun, careless of their poles.

But the vision vanished as she opened her eyes, for there stood Caleb Turner—her beloved Caleb. There he stood, embracing his weeping mother. In a moment more, he would mount his horse and ride away—just as Sam had, just as Augie had. Vivianna was grateful Caleb did not yet don a uniform. She could not have borne it—the sight of him dressed for war. Tears were filling her eyes in profusion as she glanced then to Justin.

As Caleb embraced their mother—whispered

soothing words of assurance—Justin looked on, his brow puckered with worry, the corners of his usually smiling mouth downturned. Vivianna had hoped to look to Justin and stay her own tears. Yet the sight of him only spurred more to gathering, and she could not hold them back. As tears spilled over her cheeks, Caleb released his mother, dropping to one knee before his two younger brothers. Vivianna brushed the tears from her face as she watched Caleb embrace first Nathaniel and then William. Silently she offered a prayer of thanksgiving, grateful that Nate and Willy were only six and five, too young to go to war. She knew the younger Turner boys would offer great comfort to their mother while Caleb and Justin were away. Both small boys sniffled, angrily wiping at the tears on their cheeks with the backs of their small, grubby hands.

"Now, you two take care of Mama," Caleb told his sniffling siblings. "You hear?"

Nate nodded and said, "Yes, sir," and Willy sniffled.

"And you take care of Viv for me too," Caleb added. He smiled and tousled the boys' hair. "You keep them Adder boys away from her. I wouldn't want one of them to steal her heart while I was away."

"We'll give them Adder boys a fit of fists and feet if'n they try, Caleb," Nate promised.

Caleb chuckled and tousled their hair again.

"Bye, Mama," Justin said.

Vivianna brushed the tears from her cheeks as she watched Justin embrace his mother.

"You be careful, my baby," Savannah Turner said. Her voice broke with restrained emotion, and Vivianna winced at her grimace of heartache as she hugged her son. "You come back to me. Do you hear me, Justin? You and your brother come back to your mama."

"I will, Mama," Justin said. "Try not to worry. Caleb and me . . . we'll be fine."

Savannah released her son—dabbed at the moisture on her cheeks with a linen handkerchief. "And you two be careful travelin' to Huntsville," Savannah warned as Caleb stood and Justin hunkered down to say his own good-byes to his little brothers. "Do you hear me, Caleb Turner? Just because you say north Alabama is full of Southern Unionists . . . well, it still doesn't mean it's safe for two southern boys travelin' on to enlist with the Yankees."

"We'll be fine, Mama," Caleb told her. "And besides . . . Justin and me can lick anybody who fists up a hand in our direction. Ain't that right, Justin?"

Justin nodded as he hugged Willy. "That's right. There ain't nothin' to worry about, Mama."

"The Maggee boys made it fine," Caleb explained. "Didn't they, Mama? And you know me and Justin are better men than them." Caleb shook his head. "I swear . . . I can't even imagine Boy Maggee sittin' a horse with the Alabama First Cavalry."

Justin shook his head as well. "I can better imagine Boy Maggee fightin' with the First better than I can his brother, Floydie. Now that's a sight I'm plain itchin' to see!"

"And you'll write to me," Savannah demanded, wagging a forefinger at her sons. "Every week! I need a letter from each of you every week. You hear me?"

Caleb smiled and nodded. "Yes, Mama."

His attention turned to Vivianna then, and she thought she might die from the pain tearing her heart into pieces. How she loved him! Oh, how she loved Caleb Turner! Vivianna had loved Caleb nearly as far back as she could remember. And what girl wouldn't? Tall, broad-shouldered, and more handsome than any boy or man she'd ever seen, Caleb owned Vivianna Bartholomew's full heart. Furthermore—though she had thought for years it never could be—she owned his! At times, she still could not quite believe he loved her. Yet he'd told her so often, especially in recent months. He'd even talked of marriage—just the very night before.

Caleb had come over to call on Vivianna, and Vivianna's daddy had allowed them to take a short walk together—alone! What a wonderful night it had been! A fragrant breeze cooled the air just enough to make it necessary for Caleb to place his arm around Vivianna's slight shoulders in offering warmth, and she silently swore to herself she would never forget the feel of the tender kiss he'd placed on her lips before they had returned to the house.

"You're finally sixteen, Viv," Caleb had said. "I'm plenty old enough now at twenty. And if I wasn't about to be a soldier . . . I'd sure enough ask your daddy if we could get married."

Caleb's words echoed through her mind as she watched him approach. The smile he'd forced for his mother's sake had faded—his gaze intent upon her—his beautiful blue eyes misted with emotion.

In the next moment, she was in his arms! She heard Mrs. Turner toss a slight scolding at him, but he didn't mind it—just continued to hold her.

Vivianna's tears poured over her cheeks as Caleb held her—as she held him. She inhaled the scent of his shirt—of his skin—of his hair! She pressed her cheek to his and vowed never to forget the sense of his skin against hers—the feel of being in his arms.

"I love you!" she whispered, her lips pressed softly to his ear.

"I love you," he whispered in return.

He kissed her then—in front of his mother, his brothers, and all of Alabama! Vivianna felt goose pimples race over her arms—held her breath as their lips lingered in shared affection for long moments. She wondered if this would be the last kiss she ever shared with Caleb. So many local boys had been killed in the war—so many! She feared for Caleb yet reminded herself of his strength and determination. The Turner boys were tougher than old leather. It seemed nothing could lick them, and she held to the knowledge like some unseen talisman of hope.

His lips left hers, and Vivianna fancied she felt suddenly cold and alone—even for the fact he still held her against him.

"I'll be back, Viv," Caleb said. "I promise."

He wiped the tears from her cheeks with the back of one hand. She reached up, smoothing the soft dark hair at his temple.

"I know," she breathed.

He released her—stepped back as Justin approached.

Vivianna's gaze met Justin's, sending fresh tears streaming over her cheeks.

As always, Justin's brow was puckered with a frown. He shook his head—clicked his tongue with disapproval.

"Caleb Turner," Justin began as he strode toward Vivianna, "you do know you're leavin' for war, don't ya?" he asked. "You do realize ya might never come back?"

"Justin!" his mother exclaimed.

"Of course I do," Caleb said, glaring at his brother. "Why?"

13

Vivianna was confused—overwhelmed by heartache and utterly confused. Why would Justin say such a thing? Did he want to make certain everyone's heart were as broken as hearts could possibly be?

She stared at Justin, hurt and curious.

As was ever the case when she looked at Justin, her bosom experienced an odd, rather nervous little flutter. She could never understand why Justin Turner had such an unsettling effect on her. Sometimes she fancied her mind and body reacted more ardently to Justin's presence than it did to Caleb's—even though Caleb was the one who owned her heart. Justin was handsome—not quite as handsome perhaps as Caleb but handsome enough to send the heart of every girl in the county to leaping at the sight of him. His dark hair and light blue eyes gave him a striking appearance certainly. But Justin didn't own Caleb's charm and easy manner. Still, he unsettled Vivianna somehow—especially of late.

Justin shook his head and mumbled, "Well, Caleb, it's just . . . it's just that ya done a downright pitiful job of kissin' your girl good-bye."

"I did not!" Caleb defended himself. "I done a fine job of it . . . and in front of Mama too!"

"It was a pitiful kiss for a soldier to give his girl before leavin' for battle, Caleb!" Justin scolded. "And you know it! Whether or not Mama's standin' here lookin' on . . . or Nate and Willy."

Justin's frown deepened, and he shook his head again. "We're leavin', Caleb, maybe for good, and that's all you're gonna give her . . . that choirboy peck?"

Vivianna felt her face flush crimson. She was uncomfortable with their banter. Certainly the Turner boys were known for their teasing, their bickering, and even their brawling with each other. Still, the fact they were leaving to enlist made Vivianna wish that, just this once, they wouldn't tease—not during their last moments with their family.

"First off, she ain't really my girl any more than she is yours," Caleb said. Vivianna was astonished by Caleb's utterance—surprised and hurt. Yet he added, "Not officially anyway." Vivianna sighed, somehow understanding he meant she wasn't his because he'd never spoken to her daddy about marrying her.

"You didn't talk to her daddy yet?" Justin growled.

"I ain't gonna leave Viv behind to worry over me any more than she already will, Justin!" Caleb growled. "Second off, I think the pink on her cheeks says I did a fine job of kissin' her."

Justin continued to frown as he nodded and said, "She ain't your girl, huh?"

"Not formally . . . no," Caleb admitted.

"Then I guess that gives me leave to show you how you shoulda kissed her."

Vivianna gasped as Justin suddenly reached out, taking hold of her shoulders. She held her breath, her heart increasing in tempo as he looked at her. Justin's expression softened a moment; his mouth offered a slight smile.

The frown returned to his brow all too quickly, however. "You watch out for my mama and the little boys, Viv. All right? Promise me you'll watch out for them."

Vivianna could only nod—barely managed to whisper, "Of course," in response. She was still breathless, both from the endurance of the excruciating pain of the Turner boys' leaving and from the nearness of Justin's face to her own.

"Then I'll say good-bye, Vivianna Bartholomew," he whispered, taking her face between his strong hands.

Vivianna gasped as his lips softly pressed against her own—a slow, tender kiss causing her stomach to feel light with strange, unfamiliar excitement. The gentle kiss ended, but Justin's lips lingered close to hers. He kissed her once more—more firmly—his lips slightly parted. Again he kissed her, coaxing her lips to a slight parting in meeting his. Again he kissed her—and somehow she could not keep from returning his kiss. The knowledge she might never see him again seemed to spur her to reckless abandon, and she accepted yet another kiss from him.

Justin ended their exchange, leaving Vivianna

breathless—trembling as his arms wrapped around her, pulling her against him.

Suddenly all her withheld emotion, her fear, her heartache at watching the Turner boys leave to fight the war, all of it overwhelmed her. She was glad to have had Justin Turner's kiss! She would savor the memory of it forever! No matter how inappropriate it was, she would bathe in the blissful knowledge their lips had met. War was everywhere, and she cared little for propriety in that moment.

"It's enough, Justin," his mother said.

Placing one hand at the back of Vivianna's head, he pressed her cheek against the solid muscles of his chest. Vivianna held her breath, restrained her tears, intent on listening to the strong, rhythmic beat of his heart. Oh, how she prayed in that moment that Justin Turner's heart would ever continue to beat! How she prayed no bullet or saber would strike it cold and lifeless. She clutched the fabric of his shirt in her fists, willing him not to go, sobbing as she wondered how she could care as much for Justin's leaving as she did Caleb's. She loathed herself in that moment—loathed her disloyalty, her apparent fickle-heartedness! She felt Justin press his face to the top of her head—heard him inhale deeply as he breathed in the scent of her sable hair.

Taking her face in his hands, he gazed longingly down at her. As tears spilled from her eyes and over her cheeks, she forced a smile as he smiled at her. His brow was straight and strong—free of the frown it had worn before.

"You see, Caleb," Justin mumbled, his voice filled with regret, "if battle finds me thirsty . . . I'll have the memory of lovely tears to quench my thirst. If I'm taken by nightmares—if the ghosts of men I've killed haunt me and fear threatens to overpower my mind—I'll have the sense of home and holdin' a beautiful girl in my arms to calm me. And if I die . . . I'll die with the taste of a kiss as moist and sweet as honeysuckle nectar fresh on my lips."

Vivianna released him—pushed herself away from him. Stepping back from Justin, she straightened her posture. They had to go, both of them. There would be no stopping them, and her feelings were not sorted. Her mind was muddled and confused for the sake of heartache and fear. She loved the Turner boys—both of them. But she was only *in* love with one, and she would not let the agony of war cloud her mind any longer.

"You're a poet if nothin' else, little brother," Caleb growled, his eyes narrowing as he gazed at Vivianna. Stepping forward, he reached out and took one of her hands in his own. "I . . . I guess I did do a pitiful job at sayin' good-bye. But you'll write to me all the same, won't you?"

"Of course I will," Vivianna managed. She

placed a hand to his cheek as her tears began anew.

Justin turned, strode to his horse, and mounted as Caleb dropped Vivianna's hand and followed.

"You boys take care of Mama and Vivianna for us, all right?" Justin called. Both young boys nodded, sniffling and wiping tears from their cheeks. "I love you, Mama," Justin said. He looked to Vivianna one last time, nodding at her. The frown had returned to his brow.

Vivianna watched Caleb mount—knew she would never forget the sight of the two Alabama boys leaving to fight for the Union.

"Bye, Justin! Bye, Caleb!" Willy cried out.

"I ain't watchin', Mama!" Nate cried suddenly. "I ain't gonna watch 'em ride away! Daddy rode away . . . and he never came back! I ain't gonna watch 'em!"

"Nate!" Savannah called as Nate ran off in the direction of the house.

"Let him go, Mama," Caleb said. "Don't make it any harder on him than it already is."

Savannah nodded as Willy shouted, "I ain't watchin' neither! I ain't!" and ran off after his brother.

"You all come back to us, boys, you hear me?" Savannah called as Justin set out at a gallop. "Caleb? You all come back to us!" she cried, brushing the tears from her cheeks.

"We will, Mama," Caleb said. "Good-bye, Viv," he said.

"Good-bye," Vivianna whispered.

Caleb nodded. "Get," he said to his horse.

They were gone. The Turner boys were gone to war.

CHAPTER ONE

Vivianna giggled as she watched Nate and Willy wrestling in the grass. She shook her head, wondering why boys found so much joy in torturing one another. In that moment, she was awash with gratitude and thanksgiving—grateful spring had come, thankful the war was over, grateful in knowing Nate and Willy would never have to enlist. Nate and Willy would not die in the battlefields or disappear the way Samuel and Augustus had—the way their own brother Justin had.

At the thought of her brothers—as the vision of Justin Turner settled in her mind—Vivianna drew a deep breath, silently pleading with her emotions to remain calm. Caleb was walking toward her, and she would not have him knowing she still longed for his brother.

She studied him as he approached. He was so handsome, even for the residual evidence of suffered hardship that now weathered his countenance. His smile was not so bright and carefree as it once had been, his eyes void of the radiant spark of gaiety they had once owned. Furthermore, he walked with a limp, a vestige of the war, one that would never let him forget—if forgetting such a thing were even possible. Yet

Caleb Turner was a good man, a strong man, and he had returned from the fighting when so many others never would—including his own brother.

Caleb chuckled as he glanced to Nate and Willy. "Puts me in mind of Justin and me," he said, his smile fading a little. "Do you remember how we used to fight, Viv?"

Vivianna smiled, her heart aching at the memory. "I do," she told him. "It seems the two of you were always covered in dirt and grass."

Caleb gazed at her for a long moment. She knew he was thinking of Justin too, missing his brother. A moment of unspoken understanding passed between them. Vivianna knew Caleb sorely missed his brother, and Caleb knew Vivianna's heart was broken in missing Justin as well. She sensed this was why he had not pressed her further to marry him; he knew her tender heart still clung to his brother's memory. Vivianna knew Caleb would wait until he was certain she was free of the ghost of Justin Turner before proposing to her again. In that moment, she recognized another reason for gratitude: Caleb Turner's patience.

"Do ya need anything?" he asked. "I could stop in at one of the shops for ya if ya like."

Vivianna shook her head and allowed her smile to broaden. Caleb was ever so thoughtful.

"No, thank you," she said. "I best save every-thing I have in case the critters get into the garden and we find ourselves needin' to trade our things for food. You were nothin' but skin and bones when you came home. I won't see ya skin and bones again."

Caleb nodded. "You're right. Who knows what these next months will bring?" He reached out, brushing a stray strand of hair from her cheek. "Well, you just send one of the boys after me if you or Mama needs somethin'," he said. "Repairin' bridges is hard labor . . . and I'd look forward to a reason to be called home for the day."

Vivianna smiled, though in truth she felt saddened. There had been a time when Caleb's simple touch would've sent goose pimples racing over her arms. But that was years ago—a war ago—and she felt sad that his touch no longer thrilled her.

"I'll send Nate or Willy to fetch ya if we need ya home." Vivianna glanced to the two boys still wrestling in the grass. "If I can break them up long enough to make them hear me."

"All right then," Caleb said. "I'll see ya this evenin', Viv."

"Bye now," Vivianna said, tossing a wave as he limped down the road toward town.

She watched him go—thought of the day last June when he had returned. He'd been wounded, and the injury to his leg had found him unable to fight. In truth, the doctors had feared Caleb would even lose his leg. But he didn't; he was discharged and sent home to recover.

She'd never forget the day Caleb returned—never forget the joy in Mrs. Turner's eyes. Further, Vivianna feared she'd never forget how she'd silently wished it had been Justin who had returned. She'd hated herself for two months over having had such thoughts. Caleb was a good man. She was glad he'd survived.

It was also in June that Caleb's mother told him of Justin having won Vivianna's heart. Justin had faithfully written to Vivianna; Caleb had not. Caleb seemed to understand, though he constantly scolded himself to Vivianna and his mother for letting his brother woo Vivianna away from him. Still, Vivianna was certain he had not loved her as deeply as he had once professed to. She thought if he truly loved her, he should have been angry with his brother for kissing her the day they left. If he loved her as Justin did, he should've written long letters of missing her—of loving her. But he did not. It was Justin who had written, not Caleb. Thus, Caleb—by his own admission—had no right to be angry or hurt and did not endeavor to win her away from Justin once more.

Until November—when Justin's letters had ceased in arriving. Even Mrs. Turner had received no word from him. All at the Turner home began to worry, yet they continued in owning no word of Justin having fallen. Still, as the weeks and months passed—as no word from Justin ever arrived—Vivianna and the Turners began to understand that no word would ever arrive from him—or of him. Justin Turner was lost. The war had taken him, as it had so many others. Justin would not have let his loved ones linger five months without word. Thus, Mrs. Turner, Nate, Willy, Caleb, and Vivianna had begun to accept that another Alabama son would not return from the war.

General Lee had surrendered, just three weeks past. Caleb had waited several days after the beginning of war's end before asking Vivianna to marry him. When tears began to stream down her face, Caleb at once apologized. He explained he had thought her ready to settle—mistakenly. He'd thought the love she once owned for him would somehow heal the love she'd known for his fallen brother. Still, when he realized it had not, he offered his explanation to Vivianna—told her he would wait until she was ready, even if it were a full year or more.

Vivianna had presented her own apology to Caleb. She did not wish to hurt him, for she had loved him once—yet did love him still, in a manner. Yet she suspected he had asked her to marry him more out of obligation or expectation than because he was truly in love with her. She suspected he felt sorry for her, orphaned and brotherless as she was. Further, she suspected Caleb owned the notion he and she would make a comfortable match. After all, did she not already reside with his family?

Savannah Turner had taken Vivianna into her home after Vivianna's parents had been killed by the Union soldiers raiding Florence almost two years previous. With no word from either of her brothers for those same two years, Vivianna knew the Turner family was all the family she would know. She thought perhaps Caleb felt this too—that his own tired heart reasoned it might be easier to own a wife who was already so settled in with his family.

But Vivianna's heart could not release the memory of Justin; her lips could not forget the feel of the kiss he'd given her the day he left. The memory of Justin Turner was wound about her heart—woven through her soul. It was nearly every night still that she read his letters, at least one or two of them. How could she marry his brother? How could she live with always wishing Caleb were Justin? She could not, for if nothing else, it would not be fair to Caleb.

Savannah Turner had tried to convince Vivianna that time would heal her heart. She had loved Caleb once; she could love him again. Time would be the means. Still, Savannah likewise counseled Vivianna not to marry Caleb unless she truly were able to love him—love Caleb Turner for being Caleb Turner, not merely because she'd once loved him.

Thus, as Vivianna watched Caleb rather amble-limp toward town, she thought of the good man he was, and a part of her hoped she could fall in love with him one day. Still, she closed her eyes, her mind lingering on the words written in one of her most cherished letters from Justin.

"When I return," Vivianna whispered, nearly able to hear Justin's now silenced voice speaking the words he'd written, *"we'll meet beneath the honeysuckle vine . . ."*

Awash with the sudden pain of renewed heartache, she opened her eyes. Tears filled them—tears now blurring the vision of Caleb ambling in the distance.

Turning, she left Nate and Willy to their play, brushing tears from her cheeks as she hurried toward the vine-covered arbor. It was her place of heartache—of memory. Once her secret venue of hope, the arbor heavy with honeysuckle was now the place she retreated when her tears could no longer be restrained.

The fragrance of sweet honeysuckle hung heavy on the air. Not as heavy as it would in the coming months but heavy enough that Vivianna could breath it in—almost taste the sweet nectar of the blossoms.

Mr. Turner had built a bench swing before the war and fastened it to hang under the massive arbor his own father had constructed. As Vivianna sat down on Mr. Turner's swing, she was reminded of yet another life stripped from the earth—for Mr. Turner had enlisted even before his sons. He'd

27

died early in the war. It was a widowed Savannah Turner who had watched her two eldest sons ride away to battle.

Vivianna pushed at the ground with her well-worn shoes. As the swing began to sway back and forth, she gazed up to the vine overhead. Already heavy with honeysuckle blossoms, the vine covered every space of the arbor. Even as a child, Vivianna had loved the Turners' honeysuckle vine, often spending hours upon hours beneath its shady shelter. Frequently she had imagined the vine-covered arbor was a house, a house made of honeysuckle. Certainly the arbor was as large as a small dwelling. Every year the Turners would prune back the vine at each end of the arbor; otherwise the tangle of vines, leaves, and blossoms would swallow up even the open space within it. The vine had grown unruly during the war, branching out even to the nearby trees, engulfing an old wagon abandoned nearby as well. Still, Vivianna loved it! The arbor with honeysuckle was her space of serenity—and love—for now and then she liked to imagine Justin's spirit lingered there, as if he too were finding haven in the arms of the fragrant vine.

Vivianna reached into her skirt pocket, drawing out the letter she ever carried there—the letter she had silently vowed she would always carry.

The paper upon which the letter was written was becoming fragile, weakened with so much handling and rereading. Yet carefully she unfolded the pages of Justin's cherished letter, pressing them to her face in a vain attempt to catch a lingering trace of the scent of the fallen man she so loved.

She studied the first page—traced Justin's rather disheveled script with her fingertips. She thought that all the while he had been writing it, all the while he had been thinking of her. A vision of the dead soldiers she'd seen in Florence when the Yankees had attacked entered her mind. Their faces had been dirt-streaked, pale, and often their cold, dead eyes had stared blindly at passersby or into the raining sky. A horrified shiver ran through her, yet she would not think of Justin lying dead in an open field. She would not imagine him propped up against a tree trunk, bleeding out onto the soft Georgia grass as General Sherman rode on—the Alabama First Calvary accompanying along his Savannah Campaign. No! She would only think of Justin Turner as he'd appeared the last time she'd seen him: handsome, strong, vibrant, and hopeful.

"My Darling Vivianna," she began to read aloud. New tears stung her violet eyes, as ever they did when she read Justin's letters—especially this one, for it was her most cherished.

I beg you; do not be angry with me for so intimate a beginning to this letter. By now you must know my mind addresses you as my darling . . . for you are so dear and darling to me. It is true you have always been dear to me, yet now you are even so deeply more dear, more dear than you may ever know. You have saved me, sweet Vivianna. It is many the time I have been in despair, injured, hurt, hungry, cold, or alone that your sweet letters comfort me. There is one particular I carry with me. I am hoping you will remember it if I make reference to it here. It was the letter of last June 16th, 1863, in which you enclosed a photograph of yourself—of your beautiful self, a photograph I gaze upon each night before I take my sleep, that I might rest with the vision of your loving face in my mind. Do you remember this letter, sweet Vivianna? I will write a piece here that you might remember: "The honeysuckle is heavy on your grandfather's old arbor. At times, I sit beneath it in wondering at the old arbor being strong enough to support it yet. I have gone there every day this spring and summer to think and to wish you were home . . . to wish you were here with me. It seems there are more blossoms than ever I remember seeing before, and they are soft yellow and bright pink, and their nectar more sweet than any other year, I think. Whenever I am able, I slip away to the arbor and the vine. There I imagine you are home again . . . that you and I are together on your father's swing, talking of family and friends, of long summer walks and pollywogs in puddles . . ."

Though I cannot tell you why, Vivi—for perhaps I do not know why myself—I ever think of you beneath the honeysuckle vine. I imagine you are waiting for me there, that you will be waiting there when I return. I make a promise to you now, Vivianna Bartholomew. I promise this: When I return, we will meet beneath the honeysuckle vine, and I will kiss you such a kiss as you have never known before. It is what I dream of. Amidst the nightmares of battle and death, often there comes to me a dream of you, of you and I together beneath the honeysuckle vine, and I awake improved and hopeful, for there is something for me to fight for now . . . you, my darling.

On the battlefield, or at the campfire, there are moments when your sweet face will appear before me. Those brief visions of you rescue me . . . for I will not die and never meet you beneath the honeysuckle. That is what I think—when the stench of death and fighting is all around me, when the noise of the cannons seems to echo forever in my ears, as we bury our fellow soldiers and want for food and comfort, I think of you and me there beneath that arbor, bathed in the fragrance of honeysuckle . . . sharing kisses as sweet as their nectar. You, Vivianna . . . you are why I continue to live.

I confess it . . . I confess that I love you. I have written it here in hoping you will not refuse the offer of my heart. It belongs to you, Vivianna. You alone will own my love . . . forever.

I fight for you, Vivianna. I fight to come to you . . . to live . . . so that we may linger together beneath the honeysuckle vine.

May God protect and keep you, my love.

Vivianna brushed the tears from her cheeks—let her fingers tenderly trace the lone character Justin had signed the letter with. She drew the letter to her face once more, kissed the familiar and beloved initialed signature.

"Oh, Justin!" she breathed. "I feel as if I can't go on! Sometimes I just think . . . I just think . . ."

Vivianna swallowed and inhaled a deep breath. Folding the letter, she returned it to the pocket of her skirt. She could not let her passionate emotions rise. She could not linger on thoughts of all she had lost. She would not think of her parents, of Sam or Augie. To think of them would mean collapse;

she was certain of it. It was everything she could manage to will her heart to continue to beat when the loss of Justin was so painful. She could not think of the others. Vivianna had grown to know that war was far more destructive to the human soul and heart than it was even to the landscape, towns, or cities. Each morning she awoke with thoughts of her family yet pushed them to the far corners of her mind. She could not linger on the whole of it—not yet.

She had spent enough time in misery for one day. Thus, Vivianna stood, inhaled one last breath of the sweet honeysuckle beneath which she would never meet Justin Turner, and walked. She knew where her feet would lead her, though she further knew it would only bring her more pain. Still, though she would not linger on the deaths of so many loved ones, she did not want them to look down from heaven and think she did not miss and mourn them. Thus, she wandered to the small cemetery nestled in the meadow in the center of a grove of dogwood trees. It was not more than half a mile from the house—a small cemetery belonging to the Turner family. Mr. Turner's parents and his eldest brother were among those resting beneath the cool, fragrant grass. Sadly, Mr. Turner did not rest with them, having fought and died far from home. Savannah had begged Vivianna to let her parents be interred there instead of in the cemetery in Florence.

Though there were many northern Alabamians who had silently or otherwise supported the Union during the war, the Union raids on Florence had hardened many of those hearts, as well as causing further hatred of the Union and its Yankees to grow among local Confederates. Thus, Vivianna's parents, Victor and Mary Bartholomew, were laid to rest in the Turner family cemetery where none could defile their graves for the sake of their two sons, who had been lost defending the Union.

Oddly, the short walk to the old cemetery helped Vivianna to surface from the melancholy heartache she'd been lingering in within the arbor. The dogwoods were beginning to bloom, and the wildflowers and grass were mellow and sweet in their perfumed offerings. The birds were plentiful in the trees, chirping songs of happiness, of carefree springs to come and nests filled with tiny eggs of hope in further generations—generations that would not know the scent and sight of battle and bloodshed.

As she walked, as she meandered toward the meadow and gravestones nestled midst the dogwoods, Vivianna pulled the pins from her long sable hair, allowing it to hang freely down her back. Combing it with her fingers, she wished she could always wear her hair free. She fancied it calmed her—made her feel not quite so worried and tired. Slowly she wove it into a soft, loose braid, securing it with a strand of itself and letting the braid rest over her right shoulder.

Stepping into the small clearing, Vivianna was immediately struck with the sense of warm sunshine—of peacefulness and rest. In truth, she had never feared cemeteries the way others seemed to. In fact, as a child, it was often she would wander to the Turner cemetery and sit in contemplation at the etchings on the gravestones. She liked to think that all those spirits who had left their bodies to sleep in the soft earth were watching from heaven, happy to see that a little child cared enough to read what was written over their graves. She imagined they all smiled as she wove dandelion chains or gathered nosegays of fresh violets to place by each stone. In truth, she'd learned every epitaph, every name of every person buried there, and often tried to imagine who they had been and what they had loved. Had they gathered flowers as children? Had they laughed and played, sung with the birds? Had they sat at the edge of the pond, sinking their toes into the mud as pollywogs tickled their ankles? As a child, Vivianna was certain each and every one of them had done just these things, and she had adored knowing it. Yet since the war, she'd begun to wonder how many of those who rested amid the dogwoods had known pain as well. Surely all, for pain was certainly as much a part of life as were muddy toes.

Still, as she passed the large granite monument marking Mr. Turner's mother's grave, she whispered, "Good afternoon, Mr. Turner's mother. Isn't this sunshine just lovely today?"

Thus, Vivianna wandered among the stones marking lives once lived. Oddly, it brought her more comfort than melancholy or heartache. She thought of all those who were waiting to meet Sam and Augie as they arrived at heaven's gate—wondered if Sam and Augie were there to meet her mother and father or if her mother and father stood smiling in greeting Sam and Augie. Even Mr. Turner must've been filled with joy at seeing his own parents—his earthly remains—no matter how painful a death he met, resting at last as he drifted into the arms of the Lord. She thought then that Justin too would've been met with family and friends—though she would not linger on those thoughts. Simply she wandered, tugged a few unruly weeds from places they should not be, even gathered a handful of violets to lay on the grave of the tiny baby girl Savannah Turner lost before either Caleb or Justin were born. Last, she visited the graves of the two local boys from Florence. Boy and Floydie Maggee had fought with the Alabama First Cavalry—side by side with Caleb and Justin. Yet both were wounded in the same battle and returned home, Floydie having lost both legs to amputation and Boy with a terrible injury to his head that found him unable to respond to any stimulus. Neither young man had survived the month and now rested in comfort in the arms of heaven, their earthly remains in repose at the Turner cemetery.

Vivianna kissed her fingertips and placed them on the etched name of Floydie Maggee. She did the same for Boy.

The last stones she read were those of her parents. She would not read them aloud, for she knew she could not linger, lest the certainty of her loss should overtake her. Quickly she sprinkled the remaining violets she'd gathered over the graves of her mother and father. Then—without a word— she turned.

She would think of the living—of Nate and Willy, of Savannah, and of Caleb. Caleb had returned from the war, and when he had, both Vivianna and Savannah had determined they would make certain Caleb felt no guilt in having survived when so many had not. Vivianna let her thoughts linger on Caleb—not the dead or the lost but the man that yet breathed. He was such a good man. Any unmarried woman of any age in Florence would count herself blessed in owning his heart. Vivianna determined she would try to fall in love with him. She should try. Yet even as she resolved she would endeavor to do so, Justin's words echoed through her mind.

When I return, we will meet beneath the honeysuckle vine.

Vivianna frowned as she neared the house. Nate and Willy were no longer playing in the grass nearby. The war was over, yes, but there were yet angry, renegade Confederate soldiers lurking about the countryside, beaten and desperate and not to be trusted. Thus, Vivianna frowned—felt a familiar wave of worry wash over her.

She startled when Willy rushed up behind her, taking hold of her hand and tugging at her to turn.

"Look there, Viv!" Willy cried. "Looks like two more boys are comin' home to Florence!"

Vivianna turned, her heart leaping in her bosom. It was true her heart had grown weary of leaping, only to find disappointment and renewed aching. Over the past few weeks, each time a lone soldier or a group of soldiers traveling together meandered past the Turner place on their way to Florence, Vivianna hoped. Even after years of no letters from her brothers, even after months of knowing Justin was lost, still she hoped. The pain she'd tried to leave beneath the honeysuckle vine returned, and she wondered how any human being who had survived the war continued to survive it.

"Simmer down, Viv," she whispered to herself as she raised her hand to shade her eyes from the sun, gazing down the road in the direction Willy was pointing.

"They're wearin' ordinary clothes. That means they're Yankees!" Nate exclaimed. "Two of 'em! Maybe one of 'em is Justin, Viv! Or Sam or Augie!"

"Maybe," Viv said, though she held no hope anymore—or at least very little, even for her fast-beating heart—or so she told herself.

The fact was she knew Sam or Augie would've written if they were able—if they were still alive. She knew the same would be true of Justin—especially of Justin. Instinctively she let her hand slip into the pocket of her skirt—felt the folded, well-read letter—again heard the echo of the loving words written in it.

"When I return," Vivianna whispered as she watched the distant figures advance, *"we'll meet beneath the honeysuckle vine."*

"What's that, Viv?" Willy asked. "What're you mutterin' on about?"

"Yankees," she answered. "You boys are right. They'd still be wearin' the gray if they were Rebs comin' home to Florence."

"That's right!" Nate agreed. "Only southern Yankees like Justin and Caleb come marchin' home in ordinary clothes. It might be Justin, Viv! I just know it might be him!"

"Now, simmer yourself down, Nate," Vivianna warned, though her own heart was pounding like a hammer on an anvil. "It's most likely just some men from town." She tried to steady her breathing. "We can't let ourselves get too hopeful every time . . ."

But it was too late; hope had already enveloped the two boys who so missed their lost brother. As Nate began to whistle "When Johnny Comes Marching Home," Willy ran off down the road toward the two approaching men.

"Willy!" Vivianna called. "Come here! You come back here this minute! We don't know who . . ."

Nate's whistling grew breathy—silenced. Vivianna held her breath. As Willy ran toward the two men, one of them spread his arms wide, dropped to his knees, and embraced the boy.

"It's Justin! I know it is!" Nate shouted. "Mama! Mama! Justin's home!"

"Nate!" Vivianna scolded as Nate raced down the road toward his little brother and the two men. "We don't know who they are," Vivianna breathed—even as the letter in her pocket began to warm the tender flesh of her fingers with hope.

"What's all the fussin' out here?" Savannah asked, drying her hands on her apron as she stepped off the front porch.

"Two men," Vivianna managed. "I-I think one of them might be . . ." She looked to Savannah Turner. Already tears of hope were brimming in her eyes.

Savannah looked down the road to where one

of the men still knelt on the ground, now hugging Nate as well as Willy.

"Justin!" she cried. "Oh, my baby!"

Vivianna watched as Savannah lifted her skirts, running toward the two men, who were still some distance down the road.

"It can't be," Vivianna breathed, shaking her head—still afraid to hope. Yet as she watched Savannah collapse into the welcoming embrace of one of the men, she knew.

"Justin!" she gasped.

CHAPTER TWO

Vivianna could not breathe, let alone move. It couldn't be true. It just couldn't be! After five months of no letters, no word of any kind, it couldn't truly be Justin who now embraced Mrs. Turner. It couldn't be! It was too frightening to hope—felt somehow wrong to allow the thrill to continue to well up within her.

Yet slowly—as she heard Savannah sobbing, as Nate and Willy turned, gesturing for her to join them—slowly Vivianna's feet began to carry her forward, and her eyes filled with tears.

"It's Justin, Viv! It's Justin!" Willy called. "He ain't dead after all! Look, Viv—it's Justin!"

She was running then, running toward Justin Turner, toward all her heart held dear and most loved.

Justin caught her in his arms, breathing, "Viv!" and she sobbed against his shoulder for a moment. She could feel his breath in her hair, hear his heart beating in his bosom. Justin was alive!

"I'm home, Viv," Justin said. Oh, how familiar his voice was to her—how beloved! She looked to him and took his face between her hands.

"Justin!" she breathed as she studied his weary eyes. His whiskery face was so lean, so weathered. Yet it was Justin; he had come home!

He smiled at her, the smile of a worn and weary soldier, beaten and battered by war—yet the smile she knew so well, the smile she'd so often seen in her dreams. Justin!

"You're beautiful, Viv," he whispered, and more tears streamed over her cheeks as she saw the moisture brimming in his eyes.

"And you're scrawny and bald," Willy laughed. He threw his young arms around Justin's waist then and added, "But it ain't no matter. Mama and Viv will fatten ya up now that you're home."

Justin released Vivianna, and it was only then that she noticed how weak his embrace had been. Indeed he was almost frail looking. His appearance pierced her heart with alarm, yet she was determined to cast fear aside in favor of hope. Justin was home! Weathered and weak he may be; still he was alive, and he'd come home. He'd returned to her!

Vivianna watched as Savannah ran a tender hand over the short bristles of hair on Justin's head.

"Your hair," she said.

"We shaved it," Justin replied. "I'm not sure I want to tell ya why though, Mama."

"No matter," she said, smiling and brushing tears from her cheeks. She caressed Justin's face with the back of her hand. "No matter. You're home. My darlin', you're home."

"Who're you, mister?" Vivianna heard Nate ask.

She'd nearly forgotten Justin had a traveling

companion. In truth, she'd been so overjoyed, so overwhelmed with emotion at the sight of Justin, she'd not yet looked to the man who now stood to one side.

"That's John Tabor," Justin said. "He's my friend. I owe him my life . . . more than once over."

"You look worse than Justin, mister," Willy said as the tip of one index finger disappeared into his left nostril. The young boy offered his free hand to the man, and the man shook it, though weakly.

"I suppose I do," the man said, rather coughing an amused chuckle.

"Get your finger out of your nose, Willy!" Nate scolded in a whisper, smacking Willy hard on the back of the head.

Vivianna felt her heart twist with sympathy. This man looked even more weary, weathered, and worn than Justin did. His several-days' beard growth could not hide the pale, gaunt state of his face. His clothes hung on his emaciated frame, and the knuckles of his perhaps once-strong hands looked unusually large for the lack of meat on his fingers.

"I'm Savannah Turner," Savannah said, offering a hand to the man.

"Ma'am," the man said. Yet as he reached out to accept her offer of greeting, he teetered to one side, nearly losing his balance.

"Oh my!" Savannah exclaimed. She caught hold

of the young man's arm in an effort to steady him.

"I'm sorry, ma'am," Justin's friend said. "I suppose I'm just a little worn out from walkin' today."

"Mama," Justin began, "it's the truth of it when I tell ya I wouldn't be here if it weren't for Johnny." Justin reached out and put a hand on his friend's shoulder. "I mean it. Johnny saw me through."

Vivianna smiled as Savannah gently embraced Justin's friend. Still, something in her feared that even Savannah's gentle hug might break the man in two.

"Thank you, mister," Nate began, "for bringin' Justin home."

"You can call me Johnny there, boy," he said, offering a trembling hand to Nate. Nate shook the man's hand carefully.

Vivianna glanced back to Justin. Her heart filled with so much joy, love, and emotion, she was sure it would burst!

"Justin," she breathed. He looked at her, his blue eyes weary yet still reflecting joy. "Where have you been?" She couldn't help but ask. She so desperately wanted to fling herself against him—kiss his mouth over and over with loving kisses. Yet she knew this was not the time. Justin was first and foremost Savannah's son. Second he had brothers who would require attention. Still, she could not keep from asking—for she wondered why he had not written.

"In hell," came his simple answer. The smile

faded from his eyes and his lips, and an odd sort of trepidation twisted about Vivianna's spine.

"Nate . . . run an' fetch Caleb," Savannah said.

"Aw! But I want to stay here!" Nate whined.

"Run fetch Caleb!" his mother demanded. She placed her hands determinedly on her hips, and her eyes narrowed. "Nate Turner . . . you fetch your brother this minute! It wouldn't be fair not to! He'll be as happy as the rest of us to know Justin's alive and well and come home to us. Now run along."

Nate kicked the dirt with one foot, scowled, and exhaled a heavy sigh. "Oh, all right," he mumbled. "But don't tell 'em anything 'til I get back with Caleb. Don't tell 'em one thing, Justin."

Justin grinned again at last. "All right. But you run on and fetch Caleb."

Nate smiled at his returned brother. "I will, Justin. You remember how fast I am, don't ya?" he asked.

Justin chuckled. "I do."

Nate was off then, racing toward town.

"Hey, mister . . . you don't look too good at all," Willy said.

Vivianna turned to look to Justin's friend once more.

Again she took note of the terrible condition of the man—so pallid a complexion, so thin. His brown eyes were dull, nearly void of life. His lips were parched and dry, his hands chapped and covered over with small breaks in his skin, many of which were bleeding. Even the brown stubble of his hair and beard looked weary, and she wondered why it was Justin credited this man for his return home when it appeared to her that Mr. Tabor was in worse condition than Justin.

Vivianna gasped, reached out, and caught hold of Mr. Tabor's arm as he suddenly swayed and then stumbled. It was obvious he was near overcome with the weakness of fatigue and his frail condition.

"Mr. Tabor!" Vivianna exclaimed. "It would appear you are quite unwell."

Still, the man merely shook his head and mumbled, "I just need to sit down here for a spell." He fairly crumpled to the ground, sitting down hard in the grass at the side of the road.

Certainly Vivianna herself wished to be in Justin's arms—to know, through his touch, that he was alive and home with them. But she could not ignore the poor soul who had helped him to return.

"Hey, Viv," Willy began, "I'm thinkin' you better not let that feller sit like that for too long. He might never get up again."

"Willy Turner!" Savannah scolded. "What a thing to say!"

Still, Vivianna owned the same sense as Willy— that perhaps the man ought not be allowed to linger in sitting outside.

"Mr. Tabor?" Savannah asked, bending down

before him, frowning as she studied his state. "Are you indeed well?"

Mr. Tabor nodded weakly. "I'm right as rain, Mrs. Turner," he lied.

Justin dropped to one knee before the man.

"Let's get on in the house, Johnny," he said. "I'm sure Mama's got somethin' in there that'll start in to fixin' you up."

"I just need a little time. I'll just sit here for a spell," the man mumbled.

Vivianna glanced to Justin—saw the worry in his eyes, the fear. She would not have his friend die right there in the Alabama grass before him. It was obvious Justin was weak himself; he might not endure losing his companion so soon after returning.

Kneeling before Mr. Tabor, she said, "We've killed a chicken today, Mr. Tabor. It's boilin' on the stove just this minute. Let's get you on your feet and take ya inside for some warm broth."

Mr. Tabor only shook his head a little, however. "I'll . . . I'll just sit here awhile, miss," he mumbled. "I'll just sit here awhile."

Vivianna's heart began to quicken its pace once more, again for the sake of renewed fear. She looked to Justin, praying he was stronger than this poor fellow before her. She could not bear to have Justin return only to die.

"Johnny!" Justin growled. "You get up and get in the house!"

"Please, Mr. Tabor," Vivianna begged in a soothing voice. "Let's get ya inside. Then ya can eat somethin' and rest. You'll feel better if ya eat somethin'."

"I'm . . . I'm just tired, miss," Mr. Tabor mumbled. "We walked a fair piece today. I'm just tired. I'll just stretch out for a minute and . . ."

Mr. Tabor began to lie down in the grass, and a strange sort of panic caused Vivianna to tremble. Somehow—somehow she knew he could not be allowed to rest there in the grass. Somehow she knew that if Justin's friend took his rest there, it would be his final rest. They might as well fetch a shovel and begin digging his grave as to let him linger a moment longer. She feared Justin may be lost as well—that his own will to press on in life might expire with the final breath of the man who had shared his journey home. If Mr. Tabor was allowed to lie down in the grass, well, she might as well have Willy fetch two shovels.

"Johnny!" Justin barked. "Get up, boy!" He reached out, taking hold of Mr. Tabor's arm, and began pulling him to his feet. "Don't you lie down and die here, Johnny Tabor! We're home, boy. We're home! Don't you give up now!"

"I just . . . I just need some rest, Justin," Mr. Tabor mumbled. His body was limp and too heavy for Justin to support in his own weakened state. As Mr. Tabor began to slip to the ground

49

again, Vivianna took his arm, placing it around her shoulders to help support him.

"Oh, dear!" Savannah exclaimed. "Willy! Run after Nate and make sure Caleb is on his way home. Hurry!"

"Yes, Mama," Willy said. The boy frowned. As he looked to his brother and then to Mr. Tabor, his eyes misted with fearful tears.

Vivianna wasn't certain whether Savannah were sending Willy off in search of Nate and Caleb because she truly wanted to make certain Caleb was on his way or whether she simply didn't want her youngest son witnessing the death of Justin's friend.

"Run along after Nate, Willy," Vivianna said, smiling at the frightened boy. "We'll feed Justin and Mr. Tabor so we can all sit down together when you boys return."

"All . . . all right, Viv," Willy stammered. "All right." He ran off in the direction of town, his little feet kicking up the dirt in the road as they carried him as fast as they could.

In that moment, Justin stumbled—nearly collapsed.

"Justin!" Savannah gasped. "Here . . . let me," she said, taking Mr. Tabor's arm from Justin's shoulders and placing it about her own. "You boys are so thin!"

"We'll be fine, Mama," Justin said, though he coughed into his fist and cleared his throat.

50

Vivianna's worried gaze met Savannah's near panicked one. It was obvious Justin's homecoming—though wonderful to the point of near euphoria—had not ensured his well-being.

"Let's just get you both inside and put somethin' in those empty bellies," Savannah said as she and Vivianna helped Mr. Tabor climb the stairs of the front porch.

Once inside, Justin groaned as he settled himself in a chair at the table. "Oh, Mama!" he sighed, "I never thought sittin' in a chair would seem such a pure luxury."

Vivianna helped Mrs. Turner deposit Mr. Tabor into a chair on the other side of the table.

She was frustrated—angry! She didn't want to know in her heart that Justin had returned home simply to yet linger in danger. She didn't want to nurse two more men, only to watch them die the way the Maggee boys had. She wanted laughter, love, kisses in the sunshine and beneath the honeysuckle vine!

For a moment, she feared she might burst into more tears—tears of returning hopelessness and the sore fatigue borne of enduring the seeming endless ramifications of war.

"Will you ladle some of that broth for these boys, Vivi?" Mrs. Turner asked. She was sitting at the table now, holding Justin's hand, nervously stroking it for her concern.

"I might could stomach a little bread if you've

got any, Mama," Justin said. He looked to his friend, frowning. "Though I'm not sure Johnny's up for it today."

Mr. Tabor shook his head in affirmation he did not have the strength or stomach to eat bread.

"Oh, I baked two fresh loaves just this mornin'!" Savannah said, brushing tears from her eyes. She sniffled, desperately trying to remain calm—to appear strong. Vivianna empathized with her; her own strength was waning in the wake of so much conflicting emotion.

As Vivianna ladled broth into two bowls, Justin sighed and looked around the room.

"I can hardly believe I'm here," he mumbled. "It seems a hundred years since me and Caleb left."

"Two hundred," Vivianna said.

Justin smiled at her as she set a bowl of broth in front of him. She set the other bowl of broth on the table in front of Mr. Tabor and retrieved two spoons from the cupboard. Working quickly, she cut a slice of bread from one of Savannah's still-warm loaves and then returned to the table.

"You're only prettier, Viv," Justin said, smiling as she handed him a spoon and the slice of bread. "Prettier even than I remember."

Vivianna couldn't help but smile—and blush. He was weathered, it was true. But he was still Justin—the same eyes, the same smile. Her heart leapt at the renewed realization that he was alive, that he'd come back to her. She wondered how long it would be before they could linger alone together.

Still, Vivianna was wise and tenderhearted. She had not forgotten Caleb. She would not be insensitive to his feelings. He would be glad to see his brother returned—more than glad. Furthermore, he knew Vivianna loved Justin. Still, she would press neither Caleb into letting her go nor Justin into affirming that he loved her as much as his letters had professed. He was weak—tired and worn. There was healing to be endured. Likewise, Savannah, Caleb, Nate, and Willy would want all the time they could steal with Justin. Vivianna knew she would need to find patience. She would need to allow everything to settle—to begin healing. Still, her heart beat so madly within her breast, she thought she might scream for not being able to beg Justin to hold her in his arms—to kiss her!

"Ma'am," Mr. Tabor began, "I ain't fit to be sittin' at the table. I haven't had a bath in a good long time."

Savannah looked to the worn soldier. She smiled, shaking her head. "Don't you be worryin' about that, Mr. Tabor. We'll get some broth in ya . . . see to your stomach first. Then we can see to your flesh."

"Thank ya, ma'am," Mr. Tabor said. "But I am . . . I am sorry to be sittin' in your home in such a state."

"You just eat that broth, Mr. Tabor," Savannah said, nodding toward the bowl of broth Vivianna had placed before him. "You brought my son back to me. You could sit at my table in nothin' but your skin, and I wouldn't mind it one bit."

"Thank ya, ma'am," Mr. Tabor mumbled.

"You see he eats that broth, Viv," Mrs. Turner instructed.

"I will," Vivianna promised, offering Mr. Tabor the other spoon she was holding.

Savannah's attention immediately returned to Justin, and Vivianna smiled. It was a dream! Justin—Justin was alive! She gazed at him for a moment, butterflies swarming in her stomach as he glanced at her and smiled. He dipped his spoon into the bowl of warm broth, sighing with obvious pleasure as he slurped the soothing liquid.

The clatter of a spoon hitting a bowl and then the table drew Vivianna's attention to Mr. Tabor, however. Her smile faded, and she felt a frown pucker her brow as she watched the wasted soldier struggling to pick the spoon up from the table. He dropped it again and sighed as his weak fingers tried once more to manage it.

Vivianna frowned, awed by his weakened state. Too weak to even manage to feed himself, Justin's friend would be dead in a few days if he didn't gain strength.

Picking up the spoon herself, Vivianna dipped it into the broth and held it close to Mr. Tabor's mouth. She couldn't help but grin a little, slightly amused by Mr. Tabor's obvious pride, for he would not look at her, nor would he eat from the spoon. Rather, a firm expression of defiance set itself hard on his face as his brow furrowed with a deep frown borne of self-disgust.

"You can let me feed you, Mr. Tabor," Vivianna began, "or I'll wrestle ya to the floor and pour this broth down your throat. And I think you and I both know that I well could do it."

The annoyed, humiliated man glanced at her but only briefly. He growled low in his throat but opened his mouth. Vivianna nearly giggled, thinking he looked like a pouting child as he surrendered and let her spoon the broth into his mouth. As she placed a second spoonful of broth in his mouth, Vivianna could have sworn a little color returned to his face.

"Thank ya, ma'am," Mr. Tabor mumbled, his trembling hand taking the spoon from hers. "I can do this. I can."

"Are ya certain?" Vivianna asked.

"Yes, ma'am," the man grumbled.

She watched as his weak and trembling hand struggled to ladle the warm broth into his mouth. Still, it did seem he could manage feeding himself, and she returned her attention to Justin.

"Where have you been, my darlin'?" Savannah begged, her voice breaking with emotion. "We haven't had a letter in over five months! We were certain you were . . . we were reconciled to your having . . . oh, I can't even speak it, Justin! Oh, darlin'! Why haven't we heard from ya?"

Justin's face paled; what little color he did own in his cheeks fled like rain washing new paint from a canvas. "I'm sorry, Mama," he began. "I . . . I . . . couldn't write to ya about it . . . even if they had let us write."

"Who, darlin'?"

"The guards . . . at Andersonville."

The living breath was instantly sucked from Vivianna's lungs! A cold, clammy dread crept over her flesh, and every inward organ began to quiver.

"Andersonville?" she breathed. She glanced from Justin to Mr. Tabor, struggling to feed himself. "Andersonville?" she breathed once more. As tears filled her eyes, Vivianna offered another silent prayer of thanks. If Justin and his friend had been incarcerated at Andersonville prison—if the stories of torture, starvation, and disease rampant at Andersonville owned even a little truth—then it was a pure miracle the men were alive, let alone that they'd made it home.

"Not Andersonville!" Savannah wept. "Oh no, Justin! Not that horrible place! Not that death camp!"

But Justin nodded, agony plain on his face. "Last November we were with General Sherman, after Atlanta and on our way to Savannah. And me and Johnny . . . we were out scoutin'," Justin began. He

56

paused, shaking his head and running trembling fingers over the stubble of new hair on his head. "I-I don't even remember exactly what happened. I just know that one minute I was sittin' my horse . . . and then next, I was laid out on the ground, bleedin' from my shoulder." Justin nodded toward Mr. Tabor and continued, "Johnny dismounted to help me, and in a blink, he was laid out too . . . shot in the leg. The Rebs came down on us hard then . . . drug us off to a wagon . . . and the wagon hauled us eight days to Andersonville." Justin chuckled and shook his head again. "For two years we were the best scouts in the Alabama First. Two years . . . ain't that right, Johnny? We fought hard and long and never came close to capture—not me and certainly not Johnny Tabor. No sirree! Then, as quick as that, we were captured . . . found ourselves in Andersonville."

"Andersonville," Vivianna whispered. The pain of overpowering sympathy shook her as she watched Justin's friend struggling to feed himself. The stories of the horror of Andersonville were infamous! Little or no shelter, torture at the hands of the guards, no food, filthy water, disease—how had they survived?

"Darlin'!" Savannah breathed, dabbing at her tears with her apron. "Andersonville! Nobody lived through Andersonville. They say nobody lived through it!"

Justin shrugged. "Well, not everybody had a

friend like Johnny Tabor," he said. "Johnny saved my life more times than I can count . . . and that was before the prison. But let me tell you, if it weren't for John, I wouldn't be here with you, Mama. I took awful sick last month. Winter was so cold there . . . and we didn't have much food or shelter. But ol' Johnny, he wasn't about to see me give up. I owe him my life."

"Nobody owes me anything," Mr. Tabor mumbled. "I don't want to hear that from you, Justin. I told you that."

Justin's gaze fell to Vivianna. He smiled and winked at her, and her heart fluttered as if it were a flower with petals only just caught by a sweet summer breeze.

"John don't take much to acceptin' thanks or praise," Justin said. "He's a cantankerous ol' boy sometimes, but don't let that fool ya. He's a good man."

"Justin," Vivianna began, "Andersonville! I can't hardly think on it!"

"Don't," Justin told her. "The war is over. Andersonville is no more. I'm home . . . home with you and Mama," he said. He leaned forward and kissed his mother's cheek. "The past is the past. Let's just leave it there."

"But, Justin," Savannah began, "my poor baby—"

"I'm home, Mama," Justin interrupted. "That's what matters now. I'm home."

Savannah nodded. Vivianna too understood. No doubt Justin's time at Andersonville had seemed a sentence served in hell. He didn't want to remember it—didn't want talking of it to cause the pain to return. Maybe someday he would want to or need to tell them more about it. But for now—for now, he wanted only to leave it behind.

"Well, then," Savannah began, reaching out and running a tender hand over Justin's head, "I will say I do miss those raven locks of yours. But it will grow back . . . now won't it, Justin?"

Justin chuckled and nodded. "Yes, it will. We shaved up when we were let go."

"As a symbol? A ritual of ridding yourself of the horror you boys endured?" Savannah asked, looking to Mr. Tabor.

Mr. Tabor shook his head. "No, ma'am," he answered. "We shaved up so we wouldn't carry the lice home to you folks."

"Oh my!" Mrs. Turner gasped.

Vivianna brushed a tear from her cheek as Mr. Tabor glanced to her.

"Thank you, miss," he said, nodding toward the now empty bowl. "I do feel better."

"Let me ladle you some more," Vivianna said, taking his bowl and standing.

"Just a bit . . . if ya wouldn't mind, miss," Mr. Tabor said.

"But you've eaten hardly enough to fill a kitten," Vivianna noted.

"Johnny can't handle much more than that yet, Viv," Justin explained. "I'm ashamed to say it . . . but he gave me most of his food these past two months. It's probably why the sickness didn't get me. He'll have to go slow on eatin' for a while yet."

"Oh," Vivianna said, returning the now only half-full bowl of broth on the table before Mr. Tabor.

"But I think I could use another whole bowlful, Viv," Justin said. He smiled and lifted his bowl. Vivianna returned his smile, accepting his bowl.

"And . . . um . . . and where are you from, Mr. Tabor?" Vivianna heard Savannah ask.

"Texas, ma'am," Mr. Tabor said. "And if ya don't mind, Mrs. Turner . . . my father's Mr. Tabor. I'm just Johnny."

"Of course, Johnny," Savannah said, smiling.

Vivianna placed the second bowl of broth on the table before Justin. She sighed as she sat down across from him. He was there! He was really there—there at the table! Her beloved Justin had returned from the war! She silently thanked God for the blessed miracle.

"Andersonville!" Savannah breathed, shaking her head and wiping more tears from her cheeks.

"It's over, Mama," Justin said. "Let's talk about somethin' happy." Justin smiled—chuckled. "Nate and Willy sure have grown," he said, slurping his broth.

"Oh my, yes!" Savannah exclaimed, still choking back tears. "Like weeds those two . . . growin' and growin' and always into mischief where they ought not to be."

"And Caleb?" he asked.

Savannah quickly glanced to Vivianna and then back to Justin. Vivianna willed the blush to cool from her cheeks. Suddenly she didn't want Justin to know she'd accepted he had been lost; she didn't want him to know that only an hour before, she'd been trying to convince herself she could marry his brother—learn to love him.

"Caleb's well," Savannah said. "And he'll be much better now that he has his brother back."

"He's a good man . . . Caleb Turner," Johnny Tabor mumbled.

Vivianna looked to the stranger and was startled to find he was staring at her.

"You knew Caleb?" she asked, though she was rather unsettled at the way he was looking at her— as if he somehow knew what Vivianna's recent thoughts of Caleb had been.

"Sure," Johnny Tabor said. "He scouted with me once in a while . . . until he was wounded." He looked back to his bowl of broth and mumbled, "He's a good man."

"I can't hardly believe I'm here, Mama," Justin said.

Vivianna looked to Justin, sighing with a blissful feel of hope renewed.

"Oh, Justin!" Savannah sighed. "My darlin'!"

Vivianna brushed fresh tears from her cheeks. It was wonderful—nearly too wonderful to be true! But as Justin looked to her, smiled, and winked, she knew it was true—that she was full awake, not merely dreaming.

"Would ya mind if I rested a bit out in your barn, Mrs. Turner?" Johnny Tabor inquired.

"In the barn?" Savannah exclaimed. "Nonsense, boy! Vivianna can stay with me in my room now, and you can have her room. She won't mind a breath . . . will ya, Viv?"

"Of course not," Vivianna answered. And she didn't mind a breath. The fact was she'd always felt rather too pampered having her own room. After her parents had been killed and Savannah had taken her in, she'd been nearly overwhelmed with guilt at being treated so very like a member of the family. Still, Savannah had explained how important it was for a young woman to have her own space and insisted Vivianna move into the spare bedroom. Thus, she was more than ready and willing to give up her privacy in order that a weary soldier might find respite and a space to heal.

But Johnny Tabor was shaking his head. "I just won't do that, ma'am," he said. "I don't need anythin' so fancy as a room. I just need a loft or—"

"You will stay in the house, Mr. Tabor," Savannah interrupted. "I'll have Caleb drag you in there if ya won't go just 'cause I say ya will."

"Mrs. Turner, I—" Johnny Tabor began.

"One thing you will learn, Johnny," Justin chuckled, "and that is ya won't win if ya choose to argue with my mama. If she tells you to go get your rest in Viv's room . . . then you best get to it, boy!"

"But . . . but I . . ." Johnny Tabor stammered.

"Come along, Mr. Tabor," Vivianna said, standing. "I'll take ya to your room so ya can rest awhile." Vivianna was more than willing to give up her room—and to escort Johnny Tabor to it. She wanted to sit and stare at Justin, listen to his voice, simply linger in his presence. She knew with Mr. Tabor resting comfortably, Justin would not be so worried about his convalescing friend—which in turn might offer him a respite of his own.

"Justin?" Johnny Tabor growled.

Vivianna knew he was irritated. No doubt he was not accustomed to being told what to do—at least not by anybody other than a prison guard.

"You better do what they say, Johnny," Justin said, nodding to his friend. "Neither one of us is in any fair condition to fight the will of women with a mind about 'em."

Vivianna saw Johnny's jaw clench tight. He was angry—no doubt humiliated and unhappy as well.

"Mrs. Turner, I just can't—" he began.

"You run along with Viv, Johnny," Savannah said. "You have yourself a good rest. You'll feel much better."

Johnny Tabor scowled at Vivianna as he weakly stood, and she fancied he could scare away the whole Rebel army itself with such a scowl.

"This way, Mr. Tabor," Vivianna said.

"Hurry on back, Viv," Justin called. "I ain't seen nothin' as pretty as you in over two years."

Vivianna smiled. Justin was home! As quickly as she could, she'd settle Mr. Tabor in her room and then return to her beloved. For some strange reason, her mouth flooded with moisture as she thought of Justin—the thought of perhaps kissing him soon. Oh, blessed day! Her lover was home!

"This is where you'll be stayin', Mr. Tabor," Vivianna said, stepping into her room.

"Johnny . . . if ya please, ma'am," Johnny Tabor mumbled.

"All right," Vivianna agreed as she looked at him. "And I'm Vivianna . . . Viv, if you'd rather."

Johnny Tabor nodded, weakly leaning against the doorframe of the bedroom.

"I'll bring some fresh water in for the pitcher," Vivianna said as she took his hand, leading him toward the bed. "And you just sleep as long as ya want to. I'll come in and gather up what I need later."

"Ma'am, I don't think I should . . . I ain't fit to sit at the table, let alone lie down on somethin' all covered in white the likes of that bed," he said.

Vivianna smiled. It was admirable this battered soldier should be so worried about such things.

Reaching out, she stripped the white quilt off her bed, revealing a rather tattered, old patchwork beneath.

"Does this suit ya better, Mr. Tabor?" she asked.

"Yes, ma'am," he said.

"Then I'll run and fetch a fresh pitcher for ya," she said. Quickly she lifted the pitcher from the washbasin sitting on the small table beside the bed. "You go on and lie down, and I'll be right back."

"Yes, ma'am," Johnny Tabor said.

Vivianna hurried to the well, drew a bucket of cool, fresh water, and filled the pitcher. She couldn't wait to see Justin—couldn't wait to return to the kitchen and talk with him, hear his voice, gaze into his eyes! Still, she was compassionate and worried for his friend. She would see Johnny settled, and then she could bask in the wonder of Justin's return.

Vivianna returned with the pitcher of water. Setting the pitcher down next to the basin, she gasped—grimaced with overwhelming compassion as she gazed at Johnny Tabor sprawled on his back on her bed. He'd removed his worn boots and tattered shirt, and the sight of the emaciated condition of his body caused tears to begin streaming down Vivianna's face. The rib bones of his torso were so defined, easily visible beneath his flesh. His clavicle and shoulders, though broad, were far too protruding. Already he slept, his gaunt face looking so like that of a corpse.

She could not linger in looking at him. The sight of Johnny Tabor did not cause joy to rise in her the way the sight of Justin did. Johnny Tabor seemed a stark reminder of all the horrors of war, while in the other room, Justin was the beloved evidence of war's end—and of heaven's blessings.

Vivianna went to the trunk in the corner of her room and withdrew a fresh sheet. Gently she laid it over the weathered and beaten man, more because she could not look on his condition any longer than for his own comfort.

Closing the door behind her, she hurried toward the kitchen. She could hear Justin's laughter—could hear Savannah's.

She entered the kitchen to see them still sitting at the table, smiling as they conversed.

"Is he all right then, Viv?" Justin asked as she took her seat across from him.

"I think so. He's asleep already," she said.

"Good," Justin sighed. "Now," he began, reaching across the table and taking her hand, "tell me everything." He raised her hand to his lips, kissing the back of it tenderly. Instantly, Vivianna's body was alive with goose pimples. Oh, how handsome he was! Even for his worn and weathered condition, he was handsome.

Justin was home. He was home! In that very moment, Vivianna could feel her broken heart beginning to heal. He had returned to her—to all who loved him.

"See! There he is, Caleb!" Willy hollered, bursting through the kitchen door. "I told you he'd come back! I told you all he wasn't dead!"

Caleb stepped into the kitchen and then Nate.

"Little brother!" Caleb breathed, tears filling his eyes.

"Caleb!" Justin said, pushing his chair away from the table and standing, only to collapse into his brother's embrace.

Vivianna watched and wept as the two brothers embraced, laughed, and cried with joy. Justin had come home!

Johnny Tabor listened to the voices wafting from the other room—voices raised in joy and hope. If he'd had the strength, he would have smiled in that moment, but he didn't. Still, he listened to the happy voices of the Turner family as they welcomed home their lost one.

He was so tired, so weary and sick. Yet he didn't care anymore. He'd brought Justin Turner home—brought back the man who had saved his life so many times—brought him home to his beloved family. He'd seen him all the way from Georgia to Alabama, all the way back to the pretty girl who loved him. He figured he could rest now, whether in the soft, sweetly scented bed of the girl Justin would marry or in the arms of heaven. Johnny Tabor knew he could rest at last. He'd made so many promises over the past two years—too many for one man to keep. Still, he'd managed to keep one. It had been almost two years since he'd sworn to Justin Turner he would repay him for saving his life. He could only hope that making certain Justin survived the horrors of Andersonville, that making certain he lived to return to his family and the beautiful girl who loved him, would atone for all the other promises he'd never be able to keep.

Closing his eyes once more, Johnny listened to the pretty laughter of gentle women—to the exclamations of young boys delighted to have their elder brother returned. The soft scents of spring flowers and green grasses drifted to him through the open window, and he almost smiled. It was far better to die in a soft bed under a clean sheet spread over him by a pretty girl—the sweet fragrances of fresh spring filling his nostrils—than to die drowning amidst the stench of death and disease. Yes, it would be a far more pleasant death.

As he drifted away, Johnny Tabor was glad he had seen Justin Turner safely home. He wondered then where he would take his final rest—his last thought being the hope Justin would see him buried in a quiet meadow.

CHAPTER THREE

"We were out scoutin' for the cavalry," Justin explained, "just outside a town called Waynesboro. We'd seen some small opposition—nothin' too heavy, so we weren't worried. After all, me and Johnny . . . well, we'd been scoutin' together for near to two years. Ain't that right, Caleb?"

Caleb nodded. "That's right. We scouted with Johnny right from the first of it."

"So we were just outside Waynesboro when all of a sudden I heard a shot and felt the burn at my shoulder, and then I was on the ground. In truth, the bullet only grazed me . . . here." He pulled at the left collar of his shirt, revealing a dark scar at the top of his shoulder. "But some ol' boy came runnin' outta the tree line and pulled me off my horse before I could think to move. Ol' Johnny, he was off his horse faster than lightnin' . . . drove a knife into the back of that ol' Reb who pulled me off my mount. But there were others in the trees, and the next thing I knew, Johnny was laid out beside me." Justin shook his head and continued. "They got Johnny in the leg, but luck was with him . . . and the bullet didn't hit a bone."

"Woulda shattered the bone if it had," Caleb mumbled.

Vivianna winced as she watched Caleb's hand

move to rest on his own leg. Caleb had been shot in the leg, and the bullet had hit a bone. Though the bone hadn't shattered, it did fracture. Though the injury had healed, it left Caleb with a limp.

"Indeed it would have," Justin said. Shaking his head, he added, "Johnny Tabor probably wouldn't be alive today if that bullet had hit a bone. Them doctors at Andersonville, I swear they just amputated limbs in order to decrease the prison population. I'm lucky ol' Johnny didn't find himself bleedin' out on the ground with only one leg left to him. I know I wouldn't be here if he had."

"So the Rebs hauled y'all off then?" Nate asked.

Vivianna looked to Nate and Willy, their young faces pale with imagining the horror their brother had endured.

"Yep," Justin continued. "They forced us in a wagon and headed for Andersonville. They hauled us for over a week. I suppose we're lucky we didn't die of some infection or the gangrene. Only doctorin' we had was what Johnny knew. He soaped our wounds out and stitched 'em over with a needle and thread he managed to beg off one of the Rebs."

"Was it . . . was it as awful as folks say?" Willy asked. "Andersonville? Was it really as bad as we hear tell?"

"Worse," Justin said.

Vivianna watched as Justin and Caleb both

glanced to their mother, sitting very still, endless tears streaming down her face. Vivianna brushed her own tears away, haunted by the memories of what she'd read and heard about Andersonville prison.

"But let's not linger on all that now," Justin said. He smiled and reached out, tousling Willy's hair. "The war's over, and I'm home! I want to hear what's been goin' on here all this time. How 'bout y'all tell me a bit about what the goin's-on are here about? What do ya say?"

Vivianna nodded. She knew Savannah and the younger boys needed a reprieve from such horrid stories as battle and prison camp. In truth, she wanted to put such thoughts aside as well. Thus, she was glad when she saw Willy's face lighten, a smile of excitement curling his lips.

"Me and Nate have been workin' on a fort . . . just on the other side of the old cemetery!" he said. "Caleb helped us a bit, and it's comin' right along. We'll show it to ya tomorrow if ya'd like."

Justin smiled and chuckled. "I'd like that just fine."

"And we seen Benjamin Sidney kissin' Tilly Winder out behind the ol' Libby place yesterday," Nate offered. "He was gnawin' on her face like a hound on a bone!"

"Nate!" Savannah scolded. "What a thing to say! And what a thing to be seein'. You boys stay away from that Libby place . . . and that Tilly Winder!"

"But, Mama," Willy began, "you shoulda seen it! I never seen the like . . . not in kissin' anyways. I swear, I thought he was gonna plum swallow that girl whole!"

Caleb began to chuckle, and Justin could no longer keep his amusement to just a smile.

"Sounds like little Tilly ain't changed much in the time we've been gone, Caleb," Justin said.

"No, she has not," Caleb confirmed.

"Caleb! Justin!" Savannah scolded. "Do not encourage your brothers!"

"Sorry, Mama," Justin said, still smiling.

"There's a new batch of pollywogs in the big puddle down by the barn," Willy said. "Oh, there's hundreds of 'em! Ain't there, Viv?"

Vivianna smiled and nodded. "Hundreds . . . at least," she said.

Justin smiled at her then, and she was glad she was already sitting down—for his smile caused her arms and legs to feel rather delightfully weak and spongy.

"And there's a three-legged dog in town now!" Nate added. "He belongs to Mr. Sidney. Got his foot stuck in a rabbit trap, and Mr. Sidney had to chop it off. He let me and Willy keep the leg though. We boiled it clean . . . out by the fort so it's just bones now but—"

"For pity's sake, Nate!" Savannah exclaimed. "The trouble you two get into! What am I gonna do with y'all?"

"It's all right, Mama," Caleb said. "I made 'em scrub their hands good after they brought that ol' dog leg home. I helped 'em boil the meat off. It's fine. It really is just bones now."

Savannah shook her head, placed her fingers to her temples, and began to massage. "I swear . . . four boys! What was the Lord thinkin' when he gave me four boys?" She looked up and smiled at Vivianna. "If I didn't have you, Vivi . . . I just don't know how I'd manage."

Caleb and Justin exchanged understanding glances. Vivianna knew the two elder Turner boys had been more trouble than Nate and Willy were! The difference was Mr. Turner had been alive to keep them in hand.

Justin chuckled once more, shook his head, and winked at Willy and Nate. He turned to Vivianna, his smile fading.

"You never heard anything, Viv?" Justin asked. "About Sam and Augie, I mean."

Vivianna shook her head. "No," she said. "I . . . I still ask Mr. Douglas to watch for any letters that might come to Mama and Daddy, from folks who might not know they're gone . . . but nothin' ever comes. I just figure they're up in heaven all together . . . Sam and Augie, with Mama and Daddy . . . that they're all happy." She forced a smile, and Justin nodded.

"I'm sorry, Viv," he said.

Vivianna was touched to the depths of her soul

by the moisture rising to his eyes. But she did not want the weathered soldier lingering in despair. "Thank you," she said. "But we're all here together now, and the war is over. It's in the past . . . everything about it."

Justin nodded and grinned. His eyes were entrancing! Vivianna had forgotten how mesmerizing they could be—how his gaze could hold a person awed by their overpowering depths of blue!

"Well, judgin' from the way you look, brother, and from what you've told me . . . I figure Johnny Tabor must look like hell," Caleb said.

"Caleb!" Savannah scolded. "That's not proper . . . *or* nice."

Justin chuckled and reached out, affectionately patting the back of his mother's hand. "Well, you saw him, Mama. Caleb's got it just about right . . . don't ya think?" he asked. "I'd like for him to stay on with us awhile. He ain't in any condition to travel. He'd never make it home alive if we let him leave now. We'll probably have to tie him to somethin' to keep him here . . . but he needs to stay."

"Of course he does! Oh my!" Savannah exclaimed. "You don't really think he'd try to go now, do ya? He needs his rest . . . and surely needs some meat on him. He brought my baby boy home. He can do anything he wants . . . as long as he doesn't leave! I'll never, never be able to thank him enough or to repay him in any way at all. But leastwise, maybe I can give him his health back."

"Do ya think he'll live? Do ya think he'll live so he can stay with us awhile, Justin?" Willy asked, his young eyes misted and wide with concern. "He don't hardly look like a man who has the strength to go on at all. I swear, I seen dead men in Florence who looked hardier than your friend in there."

"Willy! What a thing to say!" Savannah scolded again. She shook her head once more, sighing and saying, "I swear, Vivi . . . if I didn't have you . . ."

Justin winked at Vivianna, smiled at her, and again she was filled with wondrous delight. She still had moments of uncertainty—of not quite being sure whether she were awake. Was Justin truly sitting across the table from her, or was she lingering in a deep slumber, only dreaming he'd come home?

"Enough of this war and dyin' soldier talk," Savannah said, pushing her chair back from the table and standing. "Let's get some supper on, Viv . . . shall we?"

"Yes, ma'am," Vivianna said. She too felt the sense of despair hanging thick in the room for the trail of conversation. She wanted to think of lovely things—of love and the future—of Justin! Though Vivianna didn't want to help with supper—though she didn't want to do anything—she knew the men needed to be fed. Still, in that moment, she was sure she could simply linger, gazing at Justin forever. She sighed as she looked at him—blissful in knowing he had returned.

"Me and Nate found some nice rocks since you've been gone, Justin!" Willy exclaimed.

"Yeah, we did!" Nate added. "Some quartz . . . even a couple of pieces of marble. We could show ya if ya like . . . while Mama and Viv are gettin' supper on."

Justin smiled. "Let's do it."

"Do ya need any help, Viv?" Caleb asked.

Vivianna's smile faded a little as she looked to Caleb, reminding herself of Caleb's proposal, of his likewise wounded soul. After all, he was a weathered and worn soldier returned from war as well. She must proceed carefully. Justin and Caleb were brothers, and she would not come between them. Though she was hopelessly, thoroughly, and entirely in love with Justin, she must ever be thoughtful of Caleb's heart and feelings.

"A jar of your mama's berry preserves might be nice with supper," she told him, broadening her smile. "Would ya mind fetchin' one off the top shelf for me?"

Caleb smiled, seeming somewhat soothed. "Not at all," he said as he rose from his chair and went about the task.

Vivianna glanced back to Justin. He wore a rather puzzled expression on his face. He still smiled, but a slight frown puckered his brow. Oh, how she wanted to run to him—to throw herself against him and beg him to embrace her! How she wanted to cry, "Fear not, my darling. It's you I love! You and only you!"

Still, she knew she must not. She must wait until she and Justin were alone—until Caleb's worried, wondering eyes were not upon them. Only then could she explain; only then could she confess to him that even though it may break Caleb's heart, it was Justin who owned hers.

"Should I go look in on that feller ya brung home with ya, Justin?" Nate asked. "Do ya think he might be wantin' some supper?"

Savannah turned to look to Justin.

"Why don't I look in on him?" Caleb offered, pushing his chair back from the table. Vivianna held her breath as she felt something akin to a cold, icy-fingered hand gripping her throat. She'd seen the expression on Justin's face—on Caleb's and Savannah's. They feared Nate might wander into her bedroom, only to find that another soldier had gone to be with the angels.

"I haven't seen ol' Johnny in quite a piece. Why don't ya let me go, Nate?" Caleb said.

Vivianna held her breath—watched Caleb awkwardly amble to the back of the house.

"Nate, Willy . . . you boys get washed up for supper," Savannah said. "I swear I've never seen such dirty fingernails!"

"Yes, Mama," Willy said, though both he and

Nate stared after Caleb, watching with obvious trepidation as he entered Vivianna's room.

"Boys, I said get!" Savannah scolded.

"But, Mama . . ." Nate whined.

"Mama?" Caleb said, poking his head out of the bedroom then.

Vivianna still held her breath—glanced to Justin, who sat pale as a corpse in waiting to hear what Caleb would say.

"He's all right . . . says he'd just like to take a little supper or some broth in here . . . if it would be fine with you."

Vivianna exhaled the breath she'd been restraining—heard Savannah do the same.

"You tell him that'll be just fine," Savannah sighed. She placed a hand over her bosom, no doubt to calm her madly beating heart. "We'll bring him somethin' shortly."

Justin ran a trembling hand over the bristles of hair on his head. "I swear, there were times these past couple of weeks when we'd bunk down for the night . . . times I coulda sworn that ol' boy had quit breathin'. Times I was sure one or the other . . . or both of us would never make it home," he said.

"Well, you did make it home, darlin'," Savannah said. She went to Justin, lovingly stroking his cheek with one hand and kissing his forehead. "You're home, and everything will be just fine now."

Justin smiled. He caught his mother's hand, kissing the back of it almost desperately. "I missed you, Mama," he said, heavy moisture brimming in his eyes.

"And I missed you, my darlin'," his mother said. She smiled, squeezed his hand, and added, "Now . . . let's get some supper in you so we can put you to bed. You need your rest. I wanna see some meat on those bones of yours soon . . . and food and rest is what it'll take plenty of."

Justin nodded, and Savannah wiped another tear from her cheek.

"Would you pull the meat off those chicken bones, Viv, please?" Mrs. Turner asked. "Might be we oughta just make a stew out of it this evenin'."

"Yes, ma'am," Vivianna said, smiling as Justin winked at her again.

"Can we have 'em, Viv?" Nate asked. "The chicken bones? When you're finished, can we have 'em for our bone collection?"

"Bone collection?" Savannah exclaimed. "I hardly think a sawed-off dog leg would merit bein' called a collection."

"Oh, but we got a lot of bones out in our fort, Mama!" Willy exclaimed. "We boiled up a dead fox we found in the woods last week, and we found a dead rabbit out behind the ol' Libby place."

"And don't forget the deer head old man Marshall gave us," Nate added.

"Boys, how morbid! You can't be collectin'

79

bones! It just isn't proper," Savannah scolded, stripping several sprigs of sage from the dried stalks of various herbs hanging near the cupboard.

"Oh, let 'em be, Mama," Justin chuckled. "I'll bet ya a dollar Caleb still has the old bear skull him and me found out near the riverbed that one summer."

"Oh, don't remind me!" Savannah sighed, waving a hand in the air as if to dismiss the memory. "That ol' thing gave me nightmares for a month!"

"A bear skull?" Nate and Willy breathed in unison.

Vivianna giggled. She would've sworn their eyes were as big as dinner plates!

"Would ya rub this sage a bit, Viv?" Savannah asked, handing sage leaves to Vivianna as she plucked them from their dried stalk.

"Of course," Vivianna said.

She listened then as Justin told Nate and Willy the story of the summer he and Caleb had found the skull. It was wonderful! For a moment, it almost seemed as if the war had never been—but only for a moment. Still, Justin was home! Impatient as she was to steal a private moment with Justin, Vivianna calmed herself with the knowledge that her time with Justin would come. She forced herself to think of Caleb—of how hurt he would be were he to find her and Justin kissing beneath the honeysuckle vine when she'd only just refused his proposal. She would be patient; she had to be. Still, she smiled, hoping Justin would take her in his arms and kiss her the way Nate and Willy had seen Benjamin Sidney kissing Tilly Winder.

Vivianna slipped her hand into her skirt pocket, letting her fingers caress the worn pages of Justin's letter there. Justin was home! For a moment, her mind flitted to her own brothers—to Sam and Augie and the fact they never would return. Images of her parents entered her mind, yet she forced them away. Justin was home, and she would find her happiness again. She would!

∽

"He's a cantankerous ol' boy sometimes, Viv," Caleb said, chuckling as Vivianna entered the room with a bowl of chicken stew. "Just don't pay him any mind."

"Oh, I'm sure he's not as bad as all that," Vivianna said, sitting down in the chair next to her bed as Caleb stood up from it.

"Well, don't be too certain," Caleb said. "And his stomach is growlin' like it ain't been fed in a year."

"Then I'm glad I brought such a big bowl of stew in," Vivianna said. She tried not to frown as she looked to Johnny Tabor and noted his painfully pallid complexion, the sunken appearance of his eyes.

"It's good to see ya, Johnny," Caleb said. "We'll

have us some more time to talk when you're on the mend a bit better."

Vivianna watched as Johnny Tabor held a trembling hand out to Caleb. Caleb shook his hand.

"Good to see you again, Caleb," Johnny Tabor said, his thin, dry lips imitating a smile.

Caleb nodded and strode from the room.

Johnny Tabor was sitting up in the bed. Vivianna assumed Caleb had assisted him in doing so, for she was sure he hadn't the strength to do so of his own accord. Caleb had been talking with Johnny all the while supper was being prepared, and Vivianna was glad, for it had given her the opportunity to smile unrestrained and unguarded while speaking to Justin. She could not have felt so comfortable in doing so had Caleb still been in the kitchen. Now he was gone, and Vivianna turned her attention to the task at hand—Johnny Tabor. She was determined to ensure that Justin's friend regained his strength. She could see the worry in Justin's eyes. Each time Johnny's condition had been mentioned, Justin's eyes would darken with anxiety. Thus, Vivianna was resolute in her resolve to see Johnny Tabor strengthened.

"It's chicken stew," she said.

"Thank you, ma'am," the man said. He held out one weak, trembling hand, intending to take the bowl from her.

Ignoring his hand—for she knew he was

too weak to hold the bowl—Vivianna ladled a spoonful of stew and held it before his mouth.

Johnny Tabor's brow puckered in a deep frown, and a low, quiet growl of irritation and self-disgust rumbled in his throat.

Yet Vivianna raised one eyebrow in daring. "Open your mouth, Mr. Tabor," she ordered. "You need some nourishment."

Still frowning, Johnny Tabor opened his mouth, allowing Vivianna to feed him. He swallowed the first bite of stew, and as she ladled another spoonful, he grumbled, "Why are they makin' you feed me? You ought to be out there with Justin."

"Justin has a mother and three brothers starvin' for his company, Mr. Tabor," she said, feeding him another spoonful. "I'm not about to be selfish and spoil their first day with him."

Mr. Tabor's eyes narrowed. He seemed to be studying her. Vivianna felt her cheeks pink under the intensity of his gaze.

"You don't want to spoil Caleb's day either. Now do ya?" he mumbled.

Vivianna paused in ladling the stew. Her first thought was that there was no possible manner in which Mr. Tabor could know of Caleb's proposal to her or of her refusal. Her second thought was that perhaps Caleb had confided the fact of it to Mr. Tabor while he'd been sitting in conversation at his bedside. Had Caleb truly told Justin's friend of his offer of marriage? She thought not.

Then the realization struck her: Caleb had also known this Johnny Tabor in battle. Hadn't Justin said that Caleb too used to scout with Johnny? Perhaps this was how Johnny Tabor had come by any knowledge he owned of the Turner family. As friend to both Caleb and Justin, perhaps he knew that Vivianna had loved Caleb when the war began—likewise knowing she loved Justin at the end of it.

"Were you with Caleb when he was wounded, Mr. Tabor?" she asked, feeding him another spoonful of stew—attempting to distract him from the present subject of conversation.

"I was," he said. "He was a fine soldier . . . and he's a good man."

"And you're from Texas?" she asked, feeding him another bite of stew.

"Yes, ma'am," he mumbled. He held up a hand as she offered another spoonful to him. "Pardon me, ma'am . . . but I best not gobble . . . else it might not stay in me."

"Oh, I'm so sorry," Vivianna said, a pang of painful sympathy pinching her heart. "We'll let that much settle then."

"Do ya know if Justin sent anybody for our packs?" he asked.

"Your packs?" she asked, confused.

"We hung 'em in a tree near the road before we got too close to town. We didn't want any of the townsfolk attackin' us on our return and stealing the few things we brung with us. I thought . . . I thought maybe he'd already gone back for 'em . . . or sent someone to fetch 'em," he explained.

"Oh, I see," Vivianna said. She shook her head. "No, he didn't send anyone for them. I suspect they're still where ya left them . . . safely hidden until ya can fetch 'em yourself."

The soldier nodded but still frowned.

"Where in Texas are ya from, Mr. Tabor?" she asked, slowly ladling another spoonful of stew between his parched lips.

"San Antonio," he said. "Well, that's where I was born anyway . . . though I left to enlist from Fredericksburg."

"Fredericksburg? I've never heard of it."

"Most folks haven't. It's small."

"And your family is there?"

"No, ma'am," he answered. "Two parents, two sisters, and two brothers . . . moved north about a year ago."

Vivianna smiled and asked, "Only two parents?"

She was momentarily mesmerized as Johnny Tabor smiled then too. His smile quite lit up his face, and it was only then that she noticed what a handsome man he would be were he healthy.

"Yes. Only two," he said. Instantly, his smile faded, however, as he said, "I'm so sorry for the loss of your family, ma'am. Truly I am."

Vivianna shook her head and restrained the tears begging to well up in her eyes. "Everyone lost

85

someone in the war," she said. "But I have the Turners. They're my family now."

"Until you and Justin have your own family?" he asked. His eyes were piercing as they studied hers, as if he were trying to read the thoughts in her mind. She felt her cheeks pink with blushing, yet she wasn't quite certain if the blush rose from the thought of having a family with Justin or because of the intensity of Mr. Tabor's gaze. "Well . . . well . . . well, I . . ." she stammered.

"You haven't already promised yourself to Caleb, have ya, ma'am?" he asked.

Vivianna was astonished! She felt her mouth gape open as she stammered to respond.

"Well, no . . . I . . . I haven't. Of course . . . I have to . . . I wouldn't want to hurt him. I . . ."

"But he's asked ya . . . hasn't he?" he asked.

Vivianna sensed he already knew the answer to his own question. Therefore, she dared not lie. "Well, yes," she admitted in a whisper. "But I refused. I couldn't . . . I couldn't accept him while . . . while . . ."

"While you were still in love with his brother," he finished. Again, Johnny Tabor's dark eyes bored into her soul.

"It seems . . . it seems you know an awful lot about it, Mr. Tabor," she said, spooning more stew into his mouth.

"Bein' a friend to both boys . . . it seems I would, wouldn't it?" he asked.

86

Vivianna gasped as Johnny Tabor reached out and firmly took hold of her wrist with one roughened hand.

"I didn't bring Justin home so you could sacrifice yourself in the name of duty or pity and break Justin Turner's heart, ma'am," he rather growled as he glared at her. "I brung him home to you. So even though I know you're mindful of Caleb—and you're a good woman for it—don't do anything out of pity or obligation that might find a load of souls unhappy in the end."

"Well, I don't plan to, Mr. Tabor," Vivianna began, yanking her wrist from his surprisingly powerful grip, "but I'm not right certain that it's any of your nevermind anyway."

"Oh, it is indeed my nevermind, ma'am," he growled. His eyes narrowed as he glared at her. "I was at heaven's door not an hour ago . . . and glad to be there." He closed his eyes for a moment, his face donning an expression of peace. "I could almost see the crick glistenin' in the sun . . . almost smell the prairie grasses . . . hear the meadowlarks. I was walkin' through a meadow, and everything was green and peaceful." He shook his head, opened his eyes, and continued, "But then it come to me . . . that Caleb was thinkin' of marryin' you before the war. He told me himself, before he was shot and sent home." He exhaled a heavy sigh. "And heaven didn't let me in. It sent me back to make sure things go as they should here." He frowned and added, "I won't find my peace until things are as they should be where these Turner boys are concerned."

"Though I'm glad heaven wanted you to linger longer in life, this isn't your worry to bear," Vivianna said. "If you knew me at all, you'd know I would never marry anyone out of pity or obligation."

His eyes narrowed. "Yes, you would."

Vivianna trembled slightly—for she knew he was right. Still, she wanted to convince him—wanted to offer him any manner of peace that she could. Therefore, she set the bowl and spoon down on the washbasin table and reached into her pocket. Withdrawing Justin's letter, she held it toward Mr. Tabor.

"Do you know what this is, Mr. Tabor?" she asked. Frowning, he took the letter from her, unfolding its pages. "It's a letter from Justin to me . . . one of my favorites. I carry it with me always. Even when we thought there was no hope of his having survived to return to us, I still carried it. Even as we thought he was dead, I still kept it near me." She watched as he studied the letter for a moment. "Put your mind at ease, Mr. Tabor. I won't hurt Caleb more than necessary . . . but it's Justin I love."

Johnny Tabor folded the letter and returned it to Vivianna. She carefully returned it to her pocket.

"Then I've seen what I need to see . . . heard all

I needed to hear . . . and I can take my rest now," he said.

Vivianna's heart began to pound in her bosom. Did he mean then to die? Did he feel such a sense of having finished his calling that he would simply give up the ghost?

"No, you cannot, Mr. Tabor!" she scolded. Reaching out, she pinched him hard on the arm.

"Ow!" he exclaimed, glaring at her.

"I know you're hurt and weak, sir," she began. "But you're alive . . . and obviously heaven itself wants you that way!"

He turned his face away from her, however, mumbling, "I'm tired, ma'am . . . and I own such pain in my heart, mind, and body . . . pain beyond understandin' or endurin'. I can't even feed myself anymore. Rest is all I can think on. Rest is what I need . . . what I want."

"What you need is a good paddlin'!" she exclaimed.

Again Vivianna pinched him. Again he looked to her and exclaimed, "Ow!" Frowning, he mumbled, "Them Turner boys never told me you were so mean."

Hopping up from her chair, Vivianna stomped to her chest of drawers. Pulling open the top drawer, she rummaged around until she found the small jar of salve she kept there.

"Here," she said, returning to the bed and dropping the jar onto Mr. Tabor.

89

He breathed an "oof" and flinched as the jar landed none too gently in his lap.

"Rub this over all those scratches on your hands, Johnny Tabor. It'll soothe the itchin' and help them to heal." She frowned. "How in the world did ya get so scratched up in the first of it?"

Johnny looked at her, an expression of astonishment on his face. "I . . . uh . . . I had to hatchet through a briar patch. Me and Justin heard somebody comin' yesterday. They turned out to be Johnny Rebs . . . and we had to get off the road. It was the briars in the patch we went through."

"Very well. That salve will work wonders then," she told him. She picked up the bowl of stew once more, placing it in his lap next to the salve. "And I want you to finish up this stew! You need to build your strength. If it comes back up, you just let me know, and I'll bring ya a fresh bowl. You tell me I better not break Justin's heart, Mr. Tabor? Well, I won't see you die and do the same thing!"

Vivianna was angry with the man! How could he think of dying? How could the fight go out of such a man as this? Obviously, Johnny Tabor was a survivor! Andersonville? It infuriated her that he would consider giving up now—after all he'd fought through to live.

"Look here, woman," he began to scold. He raised a trembling index finger and wagged it at her. "I didn't bring that boy home so his little filly could corral me into—"

His words ceased as Vivianna reached out, firmly taking his chin in hand. "Thank you, Johnny Tabor . . . for bringin' my Justin home," she said. Then, before she'd even realized what she'd done herself, Vivianna leaned forward, placing a tender kiss to the parched lips of the weathered soldier.

"Now," she began, standing and smoothing her skirt, "I've said my thanks to you . . . and I expect you to mend. I won't have Justin thrown to the depths of despair by you givin' up. Do you hear me?"

"Y-yes, ma'am," he mumbled, his eyebrows still arched with astonishment.

"Fine then," Vivianna said. "Finish your stew, and put that salve on your hands. When you're finished, I'll have Caleb show you where the privy is."

Johnny Tabor nodded, picked up the jar of salve from his lap, and studied it.

"I won't have you dyin' and causin' Justin any more pain, Mr. Tabor. I won't have it," Vivianna said.

He nodded, and she sighed resolutely.

"I'll be back in a few minutes with some more stew," she said. "If what you've already eaten comes back up, just spit it in the washbasin."

Again he nodded, and Vivianna left.

As she entered the kitchen, Justin and Caleb both smiled at her.

"He can really get your dander up, can't he?" Justin chuckled.

"Yes . . . in one way or the other," Vivianna reluctantly admitted.

"You're as red as a beet, Viv!" Willy exclaimed. "What did Justin's friend do to make ya so angry?"

"Oh, it makes no nevermind, Willy," Vivianna said—though, in truth, she was still unsettled by thoughts of Johnny Tabor, by his strange readiness to give up his life so easily now that all that had threatened it was over.

Justin stood up from his chair. "Why don't ya walk me outside a bit, Viv?" he said. "Maybe that'll cool your temper . . . and I'd like to see the place before I turn in."

"The sun's settin' mighty fast, Justin," Nate said.

But Justin smiled and offered a hand to Vivianna. "Oh, that's all right, Nate," he said. "I'm sure Viv knows the way."

Vivianna's heart was pounding like a wild herd of horses was pent up inside her bosom! Still, she glanced to Caleb, worried he might be hurt if she took to Justin so soon.

Yet Caleb nodded. She saw the slight pain in his eyes, yet understanding was in them too— the unspoken understanding that he knew he had wooed her before and after the war while his brother had wooed her even through all the hardship and terrors of it.

Vivianna let her hand slip into her skirt pocket.

She clutched Justin's letter there—could not help but smile as Justin said, "I bet that ol' honeysuckle vine has really grown since Caleb and me left."

"Yes," Vivianna said.

"Then take me there, Viv," Justin said.

Vivianna bit her lip, delighted at the prospect of lingering beneath the honeysuckle with Justin. Yet she gasped, suddenly remembering the convalescing man in the other room.

"Oh, but I promised Mr. Tabor I'd bring another bowl of stew in," she explained.

"Oh, for pity's sake, Viv!" Savannah said, smiling. "I can do that. You go on and walk awhile with Justin. It'll do ya good."

"Thank ya, Miss Savannah," Vivianna said.

She placed her hand in Justin's offered one. Instantly she was warm and hopeful! His touch was startling to her senses, and she bathed in the pleasure of it.

As Justin led her from the house, he asked, "Are the honeysuckle blossoms as sweet as I remember?"

"Even sweeter," Vivianna said, smiling at him.

Justin would be her lover now; she knew he would be. All the kisses she'd never shared with Justin before the war—all the dreams she'd so long dreamt of stolen moments spent beneath the honeysuckle—they would be hers now, and this would be the first of, oh, so many!

CHAPTER FOUR

The sun was beginning its evening descent, sending bright pinks and warm purples beaming across a blue, cloud-dappled horizon. Everywhere there was color; everywhere there was fragrance! Yet no color seemed so bright and welcoming as did the sight of the vine-draped arbor; no fragrance seemed so intoxicating as that exhaled by the honeysuckle blossoms heavy upon it.

"Well, look at that!" Justin exclaimed as he led Vivianna toward the old arbor. "I guess that vine just found a will of its own without me and Caleb here to beat it back. You can hardly see that old wagon of Grandpa's anymore. That ol' honeysuckle just swallowed it whole."

Vivianna nodded as Justin paused to survey the scene. "At least somethin' seemed to thrive durin' the war," she said. "I think there're more blossoms than there have ever been this early in spring."

Justin closed his eyes and inhaled a long, deep breath. "It puts me in mind of bein' just a boy," he began. "No war, no pain, no misery . . . no death." He smiled. "It's healin' to my soul, in a manner."

Vivianna closed her eyes as well—inhaled the sweet perfume of the honeysuckle. Justin was right. In that moment, she could almost sense her childhood lingering near, almost feel those bygone, carefree days of summer, almost hear the laughter as she, her brothers, and the Turner boys played near the arbor.

"Is the swing still in good repair?" he asked.

Vivianna nodded. "Oh yes! It's often I come here and linger awhile . . . to think of you, Justin."

Justin smiled. Reaching out, he brushed a strand of hair from Vivianna's cheek. The thrill his touch sent racing through her being caused her to quiver a little—birthed goose pimples to prickle down her arms and legs.

"I've thought of you so often, Viv," he said. His voice was low, filled with longing and, somehow, a breath of regret.

"And I've thought of you every moment, Justin. From the day you left us . . . I've thought of you endlessly," she confessed, gazing into the sky blue of his beautiful eyes. "Do ya see?" she asked, reaching into her skirt pocket and retrieving his letter she ever kept there. "I carry one of your letters with me always." She giggled a little as she handed the letter to him. "This one is perhaps my favorite," she explained. "The envelope is in my room, with your other letters. But this letter . . . this is the one I've carried with me since the day it arrived."

Justin smiled and unfolded the pages, his eyes traveling over the words.

"I . . . I fear I have none of your letters, Viv," he confessed, his eyes missing some of the light they held a moment before. "My possessions are few, only a handful of things I was able to bury in a small box that day . . . the day before Johnny and I went scouting and were captured. The few things I own are waitin' now . . . way up in the branches of a tree a mile or so from here. Johnny and I, we were afraid—"

"Afraid you'd be overtaken again?" she finished for him.

He looked at her, his brow puckering into a puzzled frown.

Vivianna giggled, "Your friend Johnny told me." She reached up, placing a soft palm against his whiskery face. Oh, how wonderful it was to touch him! "Just now . . . when I took the stew to him, he asked if you'd gone to retrieve your packs . . . the ones you hid for fear ya might be set upon by lingering Johnny Rebs."

Justin chuckled and shook his head. "That Johnny. I promise to you he has fewer possessions than I do, yet I swear he worries somethin' awful about them . . . more than I do mine. I'll have Caleb go with me tomorrow to fetch what we hid." He gently ran the back of one hand over her cheek. "Still, none of your sweet letters are there." He folded the letter she'd shown him and slipped it into her skirt pocket. "I hope you understand."

Vivianna squealed with delight and threw her arms around Justin's neck in a joyous embrace. "What do I care for letters, Justin Turner?" she exclaimed. "I have every letter ya ever sent to me . . . but I'd much rather have you! Oh, now I have you!"

She felt his arms go around her body. He pulled her against him—pressed his face against her neck.

"But what of Caleb?" he asked.

Vivianna felt an uncomfortable anxiety well within her.

"In truth, I feared I might get back only to find you'd already married him," he said.

He drew back from her and studied her face, his arms still resting loosely about her.

"I won't lie to ya, Justin," she said. "He did ask me, just two weeks past . . . but I . . . I told him I couldn't. Somethin' inside me couldn't let go of you. I think he only asked me out of duty anyway. With my family gone . . . and . . . and my bein' so alone . . . I think he only asked me because . . ."

Justin drew her to him once more. "Oh, Viv! I swear I'd near forgotten how beautiful you are! I love my brother—there ain't no truer thing—but I am glad ya didn't promise yourself to him."

"How could I have?" Vivianna breathed. "How could I have promised myself to Caleb when my soul still hoped you were alive? Oh, Justin! These past five months of no letters from you . . . of no word at all . . . they were the longest, darkest days of my life!"

She felt his lips press to her cheek, and she was

rendered breathless by the blissful sensation.

"Well, I'm home now," he mumbled. "No more worries about letters . . . or whether or not I'm dead. I'm alive . . . and I'm home."

Vivianna tenderly kissed his cheek and then drew away from him. Taking his hand, she led him toward the arbor. It must be as she'd dreamt it; he must kiss her beneath the honeysuckle vine as he'd promised to do in the letter she kept in her pocket.

"You will keep your promise to me . . . won't you, Justin Turner?" she asked, smiling at him as she drew him into the arbor. The scent of honeysuckle was nearly overpowering, and she bathed in the wonder of it.

"Which one? There're so many," he teased, winking at her.

"The one you made in this letter in my pocket, silly goose! The promise you made to return and kiss me here . . . beneath the honeysuckle vine."

He smiled and chuckled, his eyes merry once more with delight.

Vivianna drew him to her, and his hands rested at her waist as he gazed down into her face. "Kiss me, Justin Turner," she whispered. "Kiss me the way ya did when ya left that day! Oh, even kiss me better!"

His smile faded, and his brow puckered with worry. "I'm still a broken man just now, Viv," he told her. "I'm not at all certain I'm at my best."

Vivianna placed a tender hand on his cheek. He smiled, encouraged by her touch.

"But I'll sure give it a try," he chuckled. His gaze lingered on her face, the back of his hand caressing her cheek.

Gently, he cradled her face in his hand—allowed his thumb to travel lightly over her lips for a moment.

Vivianna's entire body was alive with goose pimples. The swarms of butterflies in her stomach threatened to take her breath away!

Slowly—carefully—he pressed a tender kiss to Vivianna's quivering lips. Her heart leapt! She felt as if her body might fly apart. Desperately she clutched the fabric of the back of his shirt in her trembling fists. His lips pressed hers more firmly, yet he still did not kiss her as she'd dreamed he would. Was he truly yet too weak? Or was he thinking of his brother, of Caleb's heart and feelings?

Still, even as Vivianna wondered at his being so careful with her, his arms tightened around her, his lips parting as he kissed her once more. Teasingly he coaxed her into a warm and moist blending, and this kiss caused Vivianna's heart to soar into the heavens. Bathed in honeysuckle fragrance—warmed by Justin's careful and teasing kiss—Vivianna knew true happiness. Her lover had returned! All would be well.

"Justin!"

It was Nate calling out. Vivianna startled as Justin instantly released her.

"Justin! Your friend is up and walkin'," Nate said, dashing into the arms of the arbor. "He's wantin' Caleb to take him to some tree to get somethin' . . . says he don't want to leave it there through the night. He says if Caleb won't take him, he'll go by himself!"

Vivianna frowned, instantly angry with Johnny Tabor for his cantankerous ways.

Justin looked to Vivianna and smiled—regretfully smiled. "I guess I best see to it," he said. "Can't nobody keep Johnny Tabor in line when he's set his mind on somethin'." He took her hand in his.

"But you're in no fit condition to be ridin' out . . . not to fetch somethin' that'll wait 'til tomorrow, Justin," she pleaded. "Surely he can wait! You said he owns nothin' to speak of. You should wait."

"Oh, don't worry, darlin'. I won't go. I'll let Caleb ride out with him," Justin told her. "But I best see that Johnny settles himself down. He can be one stubborn ol' mule."

Vivianna frowned and shook her head. "But . . . but, Justin . . . that Johnny Tabor . . . he's weak as a new lamb! If he rides out in such a state, he might not come back."

"Ya mean he might die, Viv?" Nate asked, his eyes welling up with tears.

"No. No, I mean . . . he might try to stay the night out there . . . instead of comin' on home, and . . ." Vivianna stammered.

"You think he'll die, Viv," Nate argued. "I know ya do!"

"He won't die, Nate," Justin said, tousling his little brother's hair. "We won't none of us let him." Justin looked to Vivianna, smiled, and winked at her. "I guess we'll have to visit the rest of the place another time, Viv," he said. "I can't let Johnny linger in bein' worried about his things. I owe him my life. It's the least I can do for him."

"But, Justin," Vivianna continued to argue, "please! What could he possibly own that can't wait 'til tomorrow?"

Justin shook his head and shrugged tired shoulders. "I don't know. All he's got in that pack is a beat-up ol' tin box. I ain't never seen what he keeps in it."

"Maybe jewels! Or gold!" Nate exclaimed, his eyes widening with excitement. "What else could be worth goin' after when he's as weak as he is?"

Justin chuckled, and Vivianna couldn't help but smile—even for her worry. Nate and Willy were always hunting for treasure. She could see how a soldier's tin box would hold boundless wonder for a young boy.

"You might be right there, Nate," Justin

chuckled. "Let's get back to the house . . . before Johnny causes Mama too much worry."

He winked at Vivianna, and she was somewhat soothed. Justin was home; that was what was important, not her own selfish desires to have and hold him all to herself.

Scolding herself for such selfishness, Vivianna followed Nate and Justin back to the house. She was astonished when they arrived to find Johnny Tabor mounted bareback on Caleb's horse, Captain.

"It won't take me but a minute to saddle him, Johnny," Caleb said as Johnny Tabor took the bridle reins in hand.

"It ain't more than a mile to where we left our packs," Johnny said. "I can be there and back in near the time it would take ya to saddle him."

"Oh, Johnny!" Savannah exclaimed, worry constricting her lovely face, her hands anxiously wringing her apron. "I wish you'd wait . . . or let Caleb go for your things."

Johnny Tabor smiled at Savannah. "I'll rest better knowin' we've got our packs about us, ma'am. I promise I'll be back quick as anythin'."

"You're as stubborn as any ol' mule, Johnny," Justin said, patting Captain on the neck. "But I know better than to get in your way when you've set your mind on somethin'."

Johnny nodded to Justin. "I'll ride him easy, Caleb," Johnny said, nodding to Caleb.

"You just get back here quick as you can, boy," Caleb said. "The sun will be down in less than half the hour."

Johnny nodded to Caleb.

Vivianna startled as Johnny hollered, "Get up!"

Captain lurched into a full gallop, and Caleb and Justin both chuckled.

"Yeah, he'll ride him easy all right," Justin said.

"That boy's tougher than ol' cowhide," Caleb said. He smiled at Justin and placed a hand on his shoulder. "I'm glad he's the one who brung ya home, brother. Ain't another soldier I'd have rather seen than ol' Johnny Tabor."

"Well, it seems to me we're gonna have to tie that boy to his bed to keep him here for any length of time," Savannah said.

"Best make him feel useful if ya want him to stay, Mama," Justin said. "Johnny won't linger anywhere he's not needed."

"He can feed the chickens and gather the eggs for me, Mama," Willy offered. "I don't mind lettin' Johnny Tabor help me out with my chores . . . if it means he'll stay on and start into mendin'."

Savannah laughed and tousled Willy's hair affectionately. "I'm sure ya don't mind at all, darlin' . . . and it's mighty thoughtful of ya."

Vivianna watched Captain disappear in a cloud of dust down the road—the same road that had led Justin home. She hoped Mr. Tabor collected his things. She hoped he collected his things and that it wouldn't take him long to gain enough strength to be on his way. She sensed he was a wild sort of man, prone to belligerence, with a head thicker than a tree trunk. No wonder he'd been able to bring Justin home. It seemed Johnny Tabor's determination was unequaled. Still, as she thought of him lying in her bed earlier—scolding her for causing him to worry over whether she would be true to Justin, reprimanding her for having kept him from dying—she frowned.

"He's awful scarred up," Nate said. "Did ya see that one on his back, Willy? Near as long as your arm!"

"I stitched that one up myself," Caleb announced.

"Honest, Caleb?" Willy asked, his eyes widening in awe.

Caleb nodded. "Ol' Johnny got himself sliced near in two by a Reb saber one day. But we cleaned it out, and I stitched it up. Looks pretty good, don't it?"

"It sure does, Caleb," Nate said, nodding.

"Justin," Savannah began, "please do come and rest awhile. Can't ya just hear that spare bed in Caleb's room callin' to ya? You must be tired, darlin'. Won't ya turn in for the night?"

"Mama, the sun ain't even set yet," Justin said. "Anyhow, I'll wait for Johnny to get back with our packs. I'll rest easier once I know the ride didn't kill him."

"Well then . . . we'll all wait," Savannah said, sitting down on the top step of the front porch. "We'll wait for that headstrong friend of yours to return. Then I'll see both y'all put to bed for some good long rest."

"Bet I can lick ya 'fore he gets back with his treasure," Nate said to Willy.

"What treasure?" Willy asked as he and Nate began to circle one another.

Vivianna smiled and shook her head. She well recognized the daring attitudes and gestures of the two youngest Turner boys; a mean wrestle was about to commence.

"Now don't you boys go gettin' too all wound up," Savannah warned. "It's nearly time for bed now. Do ya hear me?"

But it was too late. Justin and Caleb both broke into chuckles, for Nate and Willy were already pulling one another down into the grass, wrestling as if their very lives depended on it.

Vivianna smiled as she watched the boys. After all, what else was to be done but to let the match play out? What else was to be done but to wait for Johnny Tabor to return—if he returned?

"You've been awful quiet today, Viv," Caleb said, coming to stand beside her. Guilt washed over her like a nauseating, bitter illness. She could not believe that mere hours before, she'd

105

been considering marrying Caleb. How utterly unfair it would've been to him—how devastating to her own soul if she'd accepted Caleb before Justin had returned.

She glanced to where Justin sat on the porch with his mother. "I guess . . . I guess I just don't have much to say is all," she said. "I mean, it's all been such a surprise . . . such a whirlwind today. I swear I don't know which way to turn. I feel like my head might spin clean off my shoulders."

"I bet you do," Caleb mumbled.

She could sense Caleb was already angry— hurting—already aware that Vivianna's heart did indeed belong to his brother. Yet she'd meant to ease Caleb into understanding and acceptance. Though she'd secretly hoped the sight of Justin returning would cause Caleb to simply forget any aspirations he'd previously held in regard to marrying her, she knew—even for her lack of experience—she knew that matters of the heart rarely worked themselves into place with such plainness.

"Caleb—" Vivianna began.

"Viv," Caleb interrupted, forcing a smile, "let's not set anything in stone yet. I know you loved my brother . . . but you loved me once too. And though you may not see it—may not want to see it—I can see he's changed some. I know my brother like nobody does . . . and he has changed.

106

So please don't make any decisions 'til he's been home a time. All right?"

Inwardly, Vivianna was infuriated! How dare he? How dare Caleb presume to know Justin better than she? It wasn't Caleb who had written to Vivianna during the war—written letters of true revelations of the heart and soul. It wasn't Caleb who had cared enough to give up sleep and comfort in order to write to her. It wasn't Caleb who had confessed his love over and over and over again. No! It was Justin! Caleb didn't know the things of his brother's heart the way Vivianna did. How could he? He hadn't even been with his brother for nearly a year. How could he claim Justin had changed? Vivianna saw no change in Justin. Certainly his head was shaven; certainly he was not full healthy; certainly there was a sadness about him. However, Vivianna did not know a man who had returned from the war without a lingering sadness about him—and that meant Caleb Turner as well.

She was angry with Caleb, yes, but she would not argue with him or injure his heart further in that moment. She must be patient. She must be patient, and Caleb must begin to understand. Her heart swelled within her with the sure knowledge that Caleb would see Justin had not changed so much. Eventually he would see it, and then he would have to accept the fact that Vivianna loved Justin—irrevocably.

107

"He's weak . . . weak and battered. I know that," she answered at last. "Like so many others," she added poignantly—but not harshly.

Caleb nodded. "I'm just askin' ya to be careful, Viv. I won't see your heart broken by me or my brother."

Vivianna frowned slightly. How could Justin ever break her heart? Furthermore, Caleb certainly never could! Other than the lingering memory of the love she'd held for him before the war and the love she held for him now as a friend, Caleb Turner had no power to break her heart. She felt sorry for him in that moment— sorry for him for thinking he held the power to do so.

Yet she felt her temper soften—and her heart. Caleb was a very fine man. Furthermore, the truth was, no matter what she'd told Justin, she'd considered marrying Caleb. She did love him in a manner, though she was not in love with him. She did own a love for him, and she did not wish to be the cause of his unhappiness. Therefore, she cooled her annoyance and nodded. After all, she knew it was purely out of concern for her that he issued such a warning.

"Nate! Nate Turner!" Savannah hollered. "You're gonna break your brother's neck! Be careful! You boys are playin' too rough! I'll have Caleb separate you two if you're not more careful!"

"Get him, Willy! You can do it! Don't give up

just 'cause he's bigger than you!" Justin called from his seat next to his mother.

Vivianna smiled at Justin, her insides thrilling when he winked at her.

She heard Caleb chuckle and glanced back to him.

"I remember when Daddy used to tell Justin the very same thing," he mumbled.

Vivianna's smile faded just a bit. "Me too," she whispered.

❧

Johnny Tabor pulled the horse to a rough halt and dismounted. He couldn't believe the sense of near panic pounding in his chest. He had to retrieve the packs he and Justin had hidden up in the tree before moving on so close to Florence; he had to retrieve the tin box inside his pack. If anybody had found it, if it had been taken—but nobody had. He could see it up high in the tree branches where he'd placed it earlier in the day.

He was tired and weak and in truth felt nearer to death than he had in a long while. Still, he had to retrieve that box! For one thing, he didn't want to die without having it near to him. He shook his head, disgusted with himself for lying in a soft bed and sleeping when his pack with the tin box full of treasure was still up in the tree. What if he'd died and left Justin to come back for the packs? What if he'd died and Justin had opened that box only to find out what a true villain Johnny Tabor was? He couldn't have it on his conscience. Justin could never know the true, wicked nature of his friend. Johnny loved Justin near like a brother—at least he had. But it didn't change the fact of what Johnny kept cached in the tin box. It didn't change who he was and the things he'd done.

With every measure of strength left in his weary, weathered body, Johnny climbed into the branches of the tree and retrieved his pack. He pulled Justin's down too, of course, letting them drop to the grass below as gently as he could.

He jumped down from the limbs of the tree and groaned, certain his weathered body would never be what it once was. A familiar hatred of the guards and circumstances at Andersonville welled up within him, but he choked it down, determined to make it back to the Turner place and hide his box of secrets and treasure where no one would ever find it if he died.

His bones ached as he awkwardly mounted Caleb's horse. It was a fine horse, befitting such a fine man as Caleb Turner. Part of Johnny Tabor—the good part—almost hoped he and Justin had returned to find Caleb wed to Vivianna Bartholomew. Caleb was true and honest; he'd make any woman a fine husband. Yet it was Justin that the girl loved, and that counted for more. It would've marked a strange thing between the

Turner brothers if Justin had returned to find his girl married to his brother—whether or not she'd understandably given him up for dead.

Johnny shook his head. Too much thinking was bad for a man in his condition. He knew his thoughts were not rational. Wasn't his riding out after his pack proof enough of that? Still, he wouldn't die with the worry that Justin might find his pack, pry open the tin box, and discover the whole truth. He'd never be able to find eternal rest in knowing such a thing.

"Get," he growled to the horse.

Caleb's mount galloped down the road to return to the Turner place.

Johnny was thirsty; his head felt heavy; there seemed to be a fog drifting over his tired eyes. He had to make it back—had to hide the box—just in case he didn't survive the night. He was nearly sure he would—but only nearly.

As he rode, the scent of night flowers filled his lungs, the sound of bug noises echoing in his ears. What in tarnation was he doing in Alabama? He should've seen Justin home and kept walking—walked all the way to Texas or until he dropped dead. That's what he should've done.

Gripping his and Justin's packs in one hand, he rode on. The sun was setting fast now, but he could see the Turners gathered out in front of the house. He'd made it! He'd fetched his box, and he'd hide it somewhere quick until morning. His secrets were safe. Johnny Tabor knew he could die now—and his terrible secrets could die with him.

"Here he comes!" Willy panted, jabbing one final elbow to Nate's ribs. "Here comes that Johnny Tabor!"

Vivianna gasped and covered her mouth with one hand as Johnny Tabor reined in and slid from Captain's back. He looked so wild! His eyes were aflame with some sort of feral determination she'd never seen before. It rather frightened her, and she wondered for a moment if Justin's friend were truly just weak and weary. Or was he indeed somewhat mad?

"I got 'em, Justin," Johnny Tabor panted. "I got 'em."

Vivianna watched as the weathered man panted with the strain of too much exertion. He held out one ragged bundle, and Justin accepted it.

"I thank ya, Johnny," Justin said. "But I wish ya woulda waited 'til mornin'. Ya look like the devil."

"I might be just that," Johnny mumbled.

Vivianna trembled slightly as Johnny Tabor's wild, narrowed gaze lingered on her for a moment. His brown eyes pierced her sense of ease; the strong features of his face purely intimidated her! Somehow, he frightened her, and for a moment, she pitied any enemy who had at any time endeavored to stand against him.

"Oh, nonsense, boy!" Savannah scolded. "Now you get on into that house and get to bed." She nodded to the bundle Johnny held in one arm. "You've got your things now, so I will see both you and Justin put to bed. I want to hear some snorin' in under fifteen minutes . . . do ya hear me?"

Vivianna was momentarily mesmerized by the manner in which Johnny Tabor's expression softened. An amused, grateful smile curved his mouth, transforming his countenance!

"Yes, ma'am," he said. "Though . . . though I don't want ya to think for a moment that I'm gonna linger in your way, Mrs. Turner."

"Linger in my way?" Savannah exclaimed. "Nonsense, boy! I've already got a day of chores planned out for you and Justin tomorrow. So ya best see yourself to bed."

"Yes, ma'am," the man chuckled. He looked to Caleb, nodding as he handed him the bridle reins. "Thank ya for the loan of your horse, Caleb. I wouldn't have rested easy at all if I hadn't fetched this." He patted the bundle under his arm—squeezed it closer to his body.

"You're welcome, Johnny," Caleb said. "Now, if ya know what's good for ya, you'll do what Mama says and get on into bed."

Vivianna watched as Johnny weakly climbed

113

the steps up to the front porch. Pausing, he lowered his head almost ashamedly and said, "I do thank you for your kindness to me, Mrs. Turner. I promise you that I most certainly do not deserve it."

Mrs. Turner smiled and took Johnny's face in her hands, raising it to meet hers. "Your kindness to me in bringin' my boy home far outweighs anything I could ever do for you, Mr. Tabor." She stood on the tips of her toes and placed a kiss on Johnny's face. "Now you run along to bed, Johnny." She looked to Vivianna. "Viv, you best get your things out of the room before Mr. Tabor retires."

"Yes, ma'am," Vivianna said.

As she passed Justin on the porch, he smiled and winked at her. Her heart fluttered, her stomach twisting with delight. She thought of their moments beneath the honeysuckle vine— the moments before Nate had interrupted them. What heavenly moments they had been! What bliss-filled breaths of spring and dreamy kisses! She wanted nothing more than to take Justin by the hand and lead him to the arbor once more. She wanted to hear him speak love to her—feel his arms around her again. Yet she knew all things must have their time, and this included rest and healing. Justin was yet weak—needed time to regain his strength.

Therefore, Vivianna entered the house,

stepping in front of Johnny Tabor as he stepped aside, gesturing with one hand and a nod that she should precede him.

"Thank you," she said to him as she started down the short hallway to her room.

"I don't feel right about puttin' you out, Miss Vivianna," Johnny said, stepping into the bedroom behind her.

"Then you're a gentleman," Vivianna said as she went to the chest of drawers to retrieve her nightclothes.

"No, ma'am," Johnny mumbled.

She felt his gaze on her—for the back of her body fairly burned with the knowledge it lingered there. "Do . . . do you have everything ya need, Mr. Tabor?" she asked, retrieving a few other items she would need.

"Yes, ma'am," he replied.

She turned to face him and was astonished by the somehow defeated expression on his face—the overall weakness about him. He opened his mouth slightly, as if he'd meant to speak but changed his mind.

"What is it, Mr. Tabor?" Vivianna asked. "Is there somethin' I can fetch for ya?"

He dropped his gaze to the floor a moment, as if he were somehow ashamed—or even frightened. "You seem an honest woman, Miss Vivianna," he said in a lowered voice.

"I . . . I hope so, Mr. Tabor," she said.

"If . . . if a person was to ask a favor of you . . . ask for your help and complete secrecy of confidence . . . would you be willin' to do somethin' for them, ma'am?" he asked.

Strangely, Vivianna was not afraid—though she thought that perhaps she should be. Still, she was not afraid—only curious, with a sudden, unexpected desire to assist the poor man. "Of course, Mr. Tabor," she told him. "What is this favor you wish to ask of me?"

He brushed a hand over his forehead, as if he estimated beads of perspiration would be lingering there.

"My . . . my pack here," he said, patting the bundle he still held. "I want to ask you to give me your word that if I finally fly to heaven to meet my maker durin' the night . . . I want ya to promise me you'll take this pack and without ever openin' it . . . promise me you'll sink it in the river. Promise me you'll never open it . . . no matter how curious your mind may be. Promise me that . . . and promise me you'll never tell a soul it ever existed or where ya sank it."

Vivianna smiled. She didn't know why she smiled, for it was an ominous request. Still, she realized it was the thought of Nate that made her smile, and she said, "Nate thinks you're hidin' gold and jewels in that pack of yours."

Mr. Tabor's eyes narrowed. "If I am . . . would

116

ya still be able to keep a promise to never open it . . . to sink it in the river?"

"Of course, Mr. Tabor," Vivianna told him, rather insulted that he should doubt her character. "Of course! You could have Mr. Booth's written confession of assassination in there, and I wouldn't care." He frowned and looked down to the bundle he held under his arm. She thought she'd somehow offended him with the suggestion of what might be in the box but said nothing more.

"Then you'll sink it if I die?" he asked. "Unopened . . . in secret . . . and never tell a soul?"

"You're not gonna die, Mr. Tabor," she told him. "Things won't seem quite so harsh and wearin' in the mornin'. I promise."

"But if I do . . . if ya come in here and find me dead—I'll put it under the bed—and if I'm dead, you'll take it, without hesitation . . . and sink it in the river?" he repeated his request again.

He was so weary! She could see he hardly had the strength to stand.

"Of course," she said. "I promise. And I always keep my promises."

"Do you?" he asked. He doubted her, yet she was not angry with him, for even as he doubted her, she knew he must have reason for trusting her as well, else he would not have asked for her help.

"I do," she assured him.

"Then I'll take my rest in peace," he mumbled.

"Oh, for Pete's sake, Mr. Tabor!" she scolded with a disbelieving giggle. "Don't say it that way! I swear, you'll give me a fit of nightmares."

He grinned, obviously amused by her outburst. "Forgive me," he said.

"I'll consider on it," she teased, reaching out and retrieving her hairbrush from her vanity. "But only if you quit talkin' so dark and deathly like," she added, wagging the brush at him.

"Yes, ma'am," he said. His eyes seemed to lighten, and he grinned at her.

"Very well," she told him. "Good night, Mr. Tabor."

"Good night, ma'am," he mumbled.

Vivianna left Johnny Tabor to his rest and walked across the hall to Mrs. Turner's room.

"What a strange man," she whispered to herself as she set her things on the trunk at the foot of Mrs. Turner's bed.

Suddenly, she gasped, "Oh no!"

Quickly, she crossed the hallway to her bedroom—rather, to the room that had once been hers alone. The door was still open, and she sighed, relieved.

"I beg your pardon, Mr. Tabor," she said. Her heart began to hammer with mad anxiety, however, as she saw he knelt on the floor next to the bed—no doubt placing his menacing pack beneath it.

118

"Ma'am?" he asked, turning to look at her.

"I . . . I only just forgot one little thing," she said, dropping to her knees beside him.

She ducked down, looking under the bed. She felt her eyes widen as she did indeed see Johnny Tabor's mysterious pack there—exactly next to the small wooden box containing Justin's letters. She reached under the bed but could not comfortably reach the box.

"Let me get that for ya, ma'am," Johnny said, obviously having noticed what she was reaching for.

Vivianna held her breath, somehow afraid the angry, weathered man might not hand the precious box to her but rather keep it from her instead.

He did not, however. As Johnny handed the box to her, Vivianna exhaled the breath she'd been holding. "Thank you, Mr. Tabor," she told him. "I hope you enjoy a pleasant rest."

"And you," he said. She watched as he started to stand—noted that it was an arduous task for him. She placed a hand at his elbow to steady him.

He nodded and forced a grin, though she sensed he was disgusted with his own weakness.

"Good night, again," she nervously giggled.

"Good night," he echoed as she hurried across the hall.

Once inside Mrs. Turner's room, Vivianna

sighed with relief. Justin's letters! She'd nearly forgotten to bring Justin's letters with her!

Quickly she opened the box and let her fingers trace the envelope resting on top. She smiled, promising herself she would read this letter before she retired for the night. Yes! Tonight she would drift to sleep with Justin's words of love in her mind and his tender kiss fresh upon her lips.

CHAPTER FIVE

Vivianna's eyes opened slowly. The sun was already shining through the window, yet she did not feel rested. Certainly she'd stayed up far past any decent hour reading over Justin's letters. She wanted to be sure she had not forgotten one word he'd written to her—wanted to think of him sleeping comfortably in another room close by instead of miserably on the hard ground.

As always, Justin's letters had so absorbed her, she'd quite lost track of the time. Thus, by the hour she finally did retire, it was to find Savannah sound asleep and snoring. The worries, fears, and losses the war had brought had caused Vivianna to become a very light sleeper. Any strange or unexpected noise woke her and kept her awake with worry and anxiety. Thus, Savannah's snore, soft as it was, had made the night seem long and void of good rest.

Yet now Vivianna sat up, stretching her arms, arching her back. She was sure the others were already up and about. This fact was made certain as she heard voices. Curious, she left the large bed she would now share with Savannah and went to the open window. The air was fresh and already heavy with moisture and fragrance.

Leaning out the window, she saw Willy inside

the hen pen. Johnny Tabor was with him, and the chickens were frantically pecking at the ground around their feet.

"Here, Johnny. Do it like this," Willy said. Vivianna watched Willy plunge his hand into the small bag of chicken feed he was holding. Withdrawing a fistful of feed, he scattered it over the ground. "Ya see that?" he asked Johnny. "And if ya want, you can talk to 'em a bit. Mama says they like that. Just say somethin' like, 'Here, chickie chickie' or some such thing. See how they like that?"

Vivianna smiled as she heard Johnny Tabor chuckle. "They sure seem to, don't they?" he answered.

"Here," Willy said, handing the bag of feed to Johnny. "You try it."

"All righty," Johnny said. He filled a hand with feed and scattered it over the ground.

"Don't forget to talk to 'em," Willy urged.

Johnny nodded. "Here ya go, hennies. Y'all eat that feed there. That's the way."

Willy looked up to Johnny Tabor with a proud smile. "Ya see, Johnny! I told Mama you'd be more'n happy to feed these chickens from now on."

Johnny chuckled, tousled Willy's hair, and said, "Oh, I bet ya did."

Vivianna giggled a little, delighted to see Johnny Tabor walking around the hen pen with

Willy. She'd been afraid she'd wake up to find he really had passed on during the night—that Justin might well have lost his friend. Furthermore, if Johnny had the strength to be doing chores with Willy, then Justin must certainly be feeling better.

Quickly she washed and dressed. She was sure Savannah had already started breakfast, and she hurried into the kitchen.

Caleb and Nate were sitting at the table as Savannah pulled a pan of fresh biscuits out of the oven. For a moment, Vivianna was unsettled, for Justin was not with them.

"Justin's still asleep, Viv," Nate said, however—and her mind was eased. "Mama says we oughta let him sleep as long as he will. But that Johnny Tabor . . . he didn't die like we feared he might. He's out feedin' the chickens with Willy."

"Well, that's nice, isn't it?" Vivianna said. She returned Caleb's greeting smile and said, "Good mornin', Caleb."

"Mornin', Viv," he said.

"I've got the biscuits ready, Viv," Savannah said. "Would ya call Willy and Mr. Tabor in, please? Oh, I hope his stomach can tolerate biscuits this mornin'."

"Yes, ma'am," Vivianna said.

Suddenly, she owned such a feeling of joy that she could hardly contain her delight. It was a beautiful day! Caleb wore a smile, Nate and Willy were happy, Mr. Tabor hadn't died, and

Justin was, at that very moment, regaining his strength. The war was over, and life was moving on—moving on down a brighter road.

Vivianna's heart felt so light, in fact, that she nearly considered skipping as she left the house and hurried toward the chicken coop. Everything seemed more wonderful! The sun seemed to shine more brightly; the sky was bluer. The grasses were fragrant and green; the flowers flaunted their blossoms in every color. Vivianna Bartholomew was happy—truly happy!

"Your mama has breakfast on, Willy," she called as she approached the hen pen. "Do ya think your stomach will manage biscuits this mornin', Mr. Tabor?"

Willy clicked his tongue and shook his head with disgust. "His name is Johnny, Viv," Willy reminded her. "Mr. Tabor's his daddy's name."

"Oh, that's right!" Vivianna giggled. "I'd quite forgotten."

Johnny grinned and tousled Willy's hair.

"And he didn't die in the night neither," Willy added.

"Johnny . . . or his daddy?" Vivianna teased, though she thought perhaps it was a little irreverent.

Willy's eyes narrowed, and he stuck his tongue out at her. "You know I mean Johnny! You've got a real smart mouth on you sometimes, Vivianna Bartholomew. A real smart mouth," he grumbled.

Vivianna giggled and affectionately tweaked Willy's nose as he stepped out of the hen pen. "Well, you just wash those grubby hands of yours, Willy . . . quick as ya can, while the biscuits are still hot," Vivianna told him. Quick as a mouse, he was off to the rain barrel.

"I suppose I better light out after him," Johnny said, setting the feed back outside the fence as he looked at his own hands.

Vivianna studied him. He did appear somewhat recovered—stronger—and there was even a hint of color in his thin cheeks. Truly, he looked quite a lot healthier than he had when she'd left him the night before. Vivianna was glad he hadn't died—and for more than just Justin's sake. She'd seen far too much death; they all had. She was glad someone near death's door had managed to drive the Reaper away. She thought for a moment that, considering it was Johnny Tabor the Reaper had come looking for, he'd probably run for the hills out of pure intimidation.

"You look near as fresh as a daisy this mornin'," Mr. Tabor," she said, smiling at him.

Johnny Tabor smiled, and Vivianna was again struck by how entirely his smile changed his countenance. He was a handsome man; she could well imagine he'd set many a female heart to fluttering in the past.

"Well, I can't say I've ever been compared to a

daisy, Miss Vivianna," he said. "The devil maybe . . . but never a daisy."

As if some mischievous imp had been eavesdropping—as if a pixie had been near and decided to mix up a bit of naughtiness—a large pigeon flew over at that very moment. Vivianna gasped, covering her mouth in dismay as the mean-hearted bird sent a stream of white bird mess to running over Johnny's right shoulder.

"Oh, Mr. Tabor!" she gasped as he frowned and looked to his shoulder. "Oh, I'm so sorry!"

She couldn't help herself, however. Oh, she tried—desperately she tried not to laugh—yet the trill of giggles would not stay trapped in her throat. "I'm . . . I'm so sorry, Johnny!" she giggled, her eyes filling with mirthful moisture. "Truly . . . I don't mean to laugh. I'm so sorry!"

Johnny looked to her, his frown giving way to a smile. His chuckles began slow, vibrating low in his throat. Yet in another moment, he laughed—wholeheartedly laughed!

This only caused Vivianna's giggles to multiply, and she covered her face with her hands a moment to try and calm herself. Yet nothing seemed to stay her laughter! As she looked at him again—shaking his head as he laughed unreservedly, a stream of bird manure as fat and as long as a grass snake dripping from his shoulder—her giggles transformed, and she was overwhelmed by a ripple of delighted giggles.

Johnny's eyes fairly danced with amusement, and he continued to laugh so hard Vivianna feared it might not be at all good for him. Yet her mother had always told her laughter was the greatest healer God had given man. Thus, as she doubled over, her stomach aching with merriment, she did not worry for the man—only laughed harder as he dropped to his knees, overcome with hilarity.

He was crouching now, on his hands and knees as he continued to laugh, and Vivianna could endure it no longer. Sitting down hard on her seat in the grass, she continued to laugh—laugh so hard she could not draw breath, so hard that her back ached. Yet she could not seem to stop laughing, and neither could Johnny Tabor.

"Oh, ho ho ho!" he laughed, tears of mirth gathering at the outer corners of his eyes.

"Oh, stop!" Vivianna breathlessly begged. "Please, stop! I'll be sick!"

Johnny drew a deep breath and seemed to hold it as he lifted his head to look at her. However, as he glanced to his shoulder and then back to her, the uncontrollable revelry overtook them again, and Vivianna was undone. Each time she or Johnny would try to settle their laughter, one or the other of them would glance to his shoulder, and the merriment would begin anew.

"For cryin' out loud, Viv!" Willy said, coming to stand next to her. "What is so funny?"

Vivianna could only shake her head and gasp. "Nothin'! Nothin' really!" Yet new peals of laughter overtook her. In her soul, she knew it wasn't just the incident of the bird mess. The laughter owning her in those moments was also a release of sorts—something she'd missed for years, since her brothers and the Turner boys left for the war. Vivianna realized that the reason the hard laughter was so entirely wracking her body with discomfort was for the unfamiliarity of it. Truly, she hadn't laughed so thoroughly in forever, it seemed. She thought the same was probably true for Johnny Tabor. As he wiped the mirthful moisture from his eyes—as he inhaled a deep breath, exhaling a contented sigh—she was certain he hadn't known such laughter in years either.

"What are y'all laughin' at?" Willy demanded. Vivianna knew he felt left out, but she couldn't breathe well enough yet to explain.

Johnny held up a hand, however, and gasped, "Just a pigeon," he began. "A pigeon flew over and targeted me with his hind end." As Johnny sat back on his heels and pointed to his shoulder, Vivianna snickered, and she and Johnny were undone once more.

Willy frowned—looked to Vivianna as she sat in the grass attempting to gain control of her spontaneous laughter once more. "Well, that ain't funny at all!" the boy exclaimed. "If a bird messed all over me, I sure wouldn't be sittin' in the grass laughin' about it!"

Johnny sighed and rubbed his moist eyes. One final chuckle escaped his throat as he struggled to his feet. Still smiling, he offered Vivianna his hand. She was certain he didn't have the strength to pull her to her feet, yet she did not want to offend him by refusing. Therefore, she took his hand and was surprised when his strength proved to be more than she had imagined.

"Willy," Vivianna began, "would ya please run on in the house and fetch one of your daddy's old shirts for Mr. Tabor? He can't possibly wear this one all day." She giggled and placed her hand over her mouth to stop. Her sides were aching— and her back! She was sure she couldn't endure another round of such overwhelming laughter.

Willy nodded—grimaced as he watched Johnny remove the soiled shirt. "Yeah, I'll get one for him, Viv," the boy said. "I couldn't hold my breakfast down at all with bird mess lookin' me straight in the face."

"Thank you, Willy," Vivianna said as one final giggle escaped her throat.

Willy hurried off toward the house, calling, "Mama! One of them naughty pigeons messed all over Johnny!"

Johnny still smiled as he wadded up the soiled shirt.

"We'll get that washed out for ya later on,

Johnny," Vivianna said. She held her hand out, indicating he should hand her the shirt.

But Johnny shook his head, frowning slightly. "Oh, no, ma'am," he told her. "I couldn't let ya wash out this mess. I'll do it after breakfast."

Vivianna smiled as he tossed the shirt onto a nearby tree stump.

"Well, the rain barrel is just over by the house. You can wash up there," Vivianna explained. "There's a towel hangin' on a nail right above it."

"Thank you," he said and sauntered past her.

Vivianna turned and watched him head for the rain barrel. She felt her brows arch at the sight of the long, dark scar marring the flesh on his lower back. Indeed, it was obviously the harsh remnant of the brutal saber wound Caleb had told them about.

Her thoughts lingered on Caleb a moment then. He was a compassionate man, a kind man, and loyal. For an instant, the tender feelings her heart had owned for Caleb before the war returned. Vivianna remembered then why it was she had loved Caleb first—why it had been Caleb who owned her heart before the war. Caleb was calm. He was not easily provoked to anger. There was a sense of stability, of steadfastness, about him that his own brother did not possess. Vivianna realized that, as a girl, these were the qualities in Caleb Turner she loved most. But that was in the past; she loved Justin now. Oh, it was true she would always be fond of Caleb—always love him in a manner. Yet, she was *in* love with Justin, and nothing would change that now.

Sighing—for she was quite worn out with laughing so hard—she started for the house.

"I'll send Willy out with that shirt, Johnny," she called. "We'll have breakfast on the table when you're finished."

"Thank you," Johnny said, smiling and nodding to her.

As she stepped up onto the porch, she heard him chuckle. No doubt this chuckle was a residual response from the previously unruly laughter. Vivianna smiled, glad that Justin's friend seemed to be mending.

Justin was sitting at the table when Vivianna entered the kitchen. At once, her heart was full and delighted! He smiled at her, and the sight of it bathed her with joy.

"Mornin', Viv," he greeted.

"Good mornin', Justin," she said. "You look quite well rested!"

Justin nodded. "And I feel it." He smiled at his mother and added, "And I can't wait for some of Mama's biscuits. I swear, Mama . . . how I've missed your cookin'!"

"Thank you, darlin'," Savannah said as she set a jar of honey on the table next to the pan of biscuits. "The eggs are about ready too, Viv. Is Mr. Tabor nearly finished out there? Willy said

131

a pigeon got him. I guess that's what all the laughin' was about. I couldn't imagine what was so funny!"

Vivianna giggled just a little. "I don't know why it seemed so funny . . . but it just tickled me so."

"I got one of Daddy's shirts, Mama," Willy said, racing into the kitchen.

"Well, take it out to Johnny then, Willy. I'm starvin'!" Nate growled.

"I'm goin'. I'm goin'," Willy mumbled as he hurried out of the house.

Vivianna smiled. Nate Turner was a bear when he was hungry. In fact, all the Turner boys were irritable when they went too long without food.

"Maybe we can finish our walk after breakfast, Viv," Justin said.

"Yes," she told him. "Of course."

Vivianna could not keep the sigh of pure delight from escaping her throat. Justin! His eyes were bright—as blue and as bright as the summer sky. Oh, how thankful she was that he seemed in fair health. She would not have had a moment's peace had Justin arrived looking as near to death as his friend did.

"I'll be workin' on that east bridge if ya need me today, Mama," Caleb said. "Just send Nate or Willy along if ya need anythin'."

"I will, darlin'," Savannah said, smiling at her oldest son.

"He's all rinsed off and ready for breakfast, Mama," Willy announced, bounding into the kitchen. Johnny entered behind him and took a seat in the chair Savannah indicated.

"Do ya think you can stomach some eggs this mornin', Johnny?" Savannah asked.

"If I can't, I'll keep 'em down all the same, Mrs. Turner. Thank you," Johnny answered.

"Then let's get to eatin'," Caleb said. "I need to get out to the bridge."

After gratitude was offered to the Lord, Vivianna watched as Justin enjoyed his mama's biscuits and eggs. He was voracious in his eating—and Vivianna delighted in it! Justin would regain his full strength—she was certain that he would—and all would be well. Furthermore, she knew her dreams would come true! For over two years she'd dreamt of the day Justin Turner would return and claim her for his own as he'd promised in his letters. It was true that for the past almost six months, Vivianna had tried to tell her heart and mind she would never know Justin—never see him again. But that was the past, just as the war was the past. Vivianna was determined to look only to the future now—to Justin.

∽

"Tell me, Viv," Justin began. "Tell me about what went on here while I was away."

Vivianna smiled—shrugged as she watched Justin sit down, lean back against the large willow, and stretch his legs out in front of him in the grass.

"I suppose . . . there isn't much I could tell you that would compare to what you endured, Justin," she said.

"Tell me anyway," he prodded. "I want to hear everything. Tell me about Florence, the family. Was your family home destroyed when your parents were killed?"

A sharp twinge of pain rippled through Vivianna's body. She preferred not to talk about her parents—about their death. Still, this was Justin, and though it was difficult to speak of the excruciating loss of her family, she was comforted in knowing he cared.

"The house is still there," she began. "The Yankees didn't harm our home at all. Not one bit. They destroyed other buildings . . . other homes . . . but not ours. It's there, and everything is just the same as it was the mornin' Mama and Daddy were killed. Everything passed to me, of course . . . but I don't go to the house often." Vivianna sighed. "I suppose I'll have to one day . . . have to pack things, sell things, sell the house. But for now . . . it's just there."

"I forget. Were they killed in the spring raid?" he asked.

Vivianna shook her head. "No . . . in December.

So much was destroyed that previous spring when the Yankees came—the cotton mills, the town hall, so many homes. But ours was preserved. Mama and Daddy were fine, and General Roddy's men beat the Union troops back that May. But in December they came again. Daddy ran out to help a wounded soldier, and Mama ran out after him. I . . . I don't even really know how or why they were killed. I was here, helpin' your mama with Nate and Willy 'cause they were ailin'. Mr. Maggee came to the door and told me Daddy and Mama had been killed . . . had been shot." Again she shook her head—choked back her tears—determined to remain in control of her emotions.

"Them damn Yankees," Justin growled.

Vivianna looked to him and smiled, even for the pain in her heart. "You're a Yankee, Justin Turner," she teased.

He chuckled. "I know . . . but I never killed nobody that wasn't a soldier. Never."

"I like to think it wasn't intentional," Vivianna began, "that it was an accident. There was so much fightin' in the street . . . and I'm sure they were just in the way." She paused and swallowed the lump in her throat. "Mr. Maggee . . . he thought maybe they were killed by Confederate soldiers . . . or someone in Florence who knew Sam and Augie were fightin' for the Union," she confessed. "I don't like to think that's true though.

135

I don't like to think that at all. Besides, I don't know of anybody other than your family and the Maggees who knew Sam and Augie were with the Alabama First. Even when Caleb came home, we didn't tell anyone he'd been wounded fightin' against the Confederacy. It's why the Maggee boys are buried in your family's cemetery. Mr. Maggee was afraid the townsfolk wouldn't take kindly to two Yankees being buried out at Soldier's Rest. There are a few Yankees buried there, but they weren't local boys like Boy and Floydie. Mr. Maggee wanted their gravestones to read that they died fightin' with the Alabama First Cavalry . . . and he didn't want the folks in Florence readin' their stones and gettin' all riled up about it. So your mama let them be buried out there in the meadow."

"It's a pity," Justin mumbled. He looked to Vivianna then, and she was warmed by the compassion in his eyes. "Boy and Floydie and your parents . . . I can't hardly imagine they're all gone."

"I know," Vivianna said. "Sometimes I wake up in the mornin' and half expect Mama will walk right through the door, smilin' and singin' the little song she used to sing to me to wake me up." She paused and lovingly gazed at Justin. "I used to imagine you'd walk through the door one day too."

"And I did," Justin said, smiling.

"Yes. You did."

He winked at her, yet his smile faded. "So . . . folks in Florence . . . they still don't know Caleb and me were fightin' for the Union?"

"They do now," Vivianna explained. "Caleb had a terrible time tryin' to find work after he started tellin' folks the truth. I guess it was Georgie Jones he first told. He and Georgie even went around awhile. Caleb came home all bloody and bruised. But in the end, Georgie understood, I think. Folks have accepted it . . . not that some aren't still angry about it. I suppose it was surprisin' to people, especially since your daddy fought for the Confederacy."

"Daddy couldn't raise his hand against Alabama," Justin mumbled, "even though he thought things needed changin'."

"I know," Vivianna said.

"Me and Caleb . . . Sam and Augie . . . we grew up with the Maggee boys," he said. "It seems strange that me and Caleb should make it through . . . while two other sets of brothers didn't."

His countenance was changing. Talk of the war was despairing, and Vivianna did not want Justin to despair—not one more day.

"Caleb has talked about movin' west," Vivianna began, smiling. "He's read about Texas and California. He thinks it might be a good thing—a new start . . . a different life where the war isn't so fresh in our minds every day. Folks don't care so much who a man fought for . . . especially in California."

Justin nodded thoughtfully. "I can see how that might be somethin' to think after. Folks hold grudges a long time after something like this war. Generations will hold grudges." He looked at her and nodded again. "Johnny, he's from Texas, and he says there're a lot of folks there who didn't want the state to join the Confederacy. He says it's beautiful there . . . wide-open space where a body can see for miles and miles. And the sky . . . he says there ain't nothin' like the sky over Texas." Justin chuckled. "I swear, I thought that boy was gonna melt out there in Georgia. Johnny says he prefers to be dry 'stead of always feelin' like he's been bathin' in somebody else's sweat."

Vivianna wrinkled her nose at the comparison, and Justin laughed.

"I guess I need to learn how to talk to a lady again," he said. "Seems the war has rusted me over a bit." Then, to Vivianna's delight, he reached out and took hold of her hand, pulling her into his arms. "I hope you can be patient with me, Viv," he whispered into her hair. "I ain't quite myself yet."

Vivianna snuggled against him—sighed at the warm, safe bliss of being in his arms.

"You're fine, Justin," she told him. "You're fine . . . and everything will only get better and better now. You're home, home here with me . . . and that's all I need to know."

Justin sighed, closed his eyes, and inhaled the sweet scent of Vivianna's soft, dark hair. Through the horrors of war and Andersonville, he'd nearly forgotten how pretty she was—how sweet. Andersonville seemed an age ago in that moment. As he sat comfortable and at peace beneath the tree, a beautiful woman in his arms, he thought he could almost forget the past—the war.

The breeze was soft, fragrant with the mellow perfume of Alabama grass. Justin could sense honeysuckle, wisteria, and violets—ambrosia to his nostrils. He listened. Gone were the sounds of battle—of misery—of men moaning in the grip of death. Now lingered the happy trilling of birds, the distant sound of Nate and Willy laughing as they worked on their fort nearby. He smiled at the thought of the two young boys, so busily collecting their gruesome bones. He remembered those days—days when he and Caleb had often gone adventuring. The memory was both sweet and painful.

It was suddenly strange to Justin Turner that he was not hungry. Yet he remembered with contentment that his mother's biscuits were in his belly—and eggs, eggs that had been flavored with the tiniest, delicious grains of salt. He could still see the salt tumbling from his mother's fingers as she'd sifted it over his plate. His mouth watered at the thought of more salt to come. A full belly—it was a wonderful awareness!

Justin squeezed Vivianna's soft form— embraced her more tightly. What a blissful sensation it was, holding her. For a moment, he briefly wondered if perhaps he had not truly returned home but rather died and these were the visions granted him of heaven. The thought frightened him, and he opened his eyes to see the green of the leafy willow wands hanging all about him. He was not dead, nor was he dreaming. He was home, and he had God to thank for it—and Johnny Tabor.

"I thought Johnny might be dead when I woke up this mornin'," Justin mumbled.

Vivianna sighed. "I was afraid too," she said. "And I didn't want you to lose your friend."

"I owe him my life. I wouldn't want to bury him . . . especially so soon," he said.

"But Johnny said he owed you *his* life," she said. "Will ya tell me one day . . . will ya tell me how you saved his life?"

Justin felt his own smile fade. Knowledge— the pure knowledge of all Johnny Tabor really was, of all he had done—that knowledge caused a chill to travel through Justin. Yet there was no need for Vivianna to bear that weight—no need for her to know who the man she'd enjoyed such a hearty laugh with out by the chicken pen that morning truly was.

Therefore, he simply answered, "Maybe one day."

"Justin! Justin Turner!" Nate exclaimed as he and Willy dashed beneath the willow tree. Breathless with agitation, Nate scolded, "Quit slobberin' all over Viv and come see! Come see what me and Willy found off in the woods! You won't believe what we found!"

Vivianna sat up, her cheeks pink with blushing at being caught so willingly in Justin's arms.

"What is it?" Justin asked as he struggled to his feet. "You two look like ya seen a ghost."

"Not a ghost, Justin," Nate panted. "Though I think I might rather have seen a ghost than what we found."

Justin frowned, and Vivianna felt the hair on the back of her neck prickle.

"What is it?" Justin repeated. Vivianna knew Justin's mind was sensing unpleasantries as well.

"A man, Justin! A dead man!" Nate whispered. "Or . . . or at least what's left of him."

CHAPTER SIX

Awash with horrified trepidation, Vivianna followed Justin as Nate and Willy led them to a place in the woods beyond the meadow and the Turner family cemetery. Surely the young Turner boys had been mistaken in what they'd seen. Surely they had! Yet as they neared the woods—as Willy's face remained void of color—she knew they had not been mistaken. She wondered what she was doing accompanying them. She'd seen enough dead men to give her nightmares for the rest of her life! Yet Justin had taken her hand—led her along with them—and she didn't know what else to do but follow him.

"See there, Justin?" Nate asked as they passed the boys' fort and made their way through the woods. "Just yonder . . . near that big oak."

"I'll stay just here," Vivianna said, stopping short in her tracks. She couldn't—she couldn't look on another dead man. The war was ending! There shouldn't be any more death!

"Come on, Viv," Justin said, looking back to her and tugging on her hand he still held.

But Vivianna shook her head and pulled her hand from his grasp. "I don't need to see another dead man," she told him. "And neither do the boys." Vivianna reached out, placing a hand on Willy's shoulder. Instantly, Willy wrapped his arms around her waist, clinging to her for comfort. Vivianna smoothed his hair and pulled him tight against her. "You stay here too, Nate," she said. "Your mama wouldn't want ya over there if ya don't need to be . . . and ya don't. You've pointed Justin in the right direction. Now come over here with me."

"Aw, Viv!" Nate argued.

But even as Justin's eyes narrowed, even as he frowned, he seemed to realize the seriousness of the situation—seemed to realize it was not in his little brothers' best interest to let them continue to linger so near to death.

"Nate . . . Viv's right," he said. "You stay here with her and Willy." He nodded, still frowning. "You're right, Viv. You're right."

He'd encouraged her—let her know he knew she and the boys shouldn't continue with him. Yet she sensed an overwhelming dread in him— and why not? Justin had returned home only a day before—returned home thinking the war was behind him, that he was finished with fighting and death, suffering and misery. And yet here was death, fresh upon his doorstep.

Justin nodded to Vivianna as Nate joined her and Willy. Inhaling a deep breath of courage and resolve, Justin turned and headed toward the big oak Nate had indicated. Vivianna waited— silent, horrified, and breathless with anxiety.

She watched as Justin reached the big oak and hunkered down. After several long moments, he stood and quickly strode back to where she and the boys were waiting.

"Nate," he said—and she could see him trembling. "You and Willy run on. Stop at the house, and have Willy stay with Mama 'til we get there. Then run on into town and fetch Caleb. Tell him to meet us at the house. Viv . . . you run back and get Johnny. Fetch him here as fast as you can."

"All right, Justin," Nate said, taking his younger brother's hand. Willy rather unwillingly let go of Vivianna. "We'll hurry."

As Nate and Willy turned to go, Justin called, "Boys!" Nate and Willy stopped, turned, and looked at him. "Don't say a word about this to anybody you see on the way. Don't even tell Caleb why we need him home until you're well away from anybody in town. Do ya hear me?"

Nate frowned, confused. "Well, yeah . . . but—"

"I mean it, Nate," Justin growled. He looked to Willy. "Willy? I mean it now. Don't you boys say one word to anybody! I don't care if someone tries to beat it out of ya. Don't say a word! Do ya understand?"

"All right, Justin," Nate said, still frowning with bewilderment. "If you say so."

"I do say so," Justin said. "Now go on and fetch Caleb home."

Nate nodded, and the boys ran off.

Justin turned to Vivianna. A quiet gasp escaped her as she saw the fear in his eyes. "Viv, you've gotta fetch Johnny quick."

Vivianna glanced behind her. Nate and Willy were well on their way—well out of hearing range. "What's the matter, Justin?" she asked. "Shouldn't we just fetch the sheriff . . . or Doctor Kindersley?"

But Justin shook his head emphatically. "No! No. We can't . . . not yet."

"But why not?" she asked.

The fear in Justin's eyes increased, and Vivianna saw something else in them too: fury!

"Because it's a Reb soldier lyin' over there dead . . . not more than a day dead. And me and Johnny know him."

"What?" Vivianna gasped.

Justin nodded. "He was a guard . . . a guard at Andersonville." Justin shook his head, his hands still trembling as he ran them over his bristly hair. "His name is Powell, Zachary Powell, and he hated me and Johnny somethin' fierce— especially Johnny. I can't figure for the life of me what he's doin' here . . . not unless he came lookin' for a fight with the two of us."

"But, Justin, we can't just leave him out here. We can't just—"

Vivianna gasped as Justin reached out, taking hold of her shoulders.

"I need you to fetch Johnny for me, Viv! Don't ya see? Me and Johnny . . . Caleb too . . . we're Yankees! A dead Confederate in the woods? Folks in town . . . they'll blame us quick as anythin'! They'll string us up without another word. I need you to bring Johnny to me, and then we'll talk with Caleb . . . figure out what to do. All right?"

"B-but, Justin—" Vivianna stammered.

"Please, Viv," he interrupted. "Just fetch Johnny. Fetch Johnny, and then stay with Mama and wait for the others. Please."

Justin was frightened. His eyes told her; his trembling hands told her. Suddenly, Vivianna was far more frightened of what Justin had implied—that he might be blamed for a dead Confederate in the woods—than she was for the fact that a dead man lay just beyond where they stood.

"All right," she said. "I'll go . . . but will you be all right?"

Justin nodded. "I'm fine. I'm fine. I just need Johnny."

"All right." Vivianna quickly kissed Justin on one cheek and then turned and ran.

Panic nipped at her heels as she ran through the cemetery; fear breathed down her neck! A dead soldier was bad enough, but she did understand the true danger for Justin, Caleb, and Johnny Tabor. The people of Florence were fairly kind to

Savannah Turner. Mr. Turner had fought for the Confederacy, so even though it was now known that Caleb fought for the Union, the townsfolk were tolerant. Yet if a dead Confederate soldier were found on Turner property, Vivianna knew how quickly the tide of tolerance could change. The war was over—or nearly over. Yet the Confederacy—the South—had been whipped, and Alabama was the South. Vivianna knew that even to those in town who had been in silent support of the Union, a dead Southerner in the woods would spur anger—and perhaps violent vigilantism.

She did not smell the sweet scents of spring as she ran—oblivious to the lazy feeling of the day. Rather, panic and fear drove Vivianna onward, and soon she could see the honeysuckled arbor a short distance away. Frantically she tried to think where she might search for Justin's friend. Perhaps Willy had already found him, when Nate had left him with Savannah. Perhaps Johnny was already on his way to Justin. Yet he would need to be led there, wouldn't he? Justin had said to send him, yet Johnny had never been to the meadow or the cemetery or Nate and Willy's fort. Yes, she would have to lead him back. She would have to . . .

Vivianna screamed as Johnny Tabor suddenly stepped into her path. He startled her so severely, tears burst from her eyes to moisten her cheeks.

"You frightened me!" she scolded as tears continued to stream down her face.

"What's the matter?" he growled, his bony hands taking hold of her shoulders. "What's happened?"

Vivianna shook her head, angrily brushing the tears from her cheeks with the back of her hands. "Justin needs you," she said. Lowering her voice, she told him, "Nate and Willy found a dead man in the woods beyond the cemetery . . . a Reb soldier. Justin says you know him . . . a guard from the prison camp . . . a man named Powell."

Already pallid, Johnny Tabor's face grew suddenly even paler, his dark eyebrows puckering into a deep frown.

"Powell?" he breathed. He released her then and ordered, "Stay here. Go into the house, and stay here until we get back."

"Justin sent Nate for Caleb," she added.

Johnny nodded.

"I'll take ya to Justin," Vivianna said. She wanted to make sure he reached Justin—wanted to make certain Justin could return to the house as quickly as possible.

"No . . . no, you stay here," he told her. "Go to the house and stay there. I'm sure it's an easy enough place to find."

"But it's in the woods . . . beyond the meadow and the cemetery," she explained. "There is a path, but . . ."

His eyes narrowed as he glared at her. "I'll find it." He looked beyond her to the path leading to the cemetery. "Just stay in the house until we return."

"But, Johnny . . . Justin's waiting. Ya have to hurry. I'll just take ya there and come back," she argued with him. She would not have him lost—would not have him leave Justin with the dead man alone. What if someone happened upon him—found Justin there with the dead Confederate? Her panic heightened. She began to panic, for the true and full realization of what such a situation could mean for Justin and Johnny—even for Caleb—was clear in her mind. "I have to make certain ya reach him, quickly! I—"

She was rendered breathless as Johnny Tabor took her chin in one hand, glaring down at her. His dark eyes burned with anger—dominance—a strength she did not think him capable of owning in his weakened condition.

"I'll find Justin," he said. "You don't need to see a dead man . . . and the others will need you. Just go to the house and—"

"But gettin' there might not be so simple as ya might think," she argued. "And Justin's waitin'! I can take ya there quick as a—"

She was silenced as Johnny's hand moved up from her chin to cover her mouth.

"I know the way, Vivianna," he growled.

149

"Please . . . just go on into the house and wait for us to return."

Vivianna's eyes widened. She was astonished at the strength in his hand as he held it over her mouth. He did not hurt her—not in the least. Yet she could feel the power in him, even for his weakened state.

She nodded, and he moved his hand from her face.

"Do you understand how important it is that ya don't say a word to anyone about the man in the woods?" he asked in a lowered voice.

Vivianna nodded. "I do," she whispered.

"Good," he mumbled. "Then run on in. I'll be back shortly . . . with Justin. I promise."

Vivianna brushed the tears from her cheeks and nodded. Somehow, she trusted his word—trusted that he would bring Justin back. After all, hadn't he brought him all the way from Georgia?

She turned and watched him hurry down the path toward the meadow. Though she still worried that he would lose his way—worried that someone else might happen upon Justin and the dead man before Johnny reached him—she tried to be brave and resolute.

As she hurried toward the house, her stomach churned with anxiety. It had hardly been one full day since Justin had returned—since he and Johnny had come walking up the road toward the house. Hardly one full day, and already their peace had vanished; already the residual horror of war was haunting them by heaping some sort of peril upon them.

Willy was in the kitchen with his mother. Savannah was weeping, cradling a frightened Willy.

"Oh, Viv!" the woman choked. "Are we never to have any reprieve from this war?"

Vivianna shook her head, overcome with her own bewilderment. She was frightened and felt helpless to offer any comfort to those she loved.

"A Southern boy?" Savannah asked. "What if he's an Alabama son? What if he's from Florence, on his way home and . . . and . . . and what could possibly have befallen him?"

"We have to wait, Miss Savannah," Vivianna said. Oh, she was worried—frightened and sickened. Yet she could not tell Justin's mother what else she knew about the dead man—not in front of an already distressed Willy. "We just have to wait for Justin to return. Caleb will be home soon . . . and Justin and Mr. Tabor. We just . . . we just have to wait."

And wait is what they did. They did not speak much—only waited. Vivianna began to count the tick-tocks of the clock on the mantel, but there were so many that she feared it might drive her mad. She forced a smile at Willy—embraced him when he left his mother for a moment to come to her. She felt so sorry for the boy, knowing he was

151

frightened—knowing he was trying to offer her comfort even for his own fear.

At long last, Caleb and Nate arrived. Though she was still near a state of panic, she did draw an easier breath when Caleb stepped into the house.

"Oh, Caleb!" Willy exclaimed, racing to his brother. Caleb knelt on the floor, catching Willy in his arms and soothingly shushing him. "It was awful! There's a man out there," Willy said in a whisper. "He ain't been dead long I don't think. But somethin' must've gnawed on him in the night . . . on his arm . . . and . . ."

"It's all right now, Willy," Caleb said. "Let's have you and Nate just run on in the other room and rest for a while."

"I don't wanna rest!" Nate exclaimed. Vivianna felt more tears in her eyes as she saw the worried expression on Nate's face. No doubt he'd figured out why Justin had ordered him not to speak to a soul about the dead man.

"You go on in the bedroom with Willy, and you boys read a book or lay down a while on your beds," Caleb said. "I promise you . . . we'll come get ya both when we get this all worked out. But ya need to let us older boys take care of what to do first. All right?"

Nate scowled but nodded. He put his arm around Willy's shoulders and began leading him toward the back room. He paused, however, turning back to Caleb and asking, "Is it all right if I tell Willy why it is we can't tell nobody about this?"

"Yeah," Caleb said, nodding. "You go on and tell him. Make sure you explain it thorough though."

"I will, Caleb," Nate said.

The moment the boys' bedroom door closed behind them, Savannah burst into tears.

"There's somethin' else about this, Caleb!" she whispered, wiping tears from her cheeks. "I can sense it. Somethin' I haven't been told yet. You're worried about the sheriff finding a dead Southern boy on our property when you and Justin fought with the Alabama First, aren't you?"

Caleb nodded. "Lee surrendered, Mama, but the war ain't over yet . . . not everywhere," he said. "Folks in Florence will want to put a noose around someone's neck if there's a dead Reb found out near our place. And if he's a local boy . . ."

"He's not a local boy," Vivianna said then. She kept her voice low and tried not to break into fresh weeping as Caleb looked to her, frowning.

"How do ya know, Viv? Just because ya didn't recognize him . . ." he began.

Vivianna shook her head and explained, "I . . . I didn't even see the man, but . . . but Justin told me . . ."

She paused—afraid to continue—afraid to tell Mrs. Turner and Caleb how far more serious the situation was than it already seemed.

"Justin told ya what, Viv?" Caleb urged, however. He rose to his feet and strode to her. Reaching out, he brushed a strand of hair from her forehead. He was so kind; there was such a calming nature about him. Caleb Turner made a body feel as if any secret could be revealed to him and kept safe—as if any worry or problem could be overcome.

"He told me . . . the man out there in the woods was a guard at Andersonville prison," she confessed. "Justin said his name is Powell . . . that he and Johnny both knew him, that this Powell man hated them both for some reason . . . especially Johnny."

Even as Savannah gasped and began sobbing— even as Vivianna felt the icy fingers of dread and doom encircling her throat—still Caleb's deep blue eyes comforted her. Caleb did not shout or yell or growl. He only nodded, as if the information she'd just offered was of little consequence.

"Caleb! Caleb!" Savannah cried. "They'll hang your brother for certain if it's known! You know they will! They'll lynch him if nothin' else!"

"Calm down, Mama," Caleb said, going to his mother and gathering her in his arms. "Just settle yourself. We'll work this out."

"Work it out?" Savannah cried. "There won't be any workin' this out! People are too angry about the war. We're fortunate you weren't beaten to death when you returned! Oh, Caleb . . . we can't tell anybody. We can't!"

Vivianna turned when she heard the door open. Justin and Johnny stepped into the house looking grave, weary, somehow defeated.

"Oh, Justin!" Savannah gasped, collapsing into Justin's embrace as he approached. "What is all this, Justin? How can this be?"

"Let's sit down, Mama," Justin said. "Let's all just sit down and do some thinkin'."

But Savannah was overcome. "We can't tell anybody, Justin! We can't! You know we can't."

"Please, Mama," Caleb said. "Let's just sit down a spell and do some talkin' on it. Everythin' will be fine. We just need to decide what to do."

As Caleb led his mother to the kitchen table, Vivianna watched as Justin turned to Johnny.

"You can run, Johnny," Justin said. "There ain't no need for you to linger and find yourself hanged just because—"

"I ain't a coward, Justin," Johnny growled. "I ain't runnin' from this. Chances are it was me Powell was lookin' for anyway . . . and you know it."

Justin nodded. "Come on then, boy," he said, following his mother and brother to the table. "We better work this out as best we can."

Vivianna looked to Johnny. He'd been standing near the front door, supporting himself by leaning on the back of a chair to one side of it. As he took a step forward, however, he lost his balance and stumbled to one side. Instinctively, Vivianna reached out, taking hold of his arm in an effort to steady him—but she wasn't strong enough to keep the weight of his body from toppling over. In the next moment, she found herself in a heap on the floor—Johnny Tabor on his hands and knees as he hovered over her.

"You need some rest, John!" Caleb scolded as he and Justin helped Johnny to stand.

"I need some backbone!" Johnny growled as Justin helped him to the table.

Caleb offered Vivianna his hand and pulled her to her feet.

"You all right?" he asked. Vivianna smiled at him and nodded. Taking her hand, he led her to the table as well.

Once they were all seated, it was Johnny Tabor who spoke first.

"Zachary Powell was a devil, Mrs. Turner. One of the worst men I have ever in my life come across. And he's lyin' dead out there in your woods," he began. "It looks to me and Justin as if he just simply fell down and cracked his head on a rock. But the fact is he's a Johnny Reb. And me, Justin, and Caleb . . ." He paused, shaking his head with something akin to disbelief. "Me and your boys will be the first ones the folks in Florence look to blame."

"No bullet? No stabbin'?" Caleb asked. "He's just lyin' out there dead?"

Johnny nodded, and Justin said, "The back of his head looks to be bashed in . . . and there's a big rock right there under him."

"Blood on the rock?" Caleb asked.

Justin and Johnny both nodded.

"Mm-hmm," Johnny said. "It would seem he just fell down and cracked his head open. Somethin' chewed him up pretty bad since though."

"Well then, that's what we tell the sheriff!" Savannah suggested. "We just tell the sheriff the truth . . . that Nate and Willy found him out there and . . . and we just leave out the part about you boys knowin' him."

Vivianna felt her heart lighten—lighten as much as Savannah's hopeful expression lightened. Surely if they simply told the truth, surely then there would be no danger to Justin and his friend or to Caleb.

"Yes!" Vivianna said. "Certainly no one would find suspicion with you boys if we just tell them the truth and they see the rock and—"

"Johnny said it *looks* like he hit his head on the rock," Justin interrupted. "It could just as easy be someone bashed his head in with the rock and then put it out there in the woods under him." He shook his head. "No . . . no. Folks would still be pointin' their fingers at us."

"Then we don't tell anyone," Savannah suggested. "We just bury him proper in our own little cemetery, and no one ever has to know we found him."

"Pardon me, Mrs. Turner," Johnny began, "but I'm sure the boy has family. It wouldn't be right not to let them know what happened to him, to let a family go for eternity without knowing if he was alive or dead . . . where he was planted." Johnny paused, glanced to Vivianna, and continued, "It seems to me that too many folks are already livin' with those kinds of ghosts."

Vivianna wondered how much Justin had told Johnny about Sam and Augie. She wondered if he knew they hadn't been heard from in over two years—that she would never know where they were buried or how they had died.

"You'd want to know about your boys, ma'am," he added. "I don't think we can simply bury the boy and not tell a soul."

"And what if someone did kill him?" Caleb asked. "If we bury him and don't tell anybody— and someone around these parts is the one who killed him—we'd be askin' for danger to come knockin' on our own door."

Justin nodded. "I say we tell the sheriff," he suggested. "Mama, Sheriff Pidwell . . . he's known me and Caleb since we were born. Surely, if we just went to him and explained—"

"Maybe he'd pretend he found the body," Caleb

suggested. "Maybe we could just tell the sheriff we found the body but explain why we don't feel safe about comin' forward. And maybe he'll just find the Reb, and we'll be done with it."

Vivianna felt hope rising in her for a moment. Yet Savannah shook her head.

"No. No," she said. "I don't trust Sheriff Pidwell. He lost three boys in the war . . . three boys who fought for the Confederacy. I don't trust that his heart is as soft as it once was."

"How long do ya think that boy has been dead?" Caleb asked.

Justin shook his head. "Johnny thinks not more'n a day," he answered. "Powell probably tracked us here. Maybe he was waitin' for a chance to—"

"Why did he hate you so, Mr. Tabor?" Vivianna asked. She was suddenly very angry. Though she didn't know exactly how, somehow she knew it was all Johnny Tabor's fault! Justin was in danger because of his friend. She knew it!

"It don't matter," Johnny mumbled. "Fact is he just hated me."

"Why?" Vivianna asked, tears welling in her eyes. "Justin and Caleb, they're both in danger because of you . . . because this man hated you. Why did he hate ya enough to follow ya all the way to Alabama?"

Johnny's eyes narrowed, and he glared at her. "Because every time he tried to beat me to

159

death . . . I wouldn't die," he growled. "Every time he'd whip me, I wouldn't holler. It's that simple. I got the best of him . . . simply by not dyin' when he wanted me to."

Justin nodded and said, "He told us . . . he told me and Johnny when we were released from Andersonville . . . he told us he'd see Johnny dead and wormy one way or the other. We just thought he was talkin' though. Just thought he was talkin'."

"I-I'm sorry," Vivianna said. She glanced away from Johnny when he looked to her. "I'm sorry, Mr. Tabor. I'm just so . . . I'm just so tired of this war . . . so tired of death and fear."

"Please don't apologize to me, Miss Vivianna," Johnny mumbled. "I've done enough things . . . things that make me not worth apologizin' to."

Vivianna wanted to run—wanted to cry, scream, and shriek! She wanted the war to be over—really over! She wanted to linger in Justin's arms under the willow tree, wanted to share kisses with him beneath the honeysuckle vine! She wanted to run and laugh—really laugh—wholeheartedly the way she'd laughed that morning when that rotten pigeon had doused Johnny Tabor. She didn't want to talk about death or dead men or prison or anything else ugly and frightening. She didn't want to think about the fact her parents were gone, that she'd never see her brothers again.

Carefully, she placed her trembling hands in

her lap and squeezed them tightly together in an effort to keep from screaming with frustration and heartache. She could not stand by and see Justin hanged—or Caleb, for that matter. Yet she also knew Johnny was right. She knew what it was to never know the fate of loved ones. She knew the haunting, the bitter sadness, the sickening nightmares. Yet what was to be done? It seemed there were only two choices before them: to sin—to lie and leave a man's family in lifelong misery—or to tell the truth and risk the death of those she loved. The dead man in the woods was the enemy, yes. He'd tortured Justin and Johnny, yes. Still, his family did not deserve to pay such a haunting and painful price. Still, she could not see Justin hanged—nor Caleb—nor even Johnny Tabor.

Vivianna swallowed. She inhaled a deep breath, attempting to calm herself.

"We could just tell the sheriff everything," Caleb suggested. "Just tell him the truth and . . . and hope folks know us Turners are good people."

"No," Justin said. "No. They'll lynch us sure. We can't tell the sheriff. Maybe Mama's right. Maybe we should just bury Powell and—"

"We can't do that, Justin," Caleb interrupted. "You know we can't."

"I do know it," Justin admitted. "Least I think I know it."

"I stand with Caleb. We just tell the sheriff," Johnny said. "If it comes to folks wantin' a hangin' . . . well, I'm the reason he's lyin' out there dead. One way or the other I'm the reason. So I oughta be the one to—"

"No!" Savannah exclaimed. "I won't see anyone hang for somethin' they didn't do . . . not if I can help it. There's got to be a way. We know everybody in Florence. Every soul! I can't believe they'd hang my boys—or even you, Johnny—without proof of wrongdoin'. I just can't believe it."

Justin sighed. Vivianna watched as he leaned back in his chair and ran a hand over his bristly haired head. She looked to Caleb, pale and worried at facing such a terrible and seemingly impossible situation. She looked to Johnny, worn, weathered, and still so weak. Savannah seemed to have aged a decade in the past five minutes. Her eyes were void of any light, the corners of her mouth downturned in a dismal frown.

She thought then of Nate and Willy. For all they knew, there was simply the horror of a dead man lying out in the woods. They knew nothing of what further horrors could come of it.

"Well, we're sittin'—all five of us—we're sittin' here until we agree on somethin'," Savannah said. "I won't see my boys hanged . . . and . . . and I do think it would be wrong not to tell someone. I'd want to know where he was if it was my son. So we'll sit here 'til we know what we're doin'."

Vivianna nearly stood up—nearly walked away. After all, of what value was her opinion? Savannah was Justin and Caleb's mother. Even Mr. Tabor had more reason to contribute, being that he was most likely the reason the dead man had come to Florence in the first place. But for Vivianna, it was one of the rare moments when she was brutally reminded that she wasn't truly a Turner—at least, not yet. Furthermore, if the people of Florence did find out about the dead Confederate near the old cemetery, she might never be.

Thus, an hour passed—an hour during which it was again considered that the dead Reb simply be buried out in the Turner family cemetery. An hour during which it was again suggested the truth simply be told. An hour during which it was again thought that perhaps Sheriff Pidwell could be trusted to help keep the Turner boys and Johnny Tabor safe from a mob lynching.

Johnny Tabor even suggested he report the body to the sheriff so the suspicion would settle only on him. Oddly, this offer of martyrdom somehow caused Vivianna to shudder with her own suspicions. No man was truly so self-sacrificing for his friends as this. She wondered if Johnny Tabor knew something they did not. Was he far more ill than he appeared? He'd been so willing to die the night before—seemed so willing to hang for the death of an enemy. She thought of the night before, when Johnny had ridden out on Caleb's horse to retrieve his pack. Was guilt eating at him? Did he know more about the death of the Confederate man in the woods than he was telling them? Had Zachary Powell come upon Johnny while he was retrieving his and Justin's possessions? Yet Vivianna shook her head. Johnny Tabor could hardly walk, let alone have the strength to kill another man.

By the time the hour had gone, everyone's temperament was strained. Always the only choice seemed to be to tell the sheriff—to have faith in a man who had lost three sons in battle against the Union that Caleb, Justin, and Johnny had fought to preserve. There seemed no other honest venue, no other road that did not include a deceit that would haunt all of them for the rest of their lives.

"Let me go," Caleb said, rising to his feet. "I've been home so long . . . people trust me again." He pointed to Justin and then Johnny. "You two only just returned. It looks bad enough . . . so let me go."

At that moment, Nate and Willy burst into the room—burst into the room by way of the front door, not by way of their bedroom.

"You don't have to worry no more!" Willy shouted, beaming with relieved joy. "Mama!

You don't have to worry about Justin or Caleb or Johnny Tabor! Everything is all worked out!"

"What are you goin' on about, Willy?" Savannah asked as everyone stood from their chairs.

It was Nate who explained.

"Me and Willy . . . we heard y'all talkin'," he began, "but don't get mad at us, Mama . . . 'cause we had to listen! We knew somethin' was wrong . . . somethin' other than just that dead man out in the woods."

"Nate Turner!" Savannah scolded.

But Nate did not pause. "So me and Willy . . . we decided we'd go out and bury that ol' dead Confederate who come lookin' for Johnny. We figured if we buried him and never told anybody, everything would be fine!"

"Nate!" Savannah began again.

"But, Mama! When we snuck out the window of the bedroom, after we got a shovel from the barn, when we got to where we first found that dead Johnny Reb . . . he's gone, Mama! He ain't there no more! I coulda sworn he was dead, one arm almost gnawed clean off by somethin'. But he must notta been dead! He's gone. He musta just up and walked away or somethin'!"

"Walked away?" Savannah asked, bewildered. "Dead men—especially ones that animals have been chewin' on—do not just get up and walk away, Nate Turner!" Savannah shook her head.

"What am I doin'? I'm sittin' here talkin' about a dead man like it's the most everyday thing in the world!"

"What do ya mean he's gone, Nate?" Caleb asked. "You mean . . . you mean you boys went out there, and there ain't no body?"

Willy and Nate both nodded, tears of joyous relief in their eyes.

"Not anymore. He's gone, Caleb," Willy said. "And me and Nate . . . we didn't do nothin'. He's just gone. We figure nothin' coulda ate him all up, and all of us . . . well, all of us were here, so none of us drug him off. He's gone. He's just . . . gone."

CHAPTER SEVEN

Vivianna pressed the clothes peg onto the line to hold one of Caleb's shirts. She sighed, glad that all the men's freshly washed shirts were hung out to dry. It would take them all day to dry, no doubt, for already the air was thick and balmy. She set the basket of remaining clothes pegs on the ground near one clothesline pole and started back toward the house.

It was a glorious Alabama morning. A large yellow and black butterfly flitted close, and Vivianna paused to watch it gracefully alight on a large purple clematis bloom nearby. The striking yellow of the butterfly against the deep purple of the flower caused Vivianna to smile with a sense of serene joy. Beauty was returning to the world, and Vivianna was thankful for it.

Over the past month, it seemed as if everything had at last begun to settle—settle into a resemblance of what life had once been. Oh, certainly there were still anger, sadness, and fatigue; certainly there was still hardship. Yet the knowledge that men were no longer fighting and dying by the thousands helped life to seem hopeful once more.

Money was a worry, yes, but the garden was thriving, and the Turners had food enough.

Certainly there was plenty of work to keep Savannah and Vivianna busy. Caring for a house and five men was enough to keep five women busy, and they were only two. Yet Vivianna was glad for the work—glad to know she was a help to Savannah.

Many were the times since Justin's return that Vivianna had considered moving back into town—back into her parents' lonely, abandoned home. This had first been a consideration when Caleb had returned, for the mere fact the towns-folk might think it inappropriate for an unmarried young woman to reside in the same house as an unmarried young man who was not kin. However, the war allotted broader boundaries, and little was said in town about Vivianna Bartholomew dwelling in the same house as Caleb Turner. Yet now—now with two other unmarried men living within the same walls—Vivianna had begun to worry more seriously. Many people in Florence were still angry with the Turner boys for fighting for the Union. Though little was said, there was gossip, and all the Turners knew there were those who disliked them for it. Vivianna had begun to wonder if the fact she was still living with Savannah and her sons might provoke even more anger or dislike. She certainly did not want to be the cause of any further unkindness to the Turners. Yet she knew Savannah needed her help—needed her company. Furthermore, she owed Savannah Turner a great debt! The woman had, without hesitation, taken Vivianna in when her parents had been killed. She'd provided food, shelter, and clothing for her—treated her like a daughter. How could she leave Savannah when she owed such a debt to her? Thus, she'd lingered in the Turner home, even after Justin had returned, even for the fact that Johnny Tabor still resided with them.

Vivianna sighed and shook her head, attempting to dispel all thoughts of worry and concern. The butterfly was beautiful, the flowers were lovely, and the sky was blue. Caleb had work, Justin was getting stronger with each passing day, and even Johnny Tabor was helping life to look more hopeful. Oddly, Johnny had recovered far more quickly than Justin, who had yet to regain his full strength. Johnny's health had returned at an astonishing rate, and now he was attempting to repay the Turners for their kindnesses to him. Johnny Tabor worked from the moment the sun broke the horizon in the morning until Savannah called him in for supper in the evening. Already he'd gathered and split enough wood to keep the oven cooking for months. He'd repaired the barn, managed the weeds in the garden, and shod half the horses in town. He'd whitewashed the fences, constructed a new chicken coop and pen, and hauled water whenever Savannah or anyone else asked him to.

Secretly, Vivianna was grateful Johnny had stayed on. His help allowed Justin to heal—to rest with a clear mind. With Johnny there to help, Justin need not worry about the physical tasks too burdensome or difficult for Savannah and Vivianna to do while Caleb was in town working. Rather, Justin knew all would be taken care of; thus he could concentrate on regaining his strength. Vivianna often thought she should offer her thanks to Johnny, for without him she was not at all certain Justin would be recovering so well. Still, something about the man—something about Justin's friend caused her to pause in thanking him, even to pause in lingering in his company. Often she wondered if it were merely the fact that, as Johnny Tabor's strength had returned, his appearance and demeanor had become even more intimidating. Like Justin's, Johnny's hair had grown in—brown and straight in contrast to Justin's dark, wavy locks. As Justin's blue eyes were bright and welcoming, Johnny's eyes were dark and brooding. Though Justin still lingered in gaining his full strength, the weakness and weariness had vanished from Johnny. Justin still struggled with lifting heavy things, his endurance still not what it would soon be. However, Johnny's musculature was now well defined and rather bulking, all for the sake of good food and hard labor. Thus, though he deserved her thanks, Vivianna could not find the words—or the courage—to thank Johnny for his service to the Turner family and herself. Rather, she simply tried to ignore his daunting presence.

Vivianna sighed as she thought of Justin—thought of his ever-strengthening health, thought of his dazzling smile and inviting gaze. As yet, he had not spoken of marriage to her, though he often implied it through teasing or in speaking of the future— -often spoke of being old together and sitting on the porch in the evenings, watching the sunset. Most every day after Justin had his breakfast, Vivianna would walk with him either to the big pond, where they would sit on a fallen tree and converse, or to the arbor and honeysuckle vine. There they would linger on the swing, lazily swaying back and forth, talking of the past and discussing all that once was. At first, Vivianna had known a fair amount of frustration in this light courting manner. The things she and Justin had written in their letters to one another during the war had seemed the stuff of deep emotion—of promise and love. Yet she'd begun to understand that Justin had endured the horrors of Andersonville since those letters—that it had weakened, frightened, and damaged him. Not only did Justin's body need rest and recovery, but likewise his mind and heart required the same. Vivianna had begun to understand this—begun to know that Justin still loved her. He simply did not feel worthy of owning her love in return.

Still, she was not too often discouraged, for she knew he would heal—mind, heart, and body. She knew he had loved her before Andersonville, for she yet held his letters as cherished treasure. Furthermore, she knew he loved her still, that he would heal and eventually fulfill every promise he'd made to her—every promise of their knowing a wonderful life together. Therefore, she was reconciled to be patient, glad in his company, delighted by each soft kiss he begged of her whenever they were alone. He would soon ask her to marry him, and then all her waiting would be rewarded, and she would know the war was truly behind them.

The yellow butterfly left its perch on the dark violet clematis, flitting off in the direction of the meadow. Vivianna frowned as her momentary respite was tainted by thoughts of the cemetery—of the woods beyond—of a Confederate soldier named Zachary Powell. Vivianna closed her eyes and forced herself to do as Caleb had suggested—tried not to think of the day Nate and Willy had first found Zachary Powell's body, the day they had later returned to find his body missing. There was nothing that could be done. Caleb, Justin, and Johnny had eventually agreed that, without a body to prove the man was dead, they could not tell Sheriff Pidwell (or anyone else) about the man's death. After all, what were they to say? Caleb had explained they simply could not wander into town and announce they'd found a dead Confederate soldier but that his body had disappeared. The situation would have been even worse than if they'd been able to lead the sheriff to Zachary Powell's body. Thus, it had been agreed upon that they would say nothing— that there was nothing to say. Yet they were all haunted—haunted by the knowledge that a man was dead, that his family would never know what had become of him. Johnny Tabor had seemed especially haunted. It was often Vivianna would awaken late in the dark hours of night to fetch a glass of water only to find Johnny sitting on the front porch whittling away on a piece of wood with the knife he kept in his boot. She suspected Johnny's guilt over the missing body of Zachary Powell was far greater than was anyone else's— even Justin's. For Johnny had hated Zachary Powell, and guilt was the constant companion of hate.

Vivianna shook her head and again determined not to think of the incident—not the finding of the body and its disappearance and not the argument she'd overheard between Justin and Johnny a few days later. Yet her thoughts had wandered there, and now she could not help but let them linger a moment.

It had been only three days following Nate and Willy's finding the dead man in the woods that Vivianna had been out searching for wild strawberries—and overheard a conversation. She'd knelt to pick a ripened bunch, and as she did, she'd heard voices. She'd remained quietly in the hidden shade of a tree as Justin and Johnny paused during their walk through the meadow—to the cemetery. They'd been arguing, and naturally, this intrigued Vivianna. Yet what she overheard had begun to haunt her nearly as much, or possibly more, than the knowledge of Zachary Powell's dead and missing body did.

Vivianna held perfectly still as Justin and Johnny stopped to argue just where she'd been picking berries that day. She fancied, in that moment, she didn't know what it was that caused her to keep still and silent—out of sight. But something did, and she'd listened.

"Don't you push me, Johnny!" Justin had snapped. "You're the one who did this . . . so you have no right to tell me how to deal it out now."

"Me? I did it?" Johnny growled. "It was you who—"

"None but you, Johnny Tabor . . . and ya know it!" Justin had interrupted. "If it weren't for you, Johnny—"

"If it weren't for me . . . you'd be dead, Justin," Johnny growled even more angrily. "Stone dead, Justin! Ya never woulda made it home. Ya woulda died, just like Zachary Powell died, only in more misery and discomfort . . . and they woulda drug ya out to a hole and shoveled the Georgia dirt over you at Andersonville. Ya never woulda made it home without me, and ya sure enough wouldn't be here all wrapped up in the arms of your pretty girl, now would ya?"

There was silence, and then Johnny spoke again. "That's right. You were the one who done this, Justin. In the very least you caused me to do it. One way or the other, it was you as much as it was me. So just do what ya have to do to make it right for your family . . . for everybody."

Vivianna had been terrified by what she'd heard! What could Justin and Johnny possibly have been arguing about—accusing each other of doing? She did not know, but her imagination began to concoct terrible possibilities—the worst being that it had been Johnny who had killed Zachary Powell! She thought once more of his lone trip to retrieve his pack the night before the young Turner boys found the dead Confederate in the woods. Still, she could not make sense of Justin's allowing a murderer to live with his family. Therefore, her mind devised a far less yet still terrifying concept. Perhaps it had been Johnny and Justin who had taken Zachary Powell's body! Perhaps, to avoid any danger to themselves or the family, they'd moved the body while Willy and Vivianna had lingered with Savannah while Nate had been fetching Caleb to the house. Perhaps it had been Johnny and Justin who had caused the disappearance of the corpse in the woods. Perhaps the entire hour that the adults in the Turner home had sat at the kitchen table discussing whether to tell the sheriff about the dead man, it had all been a ruse. Perhaps they'd known all along that the body had been moved.

Shaking her head—determined not to think on it any longer—Vivianna again started toward the house. Justin was not a liar, she was sure of it. She was not so sure about Johnny Tabor, but she knew Justin, and he would not lie over the whereabouts of a dead man. Thus, again resolved to a conclusion that all was not as it seemed— that the war was over and everything warlike had died (or disappeared) with it—Vivianna hurried into the house. Justin would be up by now and perhaps finished with his breakfast. The thought brought a renewed smile to her face and dashed away all other dismal thoughts. Though Caleb had left for work in town and Nate and Willy had had their morning meal with Johnny long ago, Justin did indeed now sit at the table enjoying a hearty breakfast.

Vivianna smiled at him, and he winked at her in response.

"He's got the appetite of a starved hog this mornin', Viv," Savannah chimed as Vivianna entered the kitchen. "He's had four eggs and two pieces of bread and butter!"

"Oh, wonderful!" Vivianna giggled.

Her smile broadened. Justin was nearly whole once more; she could sense it.

Sitting down at the table across from him, she smiled as he winked at her. Oh, he was handsome! His dark, wavy hair was mussed, his blue eyes bright as the sky, giving him a rather boyish appearance. Vivianna thought she'd never seen such a perfectly straight nose on a man—or such a dazzling smile! Part of her knew it was her love for Justin that caused her eyes to look upon him as flawless. The fact was, were he standing side by side with Caleb, it was indeed Caleb who might be chosen as the more handsome brother—by a woman who was not in love with Justin. Caleb was taller, his eyes a deep sapphire. Yet Vivianna saw only Justin's uncommonly attractive features within and without—saw the beauty in his heart as well as the comeliness of his face. She thought of his letters, of the beautiful words he'd written to her—words of love, of hope, of promise. Caleb had never written her many letters at all, let alone any filled with the deepest feelings of his soul. A piece of Vivianna's heart would always belong to Caleb, for she had loved him once. Yet Justin owned the whole of it now—and, oh, how she loved him!

"The wash is hangin' out, Miss Savannah," Vivianna told Savannah, though she still gazed at Justin, her smile broadening as he winked at her again. "Though I think it might take most of the day for it to dry."

"Well, thank you for risin' up so early and gettin' all that done, Viv," Savannah said. "I do not know what I'd do without you."

Savannah paused in clearing Justin's plate from the table. With a mother's loving expression full on her pretty face, she smiled at Vivianna, caressed her cheek, bent, and placed an affectionate kiss on her forehead. "I do swear, Viv . . . I couldn't do without you at all! I just couldn't," she said.

"Thank you, Miss Savannah," Vivianna said. She realized—as she often did—that she loved Savannah Turner as closely as was possible to the manner in which she'd loved her own mother.

"Do ya feel up to takin' me out for a walk this mornin', Viv?" Justin asked.

Vivianna looked back to him, and he winked. Flirtatiously, he reached across the table, took her hand in his, and leaned over, placing a lingering kiss on the back of it.

"Why, of course," Vivianna answered. "And where would ya like to amble today, Mr. Turner?"

Justin chuckled. "Oh, I'm thinkin' that ol' honeysuckle vine might need some tendin'," he said. "What do ya say?"

Vivianna blushed. She well recognized the expression on Justin's face—mischief. Vivianna slipped her hand into the pocket of her skirt. Justin's letter was there. She thought of his promise to kiss her beneath the honeysuckle—the promise he'd made so long ago, before the misery of Andersonville had weathered him. Oh, it was true he'd kissed her since his return—on numerous occasions. Yet she sensed he was restrained, as if he were afraid to kiss her as he truly wanted to —as she wanted him to.

Yet the twinkling mischief in his eyes as Justin sat across the table from her spoke of his being finally mended. She sensed his body was mended, his mind, and his heart. There was a light, a brightness in his eyes she hadn't seen since before the war, and the pure existence of it caused her arms to ripple with goose pimples borne of blissful anticipation.

"I say that suits me just fine," Vivianna answered at last.

Justin nodded, his smile broadening. "Well, Miss Vivianna Bartholomew . . . let's get to it then!"

He rose and offered a hand to her as she stood as well. His grasp was strong and warm, and simply the knowledge that he was touching her caused her to feel slightly breathless.

"We'll be back soon enough, Mama," Justin said.

"Oh, take your time, darlin'!" Savannah said, her eyes glistening with understanding delight.

"You two just take your time. I'll holler for Johnny if I need anythin'."

"All right then, Mama," Justin said, leading Vivianna from the house by way of the front door. "We will!"

The sun seemed brighter, the sky more blue. Vivianna could've sworn the air itself was as delighted as she was, exhaling the fragrance of a thousand flower blossoms in sharing its joy.

"Remember when we were little?" Justin began as they meandered toward the arbor. He still held her hand, and Vivianna was enchanted. "Remember how we used to play pirates . . . and me and Caleb would be pirate captains and kidnap you back and forth?"

Vivianna giggled and nodded. She did remember. After all, it had been one of her favorite games to play. "You'd have big battles. I was the princess, and each of you wanted to hold me for ransom . . . to force my father, the king—most likely Sam or Augie, dependin' on the day—to pay you in imaginary gold for my release," she said. "What fun we had then!"

Justin nodded, smiling. "We sure did." He paused, seeming thoughtful for a moment. "The day Caleb and me left for the war . . . I thought for a moment it seemed like we were still playing pirates over you. Didn't it?"

"It did," she said. "At first."

Vivianna gazed at him—studied him. She

180

remembered that day, over two years ago, when Caleb had owned her young heart—when Justin had begun to steal it. She'd known that day, the moment Justin had kissed her; she'd known that Caleb hadn't truly loved her—not the way she wanted to be loved. Vivianna wanted to be loved possessively, wanted her lover to be passionate in his love for her. Caleb had seemed only mildly vexed when Justin had kissed her. In truth, Vivianna had wondered if Justin had merely kissed her to prove a point to his brother—or to crow over him somehow. Yet as Justin's letters began to arrive, as he eventually began to confess his love for her—his professed obsessive love for her—she realized Justin had kissed her that day to prove it was he who loved her most, not simply to best his brother in wooing a young woman.

She smiled at Justin and continued, "But then you began to write . . . and slowly your letters spoke to my heart . . . and I knew you weren't simply playin' at pirates with Caleb."

Justin smiled, shook his head, and chuckled. "It's those letters," he began, "isn't it? If I hadn't written them letters, I mighta come home to find ya married to Caleb. Isn't that right?"

Vivianna shrugged. Vivianna didn't want to talk about Caleb or what might have been. The fact was Justin had written those letters, and she hadn't married Caleb. Again she thought of Caleb—of his kind manner, his calm character.

He was a great man, but he knew no passion. It seemed nothing pierced his heart to the core; nothing moved him to great emotion. Vivianna herself owned great emotion. True, she'd hidden it for long years. True, it was not often she displayed it. More often it was that she guarded her emotions quite desperately. Yet she did own deep, passionate emotion—emotions she would have had to guard her entire life had she married Caleb. In that moment, she feared she may have smothered—may have died from having had to keep herself always so calm in appearance had she'd chosen dear Caleb.

Vivianna was suddenly distracted, as was Justin. Laughter was the distraction—the mirthful laughter of Nate and Willy.

"What are they up to now?" Justin asked. "That kind of laughin' can only mean they're up to no good."

"Oh, I'm sure of it," Vivianna sighed.

It was true. If Nate and Willy were laughing so freely, it was certain that mischief was at the heart of their merriment. Nate and Willy were always up to no good, it seemed. Especially of late—especially since their summer days were now spent hunting for any kind of dead animal that might provide a bone or two for their growing bone collection. If Vivianna had learned one thing during her stay with Savannah and the young Turner boys, it was that laughter and other sounds of amusement more often than not meant naughtiness. Thus, she knew she and Justin best look in on Nate and Willy, whether or not it was still early morning.

Justin looked to her, his eyes bright with mirth. "Well, we certainly can't let that go without lookin' into . . . now can we?"

Vivianna shook her head, disappointed that their walk had been interrupted. Still, she knew it would be unwise not to see what was so thoroughly amusing to the young boys. A quick vision of weeks ago, of a pigeon dousing Johnny Tabor with his droppings, traveled through her mind, and she giggled. Perhaps it was nothing so naughty causing the boys to laugh after all. Perhaps it was simply something as silly as the antics of another mean-spirited pigeon.

"They're over there . . . near the puddle where they keep their frogs," Justin said.

Still holding Vivianna's hand, he led her through the flowering vines and bushes east of the house and toward the large puddle where Nate and Willy had been delighted to find a load of pollywogs and several new clutches of frog eggs weeks before. Many of the pollywogs had begun to transform to frogs, and the boys delighted in watching them play in the puddle each morning and evening. Vivianna enjoyed the pollywogs as well. It was often she had accompanied the boys to their pollywog hole over the past few weeks to watch Mother Nature work her wonder. Soon the tiny pollywogs would lose their tails, develop stronger legs, and leave Nate and Willy's beloved puddle. But for now, the quick-swimming pollywogs provided hours and hours of amusement for the young Turner boys.

"What's goin' on here?" Justin asked as they approached the pollywog hole to find Nate and Willy were indeed lingering beside it.

Johnny Tabor was with them. He looked up and offered a friendly smile to Vivianna. She smiled and nodded to him in return. As always, she was unsettled by the strange nervousness that rose within her whenever she was near to him.

"We're racin' pollywogs!" Willy exclaimed. "Johnny showed us how. Mine won last time!" Willy jumped up and ran to Vivianna, his hands cupped and holding a slippery pollywog and a minimal amount of water that immediately began dripping through his small, muddy fingers. "See, Viv?" he laughed. "This here's Hubert! And he beat Nate's pollywog twice runnin'!"

Vivianna smiled as she looked at the large, squirming pollywog in Willy's hands. "Ooo! He does look fast," she said, tousling his hair. "But ya better get him a drink. Ya wouldn't want him to dry out and lose his place as the winner."

Willy nodded, dashed back to the puddle, and released the pollywog.

Releasing Justin's hand, Vivianna moved closer

to the puddle, leaned down, and peered into the water. Oh, how she delighted in pollywogs! She always had, ever since she'd been a little girl. To look into a puddle and see them wildly swimming about—to feel them tickle her ankles and toes when she took off her shoes and sunk them in the muddy water—it was a true gladness.

"You boys better add a couple of buckets of water from the pond to your puddle today," she said. "It's lookin' a little low."

"That's what Johnny told us," Nate said. "He said he'd help us haul it over from the pond in a while."

Vivianna glanced up to Johnny. She couldn't help but smile as she watched him drop his own pollywog back into the puddle.

"Johnny says when they're done turnin' into frogs, we can really have some fun racin'!" Willy exclaimed. "He says he's got a real special bone he's been savin', and if one of us gets a frog that'll beat his, we can have it for our collection!"

Vivianna giggled. "Ooo! A new bone! Isn't that excitin'?"

"You bet it is, Viv!" Nate said.

"Well, seems to me that Johnny oughta be worryin' a bit less about frogs and a bit more about seein' to fixin' that broken board in the loft of the barn," Justin said.

Vivianna dropped her gaze from Johnny

Tabor—felt her cheeks go red with humiliation. She wasn't quite sure she'd heard Justin correctly. Surely Justin wasn't scolding Johnny for playing with the younger boys. Surely she hadn't just heard him imply that his friend should be working instead of enjoying a moment of carefree delight—not when Justin had yet to lift a hand to help with anything. Still, she reminded herself that Justin had been weak; he had needed time to recover. He'd been unable to help Savannah around the place or Caleb in running things or earning a wage. Yet even this knowledge did not ease the discomfort she felt over Justin's blatant lack of gratitude.

"I'll get to the loft when I'm ready, Justin," Johnny nearly growled. "That broken board will still be there come a week or two . . . but pollywogs aren't so lingerin'. Ya gotta enjoy 'em while ya can."

"Pollywogs are for children, Johnny," Justin said. "Men got responsibilities."

Vivianna watched as Johnny stood. His dark eyes were narrowed as he glared at Justin. He was much taller than Justin, his shoulders much broader. Furthermore, he was much, much stronger. This was all too apparent. Johnny had removed his shirt—no doubt to keep from soiling it while playing in the puddle with the boys and the pollywogs—revealing a strong torso built of hard work. His chest, arms, shoulders, and stomach boasted chiseled muscles the like Vivianna had never seen before. She worried that if Justin provoked Johnny Tabor much further—well, then, Justin's recovery might be set back some.

"Don't you be tellin' Johnny what to do, Justin!" Nate growled. "He's done more around here and more for Mama than you've done in your life!"

"Now, Nate," Johnny began, tousling the boy's hair, "that ain't true. And you know it ain't. Justin's right. I gotta earn my keep."

"Justin don't earn his keep," Willy mumbled.

"Willy!" Vivianna scolded in a whisper.

"No . . . no, he's right," Justin said. "I'm sorry, Johnny. I . . . I don't know what come over me."

Vivianna looked to Johnny. It was obvious he was furious. Yet he merely nodded in acceptance of Justin's apology.

"I guess I best get washed up and back to work," Johnny said.

"Oh no, Johnny! Not yet! I wanted one more race," Nate whined.

"Maybe this evenin'," Johnny said. "I'll haul that water from the pond for you boys first though." He forced a smile and tousled Nate's hair. "We wouldn't want your pollywog hole to dry up before we have our chance to beat Willy, now do we?"

Nate shook his head and smiled. Willy, however, did not.

Glaring at Justin, Willy said, "You've changed, Justin. Caleb didn't change as much as you have." Willy took hold of Nate's arm and, still glaring at Justin, said, "Come on, Nate. Let's go boil the skin off that possum head Johnny found for us."

"I guess I'll be about my business too," Johnny said. His gaze lingered on Vivianna as he nodded to her—causing a strange, fearful trembling to rise in her. "You have a nice mornin', Miss Vivianna."

"Thank you," Vivianna said.

"You too, Justin," Johnny grumbled—though his eyebrows puckered in a slight frown as he looked to his friend.

"I'm sorry, Johnny," Justin said. "I don't know what came over me."

Again Johnny's unsettling gaze lingered on Vivianna a moment. "I do," he mumbled as he strode away.

"I'm sure you plum vexed him, Justin," Vivianna said as Justin took her hand and started toward the arbor once more.

Justin shook his head. "I'm sure I did," Justin admitted. "And I don't know what I was thinkin'. If there's one thing I know . . . it's nobody oughta be ignorant enough to tangle with Johnny Tabor. Not if ya want to keep your head hooked onto your shoulders."

Vivianna frowned. "Why is he still here

anyway?" Vivianna asked. "He unsettles me so. It seems he's well enough to move on to Texas. He has family there. Why is he lingerin' here with us?"

"You and Mama nursed him back to a man," Justin said. "I suspect he knows he wouldn't have lived another day if Mama hadn't taken him in. If I know Johnny—and I do—he'll stay until he feels he's repaid Mama a debt." Justin shrugged and added, "I think he still feels beholden to me too . . . for savin' him that time I did."

Vivianna frowned as they walked into the arbor. "How did ya save him, Justin?" she asked. "Ya still haven't told me."

Justin sighed, smiled, and took Vivianna into his arms. "Oh, I don't want to talk about all that, pretty Viv," he said, smiling at her. "Not when you're standin' here with me. I'd much rather steal a kiss or two from you than talk about the war or ol' Johnny Tabor."

Vivianna smiled. "I've been waitin' a long time to give my kisses to you, Justin Turner. You don't have to steal them from me," she whispered.

Justin chuckled. "But ain't it a lot more fun that way?"

Vivianna bit her lip—shyly glanced away a moment. Still, as Justin took her chin in hand and turned her face toward his, as his lips pressed hers softly, Vivianna was astonished when the visions in her mind were not those of Justin's kiss—of his handsome face and her love for him. Rather, she frowned as she thought of Justin's haughty remarks to his friend. He'd been unkind to Johnny—to the man who had seen him safely all the way home.

Yet she buried the thoughts. Justin was still healing, and war left scars on a man—scars that the eye could not see. Justin was home, and that was what mattered.

He kissed her softly, tenderly caressing her cheek with the back of his hand as he did so. Vivianna tried to ignore the sense of dissatisfaction that began to rise in her each time Justin kissed her. She worried it was because, like the younger Turner boys, she'd once seen Benjamin Sidney kissing Tilly Winder behind the old Libby place. She worried that Justin would never take her breath away—never lead her down a path of passion the like she'd witnessed Tilly Winder wandering. Oh, certainly Tilly and Benjamin were scandalous in their behavior. Still, Vivianna often mused that Justin's letters still caused more emotion and delight to rise in her than his actual presence did.

No! Justin was wonderful! He was only being careful of her, not wanting to show her any disrespect or lead her astray in any way. His kisses would increase in passion; she was sure they would! One day he would thrill her the way his letters had—the way he'd promised to! One day he would be wholly healed, and then all her doubts would vanish.

Her mind wandered to Johnny Tabor. Somehow she could not force the vision of his hurt expression from her mind. Oh, certainly he'd been angry—even furious at Justin's condescending manner. Yet it was the expression of betrayal in his dark, smoldering eyes—of hurt at the hand of a friend—that rather haunted her.

Pressing her hands to Justin's chest, she sighed when their lips parted at her prodding.

Justin's brow slightly puckered with a puzzled frown. "What's the matter?" he asked.

Vivianna smiled at him. "Oh, nothin'," she said. "I was just wonderin' when the last time was you enjoyed a bit of honeysuckle nectar."

Justin smiled and brushed a strand of stray hair from her cheek. "Not since the summer before me and Caleb left," he answered. "Not in three long years."

Vivianna smiled, took his hand, and led him to sit in the swing. "Then I think you better be about it, Justin Turner," she said. "My mama always told me that honeysuckle nectar was somethin' to be enjoyed with each breath of summer." She reached up and plucked two large honeysuckle blossoms. Handing one to Justin, she smiled as she gently tugged at the blossom, tightly holding the small green bulb at the end. Slowly she pulled the flower until the long white style revealed a drop of sweet nectar. Carefully, she placed the drop of nectar to the tip of her tongue. "Mmm!" she sighed. "You've forgotten the simple pleasures of life, Justin. One tiny drop of honeysuckle sugar should help you to remember."

Justin chuckled and carefully revealed the droplet of honeysuckle nectar from his own flower. He smiled as the sweet nectar of the honeysuckle touched his tongue.

"It reminds me of when I was Nate and Willy's age," he admitted.

"When life was fun . . . and pollywogs were the most important thing in the world," Vivianna added.

Justin nodded. He reached up and plucked another blossom from the vine.

"We used to do this for hours . . . remember?" he asked.

"I do," she said.

Vivianna chose a large pink blossom and gently pulled it from the vine. As she watched Justin struggling to discover the nectar in his blossom, she paused—wondered if Johnny Tabor had forgotten the simple pleasures of life— wondered if he'd ever lingered in the shade of a honeysuckle vine sipping nectar.

CHAPTER EIGHT

Florence, Alabama, had been damaged by the war. Its people had been damaged. Its buildings, bridges, railroad—it seemed everything needed repair. Vivianna could see the good in this—in folks looking to the future, in seeing Florence renewed. She mused that as people watched the buildings, bridges, and streets being mended, it might well help in mending the damaged souls of those who had lived through the battle and lost so much.

Furthermore, Vivianna knew it was good for Justin to be working with Caleb in town. Over the past two weeks, she'd begun to wonder if Justin's need for a long recovery had more to do with his mind struggling to leave the war behind than his body needing to mend itself. Johnny Tabor had been looking for tasks that might afford him a wage as well, but he was not a local boy and was therefore viewed harshly for having fought for the Union, even more than Caleb and Justin were. At least folks seemed to tolerate Caleb and Justin. Oh, there was animosity enough— threats enough—but many in Florence had been in support of the Union. Perhaps many had not fought for it, but in their thinking they had known it was right. Therefore, Caleb and Justin found wages, whereas Johnny Tabor was not so easily forgiven for his part in the war. Still, the railroad was expanding, and the word was men would be hired on to help build it. Thus, Johnny lingered in fixing things at the Turner place that needed fixing, hauling water that needed hauling, splitting wood, repairing the barn, and maintaining the garden.

At first, Vivianna was somewhat unsettled that Johnny should be the only man near to Savannah, Nate, Willy, and herself during the day. He so thoroughly rattled her, and she could not quite tell herself why. She wondered if it were merely his often brooding demeanor or perhaps the fact that her thoughts still traveled to the missing body of the Andersonville guard and the conversation she'd overheard between him and Justin. There seemed so much mystery about him, as if a sort of imperceptible mist surrounded him, whispering to her that there was more to Johnny Tabor than any of them knew—even Justin. Still, the most frightening thoughts she experienced in regard to Johnny came upon her unexpectedly— on increasingly more frequent occasions when she would become conscious of an odd excitement rising in her whenever he was near. This frightened her not only because she had never experienced such sensations but also because she had begun to realize these sensations were not new to her where Johnny was concerned.

Vivianna was slowly realizing that Johnny Tabor frightened her for the mere fact that he was dangerous to her peace of mind, to her plans to find comfortable contentment in the life she'd come to know—in her life with Justin. She found she was more often than not quite distracted in Justin's presence—that her mind wandered to thoughts of Johnny, of wondering why he was so brooding, of what could be done to make him less so.

The anxious thoughts of Johnny heaped on Vivianna only grew whenever Savannah would speak to her of Justin—of her delight in one day being able to truly have Vivianna as her own daughter. Justin had not proposed marriage to Vivianna. In fact, Vivianna had begun to wonder if he ever would, for even though he doted on her as much as Justin Turner could dote on anyone, she feared he felt no passion for her— no great love the like of which he'd written of before Andersonville. She feared the horrors of war and Andersonville had broken his heart, that it would not mend, even for the sake of her love.

Each night, Vivianna would read Justin's letters. Each night, she would see his words and know that he'd written them, that once he had loved her as desperately as any man ever loved a woman. Yet where was the passion of his words now? Worse—where was Vivianna's passion?

It seemed everyone somehow fell into an uncomplicated routine. Each morning, Nate and Willy would rise and dash out to adventure, Caleb and Justin would rise and leave for town, Johnny Tabor would rise and plunge into hard labor, and Vivianna would rise and assist Savannah with the responsibilities of running the house. Yet it seemed there was nothing else—no excitement, no passion. How could they have all so quickly gone from the misery of war to such seeming utter complacency?

The wondering taxed Vivianna's mind. She was confused as to why. When she herself had been so emotional, so passionate before and during the war, why was she not more distraught over her disappointment in what was (or was not) between her and Justin? Had her heart simply been used up, emptied by longing and the nightmares of war? Or was there something else—something her mind was not allowing her to see? These thoughts weighed heavy on Vivianna—so heavy that she often chose not to think of them at all. It seemed much easier to settle into the complacency that seemed to make everyone else happy.

Even her walks to the small cemetery offered little or no emotional sensitivity. She went more out of habit and a remembered sense of duty than for any other reason. Still, she went; every few days she went—wandered to the cemetery where she would place violets on the grave of Mrs. Turner's lost baby girl, where she would not sit near her parents' graves or think too long on those of the Maggee boys.

∽

It was late afternoon. Caleb and Justin would be returning from town in an hour or two. Savannah would be asking Vivianna to help her start their evening meal soon. Yet Vivianna felt unsettled, as if the day were yet wanting, even for all she had worked over.

Slowly she ambled along the path leading to the meadow. The gardenia bushes were blooming, and the scent washed over her like an enchanting ambrosia. She could hear the bees in the apple trees—feel moisture in the air.

Vivianna paused as she stepped out of the bushes and undergrowth and into the meadow. There, near the tombstone of Mr. Turner's mother, sat Willy and Nate. Johnny Tabor was with them, lounging on his side in the grass. As usual, he wore only his trousers and boots, having explained to Savannah weeks before that the heavy, moist air of Alabama caused him too much discomfort to always wear a shirt while he was working.

"And what's them scars from?" Willy asked. Vivianna watched as Willy pointed to an area on Johnny's arm just below his shoulder. Her curiosity was piqued, and she walked to where Johnny and the boys lingered in the grass.

"Hey there, Viv!" Nate greeted. "Johnny's tellin' us about his scars! He sure does have a mess of 'em! Wanna see?"

Vivianna shrugged. "I suppose so," she replied.

"Look here, Viv," Willy said, pointing to the scars on Johnny's arm.

Vivianna almost smiled, for it was obvious Johnny Tabor was not as comfortable as he had been a moment before. She figured that telling two little boys stories of how scars came to be was a heap more impressive than telling a woman.

"See them? He ain't told us about these yet," Willy explained.

Vivianna knelt in the grass next to Johnny, studying the place on his arm where Willy was indicating. A cluster of small marks—perhaps fifty or more—formed a band of scars traveling from just below the back of his shoulder, forward over his arm, and around to the underneath of it.

"Well," Johnny rather grumbled, "these are from the lice."

"Lice?" Vivianna exclaimed, horrified. The hairs of her head stood on end as a sickening sense of being eaten by vermin filled her mind.

"What kind of lice leave scars?" Nate asked, wrinkling his nose.

Vivianna watched as Willy unconsciously

scratched his head. The thought had made her skin crawl as well.

"Lice?" she whispered again. Without thinking, she reached out, running her fingers over the cluster of small scars.

"Well . . . to be honest . . . I ain't sure whether it was the lice or the fire that left 'em," Johnny explained. He smiled, chuckled, and shook his head. "I guess in the end . . . neither one caused 'em. It was me."

"You?" Nate asked. He frowned with frustration. "Who scarred your arm up, Johnny? The lice or somethin' else?"

"We called 'em graybacks at the prison camp," Johnny said, running his own hand over the small scars. "The lice at Andersonville, they'd get near as big and as plump as a wheat kernel . . . and they were miserable. One day, I was sittin' there pickin' 'em off me. We all did it; there wasn't nothin' else to do. And they were miserable. So we figured . . . why not pick at 'em?"

Nate and Willy both nodded, as if Johnny's reasoning were as sound as the earth. Vivianna, however, frowned. She wasn't at all certain she wanted to hear stories about lice big enough to leave scars when they bit. Images of soldiers living in filth—tortured by vermin, the elements, and their captors—began to creep into her thoughts. Yet she fought the images, pushed the true horror of it all to the back of her mind.

She would not think too deeply on it; she could not.

"Well, me and this other feller," Johnny continued, "one day we just plum got irritated with the graybacks, angry about 'em gnawing on us all the time. I thought I couldn't endure another day of them eatin' me, so I got myself up and went over to the fire near where the guards were standin'. I asked for a piece of wood . . . a stick they'd had layin' in the fire. They asked me why I wanted it. I told 'em I was sick of the lice and meant to burn 'em off me. They thought I'd gone mad, of course, but gave me the smolderin' stick anyway. It was glowin' hot on the fire end—red and orange—and I couldn't wait to give it a try. I'd seen another feller burnin' off lice once. But he died pretty quick after doin' it, so I hadn't really thought of tryin' it myself . . . until that day. So I stripped off my clothes then and there and started burnin' those little sons of . . . started burnin' those graybacks off. I guess I fussed 'em up a bit 'cause the ones I burned bit me so hard that I still ain't sure if it was the bites that scarred me or the hot stick." Again he ran his hand over the scars. "Most others I picked off never scarred like this . . . so I'm guessin' it was the fire stick."

"Maybe it was both . . . the bitin' and the fire," Nate suggested.

Johnny shrugged. "Maybe. But that's why me

and Justin shaved our heads and everything else before we came home. We didn't want to bring the graybacks here to chew on all of you."

"What do ya mean by sayin' ya shaved everything else, Johnny?" Willy asked. "What could a body shave besides his head?"

Johnny glanced to Vivianna. She felt an amused smile spread across her face when she realized Johnny Tabor was blushing—truly blushing! His cheeks were near as rosy as a radish! Oh, it was a gruesome story—a horrible realization that lice could so infest a person as to offer shaving every hair as the only chance to rid a body of the bugs and their nits. Still, she could sense Johnny was entirely embarrassed—embarrassed at having mentioned something so deeply personal in front of a lady. She liked him for it—liked him more than she had even a moment before.

Nate shook his head and whined, "Willy Turner! Sometimes you're just plum ignorant. You got hair on your arms and legs, don't ya?" Nate shook his head again. "Boy, sometimes I don't think ya have a brain in your head."

"Well, I ain't as ignorant as ya think, Nate!" Willy argued. "I ain't blind neither! Justin's chest is all hairy like Caleb's now, but when he come home, it was all smooth and shiny like a little baby's bottom . . . just like your chest is now, Nate!"

"You hush, Willy Turner!" Nate growled. "I'll

sprout me some hair on my chest long before you . . . so hush!"

"Well, I don't want no hair on my chest," Willy began, "leastwise not so much like Caleb and Justin." Willy nodded toward Johnny. "I just want me enough to look manly . . . like Johnny here."

Vivianna again glanced to Johnny and giggled when she saw the lingering red on his cheeks. He was completely humiliated—so red with blushing, so uncomfortable with the course of the conversation (being that a lady was present) that she indeed wondered if he could endure it. It was delightful—his blushing, his sudden awareness that he wore no shirt.

"Besides," Willy added, "if I ever get lice . . . then if my chest ain't as hairy, I won't have to worry as much . . . right, Johnny?"

"Oh, they gnaw on ya whether or not ya've got hair on your chest, Willy," Johnny said. He wouldn't look at Vivianna, and she could tell he was still bashful. This continued to thoroughly intrigue her. Suddenly, big, mean Johnny Tabor didn't seem quite so intimidating.

He smiled at Willy then and said, "They're vermin, that's for certain. Still, they're fun to race . . . if ya ain't got anythin' else to entertain ya."

"Race?" Nate exclaimed.

"Yep," Johnny chuckled. "We'd just get us a

mess plate, line two or three graybacks up on it, and let 'em go. I found a pretty quick ol' lice bug in my belly button once, and he was fast! I won a peach and a piece of soap with him."

"How fast, Johnny?" Willy asked.

"Fast enough to win me a peach and a piece of soap," Johnny chuckled. He sighed. "But then . . . then he lost, and I had to eat him."

"Eat him?" Nate, Willy, and Vivianna asked in unison.

"Yep," Johnny said. "That was the rule. If you lost a race . . . ya had to eat the little feller ya were racin' with."

All at once, the pure horror of what Johnny was saying overwhelmed Vivianna's mind. Like a sudden illness, it wove through her body—constricted her stomach. She held her breath—tried to remain calm as she looked at the scars on Johnny's arm—scars caused from burning off body lice the size of wheat kernels. There should be no amusement in thinking of men enduring such torture. And what good could come from telling the young Turner boys about it? Suddenly, Johnny's blushing of a minute before did nothing to keep the horrid thoughts of war, prison, and misery from Vivianna's consciousness.

"That's terrible!" she exclaimed. Shaking her head in an abrupt emotional altering, she scolded, "Johnny! Racing lice? They were near eatin' ya alive!"

Johnny's smile faded. "Well, there wasn't really a whole lot else to do, Miss Vivianna."

"Oh, he's just teasin' us, Viv," Willy said. "Don't worry. I'm sure it ain't true." The boy reached out and squeezed Vivianna's arm with loving reassurance.

"It is true," Nate said. "I heard Justin tellin' Caleb about it not a week ago. He said the lice were always swarmin', everywhere . . . all over the camp, in soldier's clothes . . . on their bodies . . ."

Vivianna felt tears brimming in her eyes. It was awful! So horrible! How could Johnny sit and tell Nate and Willy such horrid things? How could she have listened so long without feeling the depth of their misery?

"Nate! Viv's gonna get upset. I was just tryin' to soothe her a bit," Willy whispered loudly.

Vivianna reached out, running her hand over the cluster of scars on Johnny's arm. She shook her head as the tears escaped her eyes, rolling down her cheeks.

"Now ya done it, Johnny!" Willy scolded, shaking his head with disgust. "Ya went and got Viv all to bawlin'. I can't stand to see Viv cry. I can't stand it."

"I'm sorry, Vivianna," Johnny said. "I'm . . . I shouldn't have told such things in front of a lady and . . ."

But Vivianna was already too overcome with

sympathetic pain to stop her tears now. She thought it odd in that moment—odd that she'd spent so many days worrying over why her emotions seemed numb. Yet here they were, violent in their rapid sympathy.

"It's not your fault, Johnny," she told him. "I just . . . I just can't think on it. I can't think on you and Justin . . . I can't think on anybody bein' so miserable."

"But he's fine now, Viv," Nate soothed. "Look . . . look at the muscles he's sproutin' lately."

"Vivianna," Johnny began. He leaned forward, placing a hand on her knee, with such an expression of guilt on his handsome face it made her feel all the worse. She'd added to his discomfort by scolding him for sharing the stories of the hell in Andersonville—stories that she well knew should be told. She'd heaped even more pain on him.

"I mean, look at these arms, Viv!" Nate said, reaching up and squeezing Johnny's muscular arm. "Like tree trunks! He's fine now. Don't go gettin' all upset like ya do. You know Willy and me can't stand to see ya upset."

"I'm fine," Vivianna said, brushing tears from her cheeks. "I-I just need some fresh air." Standing, she fled, visions of lice the size of plump wheat kernels gnawing at her mind.

"Fresh air?" she heard Willy ask. "We're outside, ain't we? I swear . . . women!"

"Vivianna!" she heard Johnny call after her. "Vivianna! Wait!"

But she wouldn't wait. The tears were streaming over her cheeks now, and she was humiliated—humiliated at having burst into tears in front of a man, a man who had endured so much and probably never shed a single tear for himself.

"Oh, come on now, Vivianna," Johnny rather growled at her heels. "I'm sorry."

Still, she couldn't let him see her weakness. Justin, Caleb, and Johnny were soldiers—soldiers returned weathered and worn. They needed strength in women, not weakness.

She was nearly back to the house—just near the arbor. Quickly, she slipped beneath the honeysuckle vine. Perhaps Johnny was far enough behind her not to see exactly which path she'd taken.

"Vivi," he said, entering a moment later, however. "I'm . . . I'm sorry. I didn't realize it would upset ya so to hear—"

"To hear how tortured y'all were, Johnny?" she asked, spinning around to face him. "Of course it upsets me! How wouldn't it? What kind of woman would I be if I enjoyed tales of torture and death?" She grimaced. "Lice races, Johnny? Lice races?"

"Louse races . . . would be the correct way of sayin' it . . . I suppose." He smiled at her, an attempt to lighten her heart. But Vivianna wasn't ready to smile. She still had imaginary lice chewing at her own flesh.

"It's not funny, Johnny," she said, angrily brushing the tears from her cheeks.

"I know. I'm sorry," he said.

Vivianna reached out, running her hand over the scars along Johnny's arm—marked in one way or the other by Andersonville's graybacks. "It's a terrible story," she whispered.

"I know it," he said. "But would ya rather the folks to come after us forget what this country endured for freedom? If we don't tell the stories, Vivianna . . . people will forget. Maybe not us . . . maybe not those of us who lived it. But those to come will. Don't you see that?"

Vivianna nodded and caressed his scarred arm again. "Yes," she whispered. "They'll forget. How will they even own somethin' to forget . . . if you don't tell them?"

"And anyway, I'm fine now." Johnny looked at the scars on his arm—fisted his hand, causing the muscles in his upper arm to harden. "I don't know if I'd say it's a tree trunk," he chuckled, "but it's a start."

Vivianna felt his muscle tense under her hand—noted that his arms were indeed profoundly muscular. In fact, she unconsciously let her hand travel up over his shoulder—down over his chest. Yes, his body was healthier—larger—indeed very muscular. It was a world of difference from what it had been when he and Justin had first arrived home.

How could she remain angry with him, after all he'd been through? Furthermore, he was right. The war could not be forgotten; it should not be. Certainly it could not be lingered upon, but history most assuredly needed to be remembered, even if it were only by way of a soldier telling stories to young boys.

"It is important. You're right. They're young, and they well might forget . . . if they're not told. Thank ya for tellin' your stories to Nate and Willy," Vivianna said, still caressing the breadth of his chest with one hand. She gazed up into the dark brown of his eyes. "And thank you for everything else, Johnny . . . for stayin' on to help us . . . for bringin' Justin home to us."

Something very deep, very strong, inside Vivianna was stirring. Not simply stirring—roaring! This man had done so much to preserve her hope of happiness, whether or not he owned a full understanding of it. How could she ever repay him? There was nothing she could offer a battered soldier—a strong, capable man.

She remembered then the first day Johnny and Justin had returned—remembered putting Johnny to bed, thinking he might never wake up again. She'd kissed him that day—kissed him in wanting to offer her thanks—in wanting to make certain the man who had saved her lover did not die without having felt one last act of tenderness.

Her attention was drawn to Johnny's lips. She wondered how long it had been since he'd felt the soft press of a kiss to them—a real kiss, not the kind she'd given him when she feared he would pass away during the night but a kiss meant to bring him pleasure. There could be no harm in offering him her thanks once more—no harm in kissing him so very lightly in showing her gratitude. Could there?

Vivianna pressed her palms to the firm warmth of his broad chest. Raising herself on the tips of her toes, she gently pressed her lips to Johnny Tabor's. Instantly, the sense of the soft, intimate touch ignited an unfamiliar and blissful delight in her. For a moment, as her lips lingered in pressing his—as she sensed his pressing hers in return—Vivianna was breathless! Such a wave of goose pimples broke over her arms and legs that she quivered with unexpected pleasure.

Thoroughly unsettled by the unfamiliar and intense sensations threatening to overwhelm her, Vivianna ended the affectionate exchange she'd instigated. She drew away from Johnny, feeling shy and knowing it was her cheeks that were now rosy with blushing. Tentatively she looked up—gazed into the smoldering depths of his dark eyes. He was so handsome, this soldier boy from Texas, and she could not help but smile at him. His hair was rather tousled, his nose quite perfectly sculpted. His jaw and chin were squared, and his lips—his perfect lips—held her attention, caused moisture to flood her mouth for the want of kissing him again!

Though she knew she should turn, that she should leave him and seek out some task to distract her from thinking on his handsome countenance, Vivianna did not move. Rather she stood quite still before him. Even when his strong hands reached out to cradle her face, she did not move.

It was then that Johnny Tabor kissed Vivianna. It was then that Vivianna allowed him to kiss her—even returned his tender, careful kiss. After all, didn't the man who saved Justin's life—the man who brought Justin home even for his own ill health and misery—didn't such a man deserve at least this small allowance, one kiss from a grateful young woman?

Johnny's hands were strong, rough, and callused from hard labor yet careful and protective all the same. The feel of them against her face heated her flesh and caused a sense of safety to rush through her—a sense she had not felt since long before the war. His kiss was careful too—overwhelming to Vivianna's mind and body, it was true—but careful. He pressed their kiss, blending the light moisture of their lips. Vivianna could scarcely remain standing. She felt weak, as if she burned, as if her entire body were aflame! Wild, unfamiliar, yet magnificent thoughts bounded through her mind—thoughts of what rapture she would know bound in Johnny Tabor's arms, of how wonderful the touch of his smooth skin felt beneath her palms. She wanted more; she wanted to kiss him more thoroughly somehow! In the next moment, as if he'd heard her thoughts, Vivianna sighed as Johnny's hands found her shoulders—slowly slid down her arms, caressing them—coming to rest at her waist. She felt his powerful hands tighten at her middle— trembled as his mouth began to coax her lips to parting.

The fragrant scent of the honeysuckle vine sweetened the breeze suddenly, and Vivianna gasped. Stepping back from Johnny, she slipped her hand into the pocket of her skirt and let her fingers caress the pages of Justin's letter for a moment.

"I'm sorry, Vivi," Johnny apologized at once. "Forgive me."

Vivianna saw the sudden frustration and self-loathing in his eyes, and she did not wish for him to worry—not over such a lovely thing as having kissed her. As she looked at him, she found her breath was still not drawn easily and that her heart was racing at an untamed pace.

She would not cause him guilt, no matter her discomfort or delight. Thus, she smiled at him and said, "I kissed you first . . . remember?"

He seemed little soothed, still frowning yet forcing a halfhearted grin.

Vivianna placed a soft palm to his cheek and added, "It was all I could think of to offer you as my thanks . . . for bringin' Justin home . . . for everything you do for us. Furthermore, don't you dare to imagine that I would ever regret that you accepted my thanks." She smiled at him, though the emotions his kiss had evoked within her frightened her to near terror. She could not let him know of the excitement he'd unleashed in her. She would only endeavor to soothe things between them.

"Now wrap me in those tree trunks of yours, Johnny Tabor," she teased, smiling at him, "so I know you've forgiven me for scoldin' you in front of Nate and Willy."

Johnny chuckled. "I imagine any man could forgive you anything, Vivianna Bartholomew."

He did embrace her then, and Vivianna melted against the warmth of his strong body—allowed her hands to slip under his arms and travel up over his back until they came to rest at his shoulders. The feel of his skin against her cheek as she laid her head against his chest was warm and wonderful—somehow intoxicating.

Such a feeling of security, of unfamiliar safety, washed over her then that she could not help but linger in his arms. Yet as her heart quickened its already mad beating pace, she drew away from him. She fancied he released her somewhat reluctantly and wondered if she'd been wise to offer affection to a man who had been so long without it. Certainly, she'd never shared such an affectionate exchange before—not even with Justin. Justin had never kissed her with such desire, in such an affecting manner. This realization disturbed her, but she would not think on it now.

"Now . . . now you run on and tell your terrible tales to the boys," she stammered, smiling at him. "But if they can't sleep tonight for fear of lice crawlin' all over them in bed . . . you'll be the one to settle them down. You hear me?"

Johnny smiled and chuckled, and the sight and sound caused Vivianna's heart to leap.

"Yes, ma'am," he said. He nodded to her, winked, and walked away.

Vivianna fairly collapsed onto the old swing, overcome by the fragrance of the honeysuckle— or perhaps the lingering bliss Johnny Tabor's kiss had drizzled over her.

Desperately she drew Justin's letter from her skirt pocket. Justin's letter would settle her whirling emotions. Yet as she read, her mouth somehow continued to water for want of Johnny to kiss her again—the flesh of her arms, neck, and face still tingling with the lingering warmth of his skin.

Still, as she read the words she so dearly cherished, she was soothed. Justin was healing just as Johnny had—just as Caleb had. Soon he would find his way back to being the man she loved. Soon he would fulfill his promise to kiss her beneath the honeysuckle vine as she'd never been kissed before. This thought caused Vivianna to gasp—to close her eyes and try to ignore the residual sensations of delight Johnny Tabor's kiss had caused her to experience. Johnny Tabor had kissed her as she'd never been kissed before. He had! Though she fought to allow her mind and body to admit it, it was true.

"Oh, Justin!" she cried in a whisper. "Don't let our letters and promises to one another die. Through all we've endured . . . don't let it all disappear! Please!"

Yet even as she read Justin's cherished letter, even as she attempted to force her thoughts to him, she could only think of Johnny Tabor— of his handsome face, his strong body, and his wonderful, wonderful kiss!

Johnny Tabor angrily wiped the perspiration from his forehead. He hated Alabama! He hated feeling as if he were never completely dry. He hated the war, hated Andersonville. In that moment, he hated Justin Turner! Still, for all his hatred, the bulk of it—the greatest seething part of it—was heaped only on himself.

What had he been thinking? He knew Vivianna loved Justin. He'd brought Justin home to her, for pity's sake! The only reason he was lingering in this God-forsaken place was to make certain Justin was well enough to follow through with all the promises he'd made to the woman he loved. But Justin had changed. Johnny knew he'd changed; hadn't he been with him when he had? Still, he'd hoped Justin would change again when he returned home—when he saw Vivianna and all she would offer him. But he hadn't, and Johnny's patience was wearing.

He stopped for a moment and leaned against a tree in an effort to calm himself. The kiss she'd given him—her kiss of thanks—nothing had ever affected him so! Neither the first time she'd kissed him nor this! He'd nearly told her the truth—nearly dropped to his knees and confessed all his evil deeds. For a moment, he'd considered telling her who he really was, what horrible things he'd done. For just a moment, he'd considered that perhaps she would look past the devil he was, forgive him his sins, and transfer the boundless love she offered from Justin's possession to his. Fortunately, the weak moment had passed. It passed the moment she pulled away from him rather than allowing him to deepen their kiss.

He growled and moved on. Justin! Justin could never kiss Vivianna the way Johnny could! Justin didn't have the passion in him. Justin owned a passion for nothing—even, Johnny feared, Vivianna. The girl deserved to be loved passionately, to be ravished with heated, demanding kisses.

Johnny feared Justin was too tainted by the war, his soul too damaged by enduring misery, to allow his heart to be free. Maybe he should never have brought Justin home. Then Vivianna would've married Caleb. At least with Caleb, she would be respected. It was certain with Caleb she would never have known passion, but with Caleb she would have known respect and comfort. Still, the thought of her with Caleb sickened him as much as thoughts of her with Justin did.

He knew he must hope—knew he had to linger. He had to stay on in the wretched humidity until he was certain all was as it should be with Justin and his family. He owed that much to the man who had saved his life.

Furthermore, Johnny owned a sense of responsibility where Nate and Willy were concerned. They had no father to lead them into being good men. Yet even in owning two older brothers, they were neglected where a man's influence and guidance were concerned. In all the time he'd been with the Turners, he'd never once seen Justin take an interest in Nate or Willy. Certainly Caleb attempted to please them with gifts of animal bones and pats on the head. But neither Caleb nor Justin spent much time in council with them—or in play. Their mother cared for them—loved them as deeply as any good mother would—it was obvious. Vivianna loved them too. It was many times, near every day, Johnny would see Vivianna playing at marbles or watching pollywogs with Nate and Willy. She slathered them with reassuring affections—pinching their cheeks, hugging them, and placing tender kisses on their foreheads. Thus, Johnny knew the younger Turner boys were not lacking in female nurturing and attention. Still, boys needed a father, or at least brothers who would teach them, and Johnny felt the burden heavy upon his own shoulders—a profound duty to Nate and Willy. No, he could not leave, not until he knew he'd well repaid his debt to Justin Turner. Not until he knew Vivianna Bartholomew was happy in having her love returned.

Johnny's stomach heaved a moment. It sickened him that Justin should own Vivianna's heart when he did not deserve it. It sickened him that he himself was such a devil, such a liar. Yet repentance through recompense was his only hope—recompense and secrecy. Some secrets must be kept in order to protect those a body loved. Johnny could never reveal to another living soul that he had fallen in love with Vivianna. He would harbor the secret forever—own a broken heart and aching soul for all eternity. Yet he deserved nothing else.

As he stepped into the meadow, he thought that at least he'd known her kiss. At least he would journey through life and then to his grave with the memory of Vivianna's kiss in his heart—that she had kissed him willingly.

"Johnny!" Nate hollered, scattering Johnny's thoughts. "Look here! Look what we found!"

A certain anxiety began to rise in his chest. It seemed any time the young Turner boys found something, it was more often than not a gruesome find. Still, they were boys, and boys were drawn to the gruesome.

"What's that?" he asked as he strode toward them.

"Right here! On Floydie Maggee's tombstone!" Willy exclaimed. "What does it look like to you, Johnny?"

As Johnny neared the boys, his heart began to hammer. Somehow, he feared he knew what the boys had found. Somehow he feared what they stood over Floydie Maggee's tombstone studying was more gruesome than most things they happened upon.

He frowned and looked down at the top and backside of Floydie Maggee's tombstone—at the dark red stain drizzled there.

"Looks like blood to me," Johnny mumbled.

"Blood!" Nate exclaimed, lowering his voice.

"That's what we think too! Don't it look just like dry blood?"

"Where do ya think it came from, Johnny?" Willy asked in a whisper.

Johnny shook his head and said, "I don't know." Still, a vision entered his mind: a vision of Zachary Powell lying cold and dead in the woods just beyond the cemetery, lying cold and dead with the back of his head bashed in.

CHAPTER NINE

Johnny was sullen at supper. Vivianna worried, for it was obvious something was gnawing at his thoughts. She wondered if it were the kiss they'd shared beneath the honeysuckle. Still, it seemed to be a different sort of distraction that held him captive, and it unsettled her.

She was likewise unsettled by her own thoughts. From the moment she and Johnny had parted earlier in the day, Vivianna's mind had been awhirl with confusion, fear, self-loathing—and delight. Her confusion was borne of her desire toward Johnny. How could she be so thoroughly attracted to a man she hardly knew? How could her mind, heart, and body be so disloyal to Justin? Her fear was borne of the strength of her want to be in Johnny's arms—to know his kiss again. Such feelings and desires were dangerous—dangerous to her peace of mind, dangerous to the happiness she'd always planned to know with Justin. It was as if Johnny Tabor had somehow stolen her heart from Justin's clasp, the way Justin had begun to steal it from Caleb's the day they left for the war. Thus, her fear led her to an overwhelming sense of self-loathing. How could she even think on Johnny after all she and Justin had shared, after all the beautiful promises they'd made to one another in their letters? She thought of Tilly Winder—of her fickle nature and easy manner with men. She would not be such a woman, swayed by any man who offered her affection. She knew she was not such a woman as Tilly and never would be.

Vivianna's self-loathing was deep, yet her good sense reminded her that Justin had not proposed to her. Even he had not confessed the true, passionate, everlasting love he'd spoken of in his letters to her. In fact, Vivianna could not convince herself that he yet loved her as he once had. It seemed to her she should feel it more deeply if he did. It seemed to her he would kiss her as Johnny Tabor had kissed her if he still loved her as he once had. She thought Justin's behavior toward her since his return was not so unlike what Caleb's had been the day they left— the day Caleb owned her heart yet did not seem unduly concerned when his brother kissed her. Thus, Vivianna's doubt of Justin's love for her deepened.

Yet it was her delight in thinking of Johnny— of his kiss—that most disturbed her. Throughout the day, Vivianna had consciously admitted to herself, silently accepted, that from the moment Justin and Johnny had arrived, Johnny Tabor had captured her attention. Oh, she'd been overwhelmed with joy—sheer bliss—at seeing Justin, at seeing her lover alive and returned.

Yet even as she'd basked in his presence—her heart soaring with elation and love—even then, Vivianna had been aware of Johnny. It was as if he'd been a spirit presence, lingering at her shoulder or whispering in her ear. She'd thought of the fact she had kissed him that first night as she'd put him to bed—kissed a man she'd never met before—kissed him soundly on the lips. Again, she thought of Tilly Winder. No one in all of Florence would be surprised at knowing Tilly Winder had kissed a strange man. Yet Vivianna Bartholomew? It was not in Vivianna's nature to offer kisses so easily.

In pondering Johnny throughout the day, Vivianna realized she'd been keeping from him—intentionally staying a distance. Previously she'd told herself this was because she did not trust him—that she suspected he knew more about the dead Confederate found in the woods than he was telling. Still, it seemed as if something in Vivianna had begun to thrive in those moments spent with Johnny beneath the honeysuckle—something that had been absent in her for months, perhaps years. The moment Johnny had kissed her, Vivianna had begun to feel her soul being freed, as if it had been trapped within a dark prison cell and Johnny Tabor was twisting the key in the lock keeping it there. Emotions she hadn't known for long, long months began to arise in her. Equally there arose in her a flaming sense of desire—of want the like she had never known before.

Even now as she sat at the table enjoying supper with the Turner family, even in those moments her flesh tingled each time she glanced to Johnny—her mouth warming at the memory of his kiss. All this was strange, confusing, frightening, and delightful to Vivianna. Yet Justin sat next to Johnny, and Caleb next to him. Vivianna glanced to Nate and Willy—to Savannah—and she was reminded of the great debt she owed to their family.

Caleb and Justin had been her friends. She'd played with them as a child, grew up with them, loved both of them. She'd once fancied herself *in* love with Caleb—thought of the letters in the small box in her wardrobe and reminded herself she was yet in love with Justin. She adored Nate and Willy and their mischievous ways—looked on and loved Savannah as any daughter loved a mother. They had become her family, and she could not hurt them. She could not allow herself to emulate the likes of Tilly Winder and give herself so easily to a strange man simply because he'd caused goose pimples to ripple over her body when he'd kissed her. No. She owed a great debt to the entire Turner family—to each and every member of it. And she would not let passionate emotions and thirsting desire allow her to cause them pain. She loved Justin. She did.

Vivianna looked to Justin then. She did love him. She was certain of it. She thought of the letter in her pocket—of all the letters he'd written to her while the war had kept them from one another. He loved her, and he would find himself and love her the way he'd promised. One day he would.

Still, as she glanced to Johnny—saw him sitting so grave in demeanor—her heart fluttered, her mouth watering at the memory of his kiss. She knew she must distract her thoughts from lingering on him. Thus, she looked to Nate and asked, "Did you boys find any good bones today?"

"Not today, I'm afraid, Viv," Nate sighed with great disappointment. "There didn't seem to be even a part of somethin' we coulda boiled up for bones today." He sighed again, and Vivianna smiled.

"We did find somethin' else in the cemetery today though," Willy began. Vivianna frowned when she saw Johnny glare at Willy, however, and heard Willy continue, "But it weren't really nothin' much to tell."

Johnny's gaze met Vivianna's. He shook his head so slightly, she wasn't certain he'd even moved at first. Yet as his eyes lingered on hers, she understood. Johnny didn't want Willy to tell what he'd found in the cemetery. She should've been unsettled—frightened or suspicious—but she wasn't.

"Well, what else did ya do today, darlin'?" Savannah asked Willy.

"Oh, nothin' much, Mama," Willy sighed. "We skipped rocks out at the pond, worked on our fort a bit . . . counted up Johnny's scars." The boy paused and wrinkled his brow pensively. "Mama," he began, "how much hair do ya think I'll have to have on my chest when I'm Caleb and Justin's age?"

Vivianna covered her mouth, barely able to keep the bite of cornbread she'd just taken from spewing out all over her plate. She muffled her giggles, only allowing one small one to escape when she saw Johnny's face reddcn up like a ripe summer cherry.

"Oh, I don't know, darlin'," Savannah answered. "Why?"

Vivianna still smiled, delighted by Savannah's easy manner with her boys. Savannah Turner simply continued to eat her meal, as if Willy's question had been the most natural curiosity in the world.

Willy shrugged. "Well, I'm just hopin' I don't have too much. I want folks to be able to count my scars easy if I'm lucky enough to get a fair amount on me."

Caleb and Justin chuckled. Vivianna still stifled the giggles induced in her bosom by the further reddening of Johnny's handsome face.

"Well, I hope you don't plan on gettin' too

many scars, honey," Savannah said. "It's usually painful . . . anything that happens to a body that leaves a scar."

"Oh, I know, Mama," Willy said. "But a man has to have a few. Ain't that right, Johnny?"

"I suppose," Johnny said, his face as bright as a radish.

"Sure enough," Justin added. "Look at this one here, Willy." Vivianna watched as Justin unbuttoned his shirt and pulled his collar down over his left shoulder. "This one here, it's from the bullet that grazed me in Georgia . . . before me and Johnny was captured."

Nate and Willy both leaned across the table and frowned with intensity as they studied Justin's shoulder.

"That's a nice one," Nate said.

"Well, that's nothin'," Caleb began, lifting his shirt to reveal a large scar running vertically over his stomach. "I got this when I was about your age, Nate. I fell out of the big tree out back and landed on a stump."

"Ooo!" Willy breathed.

"All right, boys," Savannah scolded softly. "We are tryin' to have us a nice supper. I don't care if y'all strip down naked and paint your scars red afterward. But I want to eat my supper with some semblance of propriety. You hear me?"

"Yes, Mama," Nate said.

Vivianna bit her lip to keep from laughing as

Willy mused aloud, "Still, I suppose if I do end up hairy, I could always just shave everythin' the way Justin and Johnny done before they come home." A puzzled frown puckered the young boy's brow. He looked to Johnny inquisitively and asked, "Ya never did tells us what you meant when ya said ya and Justin shaved everythin' before ya come home, Johnny."

Vivianna giggled as Savannah choked on her own cornbread, cleared her throat, and giggled.

"Now, that's enough, Willy," Savannah scolded. "You all just finish up your supper."

Caleb and Justin both chuckled, and Vivianna glanced to Johnny. He rolled his eyes and shook his head—entirely humiliated—but she adored his blushing. Simply adored it!

"Ya gotta be careful what ya say to Nate and Willy, Johnny," Justin said, teasingly nudging his friend with one elbow. "They can take anything and just run all the way to New Orleans with it."

"So I gather," Johnny mumbled.

He was so handsome! There was an attractive brutality about him—a strength in his features that neither Caleb nor Justin owned. Silently, Vivianna scolded herself for thinking such fond thoughts where Johnny was concerned. She loved Justin—Justin and the entire Turner family—and that is where her heart must remain.

"Oh!" Caleb suddenly exclaimed. "I plum forgot, Johnny." Vivianna watched as Caleb

227

leaned forward, reaching into the back pocket of his trousers. "This letter come for you. Mr. Douglas walked it over from the post station today. I'm sorry I forgot to give it to you earlier."

Instantly, Vivianna was disturbed—rather vexed. She recognized the emotions in her as those akin to jealousy. Who had written Johnny Tabor a letter? She instantly thought of the letters she and Justin had exchanged during the war. Did Johnny have a lover? Had he so deliciously kissed her beneath the honeysuckle when a lover waited for him in Texas? Immediately she scolded herself, her self-loathing returning as she thought of her own hypocrisy. After all, she'd kissed Johnny Tabor, hadn't she? And hadn't she kissed him when her own lover was only a short distance away in Florence?

Still, even though she had no right to feel the jealous and worried sensations she was experiencing, Vivianna held her breath as she watched Caleb offer the letter to Johnny— watched Johnny accept it and smile when he read the writing on the envelope.

"It's from Jeannie," he mumbled. He looked to Vivianna and said, "My sister."

Vivianna was angry with herself—angry for breathing a sigh of gladness at knowing it was Johnny's sister who had written, not a lover.

"I wrote my family weeks ago," he began, "tellin' 'em I was well and stayin' on here

228

awhile." He looked at the letter and then to Savannah. "Do ya mind, ma'am?" he asked. "Do ya mind if I excuse myself so that I can—"

"Of course, Johnny!" Savannah assured him. "You go on and read your letter. I'm so glad you're hearin' from your family."

"Thank ya, ma'am," he said, nodding with appreciation.

Vivianna watched as Johnny stood and walked across the room and out through the back door. She blushed when she returned her attention to those at the table, only to find Caleb's gaze intent upon her. He wore a rather knowing expression—a suspicious grin—but Vivianna simply smiled at him.

"Isn't that nice?" she said. "I'm sure he's so happy to hear from his family."

"I'm sure he is," Caleb said.

"Would ya like to go for a little walk later, Viv?" Justin asked then.

Vivianna's heart leapt with an odd sort of trepidation. She wasn't at all sure she wanted to take a walk—not with Justin at least. In that moment, she fully understood how confused she was.

"I swear, Justin," Nate grumbled, "you and your walkin'. I woulda thought that walkin' all the way from Georgia woulda walked ya out."

"Well," Justin began, winking at Vivianna, "this kind of walkin' is a whole lot different, Nate."

229

Vivianna blushed—smiled when Justin winked at her.

"If you say so, Justin," Nate mumbled. "Walkin' is walkin' if ya ask me."

Justin chuckled, and Savannah smiled at Nate's sweet naïveté.

"So we'll walk, Viv?" Justin asked.

"Of course," Vivianna said.

Savannah reached over then—lovingly placed a hand over Vivianna's—and she was reminded of exactly where her loyalties, and her heart, should remain.

∽

Vivianna was distracted. It was obvious to Justin that her thoughts were not on him—at least, not fully.

"You got somethin' weighin' on your mind, Viv?" he asked.

She smiled at him and answered, "I suppose." She sighed. "I suppose we all do . . . don't we?"

"I guess we do," Justin admitted. It was a warm, balmy night. The stars were bright overhead—not one cloud in the sky. He glanced to Vivianna again. "Is it somethin' ya wanna share? Or just nothin' much of anything?"

She shrugged—paused—bit her lip nervously. Finally, she answered, "The letters we wrote to one another while you were gone, Justin . . . do you remember them at all?"

Justin inhaled a calming breath. Those damn letters! He ought to bust into her room and burn the dang things!

"Of course I do, Viv," he told her. "Why?" But he already knew why. The letters—they were how he'd won her heart away from Caleb. The letters were the very reason she'd fallen in love with him. Still, Justin had changed since those letters. Andersonville had done it—Andersonville and the war. He didn't want to talk about those ridiculous letters. He wanted Vivianna to love the man he had become—the man he was now—not the lovesick fool who'd written letters full of promises Justin knew he could never keep.

"Did you mean everything you said to me in your letters?" she asked. "Truly. If your feelin's have changed, Justin . . . if . . . if ya didn't mean the things ya said to me . . ."

Justin turned and took Vivianna's shoulders in his hands. "Viv," he began, "I love you. I do. But I wish you'd quit worryin' over the man I was in them letters . . . and try to see the man I've become. I'm stronger now. I know more what I want. I see what's important and what's not. The war grew me up, Viv. It was a lovesick boy that wrote those letters. Can't ya see that? Can't ya see I'm a man now? And you're a woman . . . and we love each other. It doesn't matter how we come to growin' up and bein' here. All that matters is that here we are . . . together . . . finally together."

Vivianna nodded, yet Justin could see she was lingering in doubt. He knew he was taking too long—that he hadn't proven the depth of his love for her. He swallowed then as guilt traveled through him, for Justin knew. He knew he hadn't proven the depth of his love to Vivianna because, in truth, he wasn't certain how deep it was.

It seemed he'd lived a lifetime since he'd left Alabama—seemed he'd lived a lifetime and suffered the length of two. Andersonville had hardened him; he knew it had. Yet even though Justin felt himself softening—could almost catch hold of the feelings and sensations he'd once enjoyed—he had no idea how long it would take him or if he ever would be the man Vivianna wanted him to be.

He thought of that morning—of Tilly Winder walking past him and Caleb as they worked on the bridge. She's smiled at him—an inviting smile—and he'd been tempted. Oh, Vivianna was beautiful, and she tempted him painfully. Yet Justin knew Vivianna wanted his heart—his full heart. Tilly Winder only wanted him to spark with her a bit, and the thought quite intrigued him. He remembered sparking with Tilly before the war, and it had been far more pleasurable than anything he'd ever experienced to that time. Still, Vivianna was so pretty—so sweet. She'd make him a good wife. He couldn't hope for a better woman to love him—knew how fortunate he was in owning her love. Yet he paused in taking her to him in any serious manner, and he did not know why. At least, he told himself he did not know why.

"You're right, of course," Vivianna said. "But . . . but, Justin . . . I do sense the change in you . . . and I know you're not certain of me."

"Viv, I—" he began to argue.

But Vivianna shook her head and said, "It's all right, Justin. Truly. I-I do understand that you need more time. I-I think I might need a little time too."

Justin frowned. He did not like her easy patience with him—did not like that she seemed calm in her understanding. His eyes narrowed as he thought of what Willy had told him—that Johnny had caused Vivianna to cry earlier in the day, that he'd followed after her when she'd run off, that he'd returned to the cemetery and explained to Nate and Willy that he'd managed to soothe her.

Johnny Tabor was a liar! A liar with more evil secrets cached in his black soul than Justin cared to think on. Surely Vivianna hadn't found something to admire in Johnny. Surely Johnny Tabor hadn't managed to work his beguiling nature over Vivianna Bartholomew. Still, Justin did feel suspicion rising in him. He hid his anger, however—tried to ignore the knowledge that it was Johnny who made him swear to keep the

233

promises he'd made to Vivianna in the letters he'd written to her. Johnny Tabor owned too much old-fashioned chivalry. Why, Justin knew he could be out behind the old Libby place sparking with Tilly Winder that very minute if it weren't for that devil Johnny Tabor and the debt Justin owed him.

Still, he forced his thoughts back to Vivianna. She'd been his friend; his whole life he'd loved her. She was the best of women—a jewel—a treasure. Justin knew he needed to straighten out his mind, put his own soul back on the path it should be on. Yet the war had scarred him—scarred him just as it had Johnny Tabor and Caleb—but scarred his mind instead of his body.

Justin nodded as he gazed into Vivianna's violet eyes. "I think we both need some time, Viv. I think you might be right. We'll be lovers again, Viv . . . just as in our letters. We just need more time than we thought to get past all the ghosts hauntin' us. You lost your family; I lost myself. We both need time to heal . . . to mend ourselves before we can mend our love."

As she thought of Justin—of the letters he'd written that had given her hope and strength during the war and carried her through the loss of her family—her heart ached. Still, an unexpected sense of lightness of soul and mind breathed over her. She understood then—understood that Justin was right. He had been battered by war, and she had been cast into darkness. Until his soul was healed—until hers could find the light—they could not hope to serve each other with perfect love.

Vivianna was surprised at the lack of pain in her heart—at the sense of liberation in her heart. Still, she felt it was merely for the fact she and Justin had come to a meeting of truth and certainty.

"We do," she said.

Justin sighed, a sigh of being relieved of some heaviness. "I do love you, Viv," he told her. "I will have you . . . and you will be my wife. But only after we choose it now . . . not because we dreamed of it in letters of the past."

Vivianna nodded. She was in agreement with him. Yet a certain and frightening doubt was in her mind—a strange sense that all was not as it seemed. Still, she felt lighter of heart—hopeful. All would be well.

She nodded, and he kissed her tenderly on one cheek.

"Do you want to go in?" he asked.

Vivianna shook her head. "No. I'll just meander awhile longer."

"All right," Justin said. He kissed her cheek once more, and Vivianna fancied this kiss was more affecting to her senses than any kiss he'd ever before given her. This kiss spoke of hope—of reward borne of patience.

She watched him stride away. In that moment, Vivianna knew less heartache than she had a moment before—a day before—a month—even a year.

Closing her eyes, she inhaled a deep breath and relished the feel of the heavy, fragrant air as it veiled her. The sweet perfume of gardenia was everywhere. Savannah's gardenias had once been the talk of Florence. Folks often said Savannah Turner had a fairy's touch when it came to growing the tender and rare flowers—and for good reason. It seemed no other body in all of Florence and the surrounding area could nurture gardenias to such brilliance and perfume.

Yet as Vivianna slowly inhaled once more, it was the honeysuckle she sensed—the sweet scent of honeysuckle that breathed its breath into her lungs. Slipping her hand into her skirt pocket, she let her fingers caress the pages of Justin's letter there. She must return it to its envelope—place it in the box with the others. Justin was right. They each must heal, and Vivianna realized that clinging so desperately to the letter would not help either she or Justin to cast away the ghosts haunting them.

Sighing, she wandered to the arbor. It was, after all, her place of retreat—of privacy. Yet she was somewhat disconcerted when she stepped beneath the honeysuckle vine to find Johnny sitting in the arbor swing. Her heart leapt at the sight of him, and she felt her hands begin to tremble.

"Oh!" he said as he looked up and saw her. "I'm sorry, Vivianna. I'll let ya be." He began folding the letter he'd been reading, readying to take his leave.

"Don't be silly, Johnny," she said, however. "I'm in mind to have ya keep me company for a spell."

Taking a seat beside him on the swing, she pressed her toes against the ground and pushed a little. The swing swayed back and forth in the slightest manner that it could without being perfectly still. She watched as he finished folding the letter from his sister and tucked it into the back pocket of his trousers.

"Was her news . . . was it good news?" Vivianna ventured. "Unless . . . unless your letter is of a very private nature. I wouldn't want to impose."

Johnny nodded and smiled. "It was just a letter like any other," he said. "And it seems everybody's just fine at home."

"Are they wantin' you back then?" Vivianna asked. She felt rather unsettled in what his answer might be—as if she might be terribly despairing if his family did want him to return home.

"Yeah," he mumbled. "As soon as I can find a way to earn a bit, I'll head back. I don't want to go home empty-handed though."

"It might take ya awhile to earn enough for a

train ticket. Isn't that right?" Vivianna asked. "I mean, I certainly hope you're not plannin' to walk all the way to Texas. You and Justin have done enough walkin' by my way of seein' things."

"Well, I won't lie. I would rather ride home than walk it," he admitted. "Still, I probably should think about leavin' soon. I need to get on back . . . and everything here seems fine. I've fixed up just about everything I can find to fix, and you and Justin seem on your way to happiness. So I guess he don't need a roughed-up ol' guardian angel anymore."

Vivianna tried to steady her breathing. Yet the thought of Johnny leaving had caused her insides to quiver with trepidation. "Oh, I don't know," she told him. "We just now . . . just a minute ago . . . we just decided we need a little more time . . . a little more time to sort our feelin's out."

"What?" Johnny exclaimed, a deep frown furrowing his brow suddenly. "Did he tell you that he didn't . . . what did he say to you, Vivi?"

"Nothin' bad, Johnny," she explained. "Just that . . . he needs more time. He thinks I need more time too. So much has happened. So much is hauntin' him . . . and me, I suppose." She frowned, lost in her own self-estimation. "Sometimes I feel . . . I feel almost numb. It wasn't until today when . . ." Vivianna smiled and shook her head. Certainly, it was true Johnny's kiss had affected her. Yet she did not want him to know how thoroughly it had done so. "Anyway," she continued with a sigh and a toss of her head, "I'm glad for your letter. Letters mean the world when you're separated from your loved ones."

"Yes . . . they do," he mumbled. "My sister had another baby," he began. "A boy. She named him after me."

Vivianna smiled. "How sweet! It's very flatterin' to have a baby named after you . . . or at least I imagine it would be." She paused and studied him for a moment, causing her breath to quicken, her heart to flutter once more. "I suppose Texas isn't near as muggy as Alabama . . . is it?" she asked.

"No," he said, smiling at her. "But I sure prefer Alabama to Georgia."

"Well, we do grow the sweetest honeysuckle sugar ya ever did taste," she said, reaching up and plucking a large blossom from the vine.

She smiled as Johnny frowned when she began to separate the flower to find the sweet nectar within.

"What're ya doin'?" he asked, obviously completely perplexed.

Vivianna felt her mouth drop open with astonishment. "Johnny Tabor! You do not mean to tell me you've never had honeysuckle sugar, do you?"

"No, ma'am. I guess I haven't," he admitted with a smile and an amused chuckle.

"Hmm," Vivianna breathed. "Well, that's just plum criminal if ya ask me. Here," she said, pulling the long white thread with its priceless droplet of nectar from the flower. "Open your mouth."

Johnny's brow puckered.

"Hurry, Johnny! It'll drop off before ya get to taste it," she giggled.

Johnny opened his mouth, more to say something in response than to accept her gift of honeysuckle nectar. Still, Vivianna placed the flower style on his tongue.

She smiled when his eyes widened.

"It's good, isn't it?" she asked.

"It's almost as if . . . as if it ain't there. But . . . but . . ." he stammered.

"But it's delicious all the same?" she finished for him.

"Yeah," he admitted.

Vivianna reached out and plucked another blossom. "Here. I'll show you how to do it." She pinched the blossom, holding carefully to the tiny green cup at its base. "Ya have to pull the blossom off slow . . . or you'll crush the little green nectar cup."

She smiled as she placed another drop of nectar on Johnny's tongue. She wanted to kiss him! She did! She simply wanted to wrap her arms around his neck and kiss him.

"There now," she said instead. "You try it."

She plucked a blossom for him, giggling as she watched his callused fingers try to hold it carefully.

"I don't think I can manage it," he mumbled, frowning as he tried to tenderly disassemble the tiny flower. "You do it for me," he said once he'd managed to tear the blossom apart without even coming close to harvesting the sweet droplet of nectar it hid.

Vivianna giggled.

"Viv! Viv!" Willy called. "Help me!"

Vivianna gasped as Willy suddenly burst into the arbor.

"What's the matter, Willy?" she asked. It was obvious the boy was upset. She felt her hand reach for Johnny's arm—visions of another dead man in the woods owning her mind.

"It's the pollywog puddle! It's dryin' up! The little frogs are dryin' out, and the pollywogs will die if we don't get them to the pond!" Willy explained, breathless and near to tears. "Justin wouldn't help us. He said he's headed into town . . . and I can't find Caleb!" He reached out and took hold of Johnny's arm. "Come on, Johnny! We gotta save the frogs at least!"

Johnny was on his feet even faster than Vivianna was. "I'll fetch a bucket for the pollywogs, Vivi," he said. "You start gettin' those frogs over to the pond."

Vivianna nodded, her heart warmed by his

241

willingness to help the boys with their task.

"Come on, Viv!" Willy grumbled as he pulled her toward the pollywog puddle. "Ya don't run near as fast as you used to."

Vivianna heard Johnny chuckle but kept her attention on Willy.

As they approached the pollywog puddle, it was to see a frantic Nate stuffing handfuls of tiny new frogs into the front pockets of his trousers.

"Come on, Viv!" Nate called. "Some of 'em are already dead! I knew I should've added some water yesterday. Willy and I didn't check on 'em this morning and—"

"It's all right, Nate," Vivianna soothed. "We'll get the rest of them. It'll be all right." Lifting her apron with one hand, she began filling it with tiny frogs with the other. They were already high leapers, but she managed to keep most of them in her apron.

"They're all dyin', Viv!" Willy sniffled.

Vivianna paused and placed her free hand on Willy's shoulder. "We'll save the rest, Willy. Just help now, all right? Try not to panic. Just help me put as many as you can in my apron."

Willy nodded and brushed a tear from his eye.

Vivianna understood his pain. Too much death had touched these young boys. They didn't need to see more, even in the form of pollywogs and frogs.

Johnny arrived with a bucket. Dropping to his knees, he scooped up as many pollywogs as he could and headed to the pond.

"Come on!" he said. "Bring what y'all got so far."

Vivianna nodded, bunched up her apron, and ran after him toward the pond.

Quickly, Johnny dumped the bucket of dying pollywogs into the large pond. He plunged the bucket into the pond, filling it with water, and then turned and headed back to the puddle. Vivianna shook the small frogs out of her apron into the safe water of the pond and nodded to Nate and Willy.

"Empty out your pockets, boys. Then go back for some more," she instructed. "We'll save as many as we can."

Hurriedly they worked, Vivianna and the boys collecting young frogs, Johnny scooping up handfuls of pollywogs and dropping them into his bucket. Back and forth they went. On their last trip to the puddle, Vivianna's apron was sopping wet, muddy, and so full of frogs she wondered if she could make it back to the pond with all of them.

"That's it," Johnny said, picking up his last bucketful of pollywogs. "Me and Vivi got the last of 'em!" he told Nate and Willy with a smile. "Now, you boys run on home and tell your mama what heroes y'all are. All right? Me and Vivi will make sure they're all swimmin' happy. Go on now."

Willy and Nate nodded, smiled, and ran off toward the house.

Vivianna smiled. She knew Johnny was sending the boys away so that they wouldn't see how many frogs and pollywogs were floating dead in the water. The fish would eat the dead ones up soon enough, and then Nate and Willy could go on believing every one of their beloved little puddle pets had lived to thrive long and happy in the pond.

Johnny chuckled. Smiling at Vivianna, he said, "Well, come on, Vivi. Let's finish it up."

Vivianna giggled and followed as Johnny headed for the pond.

"I'll dump these out and help you with those," he said. Quickly he ran ahead of her a ways, dumping the bucketful of pollywogs into their new home.

Vivianna hurried. She could feel her hand slipping—feel her hold on her slimy apron loosening. She was nearly to the water's edge when she tripped and began to stumble forward.

With a shriek, she tried to keep hold of her apron—tried to pull it up so that she wouldn't land on her stomach and squish the tiny frogs she was carrying. In an instant, however, she knew it would be impossible—that she must abandoned the safety of the frogs for her own. She released her grip on her apron and squealed again as she saw the multitude of tiny frogs fly up in the air.

She fell forward and bumped into Johnny, knocking him into the pond. Somehow he turned and caught her in his arms, keeping her from falling facefirst into the muddy pond water.

Vivianna gasped for breath as Johnny pushed her back to sit on her seat only a moment before tens upon tens of frogs rained down upon their heads. Vivianna screamed as she felt their sticky feet on her face, her arms—felt them hopping around on her head.

Frantically, she helped Johnny brush them from her shoulders, out of her hair, and from her lap. It was only when she had calmed herself enough to realize that it was only baby frogs hopping around on her person—not snakes or spiders or something far worse—that she looked to Johnny.

Clamping her hand over her mouth, she tried not to laugh. Yet the sight of Johnny covered head to toe in mud and baby frogs was too delightful!

"Are you all right, Vivi?" he asked. The concern on his face was genuine—and great.

"Yes, of course!" Vivianna giggled.

"Are ya certain?" he asked, standing and offering a hand to her. She nodded and continued to giggle as he helped her to her feet. Even the deep furrow on his handsome brow, even the way he grimaced slightly as he picked a small frog from her hair, even for all his serious demeanor,

Vivianna could not stop her giggles. He was too handsome—too entirely adorable with mud splattered all over his gorgeous face, two tiny frogs clinging to his hair, three on one shoulder.

"Are you all right?" she asked at last. She reached up and gently removed one of the frogs from his hair. Wrinkling her nose, she tossed it into the pond and then reached for another.

"Me?" he asked, a bewildered look on his face.

"For goodness sake, Johnny," she giggled. "I near knocked you to Mississippi." She smiled and brushed the frogs lingering on his shoulders. "And now you're all muddy, and your pretty clean shirt is a mess."

Johnny seemed only then to realize he'd fallen too—that he too was covered in mud and frogs. He brushed at the mud on his shirt and then glanced down to the pond.

"I probably smashed half of what we saved," he mumbled. He ran a hand over the seat of his trousers and looked at it. "I don't see any legs or nothin' though." He brushed his other hand over his seat then—studied it for a moment. "No pollywog tails neither."

Vivianna clamped a muddy hand over her mouth. She could feel the peals of laughter beginning in her throat, and in a moment more, they broke the air. "Oh, Johnny!" she laughed. "Your face . . . you're so serious!" And it was true! He was still frowning, as if he were yet concerned over her.

Suddenly, his expression changed. Almost at once his frown faded, and he smiled—laughed— began to laugh so hard he could hardly draw breath! Vivianna was entirely undone. She folded her arms across her stomach as she bent over with laughing.

"I swear, Johnny Tabor!" she gasped between breaths. "It seems somethin' or other is always . . . always . . ."

"Always . . . always messin' on me?" he gasped.

Vivianna nodded as her laughter increased! She couldn't breathe, and she could see that Johnny couldn't either. He leaned forward and placed a hand on her shoulder as he hung his head in trying to cease the ripples of laughter.

Vivianna pressed her hands to his chest in trying to keep from toppling over with the force of her gasping and giggles. "Pigeons and frogs," she sighed as her laughter began to subside somewhat. "It seems they're just too jealous of your handsome face to leave you well enough alone!"

Again they each burst into laughter.

"Maybe . . . maybe they just think my shirts are too pretty," Johnny sighed, wiping the moisture from his eyes with the shoulder of his shirt— which was the only clean spot left on it.

Again they each burst into laughter. Vivianna could not seem to rein in her giggling. And Johnny certainly couldn't cork his own hilarity. He sat down hard on the muddy bank of the pond and roared.

"J-Johnny!" Vivianna begged, sitting down beside him. "P-please! I swear . . . I swear I'm gonna just bust somethin' if you don't . . . if you don't stop this!"

"Me?" he gasped. "I was . . . I was only tryin' to save pollywogs! You're the one who made it rain frogs!"

"What in tarnation is so funny?"

It was Willy. Vivianna managed to gasp and hold her breath long enough to see that Willy stood nearby, scowling at them like they had no sense at all.

"I swear, Viv. Every time I come to fetch you and Johnny, y'all are laughin' like nothin' I ever seen," the boy scolded.

Johnny drew a deep breath and sighed.

"And why're ya all muddy?" Will asked. "Y'all get into more mischief than Nate and me."

Vivianna bit her lip. It was the only way she could restrain the residual giggles still lurking in her throat.

"We stumbled a bit," Johnny explained.

Willy looked Vivianna up and down. "A bit?" He shook his head. "Anyhow, Mama sent me out to tell y'all thank you for helpin' me and

Nate." He shrugged. "I guess I'll just run on back and tell her you'll be awhile gettin' back to the house." He shook his head once more. "Y'all are a mess." He turned and trotted back toward the house.

Vivianna watched him go, smiling. When Willy was well out of sight, she looked to Johnny. His eyes were smoldering with some emotion she couldn't quite discern. Yet his smile was bright and cheerful.

Quickly, she leaned forward, pressing a quick kiss to his lips. "Thank you," she said, "for helpin' the boys with their silly frogs and pollywogs."

His smoldering gaze caused her breath to catch—caused a warm shiver of delight to travel up her spine.

"I-I should probably quit kissin' ya every time I wanna thank ya for somethin'," she said. She felt her cheeks pink with a bashful blush. She'd spoken the words out loud, though she'd only intended to think them.

"Why?" he asked.

Vivianna held her breath. The manner in which his rather predatory gaze lingered on her and the mischievous grin on his enticing mouth caused her to tremble. The manner in which he slowly leaned toward her—the way his gaze was suddenly transfixed to her lips—caused her mouth to begin to water. She wanted him to kiss her—wanted him to kiss her the way he had earlier, beneath the honeysuckle vine.

"My letter!" she gasped as the sudden realization Justin's letter was still in her skirt pocket rushed into her mind. Plunging her hand into her pocket, she removed the beloved pages. They were damp but not soaking. "Oh, it's ruined!"

She heard Johnny sigh as he reached over and took the letter from her. She watched as his brow puckered with curiosity. "It'll survive . . . but I'm not too certain it will travel on to wherever you were plannin' on sendin' it." She watched as Johnny unfolded the letter, his frown deepening as he studied it.

"Oh . . . uh . . . I wasn't plannin' on sendin' it. It was written to me," she said.

"One of Justin's?" he asked, handing the moist pages back to her.

"Yes. It's . . . it's special . . . one of my favorites."

Johnny's frown intensified into a scowl. "Then ya better get it back to the house and put a warm iron to it," he grumbled.

He stood, offering her his hand. His flirtatious manner had disappeared. And though Vivianna was disappointed in this, she knew she should expect no different.

"You run on back to the house. I'll clean up with the rain barrel out by the barn," he said. His teasing disposition was gone—his playfulness.

"All right," Vivianna said. She started to walk away from him but paused.

"Truly . . . thank you, Johnny," she said. "I know savin' those silly pollywogs and frogs meant everything to Nate and Willy."

Vivianna gasped as he reached out, slipped a muddy hand to the back of her neck, and pulled her against him.

"You're welcome," he growled a moment before his mouth crushed to hers.

Johnny's mouth was hot and moist. It was a teasingly short kiss, but it caused Vivianna's knees to buckle slightly all the same.

He held her neck as he studied her face a moment, and Vivianna nearly threw her arms around him—nearly begged him to kiss her once more.

Instead, she said, "I swear, Johnny Tabor . . . I swear I think you could lead me astray if I had a mind to let ya."

He released her then—and grinned.

"If I had a mind to lead ya astray, Vivi . . . *your* mind couldn't stop me," he said.

He turned then, striding in the direction of the barn.

CHAPTER TEN

Vivianna turned the small flame wheel of the lantern. The flame heightened, the darkness lessened, and she sighed. Reading by starlight and low lamplight had caused her eyes to grow weary, yet she wanted to finish reading Justin's letters. Carefully she drew the last letter from the box—the last letter she'd received from Justin before he'd ceased in writing to her, before he and Johnny had been captured and taken to Andersonville.

As she withdrew the letter from its tattered envelope, she felt a tear trickle over one cheek. This would be the last time she would read Justin's beloved letters. Vivianna had determined that Justin was right. He had changed since he'd written the letters, and so had she. If she were to love him, she must fall in love with the man he had become, not the man he had been. Still, thick anxiety rose in her as a vision of Johnny Tabor entered her mind—as a thrill traveled through her at the memory of what he'd said to her before leaving her by the pond.

If I had a mind to lead ya astray, Vivi, he'd said, *your mind couldn't stop me.*

Vivianna shook her head, tried to scatter her thoughts of Johnny, and returned her attention to Justin's letters. The conversation she'd shared with Justin that day—his explanation that he needed more time to heal and that she needed time too—had liberated her in many ways. Yet until she could put aside Justin's letters—until she could let go of the man he had been before Andersonville—she would never be entirely free. Thus, she lingered on the arbor swing beneath the starlit sky and honeysuckle vine, reading Justin's letters by lantern shine.

She'd read each one—bathed in the beauty of their words and promises one last time. Even she'd read the now ironed and newly folded favorite she'd kept in her pocket for more than a year. There had been no need to read it, in truth, for she knew every word by heart. Still, she'd read it aloud, determined to read them all. Finally, the letter now in her hand was the last. She would read it as well—relish it as she had the others— and then she would take the box and place it somewhere other than her wardrobe. She would remove the letters from her wardrobe—from her room—from the house. She was not yet sure where she would put them, for she was not ready to give them up wholly and burn them, but she would put them away from her own easy reach. As she unfolded the pages of Justin's final letter, a contemplation entered her mind. She would take the small box containing Justin's letters to her family home in Florence. Yes! She would take the letters there and place them in one of the trunks in the attic. There they would be safe. There they could rest until Vivianna could read them again without knowing pain and heartache for the change in the man who'd written them.

She nodded. It was a good plan. She would carry it out on the morrow. In the morning, she would walk to Florence, visit her once joyous, now empty family home, and bury Justin's letters in the warm, safe belly of an attic trunk.

Brushing another tear from her cheek, she began to read Justin's last letter.

"My darling Vivi," she whispered aloud.

Can it be true? Do you really love me? At this moment, I am sitting and listening to the warm Georgia rain beat against the tent, knowing the rain will make the battle tomorrow more miserable. And yet all I can think of . . . all I can do is wonder at the miracle of owning your love and admit I know doubt. How can you love me? Me . . . a man so thoroughly undeserving of your love? Still, I read your letters—again and again I read them—and I'm comforted. Your written words to me speak such soothing to my soul. The letter I received from you this evening renewed my certainty in owning your heart. "It is your letters that have won my heart," you wrote to me, Vivi. "For it is through them that I have come to justly know your true mind and heart . . . to see into your soul. It is for the sake of your letters that you own me, Justin, and I ponder that it seems I never truly knew you before . . . for your letters have revealed you completely—your mind, heart and spirit—and I love you for them all." Thus, your words comfort me, Vivi, and I know it is truly me you love . . . and not another. Perhaps you do not yet love me as deeply, as desperately as I love you, but you do love me, and it is enough for now.

The fighting is brutal. True that it has always been brutal. But this march with Savannah as our goal, it is so thoroughly destructive to the people of Georgia, to her cities, her very landscape. At times, it seems as if death and fire and destruction are all I will ever know. But then I dream of you, and in those dreams you promise me that the war will end. In my dreams, you place your pretty mouth to mine, kiss me, and whisper that all will be well. That war is not forever but that the love you and I have come to know is forever. Our hearts are entwined . . . and that is forever. In my dreams you promise you will always belong to me, that only I own your heart. In my dreams I can hold you, kiss you, and feel your hand in mine. It is I wonder if, perhaps, you would rather I write more of our success in battle, of the goings-on in camp. Yet as I sit here writing to you, I find I do not wish to tell of such things. I wish only to think on you—of the life we will have together when at last I can march to Florence instead of Savannah. When I come to you, and General Sherman's campaign will surely hurry the war to an end, that I may come to you and lay my claim, Vivi . . . then no one will have you but I!

I should not go on so. You will think madness has taken me if I do not write of something besides my love for you. Thus, I will tell you of Lowell. Lowell is a boy we are caring for here. I found him last week. The battle had ended for the day, and we—victorious yet overweary—were riding back to camp. I felt something hit me in the head and for an instant thought I had been wounded. I placed a hand to the place where my head was aching to find there was no injury there . . . no blood. I turned to look behind me, and that is when I saw him—Lowell. He is aged eight years, with flaming red hair and the bluest eyes I have ever seen. He'd been orphaned days before after his mother had taken ill and died. It seems his father fought and died for the Union, and he was afraid to return to town, afraid the townsfolk who knew his father had not fought to defend Georgia's soil would harm him. Thus, he had been wandering the countryside alone and frightened for several days. All this I discovered when I dismounted and asked him if he were lost. I could not leave him there, so I picked him up, sat him astride my horse, and took him back to camp with me. He has been with us ever since, for we have not yet found a family to leave him off with.

I do not know why I have written of Lowell. His is not a happy story at present. Perhaps it is because I know you will own greater empathy for him than anyone else, for your losses in this war have been far more akin to his than anyone else's. I worry in constant for him. He should not be with us, for he is not safe in the company of soldiers who are daily in battle. Yet he seems to find a measure of joy in our company. I think he feels safe with us, which of course is not at all an accuracy. Lingering with soldiers fighting for the Union on Southern soil is certainly not the safest place for a boy. Still, we protect him as best we can and in constant hope we may find him a safer place to linger soon. I have made certain that Lowell has put to memory instructions on how to find you and my family if something should happen and we are separated. I know a boy aged eight could not find his way safely all the way from Georgia to you, but it gives me a small measure of comfort. So, Vivi, if one day you are out lingering near the road and a small boy with hair as orange as a pumpkin arrives, please do look after him. He has captured my heart, and I worry for him now. I have told Lowell of you, Vivi. I have spent perhaps hours in telling this small boy of your goodness. He knows you would care for him if he and I were separated. And though I know it is impossible, I imagine he could find his way to you. Writing of Lowell may seem a strange thing to you. Still, I cannot spend all these pages in simply professing my love. Thus, I have told you of Lowell.

I will close, Vivi. I will close in knowing this letter is not the best I have written. The day was long, and my eyes are weary. I hope you will forgive me for such a lacking letter. No doubt the condition of my penmanship, weary as I am, will attest to the condition of my mind and body. Yet know that if my heart were the instrument by which I penned my letters to you, you would find no end to the pages I would send. I love you, Vivi. Oh, how I love you! Wait for me to come to you, for I will come to you. And when I do come to you—when I am able, at last, to hold you in my arms—I promise you these things: I will kiss you, and you will not be able to put me from your mind for one moment beyond our kisses. I will marry you, even if I must bind your arms and legs and carry you to the church in making it so. And I will own such a life of love, children, and happiness with you as to rival anything heaven itself could endeavor to arrange.

May God keep you safe, my love . . . my one true reason for living.

Vivianna folded the tender pages and brushed the tears from her cheeks with the back of her hand. She was angry for a moment—angry with Justin. Why had he changed? Why hadn't he endeavored to fulfill his promises of love? How her heart ached in that moment, longed for the man Justin had been. How she wished that the sight of Justin caused her heart to leap; how she wished it were Justin's kiss she longed for. Yet it wasn't—not now—not anymore. Furthermore, it was Justin's fault her heart did not beat so madly in his presence as it once had. After all, wasn't it Justin who brought Johnny Tabor to Florence? It was Justin's fault—all of it! Yet in an instant, Vivianna humbled herself once more. It was not Justin's fault, nor was it Johnny's fault. Johnny could not change the truth of his being so handsome, so thoroughgoing in his rank of attractiveness. Perhaps he might change his behavior if he wished, mask the pure magnetism of his manner. Yet Vivianna would not wish him to alter. No—she most certainly did not. Johnny Tabor had found his way into holding Vivianna's attention with his pure desirability, into piercing her heart with some intangible power she could not understand, and that was no one's fault but her own.

As she returned the letter to its place in the small box, she sighed. Perhaps she was simply not meant to love Justin Turner, just as she was not meant to love Caleb. Perhaps Justin's letters to her and hers to him—perhaps they had simply been an instrument to help both she and Justin to endure the horrors of the war. Perhaps she would one day leave Florence. Perhaps the Turner boys she had so desperately loved would become nothing but a sweet memory of the past.

Vivianna thought of Savannah then—of the

great debt she owed to her. Savannah wanted nothing more than for Vivianna to marry Justin or Caleb. It was many times Savannah had confessed this to her. Guilt and anxiety gripped Vivianna at the thought. She could not disappoint Savannah, nor Nate and Willy. She could not. Yet Justin did not want to marry her—at least, not in that moment. And she was not in love with Caleb. Either marriage would be out of obligation—either for Vivianna's part of it or for Justin's and Caleb's.

Shaking her head with utter frustration and fatigue, Vivianna sighed. Many things occurred out of a sense of obligation, including marriage. Perhaps she should have accepted Caleb's proposal. Certainly she was not in love with him, but she did love him, and he was steady. Caleb, though owning no sign of passion, was a good man—a kind and understanding man. In those moments of near despair and utter weariness, Vivianna Bartholomew wondered if she'd made a terrible mistake in not marrying Caleb Turner. After all, what good had it done her to dream over Justin, to have him return home only to find him so changed?

It was late. Vivianna knew it was never wise for a body to ponder so deeply when one was so very tired as she was. She stood, lifted the lantern with one hand, and tucked the small box containing Justin's letters under her arm. She needed rest.

The day had been long and emotionally taxing. Even in that moment, she could yet feel the press of Johnny's lips to hers. They began to rise in her then, all her emotions, every one, all the feelings she'd buried for so long—the ardor that had begun to stir deep in her from the moment she'd first kissed Johnny beneath the honeysuckle. Still, she was weary, worn from the events of the day, from hard labor, from the emotional consequences of her discussion with Justin. Yet it was the thoughts of Johnny—her confusion mingled with delight—that most exhausted her. She reminded herself that he was nearly a stranger to her. He was not someone she'd known the whole of her life as she had Caleb and Justin. He was a stranger, a stranger whom she knew nothing about, save that he was from Texas and had a family there, that his sister was named Jeannie and had named her son after him, and that he held secrets.

Vivianna thought then of Johnny Tabor's tin box, the one Justin had told her he clung to as if it contained the most valuable of treasure. She thought of his asking her to sink it in the river if he died. She thought then also of the dead Confederate Nate and Willy had found in the woods. Quickly, she buried her suspicious nature. Justin would not own a friend who was in any way wicked. He would not. Her mind was too tired—too worn out. She would return to her bed and sleep. And in the morning, she would take Justin's letters to her old home and hide them.

A cloud passed over the moon, and the darkness thickened. Vivianna was grateful she had not wandered too far from the house in seeking out pure privacy in which to peruse Justin's letters. Even with the lantern light, the thick darkness would have caused difficulty for her as she made her way to the house had she not known the path so well.

"Vivianna."

Vivianna gasped, her heart leaping so quickly within her bosom she feared it may well leap entirely from it!

"Johnny!" she scolded as she looked up to see Johnny standing before her. He held a lantern in one hand, a small, battered tin box tucked under his left arm. "You near scared the waddin' outta me! What are ya doin' out here in the dead of night?"

Johnny arched one broad brow and asked, "What are *you* doin' out here in the dead of night?"

Vivianna paused in answering. She fancied she might well tell him what she was doing and why. And before she could think to do otherwise, she did indeed tell him.

"I . . . I wanted to read Justin's letters once more . . . before I put them away perhaps forever," she said. She could not believe the confession had passed beyond her lips! Why would she tell him of her plans to put Justin's letters away?

Johnny glanced to the small box she carried.

"You're givin' them up?" he asked. "Have you . . . have you and Justin come to an agreement on—"

"We've agreed that he needs more time to heal . . . that perhaps I do, as well," she interrupted. "We are neither of us the same . . . changed since the letters passed between us. He wants me to love him for the man he is now, not the man he was when he wrote these to me."

Johnny's eyes narrowed. "But I thought ya loved him. I thought ya wanted to marry him." He paused and then added, "You refused Caleb for the mere memory Justin left in you. And now, you refuse Justin for—"

"I have not refused Justin," Vivianna interrupted once more. "He told me today . . . that he wants me to give up the letters . . . give up the man he used to be. As I said, he wants me to love who he has become."

"And will you?" Johnny asked.

Vivianna could not understand her desire, her need to be honest with Johnny. Yet honest she was as she said, "I don't know. I must confess it to someone." She paused and gazed into his handsome face. His eyes were warm—held sincere concern. "You're his friend, Johnny . . . but may I trust you with a secret?"

264

"I fear I'm the greatest keeper of secrets you'll ever meet, Vivianna," he said. She thought there was perhaps more meaning in his words than was apparent.

"Then I'll tell you this. I love Justin . . . but I love the Justin I knew here." She held the box up that he might better see it. "The Justin whose heart is written in the letters in this box. I . . . I think the Justin you brought home . . . I fear he may be lost to me forever. And I confess further that I don't know if I can love the man he is now. I . . . I don't care for some of the changes in him . . . a certain arrogance that appears every now and again . . . an impatience." She shrugged and added, "Oh, I'm sure I'm not bein' very understandin'. After all, you know what he endured at Andersonville. More than anybody else, you understand." She shook her head and restrained her tears. "My feelings go back and forth. One minute I'm heartbroken that he doesn't love me as he did, but in the next breath I feel freer than I have since before the war."

Johnny said nothing—simply looked at her, his dark eyes smoldering with an intoxicating allure. Warm and sudden moisture flooded her mouth as she gazed at him.

"Do ya think badly of me, Johnny?" she asked him. "Do ya think I'm fickle and stonehearted?"

"No," he mumbled. His eyes narrowed. "I think Justin's a fool. And if those letters you're holdin'

265

are what's keepin' your heart a prisoner . . . then burn 'em and set yourself free."

Vivianna shook her head, however—clutched the box to her bosom. "No. No, I could never burn them. But I have decided to put them away from my easy reach."

"Where do ya mean to put 'em?" he asked.

Vivianna looked at the box and studied the small treasure holder.

"I think . . . I think I'll take them to my daddy and mama's house in town," she told him. "There's a whole attic full of trunks . . . trunks and trunks filled with things my mama packed away to sort through one day. I figure they'll be safe there, and I don't visit the house often. It's too far for me to rush over in a fit of melancholy and retrieve the letters . . . yet close enough I know they're near. I figured I'd go tomorrow mornin'." She paused and glanced to the tin box still tucked under Johnny's arm. "There's a heap of trunks up there, Johnny. Most anybody could find a good hidin' place for a lot of things . . . things a body maybe doesn't want to hold too awful close . . . or things they don't want anybody to find."

Johnny glanced to the tin box. He looked back to her, frowning. "I don't want to belittle your treasure, Vivianna," he began, "but my secrets . . . what I keep in this old box are worth far more than Justin's letters. I best keep them close."

Vivianna nodded. Perhaps Nate and Willy were right. Perhaps Johnny did hide gold or jewels in the old tin box he guarded so carefully.

"I'll take ya to town tomorrow if ya'd like," he said, startling her from her thoughts.

"Pardon?" Vivianna asked.

"Ya shouldn't go into town alone," he said. "I'll go with ya."

Vivianna felt a smile spread across her face. "That's very kind of ya, Johnny. But folks in town know ya fought for the Union . . . and you're not Florence born and raised like Caleb and Justin. Aren't ya afraid folks might—"

"I ain't scared of the folks in town, Vivianna." His frown softened a little. "I'll go with ya to hide those letters . . . unless . . . unless ya don't want me to go with ya."

Vivianna's heart quickened its pace. The thought of walking all the way to town and back in Johnny's company caused such a thrill of delight to rise in her that she nearly forgot the heartache she'd been bathing in beneath the honeysuckle vine only a few minutes before.

"Oh, no! No . . . I want ya to go with me," she assured him. "I just hate to impose on your time."

Johnny shook his head, however. "It ain't no imposition," he said. "I was plannin' on checkin' in on them jobs with the railroad sometime this week anyhow. I'll be glad to go along with ya."

Vivianna smiled, though an odd disappointment

had pricked her when Johnny had said he'd planned on going to town anyway. She would've liked to believe he'd wanted to go with her simply for the sake of her company. Still, it was a kind offer, and she did look forward to his company. Perhaps having Johnny with her would make the task of letting go of Justin's letters a little easier.

"Promise, Johnny?" she asked. "Do ya promise to go with me to leave off Justin's letters?"

Johnny grinned and nodded. "I promise."

"Then I'll see ya in the mornin', Johnny Tabor," she said.

He nodded and mumbled, "Good night, Vivi."

"Good night," she told him.

Vivianna hurried to the house. She was tired, and morning would come all too soon.

"He's a good man, Viv."

Again Vivianna startled at the unexpected sound of a man's voice.

"Caleb Turner!" she scolded in a whisper as Caleb stepped up onto the porch behind her. "I swear! You nearly scared me to jumpin' right outta my skin!"

Briefly Vivianna wondered if Justin too were lurking in the night shadows. What was wrong with men? Why did they find it ever so necessary to steal up on a woman? She wondered then if perhaps their quiet, creeping ways were a lingering characteristic of war—of quiet care in scouting.

"I'm sorry," Caleb apologized. "I didn't mean to scare ya so."

"Well, you did. Shame on you," she teasingly scolded.

Caleb nodded to the box she held in her hands. "You been readin' Justin's letters again?"

Vivianna nodded. "For the last time, I'm afraid." She frowned as she studied Caleb for a moment. "You told me Justin had changed, Caleb. When he first came home . . . you said he'd changed. How did ya know he'd changed? You hadn't seen him in almost a year."

Caleb glanced away a moment. "Truth is . . . he'd changed long before I was wounded and sent home," he said.

"But . . . but that was before he and Johnny were at Andersonville."

Caleb nodded. He looked back to her and said, "Johnny Tabor's a good man, Viv. A better man than Justin . . . and probably me too."

Vivianna felt a slight blush rising to her cheeks. Had Caleb seen her talking with Johnny in the dark near the honeysuckle moments before?

"Caleb . . . how you do go on sometimes," she sighed. "What do you mean tellin' me that Johnny Tabor is a good man and that Justin's not? And why do you always put yourself under everyone else? You're a better man than most," she assured him.

"I've seen the way ya look at him, Viv," he

continued, however. "Your eyes light up when Johnny's near . . . like nothin' I ever seen come over ya before."

"Now . . . now, Caleb," Vivianna stammered, "I'm sure that's simply not true."

"It is true," he said. "And I just want you to know . . . if I can't have ya myself, then I'd rather lose ya to the likes of Johnny Tabor than to the likes of Justin."

"J-Justin just needs time, Caleb," she began to argue. Yet she wondered why she felt the need to defend Justin—for Caleb was right. Johnny Tabor did affect her in a manner that Justin did not. Yet her sense of obligation to the Turner family spurred her to protecting Justin's right to her somehow. "He just needs more time. I'm sure he'll—"

"Justin don't need time, Viv," he interrupted. "Are ya gonna stand on this porch and try to tell me that Johnny went through less than Justin did at Andersonville? When they first came home, it was plain as day who'd seen the worst of the misery Andersonville rained down." He reached out and took hold of her shoulders. "I'm tellin' ya, Viv . . . ya wouldn't marry me 'cause ya loved somebody else more. Don't marry my brother out of obligation and expectation . . . or even because of a memory. Whether it's Johnny Tabor or some other man ya find yourself lookin' to, you settle for the best man that crosses

270

your path . . . because that's what ya deserve."

Caleb paused and looked at the box containing Justin's letters. "You said you're readin' 'em for the last time. I say good! Them letters is what kept ya from marryin' me, and ya know it, Viv. Don't let them come between you and the man who was meant to have ya. Burn 'em, and look forward. That's what we're all doin'—burnin' the pain this war caused and movin' on."

"I could never burn them, Caleb," she told him. "But I won't dream over them anymore."

Caleb nodded. He smiled—a sad sort of smile—and said, "Good. Good. Now ya better get on into bed. It's late."

"You're a good man, Caleb," Vivianna said. She raised herself on her toes and kissed his cheek. "Thank you. Thank you for bein' so kind and patient with me."

"Good night, Viv," Caleb said.

"Good night," Vivianna said.

She left him then—quietly entered the house. Once she'd changed her day clothes for a nightdress, Vivianna lay in bed listening to Savannah's soft snore. It was odd that Caleb should be lingering on the porch so late, that Johnny was out near the honeysuckle vine at such an hour. *There must be something strange in the air keepin' folks from sleepin' easy tonight,* she mused.

Closing her eyes, Vivianna began to drift to

sleep. Somehow she wasn't so anxious over Justin's letters anymore. Somehow she had a notion that it might be easier than she thought to put them away in her family's attic. Though she'd shed a river of tears while reading her cherished letters one last time, she felt a renewed sense of freedom at thinking on giving them up.

She smiled as thoughts of Johnny entered her mind again. She giggled slightly as sleep began to overtake her—a vision of Johnny Tabor covered in mud and frogs heralding her dreams.

Johnny closed the tin box—fixed the lock. He should sink it in the river; he knew he should. At the very least he should hide the box containing his secrets—the proof of the blackness of his soul. He thought of Vivianna's suggestion he hide the box in one of the trunks in her family's home. How sweet and kind she was, how thoughtful and innocent.

He hated Justin Turner in that moment. Yes, he hated his greatest friend! In the least he hated the man who had once been his greatest friend. He wasn't certain exactly when Justin began to lose himself—sometime just before he'd saved Johnny's life, he thought. Still, part of Johnny—the greater part of him—was blissful in Vivianna's seeming disenchantment and frustration with Justin. Johnny had become more

272

and more certain he would rather die than see Justin actually win Vivianna—actually wed her. And now it seemed there was hope.

Justin, selfish fool he had become, had pushed Vivianna away. Fine—then she was free to love another! Justin himself had freed her. After all Justin's threats—after all Johnny's plotting—in the end, Justin had freed Vivianna, and Johnny could feel free as well—free to pursue her for his own purpose.

He thought of the kiss they'd shared beneath the honeysuckle vine—of how thrice she had kissed him in offering her thanks. It was many times he'd seen Vivianna offer her thanks to Caleb. Yet she had not placed a kiss to Caleb's mouth on any occasion of offering thanks. Johnny's entire body burned with fury as he thought of Justin's having enjoyed her kiss, and he knew Justin had. Still, he had no right to know such anger and jealousy. It had been Johnny himself that had encouraged Justin to fulfill the promises of love to Vivianna. What then had he expected?

He had expected—rather feared—that Justin may show his true weakness. Though Johnny had initially hoped Justin would return to being the man he once was—that he would endeavor to be worthy of the love of such a woman as Vivianna—he was greatly relieved Justin had failed. His relief only resulted from Vivianna's apparent lack of utter heartache. It seemed to Johnny that Vivianna truly loved Justin's letters—loved the promise of what Justin might be instead of the reality of what he was.

Johnny likewise knew Justin's kiss had not affected Vivianna as his own had. This knowledge caused him to smile. He thought of her telling him she thought he might succeed in leading her astray if she had a mind to let him. It was an honest confession—he knew it was—and it pleased him. Still, as he gazed at the tin box in his lap—as he thought of its secret contents, the contents that would prove to anyone who opened it how truly sinful and corrupt Johnny Tabor was—he knew he should not hope to win her. Yet hope was in him; he could not suppress it.

He mused that perhaps such a woman as Vivianna could forgive him his evil deeds—see beyond his wicked, deceptive nature. Perhaps she could find something in him to love. Yet he shook his head, knowing it would take a miracle for the angel Vivianna to love a devil like Johnny Tabor.

He rose from the swing, raised his lantern, and headed back to the house. He'd promised to accompany her to her parents' home in the morning—promised to be her escort as she traveled a road to ridding herself of Justin's letters. It was true he was weary. It was true any of the residents in Florence they might encounter would most likely not be welcoming to him. Still, nothing could interfere with his keeping his promise to her. After all, shouldn't someone keep one small promise made to Vivianna Bartholomew?

CHAPTER ELEVEN

"Johnny says to tell ya he's waitin' on the front porch for ya, Viv," Nate said. The boy frowned as Savannah snipped the hair around his ears with a pair of scissors. "Be careful, Mama!"

"Oh, quit your fussin', Nate," Savannah scolded. "I swear! A body would think you'd had your ear cut off before the way you carry on when I'm tryin' to shine ya up a bit."

Vivianna giggled as she watched Nate purse his lower lip in a pout and firmly fold his arms across his chest.

"Thank you, Nate," she said, quickly kissing him on the forehead.

"Where y'all goin' anyhow, Viv?" Willy asked.

"I've gotta put somethin' in the old house," she answered, tucking the small box containing Justin's letters under her arm.

"Do ya want me to come with ya?" Willy asked. "I could come with ya! I'd be more'n willin'!"

"I'm sure ya would, Willy," Savannah said. "But you need your hair looked after today too. Neither one of you boys is leavin' this house. You both look like you've been livin' in a cave."

Vivianna's smile broadened as both Willy's and Nate's eyes widened—as they looked at each other with sudden and delighted inspiration.

"A cave!" they simultaneously exclaimed.

"Now there's somethin' I'd like to do . . . live in a cave!" Nate said.

"Me too!" Willy agreed.

Savannah rolled her eyes with exasperation. Shaking her head, she looked to Vivianna and sighed, "I swear . . . if it weren't for you, Viv, I don't know what I'd do with only men for company."

Vivianna forced a smile and nodded. Yet inside she was filled with guilt and a heavy burden of obligation weighing on her. She knew she'd never marry Caleb, and she was coming to the certain realization that she may never marry Justin. What would Savannah do if Vivianna left her?

Still, she wouldn't think on it now. She had to take Justin's letters to her parents' home. She needed to release them so her thoughts and emotions could find a clearer path to follow.

"I'll be back as soon as I can, Miss Savannah," Vivianna said. "I'm just runnin' on over to the old house for a time."

Savannah smiled and nodded, though her gaze lingered a moment on the wooden box tucked under Vivianna's arm. "All right, darlin'," Savannah said. "But ya make sure you don't go further on into town without Johnny. Do ya hear me? Caleb says there are all sorts of strangers wanderin' about in Florence. Ya keep Johnny close."

"I will," Vivianna said. She kissed Willy's cheek as she headed for the door. "You boys have fun gettin' your hair trimmed up now, ya hear?"

Both boys wrinkled their noses and sneered.

Vivianna heard Nate mumble as she left the house—heard Savannah scold him. She smiled, delighted by the comfortable familiarity of the goings-on in the Turner home.

Johnny was indeed waiting on the porch. He sat in an old chair, leaning back against the house, whittling on a piece of wood.

"Good mornin', Johnny," Vivianna greeted. She smiled and felt her heart flutter madly in her bosom as he looked up to her and smiled in return.

"Mornin', Vivi," he said. His eyes were bright, his soft brown hair rather tousled, as if he'd been raking his fingers through it. It was obvious he hadn't shaved that morning, and Vivianna liked the rugged look a day's growth of whiskers gave his chiseled jaw and chin. He was wildly attractive—unfairly handsome! Vivianna thought for a moment that Johnny's overall appearance was unrivaled by any other man she'd ever met. She scolded herself for thinking that even Justin or Caleb could not match Johnny's distinctive allure. She inwardly determined there was indeed something wrong with her. How could she so be so easily affected by Johnny? She'd known Caleb and Justin all her life—loved them all her life! How could she allow a stranger to cause

278

such thoughts and feelings to overwhelm her?

She thought of the letters she carried, and again she was impressed that she must release them. She would not be able to make sense of her emotions, would not be able to think clearly, as long as they were near. They distracted her—kept her mind and heart chained to the past.

"Are ya still willin' to go with me, Johnny?" she asked. "Because I wouldn't want to press ya . . . or inconvenience ya in any way."

Johnny stood and placed the piece of wood he'd been whittling on the window ledge nearby. He tucked the knife he'd been using in his boot and smiled at Vivianna. "It ain't no inconvenience at all," he told her. "I could use a good walk to town. It ain't good for me to sit around doin' nothin' all day long."

"You never do nothin' all day long, Johnny Tabor," Vivianna said. "You work circles around the rest of us."

"I don't know about that," he said as he stepped off the porch.

Vivianna stepped down from the porch as well. "Are ya ready?" she asked.

"Yes, ma'am," Johnny said.

"All right then. Let's get to town."

As they walked down the road to town, Vivianna knew Johnny's pace was slow by way of what his stride normally was. She took two or three steps to every one of his, and she knew he was attempting to keep his pace measured for her sake.

It was a beautiful day! It was early; therefore the heat was not too miserable yet. The morning birds were busy trilling and pulling worms and bugs from the ground and grass. Everything smelled green and fresh, and Vivianna was rejuvenated.

"I really should walk to town more often," she said aloud.

Johnny frowned. "I can't say I've known ya to go to town since I've been here. Not once."

Vivianna shrugged. "I . . . I just haven't wanted to go. I don't quite know why." A small hint of a shiver traveled down Vivianna's spine. She began to think that perhaps the reason she avoided town was because Florence always ignited memories of her family. Still, she pushed such thoughts aside.

"Tell me about Texas, Johnny," she said—desperate, as always, to keep from thinking of her family. "Is it a pretty place?"

"I think so," he said. "It's warm but dry. Where my family lives now, a body can see for miles and miles. I think that's why I'm always feelin' as if I'm livin' in a hole here. I thought I'd be driven mad in Georgia. Trees and trees and more trees was all there was most of the time. Still, on occasion, we'd ride up over a hill and I could see for a space . . . but it was nothin' like Texas." He paused and smiled with obvious reflection. "Ain't nothin' like wakin' up in the mornin', steppin' out on the porch to see the cattle sprinkled over the hillside, and inhalin' that fresh mornin' air."

Vivianna smiled. It was obvious Johnny loved his home, and the visions he described made her wish she could see Texas one day.

"Tell me about your family," she said. "You said you have brothers and sisters. Two of each?"

He nodded. "Yep. Jeannie, she's the oldest. Then comes me. Then there's Oakley and Carthal, and my baby sister is Ruby."

Vivianna smiled. "And your parents?"

"My mama's name is Adelaide, and Daddy's Preston."

Vivianna sighed. She liked the names owned by the members of Johnny's family, and she told him. "I like their names! Every one of them."

Johnny chuckled. "Well, I'm glad."

"Now tell me about yourself, Johnny Tabor," she said.

"There ain't much to tell," came his response. As Vivianna moved the box of Justin's letters from one arm to the other, he said, "Let me tote that for ya."

She didn't pause. Handing the box to him, she said, "Well, I'm sure there is much to tell. Tell me about yourself."

Johnny chuckled and shrugged his broad shoulders. "I don't know what I can say that might be interestin' to ya, Vivi. I'm just a regular feller who grew up in Texas."

"Oh, there's more to you than that," she said. Yet her curiosity increased suddenly, and she asked, "Did ya have a girl when ya left for the war?" She frowned, disturbed by her next thought. "Do ya still have a girl?"

Johnny chuckled, shook his head, and said, "No, ma'am! I did not leave a girl behind me when I left."

She looked to him. "I find that rather hard to believe."

"Why?" he asked, his brow puckering with puzzlement.

"Because you're so . . ." Vivianna began. Yet she stopped herself short—just short of telling him how charming and desirable he was.

"Because I'm so what?" he prodded, however.

"Well, you know," she stammered. "You . . . you're so . . . so very nice." It was a weak explanation at best.

Johnny laughed—wholeheartedly laughed for a moment.

"What's so amusin'?" she asked. She giggled for the mere fact that his laughter was contagious. "You are nice, Johnny! Look what you've done for Justin . . . for Savannah Turner, for Nate and Willy." She paused and felt a blush brush her cheeks as she added, "Look how nice ya are to me."

"I ain't so nice as ya might think, Vivi," he told her. "First off, I owed Justin a great debt . . . a debt I have yet to repay. Second, Savannah needed help. The barn and all were near to fallin' into a heap of rubble. Nate and Willy . . . well, they're just boys. How could a body not play awhile with them two?" He looked to her, his smile fading. "As for you . . . to be honest, I ain't sure in this moment that I didn't do ya more harm than good by bringin' Justin home to ya."

Vivianna glanced to him. "First off, I wasn't even thinkin' of you bringin' Justin home when I said it. I was thinkin' more on things ya do for me . . . things like this. Ya didn't have to come with me this mornin'. I'm sure there are a heap of other things ya'd rather be doin'."

He looked at her, quirked one eyebrow, and said, "Do ya really think I'd rather be muckin' out stalls or haulin' water to the garden than walkin' to town with a pretty girl?"

Vivianna shrugged—though she smiled at the fact he'd implied she was pretty. "Maybe." He shook his head in disbelief at her insinuation, and she giggled. She thought then of something they'd discussed previously and asked, "So ya didn't have a girl when ya left for the fightin'?"

"Nope."

"How about before ya left for the fightin'? Did ya ever have a girl?" she asked.

Johnny nodded. "Two or three."

Vivianna felt oddly irritated—jealous, in fact. "What were their names?" she asked.

Johnny chuckled. "Well, I don't see what difference that makes."

"I'm just curious. I like the names of all your family members so well . . . it just puts me to thinkin' on names," she lied.

"Well, all right," he relented. "I was sweet on a girl named Jenny for a long while when I was about sixteen. She was a might older than me. 'A little too friendly' was the way my mama thought of her."

"She was flirtatious?"

"That would be the kindest way to say it, yes," he admitted. "Then Molly Brandenburg moved to town and caught my eye for a while. But she wasn't much fun . . . just pretty. I suppose it was Melba Rathbone after that."

"Did ya kiss every one of them?" Vivianna asked. She didn't know why she'd asked it—just that she felt angry inside and that the annoyance had spurred the question.

"Maybe I did and maybe I didn't," he answered, smiling suspiciously at her. "How many boys were you sweet on before Justin?" he asked.

"Only Caleb," Vivianna told him honestly.

"Caleb's a good man," he said.

"Yes, he is," she agreed. He nodded his further approval of Caleb, and she was thankful he was not as discourteous as she had been—that he did not press her for details of whom she had or had not kissed.

"Do you like Christmas, Johnny?" she asked.

Johnny stopped and looked to her with an expression of utter bewilderment. "Do I like Christmas?" he repeated. He chuckled. "Forgive me, Miss Bartholomew . . . but it utterly escapes my understandin' of how we went from you pickin' over the girls I left behind me . . . to whether or not I like Christmas."

Vivianna shrugged. "I was just wonderin'. Do ya?"

"Well, of course I like Christmas," he laughed. "What kind of a question is that? Do I seem so hard and mean that I wouldn't like Christmas?"

Vivianna smiled. "Of course not! I . . . I was just wonderin'. So . . . if ya like it so much, what's your favorite thing about it?"

He sighed, his brow puckering as he seemed to seriously ponder her question. Finally, he answered, "Besides the actual reason for it in the first place . . . I'd have to say the Christmas tree and the way my mama would gussy up our house with extra candles, holly, and pine boughs. And of course, old Saint Nick always brung us an orange and a little bag of pecans and chestnuts. Most years he left us a little toy . . . usually a cloth doll for the girls or some sort of animal carved out of wood." He paused and smiled. "I remember the year Daddy taught me to whittle

285

real well. Our old mule had stomped on Daddy's hand, and it hurt for him to do the carvin'. So he taught me to do it so that I could carve out somethin' for Oakley and Carthal to get from Saint Nicholas. I whittled and carved out a horse for Oakley and a wolf for Carthal." He chuckled, his eyes warm with delighting in the memory. "I remember Carthal thought the wolf I carved was a dog. I was somewhat offended . . . so I spent the whole of the comin' year whittlin' out the best big-antlered buck ya ever did see." He glanced at her and winked. "When Carthal saw that buck the next Christmas mornin', he said, 'Mama! Saint Nick musta spent a month of Sundays carvin' this buck out for me! Just for me, Mama!' I was pretty pleased and proud of myself 'cause Daddy trusted me to do all of Saint Nick's carvin' after that." He paused a moment and then added, "At least 'til I left to enlist." He shrugged. "I suppose it was all right I left. By then Oakley and Carthal were old enough to understand just who St. Nick's master whittler really was."

It was a thoroughly endearing response! Far more wonderful than she'd ever expected. She'd thought certainly Johnny would say his mama's pies were his favorite part of Christmas or maybe Christmas dinner. She'd never expected such an entirely enchanting reply.

"Why, Johnny Tabor," she sighed, "I swear you are the most surprisin' man."

"Why?" he asked. "Just 'cause I like Christmas?"

Vivianna shook her head. "No. And yes."

She glanced away from Johnny to the road ahead. Instantly, her delight was dampened by the sight of none other than Tilly Winder. Tilly was walking toward Vivianna and Johnny, a basket filled with wildflowers hooked over one arm.

"Oh no," Vivianna mumbled.

Johnny's attention followed her gaze, and he asked, "Who is she?"

"It's Tilly Winder," Vivianna whispered.

Johnny looked to her and quickly asked, "The girl Caleb and Justin used to take turns sparkin' with before you come along?"

"What?" Vivianna asked, stopping short and looking up to him. Instantly, Johnny's expression changed. He looked just like a little boy who'd been caught snitching a pie off a window ledge.

"Nothin'," he lied. "I was just—"

"Vivianna! Hey there, Vivianna!" Tilly called.

Vivianna had been irritated enough by the impending meeting with Tilly. But after Johnny's accidental revelation, she was even more aggravated. Still, she forced a friendly smile and said, "Hey there, Tilly," as the young woman came to stand before her.

"I haven't seen you in a coon's age! Where y'all headed, Viv?" Tilly asked—though her eyes had not strayed once from studying Johnny

287

from head to toe. "And who's this handsome man strollin' along with ya?"

"We're headed into town," Vivianna said. It took every ounce of self-control Vivianna could muster simply to appear polite. She loathed Tilly Winder! She always had. And she did not like the way the girl smiled at Johnny. "This is Johnny Tabor. He's—"

"Oh!" Tilly interrupted. "I heard tell of you! You come home with Justin Turner, didn't ya?"

"Yes, ma'am," Johnny said.

"Well, I'm Tilly Winder," Tilly said. "But you can call me Tilly."

Vivianna studied Tilly quickly. Her copper-colored hair and green eyes looked as much like the devil's as she could imagine! Oh, certainly men were drawn to Tilly. After all, her appearance was so very striking—her manner so flirtatious and easy.

"I heard Caleb tellin' Benjamin Sidney about you," Tilly flirted. "Why haven't ya been into town yet, Mr. Tabor?" the girl asked.

"I'm headed on in now, Miss Winder," Johnny answered. "I'm seein' Miss Bartholomew safely on to her family home."

Tilly glanced to Vivianna at last. Her eyes were bright and wide with what Vivianna could only identify as pure wanton lust. "Well, my, my, my, Vivianna," Tilly said. "No wonder we ain't seen a breath of ya in months. I thought for sure

288

you and Justin woulda taken your vows by now. Mmm-mmm," Tilly added, her attention returning to Johnny. "But I certainly see what's keepin' ya from it."

"We don't have much time, Tilly," Vivianna lied. "If you'll excuse us, I've gotta to get over to the house. You have a nice day, ya hear?"

"Oh, I plan to, Vivianna," Tilly said. "I hope ya enjoy your visit to Florence, Mr. Tabor. If ever ya need anything . . . you just let me know."

"Yes, ma'am," Johnny said, taking hold of Vivianna's arm and gently urging her forward.

"Bye now, Vivianna!" Tilly called.

Vivianna would've still been unsettled if it hadn't been for Johnny's seeming desperation to put as much of the road between Tilly Winder and himself as he could. The look on his face was truly amusing!

"Most men just melt around Tilly Winder," she said. "But ya don't seem at all charmed by her."

Johnny scowled as he looked at her, still holding her arm, still urging her forward at a quickened pace. "Charmed? She plum makes my skin crawl!" he said.

Vivianna was delighted—so delighted that she pulled her arm from his grasp and took hold of his hand. She held his hand for just a moment, delirious at the sense of their mutual touch. The feel of his strong hand clasped to hers was too affecting, however, and she released his hand as they continued.

"What do you know about Caleb, Justin, and Tilly Winder, Johnny?" she asked.

"Um . . . I . . . I . . ." he stammered. She glanced up to him, delighted to see his cheeks were red.

"It's somethin' they told ya when y'all were soldierin' together, isn't it?" she teased him. "Ya weren't supposed to tell me . . . were ya?"

Johnny shook his head. "They were just boys when she went after 'em," he admitted. "Just boys . . . and it was before either one of 'em was in love with ya."

Vivianna should have been upset—jealous— even furious! However, she was surprised to find that she was not. Disgusted, but not jealous or angry. She felt more aggravation in the way Tilly had ogled Johnny than she did for the fact that Caleb and Justin were part of the long list of boys and men who had practiced kissing on Tilly Winder's instruction.

"I don't imagine there's an unmarried man in town over the age of eighteen or under the age of thirty that hasn't learned somethin' about kissin' from Tilly Winder," she said.

"I guess we're nearin' town," Johnny said. "Here comes somebody else. There's too much travelin' on this road, if ya ask me."

Vivianna looked up to see that someone else was indeed approaching—a man. She smiled, however, and said, "Oh! That's Mr. Maggee, Boy and Floydie's daddy. He's the nicest man in Florence." She looked to Johnny, and for some reason, he seemed to catch her enthusiasm. "He'll want to meet you . . . bein' that you knew his boys and all."

Taking Johnny's hand once more, she tugged him forward as she called, "Mr. Maggee! Good mornin'!"

"Why, Vivianna Bartholomew! I haven't seen you in quite some time," Mr. Maggee greeted.

"This is Johnny Tabor, Mr. Maggee," Vivianna explained, dropping her hold of Johnny's hand and nodding toward him. "He was in the Alabama First with Boy and Floydie."

Instantly, Mr. Maggee's blue eyes misted, his mouth quivering even as he smiled. "My boy," he greeted, offering a hand to Johnny.

Johnny accepted his hand, and Vivianna watched, tenderhearted as Mr. Maggee seemed to rather cling to it.

"I've heard of you, Johnny Tabor," the older man said. Vivianna noted that Mr. Maggee's hair had more silver than brown now. It seemed he'd aged a decade since losing his boys.

"From Caleb and Justin?" Johnny asked.

But Mr. Maggee shook his head. "No. From my boys . . . from Floydie and Boy. It seems ya saved their hides more'n once over."

"I can't rightly say, sir . . . but it sure is nice to

291

meet the father of two such fine soldiers as your boys were," Johnny said.

"Johnny Tabor," Mr. Maggee said, still holding tightly to Johnny's hand, "I hear you and Justin Turner did a spell at Andersonville."

"Yes, sir, Mr. Maggee," Johnny said. "But we come out of it fine."

Mr. Maggee released Johnny's hand at last. Vivianna felt as if she might begin weeping, for as Mr. Maggee continued to gaze at Johnny, his eyes filled with moisture and emotion.

"Well, don't you let anybody ever disrespect you, boy," Mr. Maggee said. "You and them Turner boys . . . and my own boys . . . y'all did the right thing. Don't ya let anybody tell ya different, and don't ya let anybody ever disrespect ya or what ya done in fightin' for the Union. Do ya hear me?"

"Yes, sir," Johnny said, smiling.

"Good. Good," Mr. Maggee said. He looked to Vivianna then. "I'm on my way out to the Turner place to see my boys this very mornin', Vivianna. I hope that's all right."

Vivianna smiled. "Of course it's all right, Mr. Maggee. Miss Savannah already told ya that ya don't have to ask permission to go to the cemetery."

"I know, I know," he said. "I just always feel like I should let somebody know."

"Well, that's because you're a gentleman," Vivianna replied.

"Well, thank ya, Vivianna. Thank ya." Mr. Maggee chuckled. "I seen ol' Tilly Winder on the road ahead of me. Figure I better hang back a bit. I may be old, but I hear tell she ain't too particular who she sparks with these days . . . and I don't wanna find myself in trouble with her daddy."

Vivianna giggled. She bit her lip, however, knowing she shouldn't find mirth in such an implication.

Johnny chuckled as Mr. Maggee winked and said, "I'm only teasin', boy." Mr. Maggee wagged an index finger at Johnny and added, "But you stay clear of ol' Tilly. I bet she'd give her hind teeth to get ya alone for a minute or two."

"She ain't the kind of girl I look once at, Mr. Maggee . . . let alone twice," Johnny said.

"Good," Mr. Maggee chuckled. "Well, I'm off to visit my boys. You two enjoy the day."

"Thank ya, Mr. Maggee. You enjoy your visit now," Vivianna said. "And stop in and see Miss Savannah. She's home all alone with Nate and Willy today. She's probably pullin' her hair out by now."

Mr. Maggee chuckled. "Oh, I imagine that she is. I'll stop in on her then. Bye now. It was a real honor to meet ya, Johnny. A real honor."

"You too, sir," Johnny said, shaking the man's hand once more.

Vivianna watched as Mr. Maggee continued

293

down the road. He was whistling—whistling "When Johnny Comes Marching Home."

"That poor man," Vivianna whispered as she watched him go.

"He had a couple of good boys," Johnny said. "Real good boys."

Vivianna quickly glanced to Johnny. She'd noted the change in his voice. Meeting Mr. Maggee had brought the war to the front of his mind—caused a sad melancholy to begin to overtake him. She didn't want him to know pain or sadness. It was a beautiful day, and the war was ended. She wanted him to forget the horrors of it for a time and simply know peace of mind.

Furthermore, Vivianna didn't want to end up meeting anyone else along the way. She was on a mission—a mission to free her mind and heart. Besides, she didn't want to share her traveling companion. She owned an odd sense of wanting to keep Johnny's attention all to herself. "How do ya feel about takin' a shorter route to my parents' home . . . even if it's not so smooth as the road to town?" she asked.

Johnny looked to her and grinned. "I could do with a few less folks this mornin'," he said.

"Then come with me," she said. Taking his hand, she led him off the road and onto a small path winding through the trees. "This is the way Sam and Augie and I used to come when we were meetin' up with Caleb and Justin," she explained.

"It leads to the back of our house. Folks in town won't even know we've been there."

Vivianna's heart began to race. Home—it was just a ways more—just through the next little grove of trees and shrubbery! And then they were there. Vivianna stepped out from the tree line and into the open space behind her family home. Her heart swelled with sudden joy! The back of the Bartholomew house loomed before them. Her mother's wisteria had nearly taken over the grand gazebo nearby, and it seemed all the grasses and shrubbery were wild and rather lonesome.

"There it is," she breathed. "This is my home."

"It's awful big," Johnny mumbled as he walked past her and stepped up into the grand gazebo.

"I suppose," Vivianna whispered. "But isn't it beautiful?" Oh, it was beautiful! Perhaps the folks in Florence thought as Johnny did—that the Bartholomew house was grand and glorious. But to Vivianna, it was simply home.

As Vivianna started toward the house—as she gazed up into the windows reflecting the brilliance of the morning sun—such a feeling of home and family came over her that she sighed with momentary joy. Though she knew it was not so, she imagined her mother waited inside, tending to her needlework, while her father made ready to pay a visit to one of his patients. In those brief moments, Vivianna mused that she could almost believe there'd never been a war.

War. Vivianna felt her own smile fading. Suddenly it seemed as if the happy sun dimmed, as if a great veil of melancholy had been suddenly drawn over her eyes. She tried to fight the dark and lonely feeling welling up inside her. But somehow—for some reason—the moment was no longer bright and cheerful. The memory of war was washing over her—the inward acknowledgement of such great loss.

Vivianna closed her eyes, inhaled a deep breath, attempted to ward off the vision of her mother's face, of her father's smile, of Sam and Augustus's mirthful laughter. Yet it was too late. Suddenly awash in memory, mourning, and anguish, Vivianna opened her eyes—turned from the view that seemed so happy a moment before. It brought only misery—misery in loss and loneliness. Oh, certainly she was not alone—not with the Turners as her friends and surrogate family. Yet in that moment, Vivianna Bartholomew felt more alone than she ever had before. It was as if the war and the loss of her family—as if the pain of all that was lost—were heaped upon her in one horrid moment of true realization.

Though she could not fathom why it was her heart and mind had chosen this moment to face the certainty of life without her family—chosen that very breath to whisper to her that once she married, her family's branch of the Bartholomew name would cease to continue—still, they had chosen this moment to speak to her, and her joy was lost. She no longer imagined her mother tending to her needlework—no longer imagined her father preparing to leave the house. They were gone! Her mother, her father, her beloved brothers! All that made this house her home was gone. She was orphaned and alone; it was all she knew in that moment.

At once her cheeks were washed in tears. So violently did she tremble, with such overwhelming fear and despair, sadness, and misery, that she found she had to gasp for breath. In those moments—as she stood gazing up at her once beloved home—she felt she might die, drop dead of the pain so thoroughgoing through her! She wanted to feel her father's arms about her, wanted Sam to tease her about her freckles, wanted Augustus to push her into the pond, pleaded with heaven that she should open her eyes to see her mother waiting, arms flung wide, in an offering of tender embrace. But they were gone—all of them! It would be in another life that she would meet with them once more, and the knowledge wrought such a pain over her as to cause her to again gasp. She was certain she would die, or at least faint into darkness.

A dizziness began to overtake her—the dizziness that often accompanied collapse. Her knees weakened, and she forced herself to draw breath as tears streamed over her face.

"I cannot endure this!" she prayed in a whisper. "I cannot live so alone!"

Vivianna closed her eyes a moment, willing her heart to continue to beat, struggling to find reason and hope, but there came none into her mind.

Then—at last—she opened her eyes. Johnny Tabor stepped out of the gazebo, hunkered down, and ran one hand over the tall grass.

"Johnny," Vivianna whispered.

Johnny Tabor knew pain; Johnny Tabor knew despair. Though she did not know the reason for his occasional bath of sorrow, she knew he suffered—perhaps as she was now suffering. Yet Johnny Tabor did not die; no, he lived. Even after war and loss, even after Andersonville and the long road home he yet traveled, Johnny continued—trudged onward. Vivianna knew then: it was Johnny who would know her pain, Johnny who might teach her how to survive it.

Vivianna did not know how her legs carried her, for her entire body was weak with sudden mourning and despair. Yet, somehow, she moved toward him. Somehow she took one step—then another—and with each step toward him, she did not feel further despairing but rather further desperation. She must reach him—be with him. If she could just reach Johnny—Johnny, who was only a short distance from her—if she could reach him, she might find some hope in enduring.

He heard her approach, stood, frowned, and started toward her. "Vivianna?" he asked, concern overtaking him. "What's the matter?" he asked, setting the box of Justin's letters in the grass and reaching out to take her by the shoulders.

Vivianna shook her head and stepped back from him. She held up one dainty hand and tossed an indifferent wave. "Oh, nothin' too awful," she lied, tears streaming down her face. "I-I was just . . . I know ya own pain, Johnny," she continued. "I don't know just what causes ya to hurt . . . though I know ya've seen enough misery to make anybody's nights restless with bad dreams. But . . . but I was just wonderin' . . . how do ya . . . how do ya just keep goin', Johnny? Whatever it is that chases your smile away sometimes . . . ya just seem to fight it off. How?"

"Vivi," he began. He took another step toward her, and she took another step back.

Her mind was aching; her heart was breaking! She did not want to tell him of her pain—didn't want to heap any more pain on him. Yet she felt compelled to do so—felt as if the only way she could overcome the sudden, miserable despair was in telling him.

"I'm . . . I'm all by myself, Johnny!" Vivianna cried in a whisper. She glanced about to ensure no one else was nearby. She knew no one would be near—who would possibly be near the old, empty Bartholomew house? Still, Vivianna had kept such a tight hold on her emotions. For months she'd held them still; for years she'd kept them buried. Yet they were surfacing. They'd begun to surface the moment Johnny Tabor had kissed her beneath the honeysuckle vine. He'd turned some sort of unseen key deep within her—begun to unlock her soul. Yet now—now as she stood overwhelmed by loss and despair—she was too frightened to release her imprisoned emotions. She feared that doing so might destroy her somehow, that she might cease to exist—simply vanish. Yet as Johnny reached out, carefully taking hold of her hand, the prison door swung wide, and Vivianna's passions were freed.

"They're gone! My family! My whole family, Johnny! I-I think I might not manage it! I'm so afraid I might simply . . ."

He reached for her then, his strong arms drawing her into a safe and powerful embrace. In the next moment, she was sobbing against the softness of his shirt—against the firm muscles of his chest beneath. Frantically she clung to him—clutched the cloth of the back of his shirt in her trembling fists.

"Why now?" she begged in a whisper. "Why this moment? The war is over. Everyone is so happy. It's been so long since they were taken from me. Why can't I . . . I can't . . . I can't . . ."

She felt him sigh as he rested his chin on the top of her head, burying a hand in her hair. She clung even more desperately to him, as if releasing him would find her in some suffocating darkness.

"You haven't mourned them, Vivi," he said. His voice was strong yet soothing. It was deep—rich and comforting. "I've watched ya all this time . . . wondered why ya keep from mournin'. Ya keep your pain locked away, just like a soldier keeps it locked away. The war is over, Vivi, but ya've been fightin' so long, fightin' same as any Johnny Reb or Yankee . . . longer than some. And today . . . today the fight is finally over for ya, and ya need to mourn now. You're knowin' your own soldier's grief . . . the grief every soldier knows when the fightin' ends, when he's finally stretched out on his bedroll one night and realizes all he's lost . . . all that's been stolen from him. I know that grief. I know that pain. Ya haven't let yourself think about it before. Ya haven't let your heart admit it. You were too busy survivin' 'til now."

He took her face between his hands. She tried to look away, embarrassed by her weakness and knowing her face was red and tear-streaked. But he gently forced her to look at him.

"Ya need to grieve, Vivi," he softly told her. "Ya need to admit they're gone. Ya need to mourn them proper. Ya've bottled it all up for so long—all your pain and fear. I think ya put all your hopes in Justin's letters . . . tried to ignore anything else . . . hoped that Justin would come home and somehow everything would be all right. But it won't, Vivi. You're realizin' that now, and ya need to let go of all you've been holdin' onto so tight."

Vivianna shook her head, tears streaming down her face.

"They're gone, Vivi," he told her. "Let it hurt. If ya don't, you'll never be your whole self again. Ya ain't cold and heartless like some. You're warm and lovin', beautiful and passionate. Know your pain, Vivi . . . or you'll never know true joy again."

Still, Vivianna shook her head. "If I let it . . . if I let the pain in . . . it'll never leave, Johnny! It's all I'll ever know. If I let it take me . . . I'll be lost to it."

"No," he said. "No. You'll only be lost if ya don't face it."

"There'll only be the pain, Johnny," she whispered.

"No. Lettin' go will free ya, Vivi . . . just like puttin' these letters away will free ya. If ya face your losses, know the pain, and work your way through it, joy will come to you. A body can even know joy and pain together . . . but not if ya don't let yourself feel one. The other can't break through."

"Joy and pain . . . together?" she gasped. She shook her head. "No."

He forced her to look at him once more. "I promise ya, Vivi," he said. "You can know joy even for the hurt pain brings. I know it to be true. I promise you it's true. I've known it . . . so much pain I thought I might die. Yet at the same time, a joy that carried me through. I promise ya."

"Not for me, Johnny," she sobbed. "Don't make me a promise you can't keep. Maybe promises don't mean much to me anymore . . . but I beg, please don't make one you can't keep."

His eyes narrowed, and he released her face. "I can keep it," he growled. "I can prove to you that you can know joy . . . even for the pain you're feelin' over losin' your family."

Vivianna shook her head. "No."

Johnny nodded. "Oh yes, Vivianna. I promise."

Vivianna gasped—breathless as Johnny reached out and took her face between his hands—firmly pressed his mouth to hers.

"Kiss me, Vivi," he mumbled. "Kiss me, and I promise you that you'll know joy even for your pain."

Again he took her tremulous lips in a moist, lingering kiss. Their lips separated, but his mouth remained close—so close she could taste the warm scent of his breath. An airy thrill wafted through her heart for a moment—the lingering remnant of the joy his kiss had caused to spark within her.

"You promise, Johnny?" she asked in a whisper. "Do ya promise I'll know joy too . . . even just for one more minute?" she cried in a whisper.

"I do," he breathed.

Vivianna sighed as Johnny's lips met hers again. He kissed her softly at first, rather as if he didn't quite believe she wanted him to kiss her.

"Please, Johnny," she breathed against his mouth.

He brushed the tears from her cheeks, cupping her face between powerful hands as his mouth descended to hers once more—his open mouth—his moist, demanding, heated mouth.

Vivianna was startled at first. His manner of kissing her was unlike anything she'd ever before experienced—heated, intimate, and drawing from her a sudden and overwhelming desire. She slid her hands to his chest, over his broad shoulders, around to the back of his neck, letting her fingers travel up to be lost in the softness of his hair. His hands dropped from her face, his arms encircling her body once more as he pulled her flush to him—his mouth conducting such a passion of moist exchange Vivianna could hardly draw breath!

Colors were alive in her mind, blissful sensations erupted through her body, and she wished his mouth would never leave hers! She sensed the freshness of the morning breeze, the scent of flowers and grass. Her skin was alive with delight at his touch, her sudden thirst for his continued kiss insatiable!

Johnny's heart was locked in an epic battle of emotions! He owned her mouth—the very mouth he'd so long dreamt of tasting. He was drinking of its nectar! The feel of her body against his— of his arms wrapped around her—like a madman it drove him to kissing her more deeply, more demandingly! Yet she met his kiss with no resistance. In fact, she kissed him with as much desire and passion— or so it seemed. He knew she only kissed him in endeavoring to find comfort and distraction from her pain. Still, he wanted her. She was all he had ever wanted, it seemed, and if she wanted him for even this moment— no matter the reason—he would not deny himself the nectar of heaven.

Vivianna was a novice of passion. It had been obvious when he'd first tried to coax her into a deepening kiss beneath the honeysuckle vine. No man had ever kissed her the way he was kissing her now; he could tell as much, and he was pleased. Johnny was glad it was he who had first tasted her sweet mouth, he who had silently tutored her in the ways of impassioned kissing. No matter who won her for wife—Justin or Caleb—the imp on Johnny Tabor's shoulder affirmed to him that he had known Vivianna's mouth first. At least he would have that to carry with him back to Texas.

His innards began to tremble with too much withheld desire—too much pent-up emotion. Yet he continued to kiss her. He would not give her up—not until Vivianna was finished with him. He didn't care if she were using him to mask her pain. He didn't care if he died in trying to breathe hope and life into her with a kiss, didn't care if his very soul expired or passed from his body into hers—not if it meant he could soothe her with a measure of comfort, if it meant he could taste her for one moment more.

Tears streamed over Vivianna's cheeks. Tears of pain, yes, but also tears of splendorous joy! Johnny had kept his promise. Vivianna's heart was breaking for the sudden accepted loss of her family, yet she was captivated by the ecstasy of knowing Johnny's kiss. One moment her heart would cry out in agony, thoughts of her brothers and her parents causing so much pain to grip her she was certain she might die. Yet in the next moment, Johnny's mouth would return to hers— hot and demanding, weaving such a tapestry of passion and desire as to cause her heart to leap with resplendent elation! His arms about her caused her body to prickle with goose pimples. The heated flavor of his mouth caused her to wonder if she could ever cease in kissing him!

Her parents and her brothers were gone. Yet Johnny was there, in her arms, making love to her as she'd never imagined! His mouth left hers a moment, placing firm, moist kisses on her throat.

It was too much, the joy mingled with pain. In an instant, the walls of the prison surrounding Vivianna's emotions crumbled. She began to gasp for breath, for her heart beat madly—hammered with an abrupt understanding that her family was gone, thrashed with a rushed awareness that she was in love with Johnny Tabor!

"Johnny!" she gasped. She felt his arms tighten—felt him catch her—lift and cradle her in his arms as she was lost to sudden darkness.

CHAPTER TWELVE

Everything was dark—no light. Yet there was a voice—in the distance there was a voice. Gradually the voice drew nearer. It was Johnny's voice. Vivianna could hear Johnny Tabor calling her name.

"Vivi," Johnny said. "Come on now. Breathe deeply. Open your eyes. Come on."

Consciousness slowly returned, and Vivianna opened her eyes to see Johnny's handsome face near to her own.

"Johnny?" she breathed.

He smiled and nodded. "Yeah, darlin'. Now come on back to me."

"What happened?" she asked, feeling rather breathless—still dizzy and disoriented.

Johnny smiled. He caressed her cheek with the back of one strong hand. "I guess I smothered you with too much manly desire."

Vivianna smiled. She did remember his kiss—the ecstasy that had erupted within her because of it. She breathed a giggle and said, "You were tryin' to lead me astray, Johnny Tabor. And I guess . . . I guess I'm not too good at resistin' ya."

He smiled—smoothed the hair from her forehead.

Vivianna frowned as she noticed the heaviness of the air. The scent of dust caused her to want to cough a bit. She turned her head and glanced beyond Johnny to see that she was no longer outside but rather in a room—a parlor—her mother's parlor.

Instantly, pain began to wash over her. She felt her eyes fill with tears. She was home, lying on the chaise lounge in her mother's parlor. As her heart began to break once more, she looked back to Johnny.

"Johnny!" she whispered, panic rising in her. She did not want to know the pain again! She did not! She shook her head—took Johnny's face between her hands. As tears filled her eyes, she began to gasp for breath. "Help me, Johnny!" she begged in a whisper. She could feel unconsciousness threatening to overtake her once more.

"Vivi," Johnny said, taking one of her hands from his face and kissing the palm. "Listen to me." He kissed her lightly on the lips—tenderly. He brushed his lips to her cheek and whispered, "Breathe, Vivi. I'm here . . . and you'll be fine. Just breathe."

Vivianna endeavored to do as Johnny instructed. She didn't try to move—just lay there on her mother's chaise as Johnny placed warm, moist kisses to her cheeks and the corners of her mouth. He pressed his mouth to hers—soothingly—

lingeringly. Softly the moisture of their kisses blended, and as he held her face between his hands, he gently wiped the tears from her temples with his thumbs.

She was somewhat soothed. At least she no longer felt a faint coming over her.

When he paused in his careful kisses, his eyes gazed into hers. She fancied there was moisture in them—saw her own sadness reflected in their deep brown.

"Tell me about Sam and Augie," he said. His voice was low and calming.

Vivianna felt her lower lip begin to quiver and felt the desire to sob rising in her throat. She shook her head a little, afraid to speak.

But Johnny nodded and prodded, "Tell me . . . was Augie older? Or Sam?"

"Samuel," Vivianna whispered. Johnny nodded, and she continued, "Sam was the oldest . . . one year older than Augie. I . . . I was three and four years younger than they were."

Johnny smiled. "How about your daddy?" he asked. "Was he a kind man?"

Vivianna swallowed the lump of pain in her throat. She nodded and answered, "Yes. He was . . . he was a doctor."

"And your mama?"

"She was . . . she was always smilin' . . . always laughin'," Vivianna breathed. She sniffled, and more tears escaped her eyes. The frightening sense of panic began to rise in her again. She began to tremble. "Johnny! Johnny, I—"

His mouth was warm and moist against hers. His powerful arms embraced her, lifting her to a sitting position as he continued to kneel beside the lounge. Butterflies of bliss mingled with the aching pain in her stomach. He deepened their kiss, offering delicious affection until the panic began to subside.

He broke the seal of their lips yet continued to hold her against him. Vivianna buried her face against his neck and shoulder, careless that her tears were soaking his shirt.

"Did you always live here?" he asked. "Were ya born in this house, Vivi?"

She nodded. "Yes," she breathed. His neck was warm, and he smelled like woodsmoke and fresh air.

"Were ya happy as a child?" he whispered.

Again she nodded—breathed, "Yes!"

"Share a memory with me, Vivianna . . . a happy memory. Tell me of a time when y'all were together . . . laughin' maybe," he said. His voice was deep and resonated with tranquil reassurance.

Vivianna shook her head. "I . . . I can't think of one just now, Johnny. I can't think."

"Yes, ya can," he told her. His breath was warm and tickled her ear. "Tell me a story of your family."

311

Vivianna shook her head. Yet in the next moment a memory did enter her mind. She wept a moment more before beginning. "A wasp got into the kitchen once," she began. "Mama hated bees and wasps . . . anything with a stinger on it."

"Mmm-hmm," Johnny urged.

Vivianna tightened her embrace of Johnny, holding him closer—more desperately.

"Go on," he prodded.

"We were . . . Mama and I were bakin' peach pies, and a wasp got in through the window. It landed on Mama's hand, and she started screamin' and dancin' around like it had flown up her skirt instead of landing on her hand." Vivianna closed her eyes. A slight smile curved her mouth as she envisioned her mother dancing around the kitchen, shrieking for her daddy to come and save her from the wasp.

"What next?" Johnny prodded.

"Augustus came runnin' into the kitchen . . . but I'd dropped a peach skin, and he slipped on it," she continued. "His feet went out from under him, and he landed smack on his backside, just as Sam came runnin' in. Samuel tripped over Augie and landed on his backside too. Mama was still screamin' like a madwoman when Daddy came in and tripped over the boys. Daddy didn't fall . . . but he stumbled forward and caught hold of the edge of the table." Vivianna smiled at the visions frolicking in her mind. "But the table couldn't hold him up, and he tipped it, sending peaches and pies flyin' every which way up into the air. Mama was still screamin' and swattin' at the wasp with a towel. The pies and peaches went all over the floor when they come down . . . and I slipped when I was rushin' to help Mama. I don't think I've ever fallen down so hard in all my life! So there we were . . . Sam and Augie . . . me and Daddy . . . sittin' on the kitchen floor covered in peaches and sugar . . . watchin' Mama get out after that wasp."

Vivianna couldn't help but smile, even for the emotions causing her lips to quiver. She drew away from Johnny—brushed the tears from her eyes. He cupped her chin, running one callused thumb over her lips. She looked at him—smiled as he grinned with understanding and encouragement.

"Did she finally get that ol' wasp?" he asked.

Vivianna nodded and smiled. "It was silly enough to land on the floor . . . and to this day, I can see her grinding that wasp into the floor with the heel of her shoe. We all started laughin', and Daddy pulled Mama down onto the floor with us." Vivianna giggled a little. "One pie had somehow survived fallin' and was still in the plate . . . and Daddy took hold of it and dumped it right over Mama's head. We laughed until we were sick. I swear we did. It took us near to two hours to clean up the mess."

"It's a good memory," Johnny said.

"Yes," Vivianna whispered—though her lip began to quiver once more.

Johnny reached out, gathering her into his arms again. His kiss was more demanding when he kissed her this time. Vivianna sighed as she melted against him—savored the moist heat of his kiss. Tears still streamed over her cheeks. Yet with beautiful wings of desire, the butterflies in her stomach began to beat away the pain. Vivianna wrapped her arms around Johnny's neck—let her fingers weave through his soft brown hair as she kissed him. She felt his hands at her back—felt them move to her waist as he gently guided her body to lean back in the chaise once more.

He broke from her, his breathing labored and unsteady. "Vivianna . . . I . . . I . . ." he stammered. His eyes were filled with emotion, brimming with moisture. Vivianna could see her reflection in them, and she knew he too somehow bore her pain.

She reached out, taking his face in her hands and pulling his mouth to hers. She could not quench her thirst for his kiss! She wanted to bathe forever in the heated passion he stirred in her. He kissed her hard—near to violently—as if he could not quench his own thirst.

Suddenly he broke the seal of their lips, however. Taking her face in his hands, he gazed at her. "Love never dies, Vivi," he told her. "As long as you continue to let your heart feel joy and pain . . . to miss them and remember . . . they'll never be lost to you."

Vivianna nodded. She brushed the tears from her cheeks, even though more followed.

"I'll run on out and get that box of letters," Johnny said. "Then we'll take it up to the attic for ya, and you can show me around your family's home. How would that be?"

Vivianna sniffled and breathed a giggle as Johnny pulled a handkerchief out of his pocket and handed it to her.

"Don't worry," he said, grinning. "It's clean."

"Thank you, Johnny," she said, dabbing at her tears and then her nose. She shook her head and added, "I'm sure I'm completely melted for the rest of the day."

"And that's all right," he assured her. "Now you just sit here. I'll be right back." He stood and reached into the front pocket of his trousers, withdrawing a key. Offering the key toward her, he said, "I found this in your skirt pocket. I let us in. I hope that's all right."

"Of course," she said, taking the key from him and dropping it back into her skirt pocket. She thought for a moment that, after over a year of carrying Justin's letter in her pocket, it was strange not to feel it there when she slipped the key in.

"I'll be right back," he said.

Vivianna watched him leave the house by way of the back parlor door. She stood from the chaise and watched him through the window. Johnny hurried to the place where they'd been standing when first Vivianna's emotions had begun to boil over. Oddly, she remembered his kiss more than her pain. Johnny Tabor had been right. A body could know joy, even for overwhelming heartache. As she watched him hunker down in the grass and retrieve the box containing Justin's letters—as she watched him saunter toward her in returning—she thought of his strength, of his exceptional understanding of her need to mourn. How could he be so wise? Surely the fighting, Andersonville, and all the horror of war had given him experience to draw from. She shivered with wondering what terrible things he'd endured—what loss he'd known. She thought of the day Johnny had told Nate and Willy of burning the lice from his body. Yet unimaginably miserable as it was, it did not explain his understanding of Vivianna's having struggled against her emotions. Was he simply a man who owned a sense of reading a soul?

She watched him move closer—thought he was the most attractive man she had ever seen. Even now she wanted to kiss him—wanted to linger in his powerful arms. She was in love with Johnny. The revelation had come to her even as the acceptance of her family's loss had come to her. Yet it seemed impossible! How could she be in love with a stranger? She'd known him mere months! She'd known Justin for years—all her life—yet Justin no longer owned her heart. Certainly he would always linger in it, for one did not love so deeply and entirely and forget such a love. Yet in that moment—as she watched Johnny Tabor enter the house and offer the box containing Justin's letters to her—she knew that somehow she had fallen in love with him.

Vivianna paused in accepting the letters, distracted by wondering what Johnny would think if he knew she loved him. Surely he would think her as fickle a girl as she thought Tilly Winder was. Hadn't he brought Justin home to claim Vivianna's heart? Yet she sensed even Johnny had changed his mind about Justin. He would not kiss her so passionately otherwise. He would not kiss her at all otherwise. Johnny was nothing if not loyal; this she had observed for herself. Why then did he play at kissing the woman he meant his best friend to marry unless he'd changed his opinion of the man?

"Here," Johnny said, still offering the box to her. "Do ya still want to leave them behind?"

Vivianna fancied Johnny looked worried in that moment—as if he feared she might say she'd chosen to keep them instead of hiding them away.

"Yes," she said, accepting the box from him.

And she did want to leave them—now more than ever. "Come with me, Johnny," she said. "Come with me, and I'll show you the attic. I'll show the entire house to you if ya like."

He nodded. "Are you . . . are ya all right, Vivianna?" he asked.

Instantly, tears flooded her cheeks. Still, she answered, "I will be."

He sighed and seemed relieved. "All right then," he said. "Let's see to them letters."

⁖

Vivianna did put away Justin's letters. She tucked them safely in the bottom of one of her mother's trunks. Furthermore, she escorted Johnny throughout the Bartholomew family home—throughout her home. She led him through every room, even the one that had been hers as a child. As she wandered through the house, she felt as if she were indeed beginning to heal. Oh, certainly she wept near constantly. Yet she did not feel afraid to touch her mother's things, to look on the photographs of Sam and Augie. Her father's doctor's bag seemed a sentimental piece, not something to dread peering into any longer. Her pain was profound—excruciating at times. Yet Johnny had shown Vivianna that she could still know joy, and knowing such a thing was true helped Vivianna to know joy even in reminiscing—even for the heartache in her.

She even lingered alone awhile in her home. Johnny wanted to look in at the railroad office— wanted to inquire about earning wages. Thus, he'd suggested Vivianna take the time to sit or wander through the house—to be alone with her memories and her mourning. This she did— weeping one moment, smiling the next—and it was such a healing thing that she could not fathom it at first. Yet she did know it. The longer she wandered, trading tears for smiles, she did know that joy could still be had in life. Her emotions—held so tightly and deep inside her for so long—had broken free. Johnny had freed them, and Vivianna knew her true and full self again at last.

Johnny returned from the railroad office to announce he'd secured work. The next Monday morning, he would accompany Caleb and Justin to town and begin earning a good wage. He explained to Vivianna that he was told the labor would be hard, but he was not averse to hard labor.

As the sun hung high in the center of the sky, Vivianna locked the great bolt securing one of the back doors to her family home. She and Johnny had decided to leave the way they had come, without a living soul having seen them. They would walk the smaller path all the way home— avoid the road and any unwanted conversation. Vivianna's emotions were still ripe; she still found tears easily upon her cheeks, and she did not wish to endure Tilly Winder or anyone else's company—only Johnny's.

As they walked the long path leading from the Bartholomew home to the Turner one, they didn't speak of Vivianna's family, nor did they speak of the passion that had flamed between them. Simply they spoke of the weather, of Nate and Willy and their antics, of Caleb and his goodness. They spoke of nothing of any deep consequence.

Until, at last, Vivianna's curiosity grew too swollen to contain.

As she and Johnny wandered through a small grove of dogwoods, she began, "Justin says you saved his life . . . on more than one occasion. Yet you always maintain that he saved yours, Johnny. How did Justin save your life?" She shrugged and added, "I assume it was at Andersonville that you saved his . . . but how did he save yours?"

She glanced to Johnny then and fancied he'd paled slightly. Still, he responded.

"I was . . . I was wounded," he began. "You've seen the scar low on my back?"

Vivianna nodded. Oh, she'd seen the dark, deep scar many times. Though her attention was more often drawn to Johnny's impressive musculature when he was working without a shirt, she had studied the scar as well.

"I was matchin' sabers with a Reb . . . when another Reb come up behind me and near sliced me in two," he explained. "It was Caleb who cleaned the wound and stitched me up. So I guess I owe Caleb near as much as I do Justin." He paused, an expression of hurt or worry puckering his handsome brow. She regretted asking him abut his debt to Justin. She could see it caused him pain.

"You don't have to tell me, Johnny," she said. "I shouldn't have asked ya. It's in the past. I understand that."

He shook his head and simply said, "I was in so much pain . . . both body and mind. I'd been wounded so many times before . . . didn't think I could stand such a wound as that saber left on me. I was driftin' in and out of wakefulness . . . kept thinkin' I saw Death comin' for me. I've never known despair the likes I knew at that time. Even in Andersonville." He looked to her and forced a smile. Shrugging broad shoulders, he said, "Then Justin . . . well, Justin . . . he . . . he, uh . . ."

"There you are!" Willy exclaimed.

Vivianna startled—glanced ahead up the path to see Willy running toward them.

"Where have you two been?" he asked. "We've been waitin' forever! That boy's been beside himself with askin' when you'd be home, Johnny."

"What?" Johnny asked.

Willy shook his head with exasperation. "That

boy! That Lowell boy. He turned up on the front porch a couple of hours ago. Mama's fed him about everything she can . . . and I swear, he talks more'n any girl I ever know'd."

"Lowell?" Johnny breathed. "A little feller? 'Bout so high?" he asked, holding a hand out at his waist.

Willy nodded. "That's him. I swear he looked just like he was wearin' a pumpkin on his head when he arrived. Mama's already trimmed him up, poor feller." Willy frowned and added, "Still, I think he's a liar. He said he was soldierin' with you and Justin before y'all were captured by the Rebs. Yep . . . he's a liar."

But Johnny shook his head and said, "No, he ain't a liar, Will. He was found wanderin' in the woods . . . and we didn't have nobody to give him to. So we kept him in camp with us. I can't believe he found his way here!"

Willy shrugged. "He said some feller rode him over in the back of a wagon. He said the feller dropped him off at Rogersville, and he's been walkin' the rest of the way. Said he's been walkin' for a few days."

Johnny chuckled—laughed with disbelief and amusement. "Why, that little badger. I can't believe it!"

Vivianna smiled. She remembered Lowell, the boy Justin had found in the woods in Georgia. Justin had written to her that he'd given Lowell instructions to find the Turner family. It seems the boy had taken Justin's instructions to heart.

"Come on, Vivi," Johnny said, taking her hand. "Nothin' can cheer a body up quicker than Lowell Wheeler."

As Johnny began to lead her more quickly down the path, Willy looked up at her, frowning.

"You all right, Viv?" he asked. "You look like ya been cryin'."

"I'm fine, Willy," Vivianna explained. "I've just been to my old house . . . just missin' my family, that's all."

Willy simultaneously smiled and frowned. He took her free hand, squeezing it with affection as they walked. "Don't worry, Viv. You got me and Nate . . . and Caleb and Justin. We'll take good care of ya."

"I know you will," Vivianna said, smiling at him. "You always have."

◈

Vivianna Bartholomew had never seen the likes of little Lowell Wheeler. Pumpkin-haired and sapphire-eyed, Lowell looked like just a bundle of mischief waiting to burst into pure naughtiness. He sat on a chair at the table, enjoying a piece of Savannah's cherry pie.

"Mr. Johnny!" Lowell hollered as Willy, Johnny, and Vivianna stepped into the kitchen. "Oh, Mr. Johnny!" Leaping from the chair he'd been sitting on, Lowell ran headlong to Johnny. Vivianna smiled as Johnny dropped to his knees and caught the boy in a tight embrace.

"Lowell!" Johnny chuckled. "Boy, how did you find us?"

"I knew just where to look," Lowell answered. "It took me a time to get here, Mr. Johnny," the boy said, still hugging Johnny. "They put me in an orphanage after the war . . . and I had to escape. It weren't easy, but I done it! Then I had to catch me a ride here and there. I couldn't walk all the way."

Lowell loosened his tight hug on Johnny's neck, leaned back, and sighed. "I was worried y'all were dead. We heard they took y'all to Andersonville. Everybody said nobody could live through Andersonville. All the other kids at the orphanage . . . they said you and Justin were dead, rottin' in the Georgia ground over at Andersonville. But I know ya too well. I know y'all couldn't be licked, even by such a place. So I up and run off from the orphanage a few weeks back . . . and made my way here."

Johnny shook his head with utter disbelief. "But . . . but, Lowell, who cared for ya? What did ya find to eat?" he asked.

Lowell shrugged. "Oh, berries and such," he answered. "Whenever I'd hit a town or a farm, I'd just make myself a pair of puppy-dog eyes and beg for food and whatever else I needed."

"Puppy-dog eyes?" Nate grumbled.

"Yeah," Lowell said, releasing Johnny and looking to Nate. "You probably do your eyes that way when you want somethin' from your mama. Like this . . ."

Vivianna giggled as she watched Lowell's eyes widen—watched his young eyebrows rise in a manner of pleading. Savannah laughed as Willy and Nate looked on in bewilderment.

"Then ya add a sorry little voice," Lowell explained. "Maybe say something like, 'If only I had me a little hunk a cheese. Oh, I ain't had cheese since the war begun.' Then ya shake your head pitiful like." Lowell shook his head as if despairing. "It helps if ya add in a cough or two and tear your eyes right up." Lowell put a trembling fist to his mouth and coughed weakly. Vivianna's mouth dropped open in astonishment as his puppy-dog eyes then misted with excess moisture. "Oh, if only I could taste cheese . . . just one more time before I head to the arms of the Lord."

Johnny chuckled and shook his head with something akin to admiration. "You see what I mean?" he asked Vivianna.

Suddenly, Nate smiled—Willy too.

"That's real good, Lowell," Nate said. "Did ya get plenty of cheese that way?"

Lowell nodded. "Cheese, bread . . . even got me a half a cake once doin' it." Lowell's smile faded, his freckled face taking on a rather instructional expression. "Of course, I only done it in real times of need. I wouldn't want to use my puppy-dog eyes just 'cause I can, you understand."

"Of course not," Nate agreed. "It wouldn't be right."

Lowell nodded and then looked back to Johnny. He smiled yet seemed suddenly worried. "Is it all right that I come, Mr. Johnny?" the boy asked. "You said I could . . . you and Mr. Justin both." Lowell glanced back to Savannah. "Miss Savannah says I can stay as long as I need to." He lowered his voice to a whisper and said, "Do ya think she means it? 'Cause I can sure move on to Texas with you if she don't."

"I'm sure she means it," Johnny said, tousling the boy's hair. "But when I head on back to Texas, you can think about what you'd like to do. You know I'd be glad to have ya along."

Lowell smiled—seemed reassured. He looked up then to Vivianna, and his smile broadened. Vivianna fancied his eyes began to twinkle as he looked at her. "Vivianna! I seen a photograph of you once," he exclaimed. "You're Vivianna!"

"Yes!" Vivianna giggled.

"Oh boy! I heard all about you!" Lowell laughed. Quickly he went to the chair he'd been sitting on at the table. "Do ya mind, Miss Savannah?" he asked as he dragged the chair across the floor toward Vivianna.

Vivianna giggled, puzzled by the boy's need for the chair. In the next moment, however, Lowell pulled the chair to a stop right before Vivianna. Quickly he climbed up on the chair, standing before her. Reaching out, he took her face between his small hands.

"Yep," the boy said. "I heard all about you."

Vivianna gasped as the young boy kissed her perfectly on the lips. He kissed her! Square on the mouth, he kissed her!

"Mmm!" he sighed. Smiling, Lowell Wheeler said, "Yep! You do taste just like sugar and honey all stirred up together!"

Johnny burst into laughter, as did Savannah.

"Mama!" Willy exclaimed, however, his mouth gaping open big enough to catch june bugs. "Did you see that, Mama? Why, that boy ain't more'n eight years old, and he's sparkin' Viv . . . right here in our kitchen!"

Lowell climbed down from the chair. As he dragged it back over to the table, he said, "I'll have you know I'm nine years old. Been nine for near to six months now."

Vivianna was stunned to silence. Astonished that the young boy had kissed her, she looked to Johnny.

Johnny's warm eyes were bright with mirth. Shaking his head, he chuckled, "I told ya, Vivi . . . nobody cheers a body up like Lowell Wheeler."

"Hey, Mr. Johnny," Lowell began, tugging on Johnny's sleeve.

"Yeah?" Johnny asked.

"Bend down here a minute."

Vivianna watched as Johnny hunkered down—as Lowell whispered something in his ear.

"Nope," Johnny said.

Lowell nodded—whispered something else.

Johnny nodded. "Yep. But we'll have to see."

Lowell smiled and seemed satisfied with the answers Johnny had given him to whatever questions he'd asked.

"Hey, Lowell," Nate began, "me and Willy . . . we got us a bone collection. Do ya wanna see it?"

"Bones?" Lowell asked. "What kinda bones?"

"All kinds," Willy answered. "Johnny even found us some owl pellets to dig through. He says owl pellets gots mice bones in 'em! Little bitty, tiny bones and skulls and such."

"Oh yeah, they do!" Lowell exclaimed. "My daddy and me used to dig through owl pellets! How many ya got?"

"Nine," Nate answered. "That's three for each of us! Let's go."

"Now, hold on a minute," Savannah said. "I don't want to see any mice bones or fur or anything even resemblin' any sort of mouse remains in this house! Do you hear me, Nate? Willy?"

"Yes, Mama," Nate and Willy chimed.

"And that goes for you too, Lowell Wheeler," Savannah added. "No mouse anything in this house. All right?"

"Yes, ma'am," Lowell said. "And I'll make certain your boys wash their hands good 'fore we come home. Me too, of course."

Savannah smiled and giggled. "Thank you, Lowell."

"Is it all right, do ya think, Mr. Johnny?" Lowell asked.

"Is what all right, Lowell?" Johnny asked in return.

"Is it all right that I come here? Do ya think Mr. Justin will be glad?"

Johnny smiled and tousled the boy's hair. "I know he will be."

Lowell smiled and sighed with relief.

Vivianna giggled as the boy took her hand. "I can teach ya a little more about kissin' when I get back if ya like, Miss Vivianna. I wouldn't mind it a bit."

"Why don't ya let us older boys take care of Miss Vivi's education where that's concerned, Lowell?" Johnny chuckled.

Lowell shrugged. "All right, Mr. Johnny. But you let me know if y'all need any help."

"Oh, I will," Johnny said, winking at the boy. "I surely will."

"Come on, Lowell," Nate said. "We got owl pellets to sort and bones to boil!"

"Boil?" Lowell asked as the three boys headed for the door.

"Yep!" Willy said. "Me and Nate found us another dead fox just this mornin'!"

As the three young boys left the house, Vivianna giggled when Savannah sighed.

"My goodness!" she breathed. "That boy has more life in him than three boys put together, Johnny Tabor!"

"Yes, Miss Savannah . . . he does," Johnny chuckled. His smile faded just a bit as he added, "I'll take him on to Texas with me when I go, if ya like."

"Heavens no!" Savannah exclaimed. "If—and I do mean if—if I decide I can ever let go of ya, I won't have ya takin' that little darlin' too! Justin was tellin' me about that boy just the other day." Savannah nodded. "I think he was meant to come to us. There isn't any other way he could've made it to Florence . . . not all the way from Georgia. It's a miracle! It's truly a miracle." Savannah sighed, thoughtful for a moment. Then, dusting her hands on her apron, she said, "Still, I won't have him kissin' on girls at this young of an age . . . no, sir!" She looked to Johnny and wagged a scolding index finger at him. "That's what comes of havin' boys teach boys. What else did you tell that child that I'll have to undo?"

Johnny chuckled and shook his head. "Hard tellin', Miss Savannah. Hard tellin'."

330

"That's just what I'm afraid of." Savannah sighed. Then she smiled and looked to Vivianna. "With all this goin' on, I plum forgot to ask ya, Viv . . . how was your trip to the house?"

Vivianna felt tears welling in her eyes once more. "It was fine," she said. "I'm fine."

Savannah walked to her and pulled her into a warm, affectionate embrace. "Oh, I know it was hard, darlin'. I know it was. But ya really ought to go over more often. Time will make it a little easier. Each time ya go, it'll be less painful than before."

"Yes, ma'am," Vivianna sniffled, tears trickling over her cheeks.

Savannah released her then. "Would ya mind helpin' me pluck this chicken?" she asked. "I thought we'd have us a real nice supper. I can't imagine how long it's been since that boy had a nice supper."

"Of course," Vivianna said.

Savannah looked to Johnny. She smiled. "Did ya look in at the railroad, Johnny?"

"Yes, ma'am," he said. "They're startin' on the new line and repairs on Monday." He paused and lowered his head. Vivianna thought there was a look of guilt or shame about him. "I . . . I do thank you for your kindness and patience, Miss Savannah," he said. "For lettin' me stay on and—"

Savannah shook her head. "None of that, Johnny," she scolded. "To be honest, I won't

331

want to let you leave when the time comes. Besides bringin' my Justin back to me . . . you're a fine measure of a man, Johnny Tabor. And you've done far more for us than you'll ever know." Savannah looked to Vivianna then. "Isn't that right, Viv?"

There was thick insinuation in her words, and it caused Vivianna to feel unsettled. "Yes, ma'am," she managed. Still, as Savannah continued to stare at her—smiled a knowing smile—she was even further unsettled.

"Miss Savannah," Johnny began, "believe me . . . I don't deserve your kindness or your praise. I—"

"I would ask one favor of ya, Johnny, however," Savannah interrupted. "Would you mind peekin' in on the boys for me? I just don't like when they take up to boilin' animals alone. Would ya mind just givin' them a hand? And don't let 'em bother Charles Maggee if he's still out there spendin' some time with his sons at the cemetery. Make sure they leave him to his peace. Would ya mind?"

"Of course not, ma'am," Johnny said. "I'll look after them awhile. Lowell can be a mighty handful."

"Thank ya, Johnny. I'll send Vivianna over with some lunch for the four of you in a while. You're probably starvin'.'"

"Thank ya, ma'am," he said. He glanced to

Vivianna for a moment, smiled, and then left the house.

The moment Johnny was gone, Vivianna felt cold. The memories of her family, the ache in her heart, returned. Yet she brushed new tears from her cheeks and went to the sink to help Savannah with the chicken. She was puzzled when she saw that the chicken had already been plucked and cleaned. She looked to Savannah, curious.

Savannah smiled, took her hand, and led her to the table.

"Let's sit a moment, Viv," she said. "I'd like to talk to you."

"Of course," Vivianna said.

Once they were seated at the table, Savannah reached across the top of it, taking Vivianna's hands in hers. "How long have ya been in love with Johnny, darlin'?" she asked.

CHAPTER THIRTEEN

"Pardon?" Vivianna gasped. Vivianna was certain her heart had dropped to her stomach! An odd sort of terror washed over her. How could Savannah know of her feelings for Johnny? She'd only just discovered the depth of them herself! Furthermore, she knew Savannah wanted her to marry Justin—or Caleb, in the very least of it. Wasn't Savannah always saying she loved Vivianna like a daughter? Wasn't she always saying she didn't know what she'd do without her?

"M-Miss Savannah, I . . . I . . . ." Vivianna stammered.

Savannah squeezed Vivianna's hands once more. "That Johnny Tabor is a treasure!" she said. She giggled and winked. "And handsome as anything! I swear if I were twenty years younger, I'd try for him myself! Any man that would do what he's done for Justin . . . what he's done for us . . . he's a rare man indeed. I knew he'd steal your heart, Viv. The minute I saw him, I knew." Savannah shook her head. "My boys' heads are filled with nothin' but mud, I swear. Nothin' but mud." She sighed and continued, "They're just like their daddy . . . especially Justin and Caleb. Oh, I loved their daddy—you know how much

I did—but you need a man with somethin' in his heart besides himself." She leaned forward, lowering her voice. "Now you and I both know Johnny's haunted. It's obvious somethin's prickin' his heart. But I'm sure you can soothe whatever's worryin' him." Savannah sighed and smiled. "Neither of my boys could ever completely fill your heart, Viv . . . or love ya the way you deserved to be loved."

Vivianna was overwhelmed! She still couldn't understand how Savannah Turner could know about something she'd only just discovered—especially something so wildly unsettling.

"But . . . but, Miss Savannah . . . I . . . I . . ." Vivianna began. It was uncomfortable, sitting talking with the mother of the man she was supposed to love about the man she did love.

Savannah shook her head and interrupted. "I think it's about time you started callin' me Savannah. Don't you?"

Vivianna tried to hold back her tears. The day had been too overwhelming. Too many emotions were still battling in her—the pain of mourning her family, the bliss Johnny had stirred.

"Oh, honey, don't cry!" Savannah soothed. "It's all right. There, there now. What's all this?"

"I . . . I can't love him," Vivianna whispered. "I don't even know him."

"Oh, sure ya do, darlin'," Savannah reassured. "Just 'cause ya haven't known him your whole life, it doesn't mean ya don't know him. It doesn't mean ya can't be in love with him. He's been here for months now. I figure ya know him about as well as you know anybody." She paused, her smile fading a little. "I daresay I know Johnny better than I know Justin just now . . . and Justin's my own son."

Vivianna experienced an odd sort of relief in Savannah's having noticed the change in Justin. Caleb had seen it too. She wished she'd seen it sooner—that she hadn't been so blinded by his letters and the promises of love.

Still, even if there weren't Justin to consider— even though she had somehow fallen in love with Johnny—it didn't mean Johnny had fallen in love with her. Oh, certainly he'd kissed her— kissed her as she'd never imagined being kissed. Certainly he'd managed to unlock her emotions, her heart. But did he know he'd unlocked them, only to own them? Did he want them?

"It . . . it doesn't mean he feels anything for me," Vivianna mumbled.

Savannah laughed. "Oh, darlin'! My sweet Vivianna!"

Vivianna frowned. She saw nothing amusing in what she'd said.

"Viv . . . what do you think has been keepin' that boy here?" Savannah asked. "Surely ya don't think he enjoys fixin' up the barn and weedin' out the garden, do ya?"

"He . . . he only feels an obligation, I'm sure," Vivianna said. "He feels beholden to you for takin' him in, to Justin for savin' his life . . . however he saved it."

"Is that what you really think?"

Vivianna shrugged. "I'm afraid to think otherwise." She paused and then whispered, "After all . . . I loved Justin, didn't I? And he loved me once . . . at least I thought he did. Justin wrote professin' he loved me. And still . . ."

"Johnny Tabor isn't Justin, Vivianna," Savannah firmly reminded. She inhaled a deep breath, and suddenly, her eyes lit up with a rather mischievous light—the same light of mischief that Vivianna had so often seen in Nate's and Willy's eyes. "I'll tell ya somethin'," Savannah began. "Why don't you just give Johnny a little test?"

"What do ya mean?" Vivianna asked.

"I daresay he's kissed ya, hasn't he?"

Vivianna blushed—but nodded.

"Kissed ya good, I bet, too."

Vivianna smiled—and nodded.

"Well, see if he'll kiss ya again, Viv," Savannah suggested. "Let him know you want him to kiss ya . . . and see if he'll kiss ya again. My guess is he most certainly will."

"I don't know. Today, he—"

"Oh! Today, was it?" Savannah giggled. She shook her head and clicked her tongue. "That poor boy must be knowin' a world of confusion. First he brings Justin home to you . . . knowin' you were meant for Justin. Then finds out he wants ya for himself . . . at the same time knowin' Justin's got mud between his ears. I'm guessin' that's the only reason a man like Johnny Tabor would try for a girl that supposedly belongs to his friend. My guess is Johnny knows Justin's changed. He probably doesn't care for the way Justin's treatin' you. Still, I'm sure it's tearin' him up in one way or the other."

"I don't want him torn—not between me and Justin . . . not because of me," Vivianna said. A sense of panic was rising in her. She didn't want Johnny to feel guilt—or confusion—or anything unpleasant.

"Don't worry, darlin'. I'm sure Johnny won't linger in feeling guilty over it. Not when Justin's changed so. Johnny's got a strong character . . . and a powerful will. He's his own man," Savannah said. "So what do ya say? Will ya tempt him into kissin' ya once more? Pardon me for bein' vulgar, Viv, but a woman can tell by a man's kiss whether he's in love with her . . . or simply havin' a moment of overwhelmin' want."

Vivianna inhaled and closed her eyes. Justin had claimed he needed time to heal. It was then that Vivianna had begun to realize it was Justin's letters she loved, not Justin—not the man he'd become. Thus, she'd decided to put them away, and Johnny had offered to help her. They'd gone to her home—to where she'd once laughed and played with her brothers, once known the loving comfort of her parents—and there Johnny had finally succeeded in entirely unlocking her heart. It had been in those precious moments—no matter how painful accepting the loss of her family was—that she'd first consciously realized she'd fallen in love with Johnny. For weeks and weeks before, she'd simply thought he was simply too attractive to be ignored. Yet she realized that morning that she'd begun to fall in love with him the first night he'd arrived—the night she'd kissed him in thinking he might not live to see morning. Suddenly, the memory frightened her— even terrified her! To think that Johnny might have died—that she might never have known the wonder of his character, the bliss of being in his arms, the ecstasy of tasting his kiss. She might never have talked with him, laughed and walked with the man who had so stealthily, yet so easily, stolen her heart. She wondered for a moment if perhaps Johnny did love her—if perhaps it was why he was so determined she put Justin's letters away. Perhaps it was why he accompanied her to the house—to make certain the letters she'd pined over for so long were tucked away in the attic. Further she wondered if this was why he knew she had not mourned her family—because he loved her and had somehow seen her deeply imprisoned pain.

"Vivianna," Savannah said.

Vivianna was pulled from her thoughts and musings. She opened her eyes to see Savannah looking on her with a mother's loving gaze.

"I want you to be happy. I do love you like my own daughter, Viv. I want you to be happy and loved . . . passionately loved. Johnny loves you, I'm certain of it. Don't be afraid. Don't worry that I might mind that my boys aren't gonna win your heart . . . because I don't. Let Johnny know ya love him, Viv."

Vivianna nodded. "Maybe . . . maybe I'll try," she said. "It's been such a long day already," she sighed. "It's only midday, and already I feel wrung out."

"Oh, mercy!" Savannah exclaimed. "My poor boys! They must be starvin' by now!" Savannah lovingly squeezed Vivianna's hands once more. "Now . . . you just take the rest of the day to gather your thoughts and feelin's, Viv. I'll get somethin' together for the boys and run it on out there myself." She shook her head. "I swear, if Charles Maggee is still out at the cemetery . . . well, somebody oughta run over and save Johnny from four more hours of the tales. Charles does drag on!"

"I can run it out there," Vivianna offered, though she did feel an incredible weight of fatigue.

"And now we've got us another little wild boy to watch out for, Viv!" Savannah continued. She giggled. "I swear, he looked just like someone had smashed a pumpkin over his head when he arrived! I just had to get that hair whittled down to somethin' manageable. He's a darlin', isn't he?"

Vivianna smiled. "Yes," she said. "I suppose Justin will be surprised to see him." She thought of Justin's last letter—of his obvious affection for the boy. No doubt he'd be happy to see him safe.

"Yes, he will!" Savannah shook her head with disbelief. "And to think he made his way all the way from Georgia." She laughed. "I bet that orphanage he run away from didn't even raise an eyebrow about missin' a handful like Lowell seems to be. The way he kissed you, Viv! Mercy! I'll have my hands full with that one. But what's one more when you have four already? Isn't that right?"

Vivianna nodded. Yet in truth, she thought Lowell Wheeler seemed more than likely to equal two or three boys when it came to mischief, rather than just one.

❦

"What's takin' Justin so long?" Nate asked.

Caleb shrugged his tired shoulders. "He just said he had somethin' to do in town is all," he said.

"At suppertime?" Willy asked. "What's more important than supper?"

"Diggin' worms maybe," Lowell suggested.

Vivianna and Savannah giggled. Johnny smiled, and even Caleb grinned.

"Diggin' worms?" Nate exclaimed. "This late in the day?"

"Oh yeah!" Lowell said, his blue eyes wide with sudden excitement. "Don't y'all have them big ol' earthworms 'round here? The kind that come out mostly at evenin' and night? Them's the best kind for fishin'.""

"Well, I suppose Justin could be out diggin' worms," Savannah said. "But I'm guessin' he just had some things to finish up in town."

Caleb had come home for supper as usual. He'd been quite astonished to find Lowell Wheeler there—especially once he'd heard the tale of how Lowell came to be in Florence. Justin, however, had not returned for supper. Furthermore, Caleb seemed irritated concerning the fact. Vivianna wondered what could have kept Justin in town too. All afternoon, she'd wondered what Justin's reaction would be when he saw Lowell. She'd wondered if perhaps Lowell could touch Justin's heart—help him to find a thread of the man he used to be.

"I heard you got work with the railroad, Johnny," Caleb said, rattling Vivianna from her thoughts.

"Yes, I did," Johnny affirmed. "I figure I better start doin' somethin' before Miss Savannah tosses me out."

Savannah reached over and affectionately squeezed Johnny's arm. "You've done so much around here, Johnny . . . so much for us in so many, many ways. And I know Caleb's grateful to have you here to help me and Viv and the boys durin' the day."

"Thank ya for endeavorin' to make me feel better about stayin' on, Miss Savannah," Johnny said.

"I hear railroadin' is hard work," Caleb offered.

Johnny shrugged. "Hard work is good for a man . . . the way I see it."

"Yes, it is," Caleb agreed. "It keeps a man's mind busy and his body wore out."

"Caleb!" Willy exclaimed. "Ya oughta see the mice bones and such me and Nate and Lowell here dug outta them owl pellets Johnny give us!"

"Were there an awful lot?" Caleb asked, smiling.

"Oh yes!" Willy said.

"It was fun diggin' through the fur to find 'em too," Lowell added. "It's so soft and all."

"And we boiled up that fox," Nate said. "It smelled right rotten when we started. But once we strained out the stomach and all—"

"May I remind you boys that we are tryin' to have our supper?" Savannah gently scolded.

"Sorry, Mama," Nate said.

"Sorry," Willy added.

"Me too, Miss Savannah," Lowell offered. "I don't rightly like to think about all them fox innards boilin' around in that pot when I'm eatin' neither."

Johnny and Caleb chuckled.

"Johnny says you were out at the old place today, Viv," Caleb said then. "Is everything still in order out there?"

Vivianna nodded. Her emotions were close, but she managed not to tear up. "Yes. It's a little closed up . . . needs a good airin' out and some dustin'. But everything is just fine."

"I'm glad," Caleb said, folding his napkin and placing it on the table beside his empty plate. "It's a fine house." He leaned back in his chair and sighed, satisfied by finishing up a good meal.

Johnny folded his napkin as well. "Thank you for supper, Miss Savannah," he said. "I ain't just flatterin' when I say your fried chicken is better than my own mama's."

Savannah smiled. "Why, thank you, Johnny! A woman cannot receive a kinder compliment than bein' told she's cooked up somethin' better than a man's mama's."

All through supper, Vivianna had tried to keep her gaze from lingering on Johnny. She was afraid that if Savannah had been able to see her affection for him, then perhaps others could too.

344

She remembered that Caleb suspected too, for he'd told her, only the night before, what a fine man Johnny was. He'd told her he'd seen her light up whenever Johnny was around. Still, Vivianna was not so certain that Johnny lit up whenever she was around. Oh, his kisses caused her to think that perhaps he did. Still, she was uncertain. The day had been trying, even for the wonder she'd known in Johnny's arms. Her newly unleashed emotions were yet confusing—overwhelming— and caused a great weight of uncertainty. Just as she'd had to accept that they'd been imprisoned and lately freed, she now had to sort them—order them out before she could reason properly.

Still, though she tried not to look at the handsome man she'd fallen in love with, eventually she could not resist. Johnny was smiling—smiling as he watched Lowell trading elbow-nudges with Nate and Willy.

Vivianna felt breathless. Just gazing at him had caused her heart to begin hammering—sent butterflies to swarming in her stomach! She thought of all he'd done since he'd come home with Justin—all the chores and fixing up, all the hard work. She thought of his kindness to Nate and Willy also. It seemed Johnny was never too tired to go hunting for bones, never too tired for playing with pollywogs and frogs. She thought of the day she'd come upon him in the cemetery, of how he'd taken the time to tell the young Turner

345

boys his stories of war and the scars it leaves. He would be a wonderful father—an ideal father! The perception entered her mind that she would delight in having his children—in being as good a mother as he would be a father.

The contemplation caused her to blush, even for the fact she knew no one could read her thoughts. The warm pink on her cheeks deepened to a hot crimson, however, as Johnny glanced up to find her looking at him.

Instantly, his smile faded, replaced by an expression of concern. "You feelin' all right, Vivianna?" he asked.

Naturally, everyone's attention fell to her. Still, she simply nodded and said, "Just a little warm, I suppose."

Savannah began to fan herself with one dainty hand. "It does feel rather still and hot here," she said. "Why don't you leave the dishes for me and the young boys, Viv . . . and go on out for a walk? It's cooler outside, I'm sure. Or at least there's a little breeze."

"I'm fine," Vivianna assured her, attempting to fan away her own blush.

She might truly have done as Savannah suggested—if it weren't for the fact that she was entirely unwilling to leave Johnny's presence. She'd missed him when he'd been with the younger boys that afternoon. She fancied she'd never be able to easily leave him again!

"No, I think ya need a little air," Savannah argued. "You look like a ripe tomata! Now you go on and take a little walk. Find a bit of shade and cool off a bit. Ya won't sleep a wink if ya don't."

"Miss Savannah, I—" Vivianna began.

"I'll take ya strollin' if ya like, Miss Vivianna," Lowell offered. He smiled at her, and she was reminded of the rather brazen kiss he'd applied to her lips earlier in the day.

"That's all right, darlin'," Savannah said, patting the boy's hand. Savannah nodded to Johnny then. "Johnny . . . would you be a dear soul and see Vivianna on a walk for a little while? I think she's overdone it today. Would ya mind findin' her a bit of shade to linger under for me?"

Johnny grinned as Vivianna's blush deepened again. "It would be my pleasure, Miss Savannah," Johnny said.

"Well, I just know it will be, Johnny. Thank you so much," Savannah said.

Savannah looked to Vivianna, smiling with such entire mischief twinkling in her eyes that Vivianna felt her mouth fall agape for a moment.

"Now you go on, Viv," Savannah said, silently shooing Vivianna with one hand. "You go on and get some nice fresh air in ya."

All at once, Vivianna was nervous. All at once, the blissful memories of the time spent in Johnny's arms—the moments of their blended

347

lips—nearly overcame her with a trembling, nervous anticipation.

"I'm sure I'm fine," she told Savannah.

"You are awful red, Viv," Willy said.

"Like a radish," Nate added.

"Mr. Johnny," Lowell began, "you best take her out before her supper comes back up or the like. I can't take the sight of someone's supper comin' back up!"

Savannah gasped, and Vivianna covered her mouth with one hand as Lowell heaved a little.

"Honest, Miss Vivianna," Lowell moaned. "If you lose your supper . . . I just know I'll lose mine!"

"Viv!" Savannah exclaimed, holding her apron wide under Lowell's chin. "You go on with Johnny. Have yourself a nice walk."

Johnny stood, hurried around the table, and helped Vivianna from her chair.

"Go on now," Savannah waved, smoothing Lowell's forehead with one hand and holding her apron under his chin with the other.

"Yes, ma'am," Vivianna said as Johnny took her arm.

Savannah lowered her voice to a calm, soothing tone and asked Lowell, "When's the last time you had such a big supper, Lowell honey?"

"A might some time, ma'am," Lowell said, heaving again.

"Caleb, darlin' . . . would you fetch me a

bucket?" Savannah softly asked her eldest son. She glanced to Vivianna. "Go on. Take my Vivianna strollin' for some air, Johnny. We'll have Lowell all settled by the time y'all get back."

"Yes, ma'am," Johnny said, tugging at Vivianna's arm.

"Hold it down, Lowell!" Willy encouraged. "You can do it. You just ain't used to eatin' so much."

"Come on, Vivi," Johnny said, taking her hand and leading her out of the house.

"Oh, I hope he's all right," Vivianna said as she followed Johnny to stepping off the porch.

"He'll be fine," Johnny said. "He just ate too much. Ya gotta let your stomach get used to the food again."

Vivianna nodded and winced at the memory of Johnny the day he'd arrived. She remembered how she'd had to feed him his first few spoonfuls of broth. He'd been so weak—so near to expiring. She couldn't think on it, not after the many painful thoughts she'd already endured that day. Besides, Johnny was well—strong and healthy now. That's what mattered.

"You did seem awful pink for a moment, Vivi," he said. He reached up, placing the back of one strong hand to her cheek. "You sure you're all right? After all, you've been over the washboard and wrung out today."

"I'm fine," she told him. "Truly."

He nodded. "Good."

"Still," she ventured timidly, "I could do with a little fresh air . . . if . . . if you're still willin' to go for a little walk with me."

He smiled, his dark eyes smoldering with sudden and irresistible allure. He didn't speak—simply gripped her hand more tightly and began to lead her away from the house.

She was wildly excited—near to trembling! The excruciating pain she'd known earlier in the day—as she'd accepted and begun to mourn the loss of her family—had softened to a dull ache. Thus, her utter delight in Johnny's touch and company was able to find her joyous in that moment, not sad and despairing.

Still, she felt nervous. They'd shared such intimacy—such an exchange of mutual passion that morning. Yet they'd not spoken of it since, and Vivianna was not quite sure how to think or feel. She was grateful when it was Johnny who spoke first.

"That Mr. Maggee . . . he could talk the tail feathers off a magpie," he said.

Vivianna giggled and nodded. "Oh yes, he can!" she agreed. "I once sat and listened to him for near to two hours without sayin' so much as 'yes, sir' to him."

"Between diggin' through owl pellets and Mr. Maggee's goin' on and on . . . I'm worn out," he chuckled.

"I think Nate and Willy put Mr. Maggee in mind of his own boys," Vivianna explained. "He wanders over every once in a while to visit with them . . . or Miss Savannah."

Johnny looked to her, one handsome brow arched. "Do you think he's sweet on their mama?"

Vivianna shrugged. "Well, his wife died over two years back . . . and Savannah's awful pretty. Goodness knows she could use a hand with her boys, especially now with Lowell. I don't think it would be too awful if she liked him and he liked her . . . do you?"

"I suppose not," he admitted. "Only he might talk her to death."

Vivianna giggled. "He might. But the funny thing is . . . when she's the one talkin' to him, he listens like she was heaven's angel."

"They'd make a pair, wouldn't they?"

"They would at that."

Vivianna felt his hand tighten as it held hers— as he led her toward the meadow a ways before leaving the path and heading into a grove of dogwoods.

"Where we goin'?" she asked, delighted that he was leading her to a more secluded space.

"I found somethin' the other day. I think you'll like it," he said.

Vivianna followed Johnny, blissful in his company—delighted by the fact he still held her hand.

"Look here," he said once they'd gone a ways among the dogwoods.

Vivianna gasped and smiled. "Wild honey-suckle!" she exclaimed.

Sure enough, a massive honeysuckle vine had overgrown the remains of two dead oak trees. Lovely green leaves and bright pink blossoms climbed up one old tree trunk and all around and over its limbs to create a beautiful canopy overhead as it clung to the second old tree.

Vivianna looked through the dogwoods and bushes separating the Turner place from the dead trees and wild honeysuckle. She could see the vine-covered arbor a ways beyond.

"All these years, I just thought it was the old arbor honeysuckle smellin' so sweet," she said. "But I'm sure this one was helpin' it along."

"Do you wanna taste it?" he asked. He was smiling, and Vivianna's heart melted. He was so handsome—so kind and brave! He'd unlocked her heart—her feelings—her very life!

"Of course!" she told him. She watched as he reached up and rather roughly plucked a blossom.

"I get about one outta every five right," he said, frowning as he struggled to gently remove the styles from the flower.

Vivianna giggled as she watched his sad attempt. "Here," she said, plucking another flower. "Toss that poor thing to its grave, Johnny, and let me help ya."

Johnny sighed, shook his head, and tossed the crushed honeysuckle blossom to the ground.

Carefully, Vivianna separated the parts of the tender flower until the honeysuckle nectar clung in one large, glistening droplet to a style.

"Hurry quick!" she told him, giggling as he bent down and caught the style in his mouth.

"Mmm!" he mumbled. "You try it. I think it's sweeter than what's growin' over by the arbor."

Smiling, Vivianna plucked another blossom and tasted the nectar for herself. "Oh my, yes!" she giggled. "It makes a body feel sort of sorry for the old arbor honeysuckle . . . makes its sugar seem almost plain."

She watched him pick another blossom—bit her lip to keep from laughing as he struggled to reveal the nectar within. Still, after a time—and a fair amount of concentration—he did manage it.

"It's an awful lot of work for such a small pleasure," he said as he let the droplet of honeysuckle sugar drip from the style to his tongue.

"I suppose," she said. Vivianna stripped the flower from another blossom and savored the tiny flavor.

Johnny licked the nectar off two more styles, and Vivianna laughed.

"Oh, you're gettin' quite good at harvestin' honeysuckle sugar, Mr. Tabor," she teased.

He nodded. "Here," he said, plucking three

flowers and moving close to her. "Let me try somethin'." Carefully he held all three blossoms between his thumb and forefinger, simultaneously stripping them of their nectar-laden styles with his other hand. "Now hold still," he told her. He frowned, concentrating as he directed the three droplets of nectar to set softly on Vivianna's lower lip.

Yet honeysuckle nectar was not to be resisted, and Vivianna could not keep from letting her tongue moisten her lip in tasting nature's sweet pleasure.

"No, no, no!" Johnny chuckled. "You have to leave it there."

"I can't!" Vivianna said. "It's too temptin'." And it was true! She'd never tasted three droplets of nectar at once before! The concentration was delicious.

"Let me try that again," he said. "Four this time. A real treat for ya."

Vivianna watched him pluck four blossoms, rather awed that he would be so intrigued with a thing as simple as harvesting honeysuckle nectar.

"Now . . . hold still this time," he instructed as he stripped the flowers of their styles. "Just . . . just hold very still," he mumbled. Frowning, he placed the droplets of sugar on her lower lip again. He arched one daring eyebrow and said, "Let it stay there a minute. Don't you go lickin'" that off, Vivi . . . 'cause there's enough for two. Don't ya think?"

Vivianna gasped—instantly melted as Johnny's soft kiss pressed her lower lip—as the light touch of his tongue tasted the honeysuckle nectar waiting there! He pressed his mouth to hers, sharing the sweet flavor with her a moment before it disappeared.

He kissed her cheek—her neck—the heat of his mouth pressing the warmth of her flesh just below her ear.

"I swear, Johnny," she breathed, pulling away from him slightly.

"You swear what, Vivi?" he asked. His eyes were purely alluring as he gazed at her—as his arms went around her body, drawing her to him.

"I swear you could lead me astray if I had the mind to let ya," she confessed.

He grinned. "Why don't you just let me, Vivi?" he said. "Let me lead ya just a little astray." His voice was low and tempting—rich and dark like molasses. "I promise I won't lead ya off too far." He bent, placing his mouth against the hollow of her throat.

"Promise?" she breathed.

"I do," he whispered.

Vivianna opened her eyes—tried to keep at bay the blissful dizziness overtaking her. Overhead she saw the wild honeysuckle vine, the canopy of green leaves and sweet pink flowers.

She took his face between her hands—gazed into his smoldering brown eyes. "Then lead me astray, Johnny Tabor," she whispered. He moved to kiss her, but she placed an index finger to his lips and said, "Just a ways, mind you."

Johnny grinned. "All right . . . just a ways." He took her chin in one hand, slowly caressing her lower lip with his thumb. Gazing into her eyes, he mumbled, "Ain't nothin' in this whole world as sweet as your kiss, Vivi."

Vivianna smiled, enchanted by his words, mesmerized as they passed from his lips. "Not even honeysuckle sugar?" she asked in a whisper.

"Not a whole barrelful of honeysuckle sugar," he told her a moment before his mouth crushed to hers.

There was no soft first kiss meant to build to a passionate exchange. Rather the passion was ripe and instant between them! Vivianna sighed as Johnny's arms tightened around her—as the moist heat of his mouth bathed her in delicious bliss! She felt his hand weave into her hair at the back of her head as he endeavored to press his mouth more firmly to hers. The rough whiskers of his face prickled the tender flesh of hers, but she only reveled in the sense—further proof she was alive and knowing pleasure. For a moment, his kisses grew to such a ravenous state she was nearly unable to draw breath—but she didn't care. Her arms were around him, her hands woven through his soft hair, as she met his thirsting demands.

Breathless himself, Johnny's mouth left hers for an instant as he whispered, "Vivi . . . I . . ."

Vivianna frowned, for there seemed a deep guilt and pain in him suddenly. She fancied his eyes were moist with enduring it.

"I'm . . . I'm not a good man," he breathed.

Vivianna gazed at him—wondered at the pain in his eyes. She placed her fingertips to his lips to quiet him, and he kissed them. "You're right," she whispered. "You're not a good man. You're a wonderful man."

"No. I've . . . I've done some things . . ." he stammered.

Yet Vivianna knew she could not love a man who had done anything unforgivable—and she loved Johnny Tabor. "Yes, I know," she whispered, kissing him softly on the mouth. "You're a thief, aren't ya?"

Johnny frowned and appeared utterly astonished. "A thief?" he breathed.

"You're stealin' my heart," she said. "You've unlocked it . . . shown me that true joy can only be recognized when a person has known real pain. You've unlocked my heart, and you're stealing it for your own."

Still he frowned. She fancied the moisture in his eyes was increasing.

"You don't know me, Vivi," he whispered.

"Not really. You can't give me your heart when you don't know what I've done."

"I've already given it to you, Johnny . . . and nothin' you could tell me now would change that."

"Promise?" he asked. "Do you promise that you'll never turn from me . . . no matter what?"

"I do," Vivianna said. She was bathing in wonderment at hearing such a promise pass from her lips. Johnny was haunted—just as Savannah had said he was—just as Vivianna had known all along. Still, something whispered to her soul that whatever was haunting Johnny was not so unforgivable as he thought. "But if you're tired of me," she teased, squirming out of his arms and plucking a honeysuckle blossom, "I suppose we could go back to sippin' honeysuckle nectar."

She giggled when he took her arms tightly in his powerful hands. "I'll never be tired of you," he said—and Vivianna melted to him as he kissed her once more.

She sensed there was more to be said between them. Certainly, as they lingered beneath the honeysuckle vine, she knew she wanted only Johnny. Yet she knew her mind and heart were still spinning from his unlocking her soul. She knew the pain of the loss of her family would return—that her doubt in whether Johnny Tabor truly loved her would return. Still, there—as they bathed in the fragrance of honeysuckle and the delicious kisses borne of passion and desire—she knew only that she loved Johnny. Furthermore, in those moments, she knew that Savannah had been right. A woman could tell by a man's kiss whether he loved her or was simply overcome with momentary want. In that moment, Vivianna knew: Johnny Tabor loved her.

Justin's eyes narrowed as he watched Johnny kissing Vivianna—as he watched Vivianna willingly kissing Johnny in return. Who did Johnny Tabor think he was? After all, hadn't it been Johnny who had talked Justin into returning to fulfill his promises to Vivianna in the first place? He'd near to threatened Justin with his life if he didn't return home to keep all the promises he'd written in those damn letters! And now—now Johnny Tabor stood there owning Vivianna's affections. Furthermore, Vivianna had never kissed him the way she was kissing Johnny Tabor. He fancied even Tilly couldn't kiss a man the way Vivianna was kissing Johnny. Justin shook his head. If she only knew what a liar he really was—if Vivianna knew the things Johnny Tabor had done—he reckoned she wouldn't be so willingly caught in his arms.

Justin turned, disgusted and angry. Sure, he'd lingered in town after working all day. He'd missed supper too. But an hour or so spent with Tilly Winder was worth it. At least, he thought it had been worth it at the time—until he'd come home to peek into the kitchen window to see little Lowell Wheeler enjoying the company of his family—until he'd seen Vivianna kissing Johnny like she'd never kissed him. It had been then that Justin had begun to wonder if he truly wanted to linger on the path he'd chosen. Tilly was a fine woman! She owned a gift for causing a man to think on her all the day long—and the night too. Still, he knew she wasn't the woman Vivianna was. Tilly wasn't sweet, innocent, and tenderhearted. Tilly wasn't as pretty or as soft. Furthermore, Justin knew Vivianna had saved her passion for the man who most deserved it. That wasn't true with Tilly either.

Thus, Justin had known a moment of regret when he'd seen Vivianna in Johnny's arms. But the moment of regret quickly turned to anger—as most moments of any emotion did in Justin. He cussed the war as he lumbered back to the house—cussed the fighting, the hardship. And he cussed Johnny Tabor for managing to keep his character about him through it all. Well, most of his character. Still, Justin knew Johnny's secret— knew that if Vivianna ever found out the truth, she'd sure enough drop Johnny like a boiling hot yam.

He had a mind to tell her himself. For a moment, Justin considered revealing the truth of Johnny's black soul to her. But he thought better of it.

Telling Vivianna the truth about Johnny might well lead to Justin's own sins being revealed. He wouldn't have his mother any more disappointed in him than she already was. No. There were other ways to take Johnny Tabor down to hell. He'd wait. Justin knew that if he were patient, an opportunity would present itself. And in that very moment, understanding washed over him, and Justin realized that he wouldn't have to wait. He'd been in town, lingering with Tilly long after Caleb had left for home. Thus, he knew what had been found. He knew what questions were already being asked. Furthermore, he knew where suspicions would eventually gather.

Justin chuckled as he stepped up onto the porch. Yep, he'd wait—bide his time a little longer. He'd see Johnny get what he deserved—one way or the other. Then Vivianna could forget him—maybe finally marry Caleb. And even Justin knew that if anybody on earth deserved to be happy, it was Caleb Turner.

"Mr. Justin!" Lowell exclaimed as Justin stepped into the kitchen. "I found it! I found your place! I come all the way from an orphanage in Georgia!"

Justin smiled, laughed, and caught the boy in his arms.

"Lowell! My boy! So ya really made it, did ya?" Justin asked.

Lowell nodded. "All the way from Georgia."

Justin chuckled. Lowell was a good boy. The part of Justin's heart that still remembered the man he once was was glad to see the boy safe. He had hardly thought of him again—not since he and Johnny were taken to Andersonville. Still, he was glad the boy was safe. He smiled. Perhaps he wouldn't have to tell Vivianna the truth about the enemy she was so willingly kissing out in the woods. Perhaps Lowell would do it for him.

Still, Justin had not forgotten what he'd heard in town before coming home. He'd wait. One way or the other, Johnny Tabor was about to pay for his sins.

CHAPTER FOURTEEN

"Justin and me . . . we got along from the very first," Johnny said.

Vivianna tucked her feet under her skirt and leaned back against Mr. Turner's tombstone. As she listened to Johnny, she studied him—thoroughly studied him. She loved his manner of casually lounging—the way he rested on one elbow, his long legs stretched out in the grass. She adored his soft chestnut hair and deep brown eyes, the way his lips moved when he talked, and the square angles of his jaw and chin.

"I hate to see him so changed," he mumbled, scowling. "But he's been through a heap of misery."

"And you haven't?" Vivianna asked. "You endured the war and Andersonville too. Have you changed?"

Johnny shrugged. "A bit maybe. I ain't as quick-tempered as I once was. And I didn't laugh a whole lot . . . not for a while." He looked to her and smiled. "Not 'til that pigeon mess hit me when I was feedin' the chickens."

Vivianna giggled, delighted by the memory. "But it seems to me that those are good changes. I don't see the changes in Justin as bein' good ones," she said.

Johnny shrugged again. "War is hard on a man. Truth is I still feel a load of guilt for makin' up my mind to try for you myself." He shook his head and added, "But then I think of Justin . . . how he's altered." He paused and hung his head shamefully. "I might not be able to keep hold of ya—ya may find out the truth about me one day and change your mind about me—but I couldn't let Justin have ya. I just couldn't."

"You could tell me the truth, Johnny," Vivianna ventured. "Then you wouldn't have to worry about somebody else tellin' me whatever it is you think makes you the devil. Why don't you give me the chance to see if what's hauntin' you is really so terrible?"

"But I know it is," he said. He looked at her again. "And I can't find the strength to confess it and risk losin' your heart . . . not yet anyway."

"Hey, Mr. Johnny," Lowell began.

Vivianna glanced up to where Lowell stood studying the backside of Floydie Maggee's tombstone.

"What, boy?" Johnny asked, craning his neck around to look at the boy.

"Have you seen this here?" Lowell said, pointing to the top of the tombstone.

"I have," Johnny said, returning his attention to the rock he'd been tossing in one hand.

"It looks like blood to me," Lowell said.

"Blood?" Vivianna asked, rising to her feet.

"Yep. It sure does," Johnny said. "Probably some big buzzard dropped his prey or somethin'. Maybe a rabbit or a small fox. That would do it, I suspect."

Vivianna went to where Lowell stood. She looked at the tombstone and frowned. "It's an awful stain," she said. "Poor Floydie. I'm afraid that will tarnish his stone forever."

Lowell's eyebrows arched. "Poor Floydie? Why . . . he don't know the difference, Miss Vivianna," the boy said. "He just left his bones and teeth down there. His soul is singin' up in heaven with the angels. I don't think he cares much about somethin' like this."

Vivianna frowned, however. The memory of the dead Confederate Nate and Willy had found—of Zachary Powell—entered her mind. After Johnny and Justin had gone to look at the poor soul, hadn't Justin said it looked as if his head had been bashed in by a rock? She glanced into the woods—shivered as she realized how very close the body had been found to Floydie Maggee's resting place.

She looked back to Johnny. He was still stretched out in the grass, tossing the rock in the air over and over. Fear began to rise in her—not fear that Johnny knew any more about the death of Zachary Powell than he'd already revealed but that he shared the same frightening thoughts she'd only just had. Perhaps Zachary

Powell had fallen and bashed his head on Floydie's tombstone and not a rock. If he had, then someone had moved his body to the woods, perhaps positioning his head against the rock to make it seem as if that is where he had fallen. Perhaps the same person who had taken the body in the end—and someone had taken it. Vivianna was not able to linger in denial enough to think an animal could've dragged it off.

"Lowell, honey," Vivianna began, "why don't you run over to that mess of sweet violets we saw on our way here . . . and pick a few for my mama and daddy? Would ya mind?"

Lowell smiled and gazed up at Vivianna with a rather loving expression. "I'd do anything for you, Miss Vivianna," he sighed. "I sure am glad I finished my chores before Nate and Willy so's I could come walkin' with you today."

"Me too, sweetie," Vivianna said, kissing him tenderly on the forehead. "Now you run on and gather a few violets for me, all right?"

As Lowell nodded and dashed toward the path leading from the cemetery to the Turner home, he paused next to Johnny.

Johnny chuckled when Lowell said, "Miss Vivianna just gave me a kiss, Mr. Johnny. Ain't you just jealous as a grape?"

"You bet I am, boy," Johnny said.

Lowell turned and waved to Vivianna. She smiled and tossed a wave in return.

"I know what you're thinkin'," Johnny said, getting to his feet.

"What?" Vivianna asked as he sauntered toward her.

He shook his head and frowned as he looked at the blood on the stone. "You're thinkin' exactly what I thought when Willy and Nate showed me this awhile back . . . that this is where that devil Zachary Powell met with his Maker."

"But what if he did? It means someone . . ."

Johnny nodded. "It means somebody moved him . . . that he didn't just fall in the woods and hit his head on a rock."

"Maybe he staggered to the woods!" Vivianna suggested. "Maybe the fall here didn't kill him . . . and he staggered off to die there."

"Maybe," he said. He shrugged and added, "Or maybe a big buzzard really did drop his prey—a rabbit or somethin'—and it hit just here." He looked to her, his eyes filled with doubt. "That's why I didn't say anything. It don't change the fact that none of us know what happened . . . that folks would sure be pointin' their fingers mine and Justin's way."

Vivianna nodded. He was right. What did the blood on the tombstone change? Zachary Powell had died, his body had disappeared, and none of those residing at the Turner house knew how.

She heard Johnny breathe a heavy sigh—glanced to him to see him rake his fingers through his hair. His expression was that of fatigue, worry, and discouragement.

"What's wrong?" she asked. She studied him a moment, the way he stared at the bloodstain on Floydie's tombstone. "Is . . . is this what's eatin' you up, Johnny? Because we don't know what happened to the man who died here? Because we didn't tell anybody?"

Truth be told, the knowledge had haunted Vivianna too. Still, what was to be done?

"What can we do, Johnny? Do you . . . are you thinkin' we should tell somebody about it all . . . about this? Is that what causes your handsome brow to pucker so often?"

He looked to her and sighed as she placed a tender palm to his cheek. "Among other things," he mumbled, taking her hand from his cheek and pressing a firm kiss into her palm.

"I used to think, even just months ago . . . I used to think that when the war was finally over . . . that somehow everything would be all right. But it scars us . . . all of us," she told him.

Again he kissed her palm, somehow almost desperately. He needed her—needed her comforting reassurance. Thus, she let her arms slide around his strong body, hugging him tightly. Johnny did not pause but gathered her against him, wrapping his powerful arms around her as he kissed the top of her head.

"And yet . . . I need to confess something, Johnny Tabor," she whispered.

"What's that?" he mumbled into her hair.

Vivianna looked up into his face, tears welling in her eyes. "Sometimes—and I know it's so sinful—but sometimes . . . sometimes I'm glad for the war . . . because if it hadn't happened . . . I would never have found you." It was a terrible thing to say; she knew it was! In truth, she wasn't glad for the war. Though she knew the outcome was necessary—that freedom for every man and woman was right—she was not glad for the men who had died, for the families torn apart and left destitute. Still, she could not imagine her life without knowing Johnny—not anymore.

A slight smile curved Johnny's enticing lips. His eyes softened, and the worry seemed to fade from his face. "I know," he whispered. "I think about that too."

He took her face in his hands, lightly brushing her lips with one thumb before pressing a tender kiss to them. Instantly, Vivianna's heart soared! Her mouth flooded with excess moisture in anticipation of a more passionate exchange.

Johnny paused in deepening their kiss, however, when Lowell said, "Mr. Johnny! Is that the way you plan to kiss her? That ain't no way to kiss a woman!"

Johnny smiled at Vivianna and chuckled.

Releasing her, he turned to face the scolding little boy. "Is that so?" Johnny said.

Lowell frowned. He held a bunch of mangled violets in each hand. Vivianna bit her lip to keep from smiling as he dropped the crushed bouquets to the grass beneath his feet.

Lowell shook his head. "No, sir, Mr. Johnny! You gotta grab her tight . . . pull into ya . . . like when you're learnin' to shoot and hold the stock hard against your shoulder." Lowell nodded and added, "Now, go on. Grab her like you're a man!"

Johnny chuckled. Vivianna smiled as he indeed took her in his arms, pulling her firmly against him. "Like this?" he asked Lowell.

Lowell frowned and shook his head. "No. Pull in. Put one of your arms over her shoulder . . . the other around under her other arm . . . tight, Mr. Johnny."

Johnny did as instructed, smiling down at Vivianna.

"That's it," Lowell said. "See how she can't struggle as much now? And it gives ya a better angle to go at."

Johnny nodded and, smiling, asked, "Now what, Lowell? What do I do next?"

"Well, ya kiss her," Lowell began, "but not like she's some little girl you been chasin' after church. Kiss her once on the lips. Then ya sort of open your mouth a bit when ya kiss her again."

"Lowell!" Vivianna exclaimed.

"Well, that's how it's done, Miss Vivianna," he said. "Or so my daddy told me. He always kissed Mama like that."

Vivianna winced, knowing the boy must sorely miss his parents. She knew his pain; she shared it.

Johnny's smile faded a little too, and she knew he was thinking of the poor boy's broken heart.

"Now, go on, Johnny," Lowell urged. "Ya gotta do it before she turns yeller and tries to run away."

"Like this?" Johnny asked, kissing Vivianna sweetly on the lips twice in succession.

"Oh, no!" Lowell groaned. "No! I done told ya. The second time ya kiss her . . . ya gotta think like she's a juicy ol' plum."

"Oh! I see," Johnny said, feigning sudden understanding. "Like this."

Vivianna sighed as Johnny's mouth captured hers in a moist, impassioned kiss. As Johnny deepened their exchange, she feared the display might be a bit too lurid for a young boy's eyes, and she pulled away slightly.

"That's it, Mr. Johnny! That's it!" Lowell exclaimed. "See how she's all blushin' and tryin' to escape your charms now? That means you've kissed her right fine!"

Johnny chuckled and took Vivianna's mouth once more before releasing her. "Thanks, Lowell," Johnny said. "Don't know what I'd have done without ya here to help me out with this."

Vivianna's smile broadened as Lowell proudly nodded and said, "You're welcome, Mr. Johnny." Lowell winked at Vivianna and added, "You're welcome too, Miss Vivianna. Now you got you a beau who's handsome and a good lover."

"Why, thank you, Lowell," Vivianna giggled.

Johnny inhaled a deep breath, exhaling a rather tired sigh. "Well, I suppose I oughta see to the garden," he said. "Come Monday I won't have as much time to tend to it."

"Are ya happy to be on with the railroad, Johnny?" Lowell asked.

Johnny nodded. "I am," he said. He hunkered down and tousled the boy's hair as he looked at him. "But I'm a bit worried you might try some of your kissin' skills on my girl."

Lowell smiled and hugged Johnny. "Oh, I wouldn't do that to ya, Mr. Johnny. And anyway, I ain't tall enough."

Johnny laughed, and Vivianna giggled with delight.

"Well, you linger awhile with Miss Vivi, all right, boy?" Johnny told Lowell. "Help her put them pretty flowers on her mama and daddy's restin' places. I'll see ya back at the house in a while."

"Yes, sir," Lowell said.

Johnny smiled and winked at Vivianna. "I'll

meet you later, Vivi . . . maybe for a little honeysuckle sippin'.'"

Vivianna nodded, delighted by his inference he would kiss her later—perhaps when their instructor was not so near to give advice. "Bye-bye," Vivianna called as Johnny headed down the path toward home.

"He's a good man, that Johnny Tabor," Lowell said.

Vivianna watched as the boy bent to gather his pitiful bouquet of mangled violets. "He certainly is," she agreed.

Lowell further mashed the violets as he shoved them all into one fist so that he could take hold of Vivianna's hand with the other. Gently he began to lead her toward her parents' graves. The boy shook his head and said, "I'll tell you what . . . I sure was scared when he found me that day. I thought he was gonna shoot me or somethin'! Mr. Johnny's a mighty powerful man, and I didn't know but that he would chew me up and have me for breakfast. But then he just kneeled down and pulled me into his arms . . . and I knew everything would be all right."

"I thought Justin found you, Lowell," Vivianna asked. She remembered the last letter Justin had written to her in which he told her of finding Lowell.

Lowell shook his head. "Mr. Justin . . . he was always takin' the sunshine for things

Mr. Johnny done. I remember when we got back to the soldier's camp . . . Mr. Justin told everybody he'd found me." Lowell shook his head again. "Mr. Johnny, he never said a word. That's how I knew he cared for me. Mr. Johnny, he was just glad I was safe. But Mr. Justin . . . he just wanted everyone to think he was some sorta hero for findin' a poor orphan child in the woods."

Vivianna felt tears brimming in her eyes. She shook her head, awed to know yet another wonderful characteristic of the man she loved. She was angry too, however—angry that Justin would steal the recognition for a good deed. In the first of it, a good deed should be done simply because it was the right thing to do, not for recognition and praise. Johnny had never mentioned that he'd been the one to find Lowell. He'd just seemed happy to see the boy safe— delighted in his company. Vivianna wondered how many other stories Justin had written to her in his letters were lies.

Lowell paused and looked up to Vivianna with a rather frightened, pleading expression. "I think Mr. Johnny loves me . . . don't you, Miss Vivianna?" he asked.

Vivianna's heart nearly broke with sympathy and love for the boy. "I know he does," she said, dropping to her knees and gathering him into her arms.

"And he loves you too," Lowell sniffled against her cheek. "I can tell." He pulled away from her then, brushing a tear from his cheek. "He just needs a little more skill with his kissin'." He smiled at her then.

Vivianna giggled. "Darlin', if Johnny gets any better at kissin' . . . I swear he'll lead me—"

"Straight down the path to hell?" Lowell finished.

Vivianna's eyes widened. "Why, Lowell! What a thing to say!"

Lowell shrugged. "It's what ya meant, isn't it? Though . . . I'm not rightly certain how kissin' on Johnny could lead down to hell. I just heard a nurse woman say that once, when she was visitin' the camp. I heard her say, 'Ooo! That Johnny Tabor! He could lead me straight down the path to hell, and I wouldn't mind a bit!' That's what she said." Lowell shrugged. "Of course, I never could figure it . . . bein' that Johnny never would say a word to her." Lowell shook his head and sighed. "Sometimes grown-up folks don't make no sense at all."

Vivianna watched as Lowell then placed half the bouquet of mashed flowers on her mother's grave and half on her father's. She stifled a giggle when he kneeled down and began pinching the already mutilated blossoms with his small fingers.

"There now," he said, wiping his violet scented

hands on his shirt. "Mama used to pinch mint or sage leaves when she was cookin'. She said it released the flavors. I figure the same thing goes on with flower perfume."

"I suppose it does," Vivianna said.

Lowell was quiet for a moment—thoughtful. "Would it be all right with you if I come out here every once in a while and visited your folks, Miss Vivianna?" he asked. "I don't know where my own were buried over . . . or even if they were. It'd make me feel a whole lot better if I could come visitin' yours here and there."

"Of course, darlin'," Vivianna said, fighting back another flood of tears. "And besides, I know my mama and daddy are watchin' over me from heaven. Maybe . . . maybe since you're here too now . . . maybe your mama and daddy are together with my own. Maybe they're just sittin' up in heaven together—"

"Sippin' lemonade?" he asked, smiling hopefully.

"Yes," Vivianna said, smoothing his hair from his forehead. "Sippin' lemonade . . . with lots of extra sugar."

Lowell smiled, bent, and crushed a few more violet petals.

❧

"Lowell told me today that you found him . . . not Justin," Vivianna said. She let the droplet of honeysuckle nectar drip to Johnny's lip and then kissed it away.

Johnny smiled as he lay on his back, hands tucked behind his head, beneath the wild honeysuckle vine in the woods. "Oh, I'll take me some more of that, Miss Vivianna Bartholomew," he said.

Vivianna smiled. "Did you find him? Did you find Lowell . . . or did Justin?"

Johnny shrugged. "Does it matter? He got found. That's what's important."

"But I wanna know the truth," Vivianna prodded.

Johnny's smile faded. "The truth," he mumbled. "All right. I did find Lowell," he confessed. "I was out scoutin', and Justin was a ways behind me . . . and I found the poor boy. When we got back to camp, Justin marched in and announced he'd found a lost orphan boy. Everyone went on and on, slatherin' him with praise and compliments. I don't know why he done that. I just wanted to make sure the boy was safe." He paused, his eyes narrowing as he added, "And I ain't tellin' ya that to try and make myself shine in anybody's eyes. I just wanna make sure you know that Lowell ain't a liar." His anger disappeared almost instantly, however, and he chuckled. "That boy! He does lighten a heart . . . don't he?"

Vivianna nodded. "Yes, he does. He's a little darlin'."

Johnny sat up, and Vivianna leaned back against the old vine-covered oak as he cupped her chin in one hand and kissed her. Oh, his kiss was divine! His mouth was sweet like sugar, and the feel of it to hers caused goose pimples to ripple over her body.

He mumbled something against her mouth, yet her ears were ringing so loudly with bathing in bliss that she didn't understand him.

"What?" she breathed.

His mouth left hers, and he kissed her neck just below her right ear. "I love you, Vivi," he whispered then.

Instantly, tears sprang to Vivianna's eyes. Instantly, her heart began to hammer even more madly than it had a moment before!

"I've loved you for so long," he breathed.

Vivianna captured his face between her hands—kissed him ravenously on the mouth. He loved her! He'd said it—confessed his love. She was wild with rapture!

Throwing her arms around his neck, she wept and whispered against his cheek, "I love you, Johnny! I've loved you from the moment I first saw you! The day you and Justin returned . . . I . . . I tried not to look at you. I thought it was because you were lookin' so near to death. But . . . but now I realize . . . I realize my soul was drawn to you!"

He released her, taking her face in his hands and studying her expression.

"Remember . . . remember that day . . . when all of us thought you would die . . . that you wouldn't live until mornin'? I kissed you, Johnny! I kissed you! Oh, it probably seemed like nothin' to you, but I'd never done such a thing in my life, Johnny! To kiss a strange man? Even then my soul was drawn to you. My mind and heart were tryin' their best to love Justin . . . but my soul knew I loved you."

Johnny's eyes were moist—bright with joy but also sadness. "Do you . . . do you love me enough to forgive me anything, Vivi?" he asked.

"Johnny, I know you. There's nothin' you could've done that would change my love for you."

He looked doubtful. His brow puckered with pain.

"Johnny Tabor . . . have you murdered anyone?" she asked.

"No! Of course not," he grumbled.

"Do you have a wife and children tucked away in Texas?"

"Vivi! No!"

"Then there's nothin' you're hidin' . . . nothin' hauntin' you that would keep me from you."

"Let me taste you now, Vivi," he mumbled. His eyes began to smolder with desire as he gazed at her. "Let me kiss you for an hour here . . . beneath the honeysuckle vine. Let me have one more day of ownin' your heart . . . and then . . . then I'll tell ya. Give me time to build up my courage . . . and then I'll tell you about the devil in me. Then you can decide whether or not you can still love me . . . whether or not you can tolerate lookin' at me. All right?"

Vivianna pressed her palm to his whiskery cheek. She was not afraid. She knew Johnny; she knew his soul. There was nothing he could've done to make him unworthy of her love—to cause her to abandon him.

"Two hours," she said.

He frowned. "What?"

"Kiss me for two hours here . . . beneath our honeysuckle vine," she explained. "Kiss me for two hours. Then I'll give you until after supper on Monday to tell me of this terrible darkness that haunts you."

Johnny grinned. He glanced up to the sun in the sky. "Two hours should run us right up to suppertime," he said.

"Then two hours it is . . . two hours and Monday," she whispered.

Vivianna placed her hands against the smooth, warm contours of Johnny's muscular chest. As ever, Johnny had discarded his shirt in an effort to tolerate the unfamiliar mugginess of the Alabama summer. She wondered how he ever survived years of war while having to don a uniform.

"All right," he agreed. "Two hours and Monday."

Vivianna's entire body delighted with goose pimples as Johnny took her in his arms—as his mouth began to entwine them in a bewitching spell of mutual and barely restrained desire. There, beneath the honeysuckle vine, as Johnny's demanding, heated kisses carried her to rapture on delicious wings of bliss, Vivianna knew that these were the kisses only he could give—that Johnny Tabor was the only man she could ever belong to.

He broke the seal of their lips a moment, allowing Vivianna to catch her breath. She smiled—giggled breathlessly.

"What's so amusin'?" he asked, kissing the corner of her mouth.

"Nothin'," she whispered. "I was just thinkin' of how adorable Lowell is."

Johnny's brows arched with bewilderment. "While I'm kissin' you . . . you're thinkin' about Lowell?" he asked.

Vivianna ran her fingers through Johnny's soft hair and smiled at him. "I'm just thinkin' how sweet he is . . . to think you need instruction on how to kiss me."

Johnny's expression relaxed. "Then . . . I guess I do all right at it after all."

Vivianna nodded. "Now kiss me, Johnny Tabor. Kiss me as I've never been kissed before."

As Johnny's mouth descended to hers once more, however, Vivianna was unsettled a moment as the words from Justin's once beloved letter echoed in her mind.

When I return we will meet beneath the honeysuckle vine, and I will kiss you such a kiss as you have never known before.

She thought it somehow ironic that it was Johnny with whom she lingered beneath the honeysuckle vine, not Justin. That it was Johnny who had first kissed her such a kiss as she had never known.

As the honeysuckle blossoms quivered in the breeze, sending the sweet fragrance of nectar into the air, Vivianna was thankful—thankful to be in Johnny's arms—thankful that heaven itself had brought him to Alabama to love her and to kiss her beneath the honeysuckle vine.

CHAPTER FIFTEEN

Johnny was already gone when Vivianna rose Monday morning. The night before, he'd told her he'd be leaving before sunup. Without a horse, he'd have to walk the three miles to the railroad site, and work started at sunrise. Caleb and Justin had also left for town. Thus, as Vivianna set the pan of hot biscuits in the center of the table, it was she and Savannah who would enjoy a friendly breakfast with Nate, Willy, and Lowell.

"Can we have extra butter this mornin', Mama?" Willy asked.

"Oh yes!" Lowell chimed. "Please, Miss Savannah! I went near two years without a lick of butter 'til I got here."

Savannah smiled, tousling Lowell's pumpkin hair.

"Well, how can I refuse when ya tell me that, Lowell?" she said. "All right then, boys. Since the men didn't have time for biscuits and butter . . . y'all can have their share."

"Thanks, Mama!" Nate exclaimed, plunging a fork into the butter dish in the center of the table.

"Mind your manners, Nate," Savannah reminded.

"Sorry, Mama," Nate said, slathering a hot biscuit with butter.

"Oh, Viv!" Savannah exclaimed then. "I plum forgot. Johnny said he left something for ya . . . left it on his bed."

Vivianna smiled, even for the sudden nervous sensation swelling in her stomach. Johnny had promised to tell her what ghosts were haunting his soul. He'd promised to tell her that very day. Still, she'd expected him to wait until after supper—until they could perhaps walk a ways and be alone.

"And I'm thinkin'," Savannah continued, "that maybe we oughta have Johnny move on into town . . . before you're what he's leavin' in his bed one mornin'."

"Savannah!" Vivianna gasped.

But Savannah only giggled and teasingly winked at Vivianna. "Well, at last! I didn't know what it would take to get you to start callin' me by my given name. But . . . now I know."

"What do you mean, Mama?" Willy asked. "About movin' Johnny into town before Vivianna's what he leaves—"

"Never you mind, Willy," Savannah interrupted. "Never you mind."

"Your face is as red as my big toe was when I stepped on that hornet last week, Viv," Nate said.

"Maybe Johnny's pulled his treasure out of that ol' tin box he hides," Willy suggested, his eyes wide as saucers. "Maybe that's what he's left for ya, Viv."

"More'n likely it's a letter," Lowell mumbled, shoving half a biscuit in his mouth all at once. "Mr. Johnny was the letter-writin'est fool I ever did see. When we was in camp, I swear that's all he did. Any time he'd get a letter, he'd pine away over it like he was sick or somethin' . . . then sit down and spend an hour in respondin'."

Vivianna frowned a bit. Johnny writing letters? To whom? Yet suddenly a great suspicion rose in her, followed by a wave of nausea. She felt hot, breathless, and weak.

"Well, who was he writin' to?" Nate asked. "He writes to his sister, ever since he's been here. But I ain't never seen him—"

"Excuse me," Vivianna said, pushing her chair away from the table.

"Viv?" Savannah asked.

But Vivianna didn't stop. She was afraid if she did, she might faint. An idea—a strange under-standing—was washing over her like a spring flood.

She nearly ran to Johnny's room—burst in and went directly to the bed. His bed was neatly spread, and there was indeed something lying upon it: a honeysuckle blossom, expertly carved from a small piece of wood, and an envelope.

Vivianna picked up the carving first and held it in her trembling hand as she gazed at its perfect beauty. The carving was small, resting perfectly in the palm of her hand. The intricate detail of the carving was unlike anything Vivianna had ever seen before. She remembered all the times she'd seen Johnny whittling on the front porch or out near the garden. She remembered the story he told her of what he loved most about Christmas—of carving animals from wood for his brothers.

Overwhelmed with emotion, love, and gratitude, she pressed the delicate wooden blossom to her lips. She closed her eyes, envisioned Johnny sitting whittling, and wondered how long he had worked to create such a perfect thing of beauty.

She opened her eyes, and her gaze fell to the letter. Her name was written on the envelope, yet still she could not accept what her mind was whispering to her.

Carefully, she laid the carving on the basin table nearby. She sat down on the bed and, with trembling hands, picked up the letter.

She opened the envelope—unfolded the page therein.

Tears filled her eyes as, before reading the short inscription, she looked to the signature there.

"I love you," she whispered, reading the last line of the letter aloud. *"Johnny."*

The tears in her eyes spilled over her cheeks as her fingers traced Johnny's name—traced the letter J at the beginning of it. It was perfectly she knew his writing; it was perfectly she recognized the J at the beginning of Johnny's signature.

"Johnny!" she breathed.

Johnny had written the letters she'd loved so! Johnny had penned the beautiful promises, the pledges of true love! Johnny—not Justin! She could not fathom why. She could not fathom why Johnny would have written such things to her— why he would have allowed her to believe Justin had written them. Still, in that moment, she didn't care! In that moment, she was only euphoric with the knowledge that Johnny had loved her so long. She did not pause to think that perhaps what he'd written in the letters was false, for she knew he loved her now. Thus he must have somehow loved her before—before he brought Justin home to Alabama—before he'd kissed her so blissfully beneath the honeysuckle vine!

"Are you all right, Viv honey?" Savannah asked from the doorway.

Vivianna nodded and managed to whisper, "Yes."

She read Johnny's note then, breathing the words written upon it.

"My darling Vivianna," she whispered. *"When I return this evening, I will keep my promise. I will tell you why you may not want me . . . reveal the darkness in my soul. Still, even though I know you may despise me, I hope you will yet love me, for I have loved you longer than you know. And when I return tonight—when I have shown you the sinfulness that taints me—I pray*

that you can find forgiveness in your heart, that you might still love me. Then we will meet beneath the honeysuckle vine, and I will kiss you such a kiss as you have never known before. I love you. Johnny."

Savannah was at her side, one comforting hand on her shoulder.

"Viv," she breathed. "What is it?"

"Johnny," Vivianna whispered. She turned to Savannah, tears streaming down her face. "It was Johnny who wrote the letters . . . not Justin. It's always been Johnny I loved, Savannah."

"Johnny?" Savannah breathed, taking the note from Vivianna's hand.

"He . . . he thinks I won't love him," Vivianna stammered. "He thinks I'll hate him for lyin' to me."

"Will you?" Savannah asked. Vivianna saw the tears in Savannah's eyes as well.

"Never!" she breathed. "He loves me!" she cried. Suddenly a delicious sort of laughter overtook her. "Savannah! He's loved me all along! Oh, how hard it must've been for him . . . to watch me with Justin!"

"But . . . but why didn't he tell you sooner?"

"He thought you loved Justin," Lowell said.

Savannah and Vivianna whirled around to see Lowell standing in the doorway.

"Lowell?" Savannah asked.

"He thought . . . Mr. Johnny knew that since

388

you thought Justin wrote the letters . . . he thought you could only love Justin," Lowell said. "I heard 'em talkin' . . . arguin' the day they disappeared from camp." Lowell paused and inhaled a deep breath. "I didn't understand it 'til now. I was too upset to see Mr. Johnny and Mr. Justin arguin' that day. And then . . . and then they never came back to camp, and I was taken to the orphanage." The small boy looked to Vivianna. "But I heard 'em. I heard Mr. Justin tellin' Mr. Johnny he was a fool. I heard him say no man could love a woman he'd never seen . . . never touched. But Mr. Johnny said a man could. Then he told Mr. Justin that Mr. Justin best do what was right. 'She loves you,' Mr. Johnny told him. 'And I won't see her heart broken.' That's what Mr. Johnny said. It was you they was arguin' over, wasn't it, Miss Vivianna?"

Vivianna was trembling so violently that the sound of Johnny's letter rattling in her hand echoed through the room. "I have to go to him," she breathed. "I have to go to town and find him. He has to know I don't hate him for this." She turned to Savannah, desperation gripping her. "This is what's been eatin' him up all this time!"

Savannah nodded, brushing tears from her cheeks.

"I . . . I have to get the letters from the attic at Daddy and Mama's house, Savannah! I have to read them again now that I know the truth!" Vivianna laughed with joy and overwhelming emotion. "I've got to get to town and find Johnny!"

"I'm goin' too!" Lowell exclaimed.

"Me too!" Nate hollered from the hallway.

"And me!" Willy said, pushing Lowell aside as he entered the room.

"We'll all go!" Savannah exclaimed. She took Vivianna by the shoulders. "We'll go with ya and start takin' the covers off all your mama's fine furniture. There's no way I'm lettin' you and Johnny linger together in the same house one more night . . . not with the passion this revelation will bring!"

"Let's go now, Vivianna!" Lowell exclaimed. "Mr. Johnny needs to know you ain't gonna hate him for bein' a liar."

Vivianna laughed through her tears. Picking up the carved honeysuckle blossom—Johnny's precious gift to her—she folded the note and pressed it into her pocket. She'd put the carving in a safer place, for it was far too delicate to leave unattended, and then she'd hurry to town. She didn't care if Johnny was working; she didn't care who would be looking on when she told him. But she had to tell him. She had to tell him that, though a moment before she would've thought it impossible to love him any more desperately, she did!

"Why didn't he say somethin' when he first arrived? Why didn't he just tell ya then?" Savannah asked as she and Vivianna rushed toward town. Vivianna wished Caleb hadn't ridden Captain to town that morning. She could've reached Johnny so much quicker if she'd been able to ride.

Vivianna shook her head and stammered, "I . . . I guess . . . I guess it was that he know I thought Justin wrote the letters. He knew I wouldn't accept any other truth right off. I hadn't faced my own pain. I couldn't see that Justin was nothin' like the letters . . . not at first. I loved Justin because I thought he loved me. Johnny couldn't tell me the truth . . . not until now."

"We're almost there!" Nate called. The boys had run ahead of Savannah and Vivianna, unable to keep themselves to simply a steady walk. "Someone in town will know where the railroad is workin', Viv! Come on!"

"I hear somethin'," Lowell said. Vivianna paused as Lowell stopped dead in his tracks.

"Come on, Lowell!" Willy said, stopping as well. "Don't quit now! We're almost to town."

"But I hear somethin' . . . and it's makin' my stomach churn awful bad," Lowell said.

Vivianna and Savannah stopped; Nate stopped.

"Here comes Mr. Winder," Nate said. "He's Tilly Winder's daddy."

"Tilly Winder? The loose woman that's been keepin' Justin in town so late?" Lowell asked.

"What?" Savannah gasped, frowning at Lowell.

"Yep . . . and he looks a might upset," Willy said.

"Maybe he caught Justin sparkin' his daughter out in back of the ol' Libby place," Nate offered.

Mr. Winder did look angry. As he approached, Savannah called, "Mr. Winder! Do you know where the railroad is workin'?"

Mr. Winder stopped and snorted as he glared at Savannah. "I know where the railroad is workin', Savannah Turner . . . you Yankee lover!" he growled.

"Mr. Winder!" Savannah gasped.

"They're workin' about a mile east . . . right out where they found that dead boy this mornin'!"

"A dead boy?" Nate asked.

Mr. Winder nodded. "Yep. One of ours . . . rather, one belongin' to those of us who didn't betray the Confederacy! Looks to have been there awhile too."

Vivianna's heart was hammering, for her heart knew—she knew who the dead Confederate was that had been found at the railroad site.

She hugged Lowell and Willy tight to her as they nestled in, frightened by Mr. Winder.

"How . . . how did he . . ." Savannah began. Vivianna saw the color drain from Savannah's face. She knew Savannah was awash with the same fear as she.

"When the railroad men got out there this mornin' to start work, the buzzards were circlin'. They found him stickin' out of a shallow grave. He was half chewed up, but his uniform showed he was one of our boys," Mr. Winder growled.

"Well, where you goin', Mr. Winder?" Nate asked.

"I'm goin' to get my gun, boy!" the man growled. "We're lynchin' the man who killed that poor soldier. And if the rope don't hang him proper . . . I'm gonna shoot him right between the eyes myself!"

"Lynchin'?" Savannah gasped. "Who? How do you know anybody even killed the boy? It could be he was just some poor soul on his way home when—"

"Oh, we know who killed him, Savannah Turner," Mr. Winder growled. "It was that damn Yankee you been havin' at your house ever since your Justin brought him here."

Vivianna gasped, and Mr. Winder's eyes narrowed as he looked her up and down.

"That's right, Miss Bartholomew. You're sweet on that Yankee, ain't ya?" he growled. "Yep . . . Justin told my Tilly that you're sweet as sugar on that Yankee."

"Johnny Tabor didn't kill that soldier!" Savannah exclaimed. "Why are y'all plannin' on lynchin' Johnny? He hasn't done anything! You can't—"

"Your own boy said that Yankee knew the dead man," Mr. Winder interrupted. "Justin told Sheriff Pidwell just this mornin' . . . that him and Johnny Tabor knew the dead boy at Andersonville. Justin said he was probably huntin' down your Yankee for crimes he committed at that prison camp."

"Justin? My Justin did that?" Savannah breathed. Savannah swayed and crumpled to the ground in a heap.

Mr. Winder reached out and took hold of Vivianna's chin.

"You best hurry, Miss Bartholomew," he growled. "You don't wanna miss the hangin' of your murderin' Yankee, now do ya?"

"Don't you touch her, you dirty Reb!" Lowell shouted, kicking Mr. Winder hard in one shin and causing him to release Vivianna.

"Get your hands off her, Mr. Winder!" Nate growled. "Else you'll have to answer to Johnny Tabor!"

Mr. Winder laughed. "Johnny Tabor will be too busy answerin' to heaven, boy. Or maybe sittin' down to dinner with the devil instead."

Vivianna didn't wait. Lifting her skirts, she ran toward town, calling over her shoulder, "You boys stay here with your mama!"

"Vivianna!" Lowell called. "I'm comin' too!"

Vivianna didn't argue as the boy joined her in

running toward town. She knew Nate and Willy would look after Savannah. She knew Lowell loved Johnny too much to stay behind.

"They won't hang him, will they, Vivi?" the boy asked.

Vivianna angrily wiped the tears from her cheeks, shaking her head as she ran. "Not unless they hang us first, darlin'," she sobbed.

They were nearer to town, and Vivianna could hear the commotion. The sound of an angry mob echoed through the air.

"I told ya I heard somethin'!" Lowell told her. "I've seen lynchin's before. They just can't lynch Mr. Johnny, Vivi!"

"They won't," Vivianna promised.

It was not difficult to determine where Johnny was. A mob of townsfolk was gathered outside the jail. Sheriff Pidwell was standing at the door, shouting at the mob. Men with ropes, axes, knives, and guns were shouting. Women were crying out in anger—screaming.

As Vivianna drew closer, she saw Caleb standing near to the sheriff on the steps of the jail. He was armed—obviously attempting to help the sheriff calm the mob.

"It's Caleb!" Lowell cried. "Caleb won't let 'em hang Mr. Johnny!"

"No, he won't," Vivianna breathed. In that moment, she thanked the heavens for Caleb—for the good man he was.

"They probably got Mr. Johnny in the jail-house," Lowell said. He looked to Vivianna, his eyes frightened and pleading. "What do we do, Vivi? Oh, what do we do?"

"I'm goin' to try and help him," she said. "You stay here. Johnny loves you, Lowell. He wouldn't want to see you hurt . . . especially on his account."

"He loves you too, Miss Vivianna," Lowell sniffled.

"I know," she said. She kissed him on the forehead and hurried toward the jailhouse.

Panic and fear the like she'd never known were gripping her! Even for all that had happened during the war—even when the Union had tried to occupy Florence—in all her life she'd never known such fear and panic. Yet she'd never known a love like the love she owned for Johnny Tabor either, and it drove her forward—forward into an angry mob—forward into the bowels of danger.

Vivianna pushed and shoved—struggled to get to the front of the mob. At last she managed it, but only because the angry men of Florence were still Southern boys whose mamas had taught them to allow a lady to pass.

"Where's Johnny?" Vivianna screamed once she was at the front of the mob. "Caleb! Caleb! Is he all right?"

Caleb saw her, frowned, and shook his head.

"Caleb!" she cried as fresh tears flooded her cheeks.

"He didn't kill him! I didn't say he killed him!"

Vivianna glanced to one side. Justin was there, shouting at the mob.

"I said he knew him! That's all I said!" Justin shouted.

But the mob was in a frenzy, and his confessions went unheard.

Anger as she had never known owned Vivianna then. She pushed and shoved her way to Justin, and when he looked up—startled at seeing her— she slapped him hard across one cheek.

Justin gasped, his eyes wide with hurt and guilt.

"I didn't tell 'em Johnny killed the man," he said.

"You as good as did, and you know it," she said.

"I . . . I'm lost, Viv," he said, tears welling in his eyes. "I lost my way a long time ago. This war . . . it did things to a man."

"I know that," Vivianna said. "It wounded them . . . left them with a bad leg and a limp like it did Caleb. It ate at their bodies like the lice and disease at Andersonville, Justin. But it's no excuse. Other men came home with just as many wounds as you did, Justin Turner—many with more. But they didn't come home to be what you've become."

"They beat him bad," Justin said, tears in his

eyes. "After all he done for me . . . I stood there
and let them beat him."

Vivianna sobbed a moment—but only for a
moment. There was no time for weakness. The
slap she'd delivered to Justin had distracted the
mob—but only for a moment.

"But . . . but he's still alive?" she asked.

Justin nodded.

Suddenly the mob surged forward. Vivianna
was knocked to the ground. She heard a
gunshot—heard the mob become more frenzied
as they broke down the jailhouse door.

Struggling to her feet, she turned to see a group
of men exchanging blows with Caleb and Sheriff
Pidwell.

"Stop!" she cried. But the beating continued.

Justin shouted, pulled a man away from his
brother, and began beating him.

There were suddenly cheers of triumph, and
Vivianna gasped as two men dragged a bloodied
and beaten Johnny Tabor from the jailhouse.
Vivianna recognized one of the men—Mr.
Sidney.

"We need a rope!" Mr. Sidney shouted. "We'll
hang him at the gallows . . . where all Yankees
oughta hang!"

Vivianna brushed the tears from her cheeks as
she looked to Johnny. His face was bruised and
swollen, his lip bleeding. His hands were tied at
his front and were cut and bleeding. She glanced

around and noticed that several of the men in the mob were bleeding from their noses and lips— including the two men restraining him. Johnny Tabor was not a man to be dragged to the gallows without a mean fight. It was obvious some of the men in the mob knew it.

She was helpless! Panicked! The lynch mob would hang Johnny if she didn't find a way to save him.

Frantic, she raced forward, throwing herself against Johnny.

"Vivi!" Johnny panted. He began to struggle, trying to free himself from his captors.

"Johnny!" she screamed.

"I love you, Vivi," he breathed.

"Johnny!" Vivianna screamed once more as two men took hold of her arms, pulling her away from him. She struggled wildly—tried to escape—tried to reach for Johnny.

He was weak, yet he fought too. Vivianna watched as Johnny struggled—butted Mr. Sidney's head with his own, sending the leader of the mob reeling.

The other man landed a hard fist to Johnny's right jaw, however, and Vivianna screamed as he crumbled to his knees.

"Hang him!" someone shouted.

"Leave him be! Leave him be!" a child's voice cried.

Vivianna looked to see Lowell. He was there, a

large man holding him tightly by the arms. Nate and Willy were there too, struggling to escape the clutches of the men holding them. Savannah was shouting, two women holding her back.

"Johnny!" Vivianna cried as someone threw a noose around Johnny's neck.

"Hang him high!" someone shouted. "That damn Yankee killed one of ours! Stretch his neck long!"

"No!" Vivianna cried.

She screamed again as gunfire broke the air. She gasped as Mr. Sidney crumpled to the ground, blood soaking his shirt at one shoulder. Another shot rang out, and the second man holding Johnny reeled backward.

The mob gasped—silenced.

Vivianna followed everyone else's attention as Charles Maggee made his way through the crowd toward Johnny. He leveled his Spencer carbine at Johnny's head. Vivianna gasped—held her breath. Surely Mr. Maggee didn't intend to kill Johnny! Hadn't Boy and Floydie been Johnny's friends and fellow soldiers?

"This man didn't do nothin'," Mr. Maggee said.

"He's a damn Yankee," Mr. Sidney growled.

Instantly, the barrel of Mr. Maggee's gun met with Mr. Sidney's forehead.

"And so were you, Matthew . . . when the war began," Mr. Maggee said. "Only reason you didn't enlist in the Alabama First with my boys is because your wife said if ya did, she wouldn't be here waitin' for ya if ya lived long enough to come home. Ain't that right?"

Mr. Sidney's lips pursed in an angry, defiant expression.

"We got a dead boy on our hands! A soldier!" someone shouted.

"This here Yankee knew him!" another man shouted.

"Yes, he did," Mr. Maggee said. He stepped in front of Johnny—Johnny, who spit blood out of his mouth and still remained on his knees, panting for breath. Turning, Mr. Maggee leveled his Spencer at another man at the front of the mob.

"Fact is that's why he's dead," Mr. Maggee said. "I killed him before he could murder this fine man."

Vivianna heard Savannah gasp, "Charles!"

"I was out visitin' my boys—my two good boys, buried out there in the Turners' cemetery because I didn't think they'd rest in peace here in town . . . not with the likes of you folks around," he said. "I was out there just talkin' with my boys, when all of a sudden, here comes this Reb. He asked me what I was doin' . . . and if I know'd a feller name of Johnny Tabor or one name of Justin Turner."

Several sets of eyes suspiciously lingered on Justin for a moment.

"I said I did," Mr. Maggee continued, "leastwise I knew Justin Turner. I'd seen Justin had made it home, right that afternoon on my way to visit the boys. I seen Justin Turner and his friend here walkin' up the road goin' home."

Vivianna was desperate to get to Johnny. She started to move toward him, but he raised his eyes, slightly shaking his head as a warning she should not come to him.

"Well, that dirty Reb . . . turns out he was a guard at Andersonville . . . tried his best to beat Johnny to death and couldn't do it. He thought I was sympathetic to the Confederacy. And I am, in a manner. We all are. I love Alabama. Anyhow, the man tells me he's here to kill Johnny Tabor . . . Justin Turner too, if he can manage it. Then he looked down and seen my boys' graves. He asked me why two Yankees were buried there. I told him they were my boys . . . that they died in the fightin'. That ol' Reb, he pulled a knife from his belt and lit out after me . . . said he was gonna cut me open and I could lay out in the sun and rot like the two Andersonville prisoners he was aimin' to kill. He got me quick across the belly—nearly spilled my guts out all over the ground—so I shoved him. He stumbled backward, tripped himself over a small headstone . . . cracked his head open on Floydie's."

Johnny glanced to Vivianna, and she struggled

to keep from running to him. It was Zachary Powell's blood on Floydie's stone!

"I went over to check on the boy, even though he'd been tryin' to kill me a moment before. He was dead . . . and I knew folks would hang it on the Turner boys if I left him there. So I drug him off into the woods. He was too heavy to take too far though. So I left him while I went home and cleaned up my wounds and fetched the wagon. I come back after a while and hauled him off over there where they're buildin' the new line. I figured nobody would find him . . . or if they did, they'd think he just died in the war, like my boys."

Vivianna sobbed as Sheriff Pidwell came forward and helped Johnny to his feet.

"You killed him?" Mr. Sidney growled.

"He was tryin' to kill me, Matthew, and his death was an accident. The war weren't over yet . . . not official. I figure he's counted as a casualty, just like my boys were . . . only without any honor at all." Mr. Maggee's eyes narrowed. "He meant to murder two men that weren't soldiers no more. Way I see it, that makes him deservin' of feedin' the buzzards." Mr. Maggee lowered his carbine. He turned to face the mob, many of whom now wore expressions of guilt and sadness rather than fury. "I know how many of you were in favor of the Union. I've heard you say it . . . know you hoped for the war to end to find the Union strong," Mr. Maggee said. "I won't reveal ya, but I do expect ya to leave this boy alone . . . and to know I was only protectin' myself and two men that fought for what was right, even if it don't seem that way sometimes. Go on home. Hide your own secrets. I know ya have 'em. You're nothin' but a mob of hypocrites."

The crowd paused, each person looking to one another. Some were still angry, some humbled, some standing in utter ignorance.

Vivianna watched as Caleb helped Sheriff Pidwell to untie Johnny's hands.

She gasped when Johnny growled, landing a brutal blow to Mr. Sidney's midsection with one knee before plowing a fist into his face to send him tumbling to the ground. Johnny spit on Matthew Sidney, and no one moved to help the mob leader.

Justin approached Johnny then. "Johnny . . . I . . . I . . ." Justin stammered.

His stammering was silenced when Johnny—weakened though he was—let go a powerful fist to Justin's jaw. Caleb stood over his brother for a moment. He shook his head as he looked at him, disgust and disappointment plain on his face. Yet in the next moment, he reached down, offering a hand and helping him to his feet.

"You best keep outta my way for a while, Justin," Johnny growled.

"I'm sorry, boy," Sheriff Pidwell said, placing one hand on Johnny's shoulder.

Frowning, Johnny nodded in heroic acceptance of the apology.

"You're just gonna let him go?" Mr. Sidney asked, struggling to his feet.

"He whipped up on you and six other men before he went down, Matthew," Sheriff Pidwell said. "Unless you want me to keep him here to have another go-around at you . . . I am lettin' him go. The man ain't done nothin' wrong." Sheriff Pidwell nodded, indicating Matthew Sidney should be on his way. He looked back to Charles Maggee then and placed a hand on his shoulder.

"Let's me and you have us a talk, Charles," the sheriff said.

Mr. Maggee nodded and followed Sheriff Pidwell into the jailhouse as the crowd quickly diluted.

As Johnny stumbled toward Vivianna at last, she flew to him. He was so weak, the force of her embrace forced them both to their knees. Yet he held her tightly, stroking her hair with one bloody hand.

"Johnny!" she breathed, kissing his cheek over and over, kissing him on the mouth, careless of straggling onlookers.

"Vivi," he breathed as she kissed him, "I thought . . . I thought they were gonna hang me . . . and then . . . then I'd never be able to tell you the truth."

"Mr. Johnny!" Lowell cried, throwing his arms around Johnny from behind. "Oh, Mr. Johnny! I thought they were gonna hang you for sure!"

"Me too, Lowell," Johnny said. "Me too."

Vivianna glanced up to see Savannah standing nearby. Tears were streaming down her face as she watched Johnny and Vivianna—as she held one hand on Nate's head, the other on Willy's, to keep them from racing forward. Nate and Willy were also crying, wiping dripping noses on their shirtsleeves.

"Oh, Johnny!" Vivianna sobbed as he held her. "I love you! I love you!"

"I love you, Vivi," he breathed into her hair. "And I can't wait one more minute to tell you the truth. All I could think of . . . all I could think was that I was gonna hang . . . and you'd never know the truth."

He released her, and she watched as he struggled to reach into the front pocket of his trousers.

Withdrawing a worn, tattered piece of paper, he offered it to her and said, "This is how Justin saved my life, Vivi. Justin gave me this . . . one night when I thought I didn't have a reason to live. This is what saved me, Vivi. You saved me."

Vivianna wept as she unfolded the piece of

paper—recognized it as a page of a letter she'd written to Justin over two years before.

"Whenever I am able, I slip away to the arbor and the honeysuckle vine," she began. *"There I imagine you are home again . . . that you and I are together on your father's swing, talking of family and friends, of long summer walks and pollywogs in puddles."*

"I've carried that letter ever since, except for Andersonville," he mumbled. "I buried it in my tin box that day, just before me and Justin were captured . . . buried it with the other letters you'd written to Justin . . . the ones he gave to me . . . the ones I answered." He chuckled and coughed with the pain it caused him. "It's why it took us so long to get home once we were released. I told Justin I'd get him home . . . but that we had to go back for my tin box first. It took us a whole week just to get back to where I buried it."

"Johnny," Vivianna breathed, placing a loving hand to his bruised cheek.

"I had to go back for them, ya see, Vivi," he panted, " 'cause you thought Justin wrote the letters to you. I knew you were in love with him . . . that I had to get him home to you. But I wanted your letters with me so I'd have 'em always . . . so I could make-believe you'd written them to me and not to Justin."

He coughed again. She could tell he was in pain.

"Johnny," she said, "we have to get you home."

But he shook his head. "I'm a liar, Vivianna," he said. "I'm a sinful devil of a liar. I let you think Justin wrote those letters. All this time I let you think—"

"It's you I've always loved, Johnny Tabor," Vivianna told him. Taking his face between her hands, she forced his eyes to look into hers and said, "Don't you see? I did fall in love with the man who wrote those letters. I fell in love with you."

A tear trickled from the corner of one of Johnny's eyes. Exhausted from both the mob beating and emotion, he leaned forward, pressing his forehead to hers for a moment before finding her mouth with his own.

His kiss was hot, demanding, and as passionate a kiss as ever he'd given her.

"Best save that for lingerin' beneath the honeysuckle vine, Mr. Johnny," Lowell said.

Johnny's mouth left Vivianna's as he chuckled. "Have you been lookin' in on folks again when you shouldn't, Lowell?" he asked.

Vivianna stroked his face—smoothed the dirt and blood from his broad brow.

"Yes, sir, Mr. Johnny," Lowell admitted.

Vivianna brushed the tears from her cheeks and pressed one last kiss to Johnny's lips as Caleb, Savannah, and the younger Turner boys approached.

"You're a hard man to bring down, Johnny Tabor," Caleb said, helping Johnny to his feet.

"Oh, my darlin'!" Savannah sobbed, reaching up to dab at the blood near his mouth with a lace handkerchief. "I am just so sorry! Oh, my dear boy!"

"Thank ya, Miss Savannah," Johnny mumbled.

Johnny looked to Nate and Willy, still wiping tears on their shirtsleeves.

"It's all right, boys," Johnny said, tousling their hair. "I'm fine. Everything is fine."

Nate and Willy rushed forward, flinging themselves against Johnny and hugging him desperately. Vivianna watched as Lowell joined them, smiling at the pure joy displayed on his young face.

The mob had nearly succeeded in hanging Johnny. Justin had been the cause of it. Vivianna looked to Justin, and he shook his head in an expression of guilt and self-loathing. She wanted to go to Justin—to slap him once more. Yet the knowledge she'd nearly lost the man she loved began to wash over her like a sudden illness, and she began to sway—felt the bleak darkness of a faint overtaking her.

"Vivi!" she heard Johnny say—and she was in his arms. He kissed her cheek, her mouth—and she was invigorated before the faint took her.

"Johnny!" she breathed. "I nearly lost you! What if they'd . . . what if they'd . . ."

409

"They didn't," he told her. "They didn't. I'm here . . . and I'll never leave you, Vivianna. I love you." He brushed a strand of hair from her cheek, grinned, and added, "But I do hate Alabama. Do you think you could marry me quick and let me take you home to Texas?"

Still trembling with residual terror, she nodded, wrapped her arms around Johnny's neck, and whispered, "Yes! Oh yes, Johnny! I love you. Oh, how I love you!"

"Kiss her again, Mr. Johnny," Lowell said. "The way I taught ya now."

Vivianna watched as Johnny looked to Lowell. He chuckled and nodded at the boy.

"Pull her in good to ya . . . like a gun stock to your shoulder," Lowell instructed.

Johnny did as he was told—pulled Vivianna into a commanding embrace.

"Now kiss her good and hard . . . like I told ya," Lowell said.

"He's a bossy little cuss, ain't he?" Johnny asked, gazing into Vivianna's eyes.

"Yes," Vivianna breathed. Johnny was holding her; she was in his arms! Her boundless joy was overwhelming.

"Still, I guess I better do what he says," Johnny mumbled.

"I guess so," Vivianna whispered.

"That's the way, Mr. Johnny!" Vivianna heard Lowell giggle as Johnny's mouth melted to her own. "Step up and see how it's done, fellers! I taught him everything he knows about kissin' women, Miss Savannah."

"Then heaven help me, Lowell!" Savannah laughed. "Heaven help me!"

EPILOGUE

Vivianna closed her eyes. Inhaling the sweet scent of the crisp autumn air, she smiled. Johnny had been right; there was nothing like Texas! She opened her eyes, gazing out across the landscape to the cattle grazing on the hillside—reveling in the feel of the fresh, fragrant breeze weaving through her loose hair.

She wondered if she would ever miss the balmy feel of Alabama. She was certain she would; she must. One day she might miss it, for she was born there, had known her family there. Yet she felt it would be a far-off day. More than Alabama, she missed Savannah and the boys—Nate, Willy, Caleb, and Lowell. Even at times she missed Justin—the Justin she'd known as a child. Yet she did not miss Alabama, for the dryer, fresher air of Texas—the unimpaired vision of the far-reaching landscape—it gifted her very soul a sense of freedom.

She heard the drumming of horse hooves and turned, smiling as she saw Johnny riding toward her. Though it seemed quite impossible, each time she saw him, her heart swelled for knowing his handsome countenance. He sat tall and straight in the saddle—a very commanding vision indeed. Oh, how she loved him! As her heart began to beat madly—as butterflies took flight in her stomach—she smiled and waved as he rode toward her.

She thought of the moment earlier that morning when she'd awakened in the warmth and power of his arms, just as she had every morning since they'd wed a month before. There was nothing in the world so wonderful to Vivianna Tabor as waking up in Johnny's arms—knowing his kiss as her first pleasure of the day. She thought of the nights spent in his arms as well, blushing with delight in thinking of the passion the moonlight ever led them to sharing.

Johnny reined in, dismounted, and gathered Vivianna into his arms. "It's a bit chilly out here, darlin'," he said, pressing his warm mouth to hers. "Let me warm ya up a bit." He kissed her again, and Vivianna's arms encircled his neck as she bathed in the sweet, moist flavor of his mouth.

He broke the seal of their lips, smiling as he raked a strong hand through her hair. His dark eyes smoldered with the love he owned for her. Vivianna could see her own reflection in them, and she could not resist kissing him once again.

"I've got somethin' for ya, Vivi," Johnny said.

"What?" she asked.

He looped the bridle reins to a nearby post. Reaching into the back pocket of his trousers, he smiled as he produced a letter.

"I think we are about to be thoroughly entertained, my angel," he chuckled.

Vivianna smiled—bit her lip with delighted anticipation.

"From Lowell?" she asked.

Johnny nodded and handed her the letter.

Vivianna giggled with delighted anticipation. Taking Johnny's hand, she led him to one of the large logs sitting around the firepit. They were some ways away from the house, and Johnny's parents were due to arrive any time to help bring in the cattle. Still, Vivianna knew Johnny would hear them coming, so she figured there was no harm in taking a moment to read Lowell's letter.

She felt excitement rising in her as she opened the envelope and removed the pages of the letter. Lowell's letters were always amusing—and informative.

"Are you ready, darlin'?" Vivianna asked Johnny.

Johnny smiled, nodded, and stretched his long legs out before him.

"This will be good. It always is," he chuckled.

Vivianna cleared her throat and looked at Lowell's letter.

"Dear Johnny and Vivianna," she began reading, *"I am sitting here in the cemetery. I have just been watching Miss Savannah and Mister Maggee sparking in the old arbor. Mister Maggee does not need any lessons in kissing*

*women. I think that is good for Miss Savannah.
I hope Johnny is still doing fine with kissing you,
Vivianna. I tried to teach him well. Please write
to me if he needs my advice.*"

Instantly, Johnny and Vivianna burst into
laughter. Such a hard laughter made continuing
to read difficult, for Vivianna could not catch her
breath. Johnny doubled over with laughing so
hard! Still, at last they were able to sigh, wipe the
moisture from their eyes, and continue.

Vivianna sighed and read.

Miss Savannah is very happy that no
one wanted to hang Mister Maggee for
knocking that Reb's head on his son's
tombstone. The sheriff has said that it was
an accident and that Mister Maggee is
fine to go about his life. I think Nate and
Willy will have a new daddy soon.

The sheriff wrote a letter to that dead
Reb's mama. I think that is a kind thing. I
do not know if I would have wrote a letter
to her. Still I think it is the right thing
to do. So I will not hate the sheriff for
writing it.

Justin and that loose woman Tilly
Winder married one another. I heard
Miss Savannah tell Mister Maggee that
Tilly Winder's father demanded that
Justin marry her. I hope they will be

happy. Well . . . that is a lie. I am still angry with Justin for almost causing Johnny to hang. I will try to feel better about that someday.

I have seen many things of late. I have seen Caleb sparking with a pretty girl with dark hair. Her name is Emily. She is pretty, but I do not care for her name. I knew a girl with that name, Emily, before and she was a mean girl. She once put a snake down my back, and I hate snakes. So I do not like girls named Emily. I will never kiss one. The only one I may kiss is Caleb's Emily if she wants me to kiss her.

Again Johnny's laughter caused Vivianna to giggle. Still, biting her lip she continued—determined to finish Lowell's sweet letter.

I am well. I miss you both. Sometimes I think I should have gone with you to Texas as you asked me to. But most times I am glad I am here with Nate and Willy and Caleb and Miss Savannah. Miss Savannah loves me and tells me I am her son as much as Nate and Willy. Also, me and Nate and Willy have great fun. We are still finding bones. We found a dead skunk. We skinned it and boiled it. Miss Savannah made us sleep in our fort for a week. She said we smelled bad. Still, the skunk boiled up good, and we have his bones in our collection. So, even though I miss you, Mister Johnny, and you, Miss Vivianna, I am happy.

I must go now. Nate has found a dead bull snake. We are going to skin it. I will write to you again. Please write to me. I love you both and will remain yours forever, Lowell.

Vivianna folded the letter—sighed with both gladness and melancholy.

"I miss him," Johnny mumbled.

Vivianna looked to her handsome husband—saw the moisture in his eyes as he gazed out to the horizon. "Me too," she whispered, feeling tears in her own eyes.

"Vivi?" he said then—and she glanced back to him.

"What, darlin'?"

Johnny's brow drew into a frown, and he slowly stood—his attention still fixed to the horizon.

"I need my gun," he mumbled.

Vivianna followed Johnny's gaze. As he hurried to his horse, pulling his rifle from the rifle sheath of his saddle, she raised one hand to shade her eyes from the bright Texas sun.

Two riders were approaching. They were already close enough that Vivianna could see

417

they were not Indians. She and Johnny had been so enchanted by Lowell's letter they had not heard the riders approach. Vivianna's heart began to beat with fear. Of late, there had been no incidents in or around Gainesville that should cause worry. Still, renegade soldiers, still angry over the war, yet appeared now and again.

Johnny stepped in front of her—readied his rifle as Vivianna watched the men ride closer. Closer they came—closer—and as they became more easily visible, Vivianna's eyes widened. She thought certain her heart would beat from her breast—for each man sat tall in his saddle. Each man had a distinct manner of riding—a manner that Vivianna recognized. Yet it couldn't be! It couldn't!

"Samuel!" Vivianna breathed. "Augie!"

"What?" Johnny asked, frowning to her—still aiming his rifle at the approaching men.

"It's Sam and Augie!" Vivianna cried. "It's them, Johnny! I swear it!"

"Vivi," Johnny began. Yet he lowered his rifle as the two men reined in before him.

"Vivianna?" one of the men asked.

Vivianna's heart hammered wildly, and tears misted her eyes, yet she recognized her own violet eyes looking back at her—her mother's beautiful blue-violet eyes!

"Samuel!" Vivianna cried, racing forward as the men quickly dismounted.

At once, Sam caught her in a powerful embrace. "Viv!" he breathed, his voice breaking with emotion.

Vivianna looked beyond Samuel—left his arms to enter those of Augustus. "Augie!" she cried. "Oh, Augie!'

"Baby sister," Augie chuckled. "We thought you were dead, darlin'! We thought you were dead!"

"Where have you been?" Vivianna cried with simultaneous joy and pain. "Where have you boys been?"

She drew away from Augie and brushed the tears from her cheeks as more followed. She looked from one to the other—from her brother Samuel to her brother Augustus. She wasn't sure it was real! Could they really be there with her— with her and Johnny?

"We heard the family had been killed," Sam explained, wiping a tear from the corner of his eyes. "We thought you'd been killed too. We didn't write, because we thought there was no reason to . . . thought nobody was there to receive the letters."

"Vivianna," Augie said, leaning forward and kissing her cheek. "We thought you were dead! It wasn't 'til we decided to go back and see what had been done with the house . . . to visit y'all's restin' places that we found out the truth! Thank the Lord we stopped in at the Turner place, Viv. Thank the Lord!"

Vivianna sobbed—buried her face in her hands and sobbed with overpowering joy and relief! Her arms and legs felt weak, and she was grateful to suddenly find herself sobbing in Johnny's arms—held close and protected against his strong body.

"I'm Johnny," she heard Johnny say.

She felt him shake hands with each of her brothers.

"We heard a lot about you, Johnny Tabor," Sam said. "It seems you're a man to be reckoned with."

Somewhat recomposed, Vivianna turned to face her brothers again. Sam and Augie! She could not believe they stood before her.

"From what Miss Savannah told us, you're right worthy of our baby sister," Augie added.

"Well, I don't know about worthy," Johnny began, "but I couldn't live without her."

"Oh, Viv!" Sam said, chuckling and drawing Vivianna from Johnny's arms and into his own once more. "Viv! I'm sorry we caused you so much pain! We didn't know you were alive. We were ignorant not to make certain you'd been lost with Daddy and Mama before now. I'm so sorry."

Vivianna wept—wept with whole and complete joy as Augie took her in his arms again then.

"I'm so sorry, Viv," he said, his voice breaking with emotion. "I'm so sorry."

"It doesn't matter," she whispered. "You're

here. You're alive, and you're here. That's all that matters now."

Augie released, her and Vivianna smiled at him.

"Heard you did your worst of it at Andersonville, Johnny," Sam said.

Johnny nodded. "I did. I sure did. And you boys?"

Augie chuckled. "Well, we're hopin' there's somethin' 'round Guinesville for two men lookin' for work to do. I figure we'll all need a lifetime to tell the stories between us."

Johnny nodded. "Well, if you boys don't mind cattle . . . me and my daddy can keep ya busy for the rest of your lives."

Both Sam and Augie nodded.

Sam reached out and caressed Vivianna's cheek with the back of his hand. "I wouldn't mind anything that kept me near my baby sister," he said.

"Well, y'all unload your gear in the barn. We'll give your horses somethin' and then head for the house," Johnny said. "We all got a lot of talkin' to do."

"Thank ya, Johnny," Augie said.

Sam nodded, brushed another tear from his temple, and kissed Vivianna's cheek. "Baby sister," he said, shaking his head. "Oh! I almost forgot," he exclaimed suddenly. Moving to his saddlebags, he opened one, removing a book.

421

Vivianna frowned with curiosity as he handed it to her.

"It's from that little red-haired feller Miss Savannah took in," he said. "He says the book ain't the gift. It's what's inside. He said he wanted to make certain you and Johnny had a little piece of somethin'."

"Head on over to the barn, boys," Johnny said, nodding toward the barn. "I'll be right behind ya."

"All right. Thank ya, Johnny," Sam said.

Augie nodded and said, "Thank ya."

As her brothers started toward the barn, Vivianna frowned as she opened the book. She gasped—more tears moistening her cheeks as she saw the sprigs of honeysuckle vine and blossoms perfectly pressed between the pages of several sections of the book.

A small piece of paper slipped from the book, floating gently toward the ground. Johnny caught it, however, and read, *"To Mister Johnny and Miss Vivianna. I went out to your special sparking place and picked a few vine parts for you. I don't know if there are any pretty honeysuckle vines in Texas . . . so I thought I would send these. From Lowell."*

Johnny smiled as he looked at the pressed flowers and leaves between the pages of the book. "That boy has more sense of things than anybody I ever knew," he said.

"Yes, he does," Vivianna said. She glanced to Sam and Augie, smiling as she watched Sam point to several cattle grazing nearby and nudge Augie with his elbow. "It's a miracle, Johnny. I still can't believe it," she whispered.

Johnny shook his head in mutual disbelief. "It is a miracle . . . them comin' here . . . bein' alive."

Vivianna looked to Johnny—placed a tender palm to his rugged cheek. "Yes. Sam and Augie are a miracle too," she said. "But I mean you. The miracle heaven sent for me . . . was you."

"I love you, Vivi," Johnny whispered as he gathered her into his arms.

"I love you, Johnny," Vivianna breathed.

"Now, my own little honeysuckle blossom," he mumbled, "give me that nectar you keep in your mouth."

Vivianna smiled as Johnny kissed her—held tight to the book between whose pages a young boy had pressed the sprigs of a wild honeysuckle vine.

AUTHOR'S NOTE

I was in fifth grade the year I read *Gone with the Wind*. Not only was Margaret Mitchell's Civil War (and beyond) epic the first real novel I read, but it also still stands as the thickest, longest, highest page count novel I ever read! In fact, I believe that it was because of that reading experience that I'd always look at the page count of a book after that, and if it was longer than four hundred pages, I wouldn't even crack the spine. But I digress.

Reading *Gone with the Wind* was incredible, inspiring, and eye-opening, and I have to say, I think it impacted me so greatly that it actually helped mold who I became. Oddly enough, I don't like sad endings (as you well know by now). There's enough going on in reality incorporating sad endings that I never have any desire to experience one in fiction. Thus, it seems strange to me that I did love *Gone with the Wind* so much. But as you know (if you've been lost in that book), it's a historically fascinating journey—and I love history!

Shortly after I read the book, the movie version of *Gone with the Wind* experienced a limited rerelease, and I was able to go to the old Hiland theater house in Albuquerque (when the plush seats and other original decor still existed) and watch the enormous, crushed red velvet, gold-tasseled curtains part just before the movie started. Then there was the sound of the movie reel beginning (something I'm sad that children today will never experience), the lights on the screen, and voilà—*Gone with the Wind* as no one has ever seen it since! The movie affected me just as deeply as the book had. I thought (and still think) that Vivien Leigh is one of the most beautiful women ever, and the sheer scope and lavishness of the cinematography dazzled and inspired me like no other movie I had ever seen.

You might be wondering why I'm spending so much time babbling on about my *Gone with the Wind* experience. Well, it was *Gone with the Wind* that planted my passion for Civil War history deep into the very core of my heart. Once I'd read the book and seen the movie, I was ravenous for Civil War history knowledge—especially Southern history. The South intrigued me—not simply because I couldn't understand the whole ignorant thought process around slavery and how it could have ever existed but because of the customs, the fashions, the architecture, the easy, relaxed manner of culture, the Spanish moss and cypress trees, Reconstruction, industrialization, and so much more. Thus, it was my passion for Civil War history and the people that lived through that terrible conflict that led me to writing not only *The Fragrance of Her Name* but also this book—*Beneath the Honeysuckle Vine*.

Beneath the Honeysuckle Vine is a soul-written book for me—meaning it incorporates feelings, opinions, and emotions that my very soul has experienced over and over through the years. Though all my books were birthed in my heart, some of them go deeper than that, and *Beneath the Honeysuckle Vine* is one of those.

Ironically, where readers are concerned, it's not my most popular book. It seems readers either love it and list it in their top favorites or they list it at the very bottom of their list. In conversation with people who own different opinions of the story, I've come to this conclusion: those who love this book, whose hearts it touches so deeply, love it for its historical value and nostalgic sense of a time we could never empathize with. They recognize the sort of love borne through heart-felt letters and not just visual or physical attraction. It's an old-school concept, lost to time and technology. The other side of the coin (for those who don't list this book as a favorite) is that *Beneath the Honeysuckle Vine* begins with a sense of sadness, struggling and wounded bodies and souls. Furthermore, in regard to the love letters between Johnny and Vivianna, as one reviewer on one of the social networks said, "I felt they needed a better reason to fall in love." (Yep! I can be inspired by negative things just as well as positive things—sometimes!) I'm not offended that some readers do not like this book as well, because if anyone understands wanting everything to be pretty and happy, it's me! And I know that the human interest in history isn't as prolific as it was, or should be. Therefore, *Beneath the Honeysuckle Vine* certainly appeals more to some readers than to others.

Now the other big part of this story that is very significant in my own life history is the letter writing between Johnny and Vivianna. To the reader who thought they needed "a better reason to fall in love" (and I *really* loved writing that book, by the way, so I thank you, whoever you are, for that line that inspired me!), what she didn't know was that part of the plot was based on my own falling-in-love story.

My husband (Kevin from Heaven) and I did meet in person, but shortly thereafter, I left to attend college out of state. (Some of you already know this story, so sorry for the repeat.) Back in the olden days of 1983–1984, card and letters were still the main technique of correspondence, other than landline telephones (which would often cost $1 per minute long distance). Thus, Kevin and I began exchanging letters. For nearly ten months, during which I was in a different state, we wrote back and forth, discussing everything from what we'd had for lunch to information about our families. Almost immediately, however, our letters took on a very romantic tone. We were writing what might be called "serious but with a teasing delivery"— the first part of the letter being an attempt to write romance to one another, with the second part of the letter being about everyday thoughts, experiences, and feelings.

Being that people will often say things in letters that they would be too afraid to confess or say face-to-face, Kevin and I were able to get to know each other in a way that most people don't. Although we were definitely attracted to each other the instant we met (wildly so, I might add), we found that through our letters, there was an even deeper connection that we might not have experienced as early as we did otherwise. To this day, our letters to each other are one of my most treasured earthly possessions. Fraught with scandalous flirting, humor, and drama, those letters tell the story of our falling in love—and they are a profound insight and inspiration.

Interestingly enough, my daughter and her husband had a similar experience. Having met at college, they found themselves in different states during the summer break. Texting was their letters, and then they talked on the phone every Sunday for, like, eight hours (and that's not an exaggeration)! Therefore, similar to the story of Kevin and me, Sandy and her heroic Soren were already in love by the time they returned to college. But where Kevin and I waited an entire two weeks after we were finally together in body as well as spirit, Sandy and Soren waited almost a whole month! Ha ha!

My son Mitch and his wife, Mallory, also had the beginnings of their romance through letters via e-mail during their separation. Actually, their story is even more incredible—for they'd never even met in person when they began e-mailing! But once they met (and I'll never forget the look on my son's face the first time he sat in the same room with Mallory)—well, the rest is history! They met in person for the first time the very end of March and were engaged by the very beginning of April.

And so, my own experience is where I found the inspiration for the letter writing between Vivianna and Johnny—their means of falling in love. It was a common way to fall in love all through history—*if* you were given the choice to fall in love, that is.

It breaks my heart to know that letters and cards (correspondence via tangible mail) are vanishing things. People do not realize what is being lost, I'm afraid. Just the other day, I heard a statistic that in ten years children will have no idea what receiving a birthday card in the mail is like. That makes me so sad! Especially when I remember receiving that unexpected birthday card—a handwritten note from my grandma or grandpa inside and the ever-impressive two-dollar bill enclosed. It was wonderful! I still love receiving mail, though letters and cards are very few and very far between. We will live to regret the day personally written letters are lost forever. It takes time and thought to sit down and handwrite a card or letter. E-mails are not the same.

There's a quote I love. It was included on the cover of a little folio of Victorian notecards a friend gave me some years ago. I'm actually going to have it framed for display in my home very soon. But it says so much—expresses such a deep and meaningful truth—a truth that will be lost to technology and time. It's an excerpt from the Royal Gallery, 1897, and reads thus:

> Never burn kindly written letters; it is so pleasant to read them over when the ink is brown, the paper yellow with age, and the hands that traced the friendly words are folded over the heart that prompted them. Keep all loving letters. Burn only the harsh ones, and in burning, forgive and forget them.

The line, "It is so pleasant to read them over when the ink is brown, the paper yellow with age, and the hands that traced the friendly words are folded over the heart that prompted them," is so affecting to me. I think of my sweet grandmother

(Opal Switzler States)—her mortal remains now resting in a quiet, beautiful space in Canyon City, Colorado, her once warm and gentle hands still folded over the place where her heart used to beat—and whenever I read one of her letters I can envision her sweet smile and her still warm and gentle hands waving to me from the peace and happiness of heaven. Without the letters she'd written that I now have, that helped me to see into her thoughts and heart, I wouldn't know her as well as I do, and I wouldn't have a tangible something written in her very own pretty little script, explaining feelings, memories, and the prices of shortening and eggs in 1936. The world is losing something profound in giving up letters to e-mails and texting. It haunts me to my very core, and I feel sad for she who thought Johnny and Vivianna needed "a better reason to fall in love"—because she'll never know that manner of expressing emotion: the love letter.

Another thing that I did choose to include in this book is a little more gruesomeness—and I chose to include it for the mere fact that we, in this country and in this day and age, are spoiled rotten when it comes to physical hardships the like endured by men and women during the Civil War. Believe me, Johnny's descriptions of his time in Andersonville do not begin to convey the true horrors of it all! And as much as I believe we all need escape through fluff and romance and things that don't tax our already overtaxed minds, I do believe that once in a while, we need to remember what our ancestors endured and be more consciously respectful and grateful for it, and for them. I won't hop up on my political soapbox, but I will say that Americans have forgotten what it is to suffer for the freedoms we enjoy. Most of us didn't even have to experience a war on the scale of World War II. Furthermore, the men and women who fight to protect our freedoms and the freedoms of other—the media skirts them, disrespects them, and would have us forget what they're enduring. Therefore, once in a while, I feel the need to remind and remember.

And now I'll leave the sad stuff behind and push forward with a little insight into some other things about *Beneath the Honeysuckle Vine*. First of all, I certainly hope that everyone out there had the opportunity as a child (or adult) to sip the nectar from honeysuckle. What a wonderful childhood memory that is for me! The hours we'd spend sitting in our backyard, plucking honeysuckle blossoms and carefully picking them apart to finally enjoy that one tiny little droplet of nectar! Oh, I miss those carefree childhood days, don't you? Tadpoles hold the same mesmerizing wonder for me and were an indispensable part of my childhood too—thus the tadpole and pollywog scene in the book.

And then there's the bone collection of Nate,

Willy, and eventually Lowell. Well, you know the side of my family that is intrigued with black widow spiders? That same side of the family likes anything interesting and gruesome—including bones! My favorite "family bone" story is one that I wasn't aware of until just a few years ago. Now, I may or may not have already told you this story in another Author's Note, but since I can't remember off the top of my head, here it comes either way.

I have these two really cool uncles, Uncle Wayne and Uncle Russell. You've met them before in Author's Notes. Well, this story involves my Uncle Wayne as the hero. Way, way, way back (I believe it was the late '60s), my Uncle Wayne and a friend of his were wandering along an old riverbed. Now, you must understand that Uncle Wayne has the eyes of a hawk! This is the guy who spotted a tarantula on the side of the road as he was driving home one pitch-black night from Canyon City and stopped to collect (being that he must've always had a jar in his trunk for just such occasions). Anyway, my hawk-eyed Uncle Wayne and his friend were roaming along this old riverbed when all at once Uncle Wayne looks up and sees a sort of spherical something slightly protruding from the dirt of riverbank wall. (The river was low, so the bank was vertically higher than normal.)

Well, naturally Uncle Wayne reached out.

digging his fingers around whatever the thing was. And lo and behold, what does he pull out but a human skull! That's right, a human skull! Now, being that Uncle Wayne is as smart as he is hawk-eyed, he studied the riverbank awhile and surmised that the skull must be of Native American origin and very old. Nowadays, you'd be obligated to report this kind of a find to the state or something, but Uncle Wayne (being interested in all things natureish and scientific of any kind), simply kept the skull. Seriously. He just set it in his closet and hung onto it for years.

Eventually, my uncles and my auntie (you remember Auntie from other stories, right?) all shared a house when they were in their twenties and none of them were yet married. This meant that Uncle Wayne moved all his stuff (including the skull) into Auntie's place.

Time passed, as it often does, Uncle Russell got married and moved out, then Uncle Wayne moved out, and then Auntie got married to my now Uncle Ken. Well, as you know, when you move, sometimes you leave things behind on accident, or intentionally if you don't (especially if you're not sure what to do with them). The skull must've been one of those things Uncle Wayne wasn't sure what to do with because it ended up sitting on a shelf for a time before my Uncle Ken went downstairs and found it one day.

Of course, he instantly went on a rant about how someone was going to come into the house and see a human skull and think he and my auntie were murderers or something. (He's a funny man, always laughing, but the skull must've wigged him out—understandably.)

So Auntie gave the skull back to my Uncle Wayne. But Uncle Wayne was still uncertain about what do with it or how to display it in his house, so he gifted it to a woman he was dating at the time who worked at a museum.

My reaction to hearing what Uncle Wayne had eventually done with the skull was thus: "Are you crazy? You just gave it away? I would've *loved* to have had that!"

Well, feeling regretful at that point, my Uncle Wayne soon sent me a mummified toad he'd found in his basement one year. So it all worked out for the best. I will never have to explain to anyone why there's a human skull in my closet, and I added a mummified toad to my collection of rarities amassed thanks to my Uncle Wayne, grandparents, and mom. So in the end, all is right with the world.

As a side note, my kids are the same way; I think most kids are. I remember the Thanksgiving when Mitch was about four or five and was so intrigued with the turkey bones that my mom boiled all the meat and remains off our Thanksgiving turkey, bleached the bones, drie them out, and put them in a shoebox, which she gave to Mitch for Christmas, I think. He was elated, and he and my mom spent several hours going through those old turkey bones. I love Christmas gifts like that!

Anyway, I've always been intrigued with bones, dead animals, and so on—and so were Nate, Willy, and Lowell.

Speaking of Lowell, I have to admit that he is one of my favorite secondary characters ever! He's so funny—so brave and brazen too, to kiss Vivianna like that when he first met her! Many readers have written to me concerning their adoration of Lowell, and I am so touched, tenderhearted, and grateful that you all love him as much as I do. He's such a little dickens, and I love him!

I love this book! It springs from something embedded deep within my soul, and whether or not it's a favorite of yours, I do hope you enjoyed it. At least the kissing was good, right? (Winky wink!)

Beneath the Honeysuckle Vine Trivia Snippets

Snippet #1—Guess what my major was in college? Yep, that's it! For practical reasons (at the time), I majored in Secretarial Science. However, my minor was in something I loved—story!

Snippet #2—The Alabama First Cavalry was a real cavalry unit, not one I made up. The Alabama First Cavalry comprised rich men, poor men, black men, and white men who were loyal to the Union, even for the fact they were Alabamians, and volunteered for service. Southerners who fought for the Union were called Southern Unionists and were viciously persecuted by loyal Confederates. In fact, you may or may not be aware that more than one in ten southerners who fought in the Civil War enlisted in and fought for the Union Army. And with the exception of South Carolina, every Confederate state raised at least one Union battalion. Interestingly enough, you don't often hear about all the southerners who abhorred slavery during the Civil War, and I think that is a distortion in reporting true history.

Snippet #3—Now, at the risk of leaving you on a little of a melancholy note, I've decided to really stick my neck out and share something very personal. Years and years ago, I woke up one morning after having a very vivid dream—a dream of a story in the form of a poem. The dream was so powerful that I immediately wrote down the poem I had dreamed. Now, could I have had a Stephanie Meyer type dream that turned into a multimillion-dollar franchise? Nope. I just had a dream about two brothers—two Civil War soldiers. It's not anything profound, and it *is* very melancholy, so if you're feeling down or not in the mood for an emotional journey, you can skip it and go right to the teaser chapter for *The Fragrance of Her Name*. But since it does have something to do with my inspiration for this book (even just a little), I thought I'd share it now. The brothers in this poem struggled with exactly the same emotions that Robert E. Lee did—a love for the South and his home but a disgust for the evil of slavery. It's something we will never understand or have to endure, thank heaven, but many of our ancestors did, and perhaps it was just given to me for that reason. Again, it's a sappy little ditty, so if you're not in the mood, that's fine. Just grab some chocolate and a season of your favorite TV series on DVD and have at it instead! But for anyone who may be interested, here it is—a powerful dream I once had when my mind wasn't so smushy. ☺

Donnin' the Gray
By Marcia Lynn McClure

He wore the gray when he passed away at
    a ripe ol' hundred and one.
He donned the gray, and was buried that
    way in 1941.

He said, "Don't grieve," before he went.
    "I'm more' n happy to go.

I'll go where my brother was early sent
　'round 'bout eighty years ago.

"I know I've told you before," he said,
　"at one time or another,
And I'll tell you again on my own
　deathbed, 'bout my own departed twin
　brother.

"That ol' war 'tween the states, son, it jest
　had to be to put this great country at
　rest.
And we know'd it, son, brother Joe and
　me, an' we know'd we'd be leavin' the
　nest.

"Both of us know'd that the Union side
　was right in the words from its mouth.
But both of us know'd that if'n we died,
　it'd be defendin' our beloved South.

"Slavery was a sin, son. It was terrible
　wrong! Them slaves was jest folks like
　me.
They shouldn'ta had to suffer so long. We
　shoulda jest let 'em be free.

"And if'n that'd been the only reason for
　the war that took me and Joe,

It wouldn'ta lasted one whole summer
    season, 'cause most of us Rebels was
    po'.

"Folks is folks, son—no matter their skin.
    We know'd they should been freed.
But there was other reasons that the war
    took our kin and caused North and
    South to bleed.

"Our way of life, our homes . . . our
    settled back ways. I know'd progression
    must come.
But I loved Carolina and those warm
    fragrant days, and could not fire 'gainst
    my home.

"Me and Joe, we talked . . . we discussed
    it a while. We know'd the Union must
    live.
We talked and considered over ten
    country mile, 'bout what we two oughta
    give.

"One oughta fight to save the U-nited
    States . . . one for the sake of fam'ly.
So we made up conditions with mighty
    high stakes. We decided what to do, Joe
    and me.

"We flipped up a coin, and it flied in
the air. I hollered out 'heads,' Joe said
'tails.'
It headed for ground and then landed
there . . . right 'tween two rusty ol'
nails.

" 'I win,' said Joe. 'or I reckon I do. So I
get to choose where I go.
And tho' I'm jest as torn 'tween 'em as
you, I'll don the blue,' said Joe.

" 'I'll carry our face and our hearts, yours
and mine, for the future and what hasta
be.
You don the gray for the South—you'll
do fine—and that way you'll represent
me.'

"So we said good-bye. He left me right
then, and I went home to tell Mama.
And when he come home at a quarter to
ten, Mama done told it to Papa.

"They know'd we done right. We'd done
all that we should, they said when I left
to enlist.
'Keep your eyes out for Joe.' They
know'd that I would, and then my
Mama I kissed.

"Won't go into war stories," he paused
for a tear. "Them's long passed already
been told.
But I'll tell you 'bout Joe, if'n you're
wantin' to hear. My goodness! I am
gettin' old.

"It was after a battle that I seen him at
last. Ol' Getty—she took lotsa blood.
I found him up there, and we talked 'fore
he passed, right there in that old Getty
mud.

"He's been 'mortally wounded,' is the
way they described it, and I know'd
Joe's time was a-comin'.
When I found him I seen how bad he'd
been hit, and I heard brother Joe
a-hummin'.

"It was Dixie he sang—not the song of
the Yanks. I could hear as I sat down
beside him.
I give him a drink, and he gave me his
thanks, and said, 'Tom, you look awful
slim.'

" 'I'm glad it's you, Tom . . . glad you
finally found me. I'm so awful glad that
you're here.

It's you that I been so a-longin' to see.'
  And he let go a lone single tear.

"His breath, it was shallow, and it gave
  him great pain, but we talked 'bout
  missin' each other.
And there in that field in the mud and the
  rain, I said good-bye to my brother.

" 'I'm glad to go, Tom. Our grandpa's up
  there, and our little sis, Marianne Sue.
I've missed 'em all so since they left us
  down here, but now I'm gonna miss
  you.'

" 'Tell Papa I love him. Tell Mama be
  strong, 'cause the South's more'n likely
  to lose.
To fight for the North . . . I know it
  weren't wrong, but it wasn't the first
  side I'd choose.'

" 'Tell Mama for me,' and he smiled
  (tho I cried), 'that I love her and South
  Carolina.
I love you too, Tom,' he said as he died,
  'and I'll wait up in Heav'n for ya.'

"So I'm wearin' the gray as my bones
  take their rest, jest as dear brother Joe
  wore the blue.

Ma always said we were lookin' our best,
with one donnin' gray and one blue.

"But when I've departed to my loved
ones above, to my wife and Joe and all
ours,
Cover my coffin, son, with the flag that
I love—the striped one with the forty-
some stars."

Then a smile crossed his face, and he
looked right past me and said, "Joe!
Why, you look mighty fine!
I was layin' here wonderin' how much
longer you'd be, but I know'd you'd
come in good time."

Then his eyes slowly closed, and with his
last breath, he said, "Violet . . . my wife
sweet and dear—
Thanks for bringin' her, Joe, to help me
through death. Now y'all help me walk
over there."

His breath stilled and silenced, his lips
donned a smile, and he left me there
holding his hand.
I sat there just thinking for an awfully
long while 'bout my kin that had fought
for this land.

ABOUT THE AUTHOR

Marcia Lynn McClure's intoxicating succession of novels, novellas, and e-books—including *Shackles of Honor*, *The Windswept Flame*, *The Haunting of Autumn Lake*, and *The Bewitching of Amoretta Ipswich*—has established her as one of the most favored and engaging authors of true romance. Her unprecedented forte in weaving captivating stories of western, medieval, regency, and contemporary amour void of brusque intimacy has earned her the title "The Queen of Kissing."

Marcia, who was born in Albuquerque, New Mexico, has spent her life intrigued with people, history, love, and romance. A wife, mother, grandmother, family historian, poet, and author, Marcia Lynn McClure spins her tales of splendor for the sake of offering respite through the beauty, mirth, and delight of a worthwhile and wonderful story.

Books are produced
in the United States
using U.S.-based
materials

Books are printed
using a revolutionary
new process called
THINKtech™ that
lowers energy usage
by 70% and increases
overall quality

Books are durable
and flexible because
of smythe-sewing

Paper is sourced
using environmentally
responsible foresting
methods and the
paper is acid-free

Center Point Large Print
600 Brooks Road / PO Box 1
Thorndike, ME 04986-0001 USA

(207) 568-3717

US & Canada:
1 800 929-9108
www.centerpointlargeprint.com